KING SOLOMON'S
CURSE

ANDY McDERMOTT

KING SOLOMON'S
CURSE

HEADLINE

First published in 2017 by
HEADLINE PUBLISHING GROUP

1

Cataloguing in Publication Data is available from the British Library

Hardback ISBN 978 1 4722 3685 2
Trade paperback ISBN 978 1 4722 3686 9

Typeset in Aldine 401BT by Avon DataSet Ltd,
Bidford-on-Avon, Warwickshire

Printed and bound in Great Britain by Clays Ltd, St Ives plc

HEADLINE PUBLISHING GROUP
An Hachette UK Company
Carmelite House
50 Victoria Embankment
London EC4Y 0DZ

www.headline.co.uk
www.hachette.co.uk

For Kat and Sebastian

Prologue

Tenerife,
the Canary Islands

Eddie Chase entered the arrivals hall of Tenerife-Sur airport and greeted the man waiting for him with a mocking grin. 'So you've been demoted to my chauffeur, Alderley?'

'Actually, I've been promoted since we last met,' replied Peter Alderley. 'Avoiding you does wonders for my career.'

'Bell-end,' said Eddie, though with humour. The two Englishmen shook hands. Neither would have described the other as a friend, but the past dealings of the former SAS soldier and the MI6 officer had at least given them a grudging mutual respect. 'Promoted, eh? Things must be going well.'

Alderley nodded. 'I'm in charge of the Africa desk, reporting directly to C.'

'And who does C report to? B?' Eddie grinned again, knowing full well that 'C' – not 'M', despite the claims of the James Bond novels and movies – was the codename for the director of Britain's Secret Intelligence Service.

The older man's drooping moustache twitched with both amusement and faint exasperation. 'Your sense of humour hasn't changed. Sadly. But I understand other things have. You're a dad now?'

Eddie beamed proudly. 'Yeah. Me and Nina've got a little girl,

Macy. She's two.' He showed off her picture on his phone's lock screen.

'She's got Nina's looks,' said Alderley of the smiling young redhead. 'Luckily for her.'

'Yeah, sod off.' His expression and tone became more businesslike. 'But you didn't ask me to come all the way from New York to see my baby pictures. You said this was about Mukobo.'

'I'll tell you on the way.' Alderley led the way to a car park. His anonymous Peugeot 308 was unpleasantly hot inside; the Canaries were off the coast of North Africa, and the sun was blazing relentlessly down on the dry landscape.

'Not much of a spy car,' said Eddie. 'Still, it's better than your rubbish old Ford Capri.'

Alderley huffed as he started the car. 'My Capri is officially a classic.'

'That just means *ancient*, though, doesn't it?'

'And this one's rented. Budget cuts, across all the intelligence agencies. If it's not related to Islamic terrorists, Russia or Brexit, its spending's been slashed. Same for the armed forces,' he added.

Eddie had a long-standing antipathy to the intelligence services, but anything that made the job of the soldier on the ground more difficult made him bristle. 'Ugh. Politicians.'

'Yeah, whoever you vote for, some bugger wins,' said Alderley as he headed for the airport's exit. 'Anyway, we can talk now. All this is top secret, of course.'

'You don't need to tell me the rules. I signed the Official Secrets Act when I joined the forces.'

'So you haven't told Nina why you're here?'

'Nope, and she's not happy about it. I just said you needed my help. She didn't think that justified swanning off and leaving our little girl, and she's probably right. But I came anyway.' The Yorkshireman regarded Alderley intently. 'Mukobo. I assume he's here.'

Alderley nodded. 'We wouldn't have asked you to come otherwise.'

'You need me to ID him?'

'You're the only person we know of who's met him face to face. Who's still alive, anyway. Philippe Mukobo has been, ah . . . *proactive* about maintaining his privacy. Hardly surprising when he's high on Interpol's Red List, to say nothing of the Yanks wanting to get their hands on him.'

'For killing those aid workers.' It was not a question but a grim statement of fact. 'And a load of other people. I should've shot him when I had the chance.'

Alderley hesitated as if about to say something reassuring, but then continued with his briefing. 'Anyway, GCHQ picked up chatter that he'd made it over here by sea. He's since been in phone contact with a man called Provone who's arranging a fake European Union passport for him. As the Canaries are Spanish territory, once he gets it he can travel freely from here to anywhere in Europe – even Britain, since we haven't finished the Article 50 negotiations and left the EU yet.'

The Peugeot merged on to a motorway. 'You know where he is right now?' Eddie asked.

'In a villa outside Playa de las Américas.'

'So why haven't you grabbed him already?'

'As I said, we don't know what he looks like. There are no known photos of him. And he has at least nine guards at the villa, all armed. We don't want to risk a bloodbath. We want him alive.'

Eddie cocked an eyebrow. 'Why? If it were up to me, I'd just shoot the sod and be done with it.'

'Not my department, I'm afraid,' said Alderley. 'This is a field operation, so technically I'm only here to advise the officer in charge. Okay, *technically* I'm not here at all, but you know what I mean.'

'So who's the OIC?'

'John Brice, one of our top field men.'

'John Brice?' Eddie echoed, scoffing. 'What *is* it with spies having the initials JB? James Bond, Jason Bourne, Jack Bauer, and now this guy. Surprised you didn't change your name to Jethro Bollocks or something.'

Alderley chuckled. 'Not sure my wife would have wanted to become Mrs Bollocks. Anyway, he's got surveillance photos of the men in the compound. If you can ID Mukobo, Brice can take it from there.'

'You couldn't have just emailed me the pictures?'

'MI6 doesn't generally send classified imagery via Gmail.'

'Suppose not,' said Eddie, amused. 'All right, let's get this over with.'

Alderley brought him to one of Playa de las Américas' numerous hotels – and then to its bar. 'Why aren't I surprised to find a spy hanging out in here?' said Eddie.

'There he is – oh,' said Alderley, with distinct disapproval on seeing that the man they had come to meet was seated in a corner with a tanned young woman in a bikini. Brice whispered to her, then stood to usher her away with a swat to her backside as the visitors approached. She headed for a swimming pool outside. 'Who was that?'

'Nobody,' said Brice, shaking Alderley's hand. 'Peter.' He faced Eddie, blue eyes looking the stocky, shaven-headed Yorkshireman up and down and not appearing particularly impressed. 'And Eddie Chase.'

'That's me,' said Eddie, giving Brice an assessment of his own. Late thirties, tall, sharply handsome, jet-black hair conservatively yet carefully styled. His clothing was similarly neat; overdone for the climate, but the athletic MI6 officer didn't seem the kind to break a sweat for much. There was a glass of whisky before him.

'John Brice.' He briefly shook Eddie's hand, then sat again. 'I assume Peter's told you why you're here.'

'Yeah, Mukobo,' said Eddie. 'You need me to ID him for you.'

'That's right.' Brice opened a slim laptop. 'Our pictures of the men in the villa are here.' A few clicks, then he slid the machine to Eddie. 'Oh, screen facing the wall, if you don't mind. Wouldn't want anyone looking over your shoulder.'

'Your girlfriend have clearance, did she?' said Eddie, irked by the younger man's patronising tone. He sat with a wall behind him, then regarded the screen. The image, taken with a telephoto lens, was of a scowling black man in mirrored sunglasses. 'That's not him. Too young.'

'Swipe through to the next one,' said Alderley. Eddie did so. The next man was older, but also unfamiliar.

'By the way, I read your file, Chase,' said Brice. 'Interesting career you've had.'

'Yeah?' Eddie replied, bringing up the next image.

'Yes. Edward Jeremy Chase, born 1975. Joined the army at sixteen the day after finishing your GCSEs, so the earliest possible time allowed by law. Problems at home?'

'None of your business,' was the irritated reply.

'Served competently but unremarkably,' Brice went on, unfazed, 'as a squaddie for six years with a promotion to corporal, then applied to join the Special Air Service. On your first selection attempt, passed the endurance, jungle training and escape and evasion phases, but failed on tactical questioning and returned to unit.'

Alderley was surprised. 'You didn't pass first time?'

'"Tactical questioning" is basically being tortured,' said Eddie. 'Whatever they do, you're only supposed to give 'em your name, rank and serial number, or say "I'm sorry, but I can't answer that question."'

'So what did *you* say?'

'One of the interrogators started on about how he'd shagged my mum. So I told him I'd shagged his girlfriend. Which . . . I had.' He grinned, exposing the gap between his front teeth. 'He got pretty annoyed with me.'

'I can imagine!'

Brice exhaled impatiently. 'Reapplied the following year, this time succeeded. Joined 22 SAS "A" Squadron, promoted to sergeant in 2000, court-martialled and demoted back to corporal following an incident in Afghanistan when you struck a superior officer. Redeemed yourself in 2002 when you were awarded the Victoria Cross' – a hint of disbelief, as if unable to accept that the man before him could have received the British military's highest honour – 'for rescuing your wounded commanding officer while under fire. Married Lady Sophia Blackwood in 2004 after saving her from terrorists in Cambodia, left service in 2005, divorced in 2006.'

Eddie looked up from the laptop. 'You got all this fu— . . . flippin' memorised?' He caught himself before saying something stronger; he had promised his wife – and himself – when Macy was born that he would stop his habitual swearing for his daughter's sake. 'Thought you were a spy, not presenting *This Is Your Life*.'

'I like to know as much as possible about the people I deal with.' He indicated the laptop. 'Have you seen Mukobo yet?'

'Nope.'

'Then keep looking.' Eddie frowned, then turned back to the screen. 'After that, you worked as a mercenary in numerous countries. Including Rwanda, where you encountered Mukobo . . . and let him go.'

The Yorkshireman's gaze returned to Brice. 'Got something to say?'

He shrugged. 'Merely an observation.'

The dismissive response annoyed Eddie still more. 'Our convoy ran into him by fluke – he wasn't expecting trouble, or he'd have had more than one bodyguard. He was outgunned, and surrendered. I wasn't going to shoot a prisoner, so we took their weapons and told 'em to piss off. I didn't know he was a warlord who'd been killing and raping people in four different countries. If I had . . .'

'You would have done something about it?'

'Turned him in, at the very least.' A shake of the head. 'But I didn't, so now we're here. None of these guys are him, by the way.'

'Damn,' said Brice quietly. He retrieved the computer. 'Then I'll need you to come to our observation post and see if you can identify him from there.'

'I was planning to be on a flight back home tonight.'

'As soon as you ID him, you can go.' Brice finished his whisky in a single slug. 'All right, let's move.'

Playa de las Américas was a relatively new resort, still expanding into the surrounding arid hills. The unfinished shells of apartment blocks and ranks of tightly packed little houses rose up the slopes like a concrete cancer, aesthetics and interior space secondary to giving as many future buyers as possible a view of the sea, however distant, from their place in the sun.

The trio's destination was beyond the sprawl, however. The hilltops had already been claimed for the rich, expansive villas imperiously overlooking all below. 'That's the target,' said Brice as Alderley guided the Peugeot up a dusty road.

The red-roofed villa was about half a mile away. What Eddie could see of it over its high surrounding walls was impressive. 'Nice place. Where's the observation post?'

'That ridge,' Brice told him, pointing. Another dusty hill rose ahead.

Before long, Alderley turned on to a dirt track, the 308 jolting uphill behind the ridge. Eddie looked up to its top, spotting a man lying beneath a camouflaged sunshade – then tensed as a sixth sense developed from training and experience told him the watcher was not alone. 'Who else is up here?'

'Three-man snatch team from the Increment,' said Alderley as he stopped behind a dusty Land Rover Discovery. 'Well, a sub-unit, GB63.' He pronounced it *six-three*. 'We call them the Removal Men. Because, ha ha, they remove—'

'Yeah, I get it.' The Increment was one of several codenames for a top-secret MI6 unit, its members drawn from the SAS and other British special forces. Eddie tried to locate the other two men. It took a few seconds to spot one watching them from behind a rock, but the last remained unseen. 'Anyone I know? Always wondered who the Increment took on.'

'You were almost one of them yourself, Chase,' said Brice, exiting the car.

Eddie followed. 'You what?'

'You went on a selection exercise in summer 2001.'

'First I've heard of it.'

Brice gave him a patronising smile. 'They wouldn't have told you what it was. You don't ask to join the Increment – you're chosen for it. You went to an SIS training facility. We call it "the Funhouse".'

A memory surfaced; Eddie recalled being unexpectedly summoned by his commanding officer and taken in the back of a windowless van to a building somewhere in the English country-side, where he had taken part in an unusual exercise. 'What, the place set up inside like an Iraqi village?'

'Oh, that's what you had?' said Alderley with interest. 'Every MI6 field officer gets tested in the Funhouse, and everyone gets a different scenario. They must have at least a dozen sets they can swap around. Mine was a half-flooded submarine.' The recollection did not seem pleasant.

They started up the hill, Eddie still searching for the third man. 'So I was being tested to join the Increment?'

Brice nodded. 'You were. But you failed.'

'Like fu— . . . like hell I did,' Eddie protested. 'I shot every single one of those animatronic dummies guarding the hostages.'

The smug smirk returned. 'Sometimes, being a good shot isn't enough. Killing the kidnappers wasn't the mission, was it? You were supposed to eliminate the leader and recover his laptop without being detected; the hostages were irrelevant. You prioritised wrongly, so you failed the test.'

'I didn't even know I was taking it!'

'Which was the point.' They approached the top of the ridge, Brice nodding to the man behind the rock. Eddie looked back at the car – and to his surprise saw that the third Removal Man had materialised from nowhere, silently following them. Of course; while a casual passer-by would see nothing, someone specifically investigating the area would eventually spot the first two men . . . but by then, the third would have moved in on *them*.

Brice hunched down as they reached the hilltop. 'Any activity?'

'Just the guards patrolling the perimeter,' the man replied. He glanced at Eddie. 'This the source?'

Eddie extended his hand. 'Eddie Chase, 22 SAS.' The man – no older than thirty, he guessed, so too young even to have started special forces training by the time he left the SAS twelve years earlier – nodded, then turned back to the binoculars. 'Nice to meet you too,' the Yorkshireman said sarcastically.

'Check the compound for Mukobo,' Brice told him. The man on the ground shuffled aside so Eddie could take his place at a pair of powerful binoculars on a squat tripod.

The view through the lenses reduced the mile-wide gap to virtual yards. 'Okay, so we've got . . . three armed men on watch,' he reported. 'Two big SUVs, and a guy near them having a smoke. None of 'em are Mukobo.'

'We can cross them off, then,' said Alderley.

'You thought he'd be doing his own bodyguarding?'

'Mukobo got this far by staying hidden,' Brice said. 'Posing as one of your own security detail to protect a decoy is an old trick.'

'Yeah, I saw *The Phantom Menace*. And, y'know, I've done security work for a living.'

'I know.'

Eddie snorted. 'Course you bloody do, you've memorised my file.'

'Hired by Norwegian industrialist Kristian Frost to act as bodyguard for Dr Nina Wilde in 2008 during her search for the lost city of Atlantis, and married her three years later,' Brice recited as Eddie continued with his observations.

'I'm seeing something of a pattern,' Alderley cut in with a smile.

'Since meeting her,' Brice continued, 'you and Dr Wilde have discovered several major archaeological sites – as well as averting a number of biological and chemical terror attacks, stopping a missile strike on the G20 summit, and preventing your ex-wife from detonating a nuclear device in New York City. James Bond would be proud.'

'If it's the Roger Moore Bond, that's good,' said Eddie. 'Raised eyebrows and quips, that's all I want from a spy – ay up, hold on.' The smoker and one of the guards hurried to the front doors. Another man appeared, issuing instructions.

A tablet computer was attached to the binoculars by a fibre-optic cable, relaying what Eddie was seeing; Brice snatched it up. 'The man who just came out is a driver,' he noted. 'They must be going—' He broke off as his phone trilled. 'Brice. Yes? Okay, get me the translation as soon as you can.'

'GCHQ?' asked Alderley.

'Yes. Provone just called. We'll know what he said in a minute.'

'Maybe he wants to meet Mukobo,' said Eddie, still watching the villa. More men emerged from the house. All wore similar outfits: dark slacks, white shirts under dark jackets, mirrored sunglasses. Another old trick, making it harder for onlookers to tell the guards from the client—

'Wait, wait, that's him!' he gasped. 'That was Mukobo, I'm sure of it!'

'Which one?' snapped Brice, staring at the tablet.

'I've lost him.' The briefly glimpsed face had vanished in the crowd. 'Short hair, he was putting on his sunglasses.'

'They've *all* got short hair and sunglasses,' Alderley complained.

Eddie tried to find him again, but with no luck. The men split up to board the pair of vehicles. 'I couldn't see which truck he got into.'

'Orders, sir?' the watcher asked Brice.

Brice was about to reply when his phone rang again. 'That was the translator – they're meeting Provone,' he reported. 'The papers are ready.'

'Where?' asked Alderley.

'He just said "the place we arranged". We'll have to follow them – once he gets a new passport, there's nothing stopping him from leaving the country.'

The group hurried back downhill. 'Why don't you stake out the airport and grab him there?' said Eddie. 'I can spot him for you.'

'Tenerife has two airports,' Alderley pointed out. 'You've got many talents – well, a few – but I don't think bilocation is one of them.'

'You're bloody *spies*! You must have cameras and satellite links. Or just put me on FaceTime, for God's sake.' He gestured at the watcher's tablet. 'You recorded everything, right? Let me find a frame showing him, then email it to passport control. They'll catch him.'

'Not an option,' snapped Brice as they neared the cars. 'This operation is both low profile and solely British. We don't want Mukobo being picked up by some dago customs officer.'

Eddie was surprised by the MI6 man's use of the racist insult. 'Did I go through a time portal back to the 1970s?' He shook his head. 'You bloody spooks think every other country's our rival – or our enemy. Even our allies!'

'In this business, the only people you can trust are the ones you totally control,' was the dismissive reply.

'You must have a really healthy marriage,' said Eddie mockingly, though he then noticed that Brice wasn't wearing a wedding ring. The discovery did not surprise him. 'Anyway, Mukobo's on the Red List; he should be arrested on sight.'

'That's not the mission objective.' They re-entered the Peugeot, Brice taking the wheel, as the Removal Men jumped into their Land Rover.

'Then what is?'

'All you need to know is that our capturing Mukobo serves British interests. And I expect you to help us achieve that.' Brice reversed into a turn, kicking up dust, then took out a walkie-talkie. 'We've got to catch up before they reach the main road,' he barked into it. 'But don't get too close.' The men following in the Discovery responded with curt affirmation.

The villa came back into view as they emerged from behind the ridge. The two SUVs, identical black Chevrolet Suburbans, drove through its tall gates and started downhill. 'This road, does it meet up with theirs?' Eddie asked.

'Yeah, about a mile away,' said Alderley.

'We passed a freeway entrance coming up here. They could be going anywhere on the island.'

'They won't get away from us,' Brice said, before adding snidely: 'And "freeway"? You really have lived in the States for too long.'

'I'm remembering why I left in the first place,' Eddie shot back.

'Just remember whose side you're on – to whom you pledged loyalty.' Brice swung the car back on to asphalt and accelerated down the hill. The Discovery followed. Both Suburbans were ahead on the other side of the dry valley. He judged their speed, then raised the walkie-talkie again. 'Okay, we have clear sight. Ease off.'

The Land Rover dropped back. The two roads met, Mukobo's little convoy heading towards the heat-shimmering sprawl of Playa de las Américas below. Their pursuers kept pace, until—

'They're splitting up!' Alderley said in alarm. The second Suburban peeled away to the right as the leading vehicle continued straight on.

'We'll have to do the same,' said Brice, lifting the radio again.

'Wait,' Eddie said. 'The second SUV had more guys in it, didn't it?'

'Four in the first, five in the second, yes.'

'We should follow that one. Even when you use decoys, you still need bodyguards, *plus* the client. And I don't think Mukobo'd short-staff his own protection.'

Brice spoke into the walkie-talkie. 'Follow the first vehicle. We'll take the second.'

'What? Oh, for . . .' Eddie said, exasperated. 'I know what I'm bloody doing! Mukobo's in the second car – and now we'll be outnumbered!'

'I can't take the chance that you're wrong,' Brice replied. He guided the Peugeot after the second SUV as the Land Rover continued onwards. 'We need to cover both vehicles.'

'What's the point of me being here if you're not going to listen?'

'I'll say it again, Chase: the *only* reason you're here is to identify Mukobo. Just shut up and do what I tell you.'

'Arsehole,' Eddie growled, immediately annoyed with himself for breaking his own promise. 'Was *that* British enough for you?'

Brice glowered at him in the mirror, then returned his attention to the road. The highway came into view ahead, but the Suburban's destination was closer. 'Are they going *shopping*?' said Alderley, incredulous, as it entered a mall's car park.

'Mukobo must be wanting to buy a handbag,' Eddie joked.

Brice drew in after the Chevrolet, keeping his distance. It took a handicapped space near the entrance. He continued past it, stopping a couple of rows away. The three Englishmen watched as the Suburban's occupants emerged. 'Is Mukobo with them?'

Eddie squinted into the bright sunlight. 'Can't tell.' All five men were facing away from him as they crossed the parking lot.

'We'll have to follow them. Don't get too close, Chase,' Brice warned as they got out. 'You remember him – so he might remember you.'

'How close did you get to him when you met?' Alderley asked.

Eddie held his hands a foot apart. 'About this close.'

'Ah. So he *will* remember you, then.'

'I dunno, I had more hair then.' He grinned, then regarded the shopping centre. It was fronted by a large wooden portico in an ersatz-Asian style, the name *Siam Mall* emblazoned across it. The five men went inside.

'We can't lose them,' said Brice. He made a call. 'Snatch team, we're at the Siam Mall. Will advise if we locate Mukobo.'

The mall's interior was considerably cooler than outside. A large supermarket was on the left, smaller shops to the right, but the men they were tracking were ascending an escalator directly ahead. The rearmost of the group turned to survey the scene behind him. 'He's not Mukobo,' Eddie said. 'So he's one of the other four.'

'If he's here at all,' said Brice. They started up the escalator. A breeze blew in from above, the top floor only under partial cover. There were a couple of shoppers between them and the rear guard, whose mirrored gaze remained fixed on those below – until he looked around as a line of fountains on the ground floor gushed to life. The distracted man smiled at the sight.

Eddie pretended to watch the aquatic display as the escalator carried its passengers higher. The five men reached the top and headed left. When their three tails arrived at the upper floor, Brice went right, going back around the escalators towards the mall's front. Alderley and Eddie trailed him, surreptitiously watching their targets move out into bright sunshine.

A display of several Hyundai cars had been set up beneath the canopy. Eddie pretended to examine a Santa Fe SUV. 'You need to call the other car in.'

'We still don't know if Mukobo's one of them.' Brice waited until the last man passed out of sight behind a shop, then followed.

Eddie waved away an over-attentive salesman and went after him, Alderley in his wake. 'I know I'm just some stupid squaddie and you're an Oxbridge super-spy, but trust me, he's here.'

'I need proof, not instinct.' Brice halted at the shop's corner. In the far corner of a broad terrace were several gazebos, covered outdoor seating for a restaurant. The five men headed for them. A figure waved from one of the shelters. 'They're meeting someone.'

'Must be Provone,' said Alderley.

'Provone's got mates with him,' Eddie observed, seeing other figures within the gazebo. The intense sunlight reduced them to silhouettes. 'Bodyguards?'

'Probably. I doubt he trusts Mukobo any more than Mukobo trusts him.'

The Yorkshireman glanced back towards the escalators. The

mall was not busy, but there were still shoppers milling about. 'I don't like this. If something kicks off here, civvies're gonna get hurt. Call your boys in so they can pick up Mukobo once he's back outside.'

'For the last time,' Brice snapped, 'we aren't going to do anything until we *confirm that Mukobo is here*. All right?'

'Okay, then,' said Eddie, looking into the shop, 'I'll *get* you confirmation. Alderley, you got money?'

'Er, yes?' said Alderley, surprised.

'Good. Give me fifty euros.'

'Why?'

'So I can buy a bloody lottery ticket. Just give it to me!' He held out a hand, waiting until the older man reluctantly produced a banknote, then snatched it from him and entered the shop.

Two minutes later, he emerged again. Brice stared at him with wordless contempt. 'Oh, God,' sighed Alderley.

'What?' Eddie protested. 'It's the perfect disguise. No undercover cop'd wear this. Or spy.'

'No sane *human* would wear that.' The Yorkshireman had donned a wide-brimmed fabric sun hat emblazoned with images of SpongeBob SquarePants, a Hawaiian shirt exploding in rainbow colours and a pair of oversized sunglasses with bright cyan frames. 'You look like . . . like Elton John vomiting a packet of Skittles.'

'So, a tourist.' He took out his phone. 'Okay, I'll be right back – and I'll have your confirmation,' he told Brice as he started towards the tents.

'Er . . . my change?' Alderley asked hopefully.

Eddie ignored him, keeping his eyes fixed on the silhouetted figures. Mukobo – he was certain the warlord was here – and his bodyguards were with another four men, one from each group standing to keep watch on the mall. Mirror shades turned towards him, but he kept going, heading for the terrace's edge. Both guards lost interest, dismissing him as a harmless tourist.

Relieved, Eddie held up his phone and slowly turned, pretending to take a panoramic photo of Playa de las Américas and the blue Atlantic beyond. From here, he could see more in the gazebo's shadows. A Caucasian man – he assumed Provone – was talking, gesticulating with Mediterranean flourish. An open briefcase sat on the table. He still couldn't tell which of Provone's guests was Mukobo, though.

The wind flapped at his hat. That gave him an excuse to turn away and face the gazebos directly as he secured his headgear. He regarded the seated men over his sunglasses. The farthest away was definitely not Mukobo, his face the wrong shape. The two nearest were too young, and too tall. That left . . .

Provone took a large white envelope from the briefcase and handed it to the fourth man. Sunlight glaring off a wall behind him briefly reflected from the pristine paper, illuminating his face—

Eddie felt a small shock of recognition. Over a decade had passed since their meeting, and the Congolese warlord was now more hard-featured, but it was definitely Philippe Mukobo.

Confirmation.

He pocketed his phone and started back towards the shops. A sidelong glance at the gazebo as he passed . . .

Mukobo was staring at him.

Eddie forced himself not to react, maintaining his pace. The African's gaze did not waver as he slowly rose to his feet. His men responded to their leader's movement with growing alarm. Hands reached into jackets.

'Oh . . . botheration and flippery,' Eddie muttered, walking faster. He didn't know why he had caught Mukobo's attention, but something had prompted him to look through his disguise . . .

17

The wind gusted again – and he realised what had blown his cover.

He thought he had removed all the tags from his hastily bought clothing, but now felt an overlooked label flapping at his back on a length of thread. The incongruity had aroused Mukobo's suspicions, and now his eyes were fixed upon him.

Recognition dawning—

'*Chase!*' The name was a bark of fury.

Eddie ran, his hat flying off. There was no cover on the terrace; all he could do was sprint for the shops and hope Mukobo's bodyguards weren't crazy enough to start shooting in a public area—

That hope evaporated as a sharp boom came from behind – and one of the shop windows ahead burst apart in a crystalline cascade.

Shoppers screamed. He ducked, risking a rapid glance back. The gunshot had come from Mukobo himself, the warlord wielding a large gold-plated revolver. His bodyguards leapt into the open to protect him, drawing their own weapons.

Brice and Alderley darted around the corner, guns raised. 'Chase!' shouted Alderley. 'Move, hurry!'

'What do you bloody *think* I'm doing?' Eddie yelled, swerving. Another thunderous report came from Mukobo's Magnum, the round searing past and shattering brickwork. The two MI6 men jerked back into cover.

More screams, people running in panic. Eddie dived around the corner. Gunshots followed him, another window exploding. He rolled against a pillar and glanced around it. Mukobo and his men were running along the terrace, heading behind the shops towards the escalators. The warlord yelled into a phone. Provone and his own bodyguards rushed from the tent after them.

'Damn it!' Brice snarled. 'Chase, you've blown the mission!'

'We can still catch them at the escalators,' said Alderley. 'Come on!'

The three men ran along the arcade. Alderley reached the next corner – then threw himself back as more bullets cracked past. He retreated into a shop doorway, Brice and Eddie joining him. Mukobo and his goons raced for the escalators. Another barrage of gunfire hit pillars and blew out windows, the three Englishmen shrinking into their cover.

Mukobo hurled a cowering woman over the guardrail to clear his path as the five Africans pounded down the escalator. 'Just bloody shoot them!' Eddie yelled.

'We need Mukobo alive!' said Brice. He was about to move when Provone and his guards sprinted into view. One man stopped and aimed at them—

Now Brice whipped out his sidearm, locking on with laser-like precision and firing three rounds. Red spots burst open across the bodyguard's chest. He backflipped over the balcony and crashed down in the fountains below. The plumes of gushing water turned pink.

Provone gawped at the dead man, then he and his remaining guards unleashed a furious barrage at his killer. Brice retreated as more windows shattered, a shopper taking a hit to his shoulder and falling with a scream.

Provone scurried to the escalator. His men followed, still firing at the trio's hiding place. 'We're pinned down!' cried Alderley.

A thump caught Eddie's attention. He glanced into the shop to see an open emergency exit at its rear. The employees had fled through it to the terrace . . .

He ran into the shop, vaulting the counter and charging through the exit into the open. The shop workers hared for cover to his right – and on the left were the Hyundais beneath the sunshade. Eddie dashed to them, seeing the salesman quivering by the SUV's nose.

More shots from the escalators as Provone and his men descended after Mukobo. The Englishman spotted a bulge in the salesman's chest pocket and snatched out a key fob. He pushed a button; the Santa Fe's headlights flashed. He dropped low and sidestepped to the driver's door.

One of Provone's men saw him and fired, a glass panel between them disintegrating. Rounds clunked into the Hyundai's tailgate. Eddie yanked the door open and dived inside, then stabbed at the starter button. The engine chuntered to life.

He grabbed the mirror and angled it to see the view behind. A glimpse of Provone and his two remaining men before they dropped out of sight. He fumbled the gear selector to reverse – then stamped on the accelerator.

The SUV surged backwards. Eddie clutched the steering wheel with one hand, aiming the vehicle at the descending escalator, then braced himself—

The Hyundai smashed tail-first through the damaged barrier and arced down at the moving stairway.

Provone looked up – and was hit in the face by two tons of metal. The Santa Fe demolished a section of the escalator's sides, mashing him and a bodyguard into gory chunks against the sharp-edged steps, before tipping forward and slithering down the surviving guardrails.

The remaining man stared in shock at the splattered remains of his boss, then aimed at the sliding vehicle – only for another three shots from Brice to spin him through the crushed rail to demolish a stall selling scarves below.

The Hyundai reached the escalator's foot and rolled off the guardrails, landing with a crunch. Eddie disentangled himself from the deflated airbag and pulled himself upright. 'Chase, are you okay?' Alderley cried as he and Brice ran down the escalator.

'Forget him, they're getting away!' yelled Brice. He spoke into his phone. 'Snatch team, get here, now! Mukobo is on the move!'

Eddie squinted into the sunlight outside. Beyond the mall's main entrance were five running figures: Mukobo and his bodyguards, heading for their vehicle.

Rubber shrilled as the second Suburban skidded to a stop near its twin. The rest of Mukobo's guards spilled out of it to protect their leader – and to aim at something approaching from behind. The Removal Men had followed them, forced to blow their cover to keep pace.

The guards opened fire. Another screech of tyres as the Discovery braked hard. Mukobo reached his parked 4x4, two men taking the front seats as he scrambled into the rear behind them. The rest of his companions joined in the shootout, taking cover behind the second Suburban—

The Hyundai's engine was still running. 'Oh well, why not?' Eddie growled, shoving the gear selector into drive and flooring the accelerator again.

The SUV leapt forward. The chassis had been buckled by the crash, making the vehicle veer off course. He forced it back towards the doors, ignoring Brice's angry shout of 'Chase!'

The supermarket whipped past. Outside, the three MI6 operatives returned fire – and the Yorkshireman saw with dismay that the Suburbans were bulletproof, rounds smacking uselessly against their armoured bodywork. Mukobo's 4x4 powered away. More bullets twanged ineffectually off its rear.

Eddie knew the crippled Hyundai could not keep pace. Instead he aimed at the second Suburban beyond the mall's doors—

The SUV burst through them, the impact crumpling its nose. He fought to keep control as it lanced into the car park. The bodyguards reacted in surprise – then fired at him.

Eddie ducked. The windscreen burst apart, but he kept his foot down—

A flat thump as he hit one of the gunmen – then came a huge

bang as the Hyundai ploughed into the Suburban's side. Even the extra weight of the Chevrolet's armour was not enough to resist the impact. It swung around like a scythe, mowing down two of the bodyguards sheltering behind it and crushing a third between it and a parked car. Another man was knocked over, the last leaping aside just in time – only for a Removal Man to pop up from behind the bullet-riddled Discovery and put a round in his head.

Eddie clambered out of the Hyundai. A shout in French came from the Suburban's far side – followed by another shot from an Increment member. The last bodyguard slumped dead over a car's bonnet.

The Yorkshireman saw that one of the Removal Men had taken a hit to his arm, a comrade hurriedly examining the wound while the third man ran to the wrecked Suburban to police the bodies. Brice and Alderley rushed from the mall. 'Where is he?' demanded the former. 'Where's Mukobo?'

Eddie pointed at the Suburban as it roared across the car park. 'There!'

'Damn it! Peter, come on!' Brice sprinted for the parked Peugeot, Alderley behind him. Eddie hurried after them.

The field agent started the car before Alderley was fully through the door. He pulled out, Eddie having to block his path to force him to stop. 'Get out of the way!'

Eddie jumped into the rear. 'I'm coming with you!'

'Why? You've already caused enough trouble!'

'Can you shoot and drive at the same time? Gimme your gun!'

Brice pulled away in pursuit of the Suburban, reluctantly passing back his sidearm. Eddie quickly checked the weapon – a nine-millimetre Glock 17, ten rounds remaining in the magazine and one in the receiver – then readied it.

Mukobo's vehicle made a skidding right turn at the top of the exit ramp to avoid an approaching bus. 'Oh, God,' Alderley said in dismay. 'He's going down into the town!'

The Suburban cut the wrong way around a roundabout, crossing a bridge over the freeway to head for Playa de las Américas. 'Great, right into a place full of tourists!' Eddie said. 'We've got to stop 'em before someone gets hurt.'

'That *is* the plan,' Brice told him sarcastically.

He skidded the Peugeot through the roundabout. Ahead, the Suburban charged down a sweeping road past a large piece of modernist concrete architecture – but movement outside a more mundane structure caught Eddie's attention. 'Cops!' he shouted, seeing several police cars peeling out from its grounds. 'We're going right past the local nick!'

'We can't let them catch Mukobo,' said Brice.

'It's their bloody jurisdiction, and Mukobo shot up a shopping mall! They won't let you walk out of here with him.'

'It's vital to British interests that we bag him. That's our top priority – our *only* priority.'

'Why? Why's some mass-murdering rapist from the arse of Africa so important to Britain?'

If Brice was about to deign to answer, he was cut off as the Suburban vaulted over a grassy reservation at a junction. The kerb was too high for the pursuing car to risk traversing, forcing him to brake and go around it. The SUV pulled away, Brice accelerating after it with a curse.

'Cops have seen us!' Eddie warned. Three police cars were closing fast. 'Does MI6 give you "get out of jail free" cards with your licence to kill?'

'They haven't caught us yet.' The Suburban turned hard left on to a side road. Brice followed – only to react with a start when he saw more police cars skidding to block its far end.

Mukobo's driver also responded with alarm, the SUV ramming a parked car aside to reach the pavement before another frantic turn brought it on to a descending ramp. Brice sawed at the wheel to bring the Peugeot in pursuit.

The Suburban smashed through a fence at the ramp's bottom and leapt into a flood control channel. Brice followed. The only water in the concrete river bed was a thin, rancid stream, the SUV kicking up a dirty spray as it rushed along. 'There's nobody around – we've got clear shots!' Eddie yelled. He lowered a window and leaned out, bringing up the gun. 'It's bulletproof, so go for the tyres!'

He fired three shots. The first grazed the SUV's rear bumper, the others hitting the wheel below as he refined his aim. A chunk of rubber flew off – but the tyre remained intact. Alderley's shots had no more effect. 'It must have run-flats!'

The truck's occupants heard the impacts – and moved to retaliate. Movement behind the tinted windows as someone opened the sun roof. The bodyguard in the front seat stood – and opened fire on the Peugeot.

Brice swerved across the channel in a spume of filthy water. A bullet punched a hole through the roof above Eddie as he ducked, another scarring the windscreen—

Alderley cried out, falling back into his seat and clutching his right arm. 'Jesus, I'm hit! I'm hit!'

Eddie leaned back out. The bodyguard, smiling at his success, brought his gun around at the new target—

Five rapid shots exploded from the Glock, blowing a bloody chunk from the African's head. The SUV swerved crazily as the dead man collapsed on to the driver.

'Sometimes it *is* about being a good shot,' Eddie told Brice. 'Alderley! You okay?'

'Just – winged me,' the older man replied in a strained voice.

The Suburban's driver regained control. Taller buildings rose on either side of the flood channel: hotels. They were approaching the heart of the resort. Eddie looked ahead. A road bridge crossed over the waterway – and beyond it, he glimpsed blue water. 'We're almost at the beach!'

There was an obstacle between them and the sea. Past the bridge was a piled mound of grey sand and rocks running across the channel. The 4x4 would be able to traverse it with relative ease; the Peugeot, an ordinary family car, less so.

Brice had seen it too. 'Damn it! Hold on!' He accelerated.

'You'll never get over that,' Eddie cautioned.

'We don't have a choice! We've got to get Mukobo!'

The Suburban whipped under the bridge. The 308 followed, juddering as it drove on to accumulated silt and stone. The 4x4 reached the mound, reeling drunkenly over ever-larger rocks – then it went airborne, thumping back down in an eruption of sand. Brice tried to follow—

He and Eddie both saw the sharply protruding stone at the same moment. The agent braked hard – but too late.

A tremendous *bang* – and part of the car's suspension was ripped away by the unyielding point. The Peugeot slewed across the debris pile, almost rolling on its side before lurching to a standstill. Alderley cried out as his injured arm hit the door.

Even braced, Eddie had also been flung sideways. Shoulder throbbing, he straightened. 'Everyone okay?'

The steering wheel's airbag had deployed, protecting Brice but leaving him dizzied. 'Yeah. I think so.'

'Been better,' Alderley gasped, face pale.

People on the beach were gawking at the wreck, but the Suburban was still mobile beyond them. 'Mukobo!' Eddie cried, jumping from the car.

'Chase! Wait!' Brice tried to follow, but his door was jammed. 'Wait! That's an order!'

Eddie ignored him, running after the SUV. 'Move, move!' he yelled. Tourists scattered in fear on seeing his gun. He scrambled on to a paved walkway along the beach's edge just as the

Suburban cleared the sand ahead of him. It hit an obese man in shorts, throwing him bloodily over a low wall, then swerved up a ramp. People screamed, flinging themselves out of its path. A flat thud told Eddie that someone else had been mown down in Mukobo's merciless desperation to escape.

He pounded up the ramp. The 4x4 was now hemmed in, a wall on one side and packed seating outside bars and pizzerias and steak houses on the other. More shrieks of terror as the Suburban ploughed through the tourists on the waterfront. Another harsh bang, a woman spinning over the wall to the beach below. It would be a massacre, unless he stopped it—

Eddie halted, whipping up the gun and locking on to the damaged wheel – then emptied the Glock's magazine into it.

This time, the tyre blew out.

The Suburban swerved sharply – and hit a palm tree.

Even bulletproof armour yielded to a two-foot-thick column of solid wood. The SUV slammed to a stop, its nose folding around the obstacle.

Eddie ran towards it. If he could catch Mukobo while he was still stunned from the crash . . .

The warlord stumbled from the Suburban – and saw him.

Mukobo's golden revolver came up, a thunderclap erupting from its barrel—

Eddie vaulted over the wall, hitting sand as the Magnum round cracked above him. More screams from the tourists. He expected another shot, but the Congolese had turned to run.

He jumped back over the wall and raced after him. A glance into the Suburban as he passed told him that the driver would pose no further threat. He had been thrown face-first into the bulletproof windscreen, leaving a good chunk of his features stuck messily to the glass.

Ahead, he saw that Mukobo was limping. He would soon catch up – but the warlord still had his gun and, depending on whether or not he had reloaded in the car, anything from three to five bullets. The Glock in the Englishman's hand was literally an empty threat.

High fencing around a twin-towered hotel complex lined the path's inland side, and the beach narrowed below the wall on the other. Mukobo was being channelled, trapped – and a trapped foe was the most dangerous.

Mukobo had realised the same thing. He fired a wild shot over one shoulder. The Yorkshireman swerved behind a tree. The African opened up the gap a little, but was still limping. Eddie closed again—

A couple emerged from a high metal gate in the fence. Mukobo knocked them aside, darting through – and slamming the barrier behind him. Eddie reached it seconds later, only to find that it had a key card lock.

Mukobo grinned – then fired again. Plasterwork exploded from concrete as Eddie dived behind a gatepost. Sunbathers screamed and scattered. The warlord hurried towards the hotel.

Eddie stuffed the Glock into a pocket, then scaled the gate. Mukobo was almost at the hotel's entrance. He hared after him.

The African ran through the doors, finding himself in an expansive marble lobby. He slowed, searching for the best escape route. A bearded man was at the nearby reception desk, complaining to the concierge. 'Look, we specifically asked for a quiet room for our baby, and you've put us right above the disco!'

The concierge smiled smugly. 'I have worked here for fourteen years, I know which rooms are quiet—'

The boom of a gunshot shattered the air-conditioned calm as Mukobo saw Eddie approaching the glass doors and fired at him. The Englishman saw the glinting gun just in time to dodge as the bullet exploded the pane. Mukobo ran through the nearest exit.

'I will find you something quieter,' said the trembling concierge.

Eddie hopped through the hole in the door and chased the warlord into a large cafeteria – with no way out at its far end. Mukobo spun to face his pursuer. The golden gun came up—

Click!

The hammer fell on an empty casing. Mukobo *hadn't* reloaded during the car chase. The Congolese glared at the revolver as if it had betrayed him personally – then charged.

The two men collided, Eddie crashing backwards against a table stacked with glasses. Several shattered beneath him, dozens more smashing on the floor. 'I did not think I would ever see you again, Chase,' snarled Mukobo, forcing his forearm across the other man's throat. 'But now I have, I can finish what we started!' He pushed down harder, trying to choke him. Something heavy clunked across the surface behind the Yorkshireman as the table shook.

Eddie felt the cartilage of his Adam's apple crunch. Broken shards stabbed into his back. He clawed at the tumblers, but they skittered away from his fingertips. Mukobo leered in triumph—

The Englishman's hand found a curved handle. He grabbed it, swung – and a large glass jug burst apart against Mukobo's head. The African reeled away. Eddie jumped up and grabbed him, swinging around to propel him into one of the buffet counters. 'Only thing you're finishing,' he growled as he delivered a savage kidney punch, 'is lunch!'

He slammed the gasping Mukobo on to a metal tray of greasy bacon strips. The warlord yelled as runny fat burned his face. He jumped up – and hit the heat lamp above, smashing the bulb and driving spears of hot glass into his scalp.

Eddie hauled him out and punched him, then grabbed him in a fierce headlock. It would only take a twist and squeeze to snap his neck. He was sorely tempted – but instead forced him along the buffet, knocking abandoned trays to the floor. A large metal vat of baked beans stood under another heat lamp at the counter's end. He shoved down Mukobo's shoulders and ran him headlong into the pan with a flat *bong*. The dazed warlord staggered back – and Eddie swung the vat against his opponent's head. Mukobo crashed to the tiled floor. Eddie tipped the beans over him, then dropped the empty pan after them. 'You've bean done, mate.'

Shouts from the entrance. He looked up – to see several policemen rush into the cafeteria, guns raised. He immediately lifted his hands in surrender as a cop screamed at him in Spanish. 'Don't shoot, don't shoot!' he replied. *'No hablo español.* I got your guy.'

Most of the officers advanced on the two men, the remainder ordering onlookers away. Brice ran in, only to be told in no uncertain terms to move back. 'Chase!' he shouted. 'You idiot, what have you *done*? Now the local police are going to arrest him!'

Eddie knelt in response to a gesture from a gun-wielding cop. 'You're lucky I didn't kill him. And I caught someone on Interpol's most-wanted list! What difference does it make who arrests him?'

The MI6 officer seemed about to reply, but held back, aware that he was in a public place with numerous civilians. He settled instead for glaring at Eddie as he was handcuffed. Alderley caught up with him, one hand to his bloodied arm.

Mukobo had already been identified as responsible for the carnage along the seafront, other cops hauling him up and cuffing him with no small amount of force. Eddie was also pulled to his feet. 'You'd better bloody get me out of this,' said the Yorkshireman as he was hustled past his two countrymen.

'I should let you rot,' growled Brice.

Alderley gave Eddie an unhappy look. 'I'll see what I can do.'

'You'd better,' he replied, 'or I might tell 'em why we were here in the first place!'

Brice prickled with anger, keeping pace with Eddie on the

other side of the police cordon. 'The Official Secrets Act still applies to you, Chase. Don't tell them anything! That's an order!'

'I don't work for you. But sort this out and I won't need to tell 'em, will I?' The cops took Eddie and Mukobo through the exit, an officer preventing the furious Brice from following. 'And Alderley?'

'Yeah?' Alderley replied.

'For God's sake, don't tell Nina what's happened!'

'Hi, honey,' said Eddie as he entered his apartment two days later. 'I'm home.'

His wife's silence warned him to expect a frosty reception. He grimaced, then went into the living room. Nina Wilde was waiting on the couch, arms folded. 'So,' she said. 'What happened?'

'Nothing happened. Where's Macy?'

'Napping in her room. And what do you mean, "nothing happened"? You were supposed to come back yesterday!'

'Things were a bit more complicated than I expected.'

Nina stood, eyeing him suspiciously. 'More complicated? How?'

He decided not to tell her that he had spent a night in a cell, Alderley getting the British Consul to intervene the following day. Diplomatic strings had been pulled to suggest that delivering Mukobo to Interpol through the local police had been the objective all along. 'I had to help Alderley with the paperwork,' he said instead, giving her a *technical* truth. 'But everything's been sorted out now.'

'And you're still not going to tell me exactly what it was all about? I'm assuming it was something for MI6 since Peter got you involved.'

The restrictions of the Official Secrets Act meant he wasn't supposed to confirm or deny, but he knew that after nine years together Nina would read his expression easily enough. 'Someone needed my help, and I helped them,' was the best he could manage. 'The world's a better place for it, trust me.'

'I *do* trust you, Eddie, you know I do. But I don't like being kept out of the loop.'

'I know, and I'm sorry. I really am.'

She finally thawed, giving him a small smile. 'The main thing is that you're back. Come here. Give me a kiss.'

He did so, embracing her. 'Glad to be home.'

'I'm glad too.' Her smile widened into a grin. 'Because our daughter has a smelly diaper that needs dealing with.'

Eddie sighed. 'Yep. Welcome home.' He released the redhead and started for Macy's bedroom.

'Eddie,' said Nina, the concern in her voice halting him. 'This thing . . . it's finished, right?'

'Yeah,' he assured her. 'It's all over.'

1

The Atlantic Ocean

Two years later

Deputy US Marshal Art Garrison peered through a porthole at the empty azure sea thirty-seven thousand feet below, then looked back at his prisoner. Younger and cockier men would have made a sardonic comment about it being the last good view the shackled man would ever have, but the craggy team leader merely gave him a cold stare, getting a sneer in response, then turned away.

It had taken almost two years of legal wrangling for Philippe Mukobo, a native of the Democratic Republic of Congo but whose reign of terror had bloodied several other central African nations, to be turned over to the custody of Garrison and his two fellow marshals. Mukobo was high on Interpol's most-wanted list for numerous crimes including mass murder, rape and drug running, but the diplomatic weight of the United States had decided for which he would stand trial – and where.

The Skyblue Airlines 747-8 was on its way from Paris to New York. Mukobo's lawyers had fought a long but ultimately futile battle at the European Court of Human Rights in Strasbourg to prevent his extradition for the murders of a group of American aid workers six years prior. All avenues now exhausted, the warlord was being taken in chains to face justice.

The thought brought a brief smile to Garrison's stern face. Mukobo was a monster, plain and simple, and he would finally get what he deserved. Life without parole in a federal penitentiary was the best he could hope for; execution was more likely. Though the plane was heading for New York, his trial would take place in nearby New Hampshire. Partly because three of his victims were from that state, but also because it maintained the death penalty. Those pushing for Mukobo's prosecution wanted every possible sentencing option.

He glanced at his watch. Four hours before landing; halfway across the Atlantic. Garrison permitted himself to relax a little, leaning back in the comfortable business-class seat. The Justice Department had booked every seat on Flight 180's upper deck to isolate Mukobo from the other passengers, any displaced travellers getting upgrades to first class courtesy of Uncle Sam. Pricey, but less so than despatching a US government jet solely to transport one prisoner.

A quick check on his team. Radley was behind him, guarding the spiral staircase down to the main deck, while Szernow sat by the cockpit door. Should anything happen, they were ready for it.

Another look through the porthole. The sky was clear. It would be a smooth flight.

'You okay, Pierre? You look a bit airsick.'

Pierre Noret, the 747's co-pilot, laughed to cover his nervousness. 'I'm okay. Thirsty, that's all.' He looked at his watch, then drained a plastic water bottle.

The plane's captain, Paul Watley, nodded. 'Call one of the girls, have them bring you some more water.'

'No, I'm okay.' Noret stood. 'I have some in my bag.'

'Don't get lost,' said Watley with a chuckle.

Noret smiled thinly, then headed aft. Despite its size, the 747 was designed to be flown by just two pilots; he and Watley were the only people in the cockpit. With the reinforced door locked, the only way for anyone else to gain access was if one of them allowed it.

There was a small crew rest area at the cockpit's rear. The Frenchman entered, collecting his bag. He suddenly felt hot, sweat prickling his skin. Nervousness became nausea as he took out a fountain pen. It appeared perfectly ordinary, if pricey, but airline pilots were well known for ostentatious accessories. Certainly this one had drawn no attention at the security check.

Noret carefully removed the cap, realising his fingers were trembling. *Calm, calm.* If he aroused Watley's suspicions, his only hope of making a fresh start free of his mounting debts and rapacious ex-wife would be over before it even began.

His hands steadied. He slowly turned the pen's body. A slim needle extended from the nib. The Frenchman hesitated, then tipped the pen downwards, as he had been instructed. A tiny dewdrop of colourless liquid swelled on the silver sting's point.

One last tense time check, then he headed forward, the pen clutched in his right hand like a dagger. Watley, reading the news on an iPad, didn't look around at him. Noret advanced on the American, eyes fixed on his target: the right side of Watley's neck, just above his collar. He would only get one attempt . . .

The captain sensed the co-pilot's approach. 'When we land, it might be worth you seeing the company doctor.' He turned his head. Noret froze. 'You really didn't look well – and God, you look even worse now! Are you sure you're okay?'

Noret felt sweat sting his eyes. 'Yes, I'm fine.' He didn't dare move, terrified of drawing attention to the object in his hand.

Watley gave him a look of concern . . . then returned his attention to the iPad. 'Just so long as you—'

The Frenchman lunged, stabbing the pen's tip into the pilot's neck. There was a flat *phut* as a gas injector forced its contents into Watley's bloodstream.

The captain gasped and jumped up. 'What was – what the *hell*?' He stared at the pen as the Frenchman drew back. The needle was still clearly visible, its tip red with blood. He clambered from his seat, Noret fearfully backing away. 'What did you . . .'

Watley staggered, clawing at his co-pilot . . . then crumpled to the cockpit floor.

Noret stared at him, breathing heavily, before checking Watley's pulse. He was unconscious, but alive. The sedative had worked as promised.

He dragged the taller man back into his seat and fastened his belt, then went to the engineering consoles and switched the circuit breakers to cut off power to a specific system: the satellite link connecting the aircraft's wi-fi and telephone services to the outside world. Now, the only working communication channel was via the cockpit radio.

There was one more breaker to open. He hesitated, then tripped it – deactivating the cockpit voice recorder. There would be no audio record of what was about to happen.

Noret returned to his own seat and belted up. Wiping away sweat, he redonned his headphones and tuned the radio to a memorised frequency. 'Dragonfly, Dragonfly, do you hear me? This is Papillon. Do you hear me?'

No response for several seconds, then: 'Papillon, Papillon, this is Dragonfly.' A man's voice, electronic masking rendering it almost robotic. 'We hear you. Situation?'

'Phase one complete,' said Noret, surprised at his own ability to reduce the enormity of what he had just done to a euphemism so quickly. 'Where are you?'

'Flight level three-eight-zero, one kilometre directly behind you. Are you ready to commence?'

He had to compose himself before answering. Assaulting Watley was one thing, but what he was about to do was the antithesis of every commercial pilot's instincts. Even if everything went perfectly, there was still an element of risk to the three hundred and five passengers and crew. 'Yes. I'm ready.'

'Proceed.'

The voice went silent. Noret took a deep breath as he reached the point of no return . . . then disengaged the autopilot and shoved the control yoke forward, throwing the 747 into a steep dive.

Nausea rose in his stomach as the huge aircraft dropped towards the ocean. He could hear screams through the floor from the passengers below. Trained responses kicked in: he hit the button to turn on the seatbelt lights, then activated the emergency oxygen supply. Muffled bangs echoed through the fuselage as ceiling panels disgorged breathing masks. He switched on the intercom. 'This is the co-pilot! All passengers must return to their seats immediately! Remain calm and put on your oxygen masks. We have a system malfunction, and are descending to a lower altitude for safety. Everything is under control.'

He eased back the four throttles to lower the stress on the airframe. The altimeter spun downwards, nothing but ocean visible ahead. Passing thirty thousand feet, twenty-nine. He needed to get the airliner to no more than eight thousand feet above sea level and hold it just above stall speed, which in the current conditions would be about one hundred knots. It was balancing on a knife-edge, but Noret was confident in his skill as a pilot.

A voice came through his earphones. 'Captain! What's happening, what's going on?' Rose Dewar, the chief purser. 'Captain Watley! Are you there?'

'This is Noret,' the Frenchman replied. 'We're losing cabin pressure. Everything is under control, so please keep the passengers calm.'

'But – but the cabin pressure seems okay down here.' Dewar was a highly experienced flier, and even through an oxygen mask he could hear her confusion.

'We don't know exactly what's wrong, but there is definitely a major malfunction. The captain is taking us down before it gets any worse.'

He switched off the intercom and checked the altimeter. Twenty thousand feet and still descending rapidly. Someone hammered on the cockpit door. 'Captain! What's going on? Captain, answer me!'

'Go back to your seat!' Noret shouted. He had been warned that the US marshals would try to assert their authority once it became clear something was wrong.

More pounding. 'We have a high-risk prisoner here – I demand to know what's happening!'

'What's happening is that we are trying to keep this plane in the air!' Noret yelled back, still watching the altimeter. Sixteen thousand. 'Sit down and put on your seatbelt! Our first priority is the safety of this aircraft and its passengers, so let us do our job!'

Garrison started to say something else, then stopped. Noret assumed he was returning to his seat, but even if he was not, there was no way he could enter the cockpit.

Thirteen thousand feet – and now the co-pilot pulled back the yoke, easing the Boeing out of its dive. Ten thousand, the blue horizon sliding back into view. He reduced the throttles still further. The airspeed indicator dropped, two hundred knots, one-fifty. A course adjustment to bring the airliner directly into the wind, giving him the maximum possible lift.

Eight thousand feet. He levelled out. One hundred and twenty knots, still slowing.

Phase two was complete.

As if in response to his thought, the flat voice returned to his headphones. 'Papillon, Papillon. Status?'

'This is Papillon,' Noret replied. 'Holding at flight level eight-zero, bearing two-four-seven degrees, slowing to one hundred knots.'

'Roger. We are moving to transfer position.'

Noret leaned forward and looked up. Nothing but empty sky – then a white shape hove into view overhead.

Another aircraft.

He felt a flash of fear. The second plane – a Bombardier Global 7000, a long-range business jet – was less than a hundred metres above, well within the distance considered a 'near miss'. Every part of his training told him to veer away, but he forced himself to hold course. The sleek metal crucifix slid into full view.

Its forward hatch opened.

The Bombardier shimmied, the pilot battling to keep it steady as a hundred-knot wind blasted into the cabin. Noret's breath caught. If the plane went out of control, it could tumble right into the 747 . . .

It stabilised – then juddered again as something else disrupted the airflow. A thick metal bar swung out from the open hatch, a steel cable extending from a pulley flapping in the slipstream. Something resembling a boat anchor was attached to the end of the line.

'Papillon, Papillon,' said the radio voice. 'We are in position for phase three. Are you ready?'

'Engaging autopilot,' the Frenchman replied. 'Preparing to receive.'

He switched the computers back on, then unbelted and stood. Watley was still slumped in his seat. He crossed the cockpit to stand behind the captain's position.

A plastic cover was set into the curved ceiling. Noret pulled it away, revealing what was built into the hull behind.

The escape hatch.

The Boeing 747's unique design had created safety headaches

for its engineers, the cockpit so high up compared to other airliners that jumping to the ground in an emergency could be fatal. They had solved the problem in an inventive way. The cockpit crew could open the hatch, then use a set of cable reels mounted in the ceiling to make a controlled descent to earth, rappelling down the aircraft's flank.

Noret had no intention of using the cables, though, and going through the hatch was the very final part of his plan. Instead he braced himself, turned the yellow-painted latch handle until he heard the thunk of bolts . . . and pulled.

The hatch swung downwards – and a hurricane-force wind screamed into the cockpit.

Alarms howled, the 747 shivering as its aerodynamics were disrupted. Noret locked the hatch open and staggered to his seat. The autopilot was handling the disturbance, but he wanted his hands back on the controls. 'Dragonfly!' he shouted into the microphone as he disengaged the computers again. 'Ready for transfer!'

He looked up at the other plane. The anchor wavered in the wind, then dropped towards him. Noret held the 747 steady, flexing his fingers as the wind chill bit. He switched the inter-com back on to address the cabin crew. Dewar's near-panicked voice immediately came through the earphones. 'I'm here, I'm here,' he told her. 'We've lost pressure in the cockpit. Keep the passengers in their seats – including the men on the upper deck. When we get the situation under control, we'll divert to Greenland or Iceland.'

'What's wrong with the plane?' Dewar asked. 'Are you both okay?'

'We're good,' he replied, giving Watley a brief glance. 'We don't know the cause of the malfunction. As soon as we do, we'll update you. Out.'

He looked up. The cable was still unreeling, the Bombardier's pilot making small attitude adjustments to guide the anchor towards the opening in the 747's humped fuselage.

It came closer, closer. He could now see what he had been told to expect; the mechanism was folded so it would fit through the hatch, with a long dangling strap at its base. When it was just ten metres away he reactivated the autopilot and hurried to the emergency exit. The wind lashed at his face. He shielded his eyes with one hand, holding the cockpit wall with the other.

A bang as the anchor hit the hull, scraping along the metal before the slipstream flicked it away. Noret grimaced, but held his position. He glimpsed the other plane's wing as it slipped sideways to bring the cable into line with the hatch, but his eyes were fixed upon the opening's forward edge, waiting—

Another thunk – then the black strap flapped past. He snatched at it, but missed as the anchor rattled over the fuselage. He suppressed his panic and waited for it to reappear. Another frightening impact outside as the cable swung back – and this time he caught the strap. 'I've got it, I've got it!' he shouted into the headset. 'Give me some slack!'

The Global 7000 descended slightly. The anchor slid over the hatch's edge, and he yanked it into the cockpit.

'I have it!' he called. 'Deploying now!'

The mechanism he had just received was spring-loaded, restrained in its folded configuration by a thick metal clip. He wrestled it into position, holding it against one corner of the open hatchway, then forced off the restraint. It expanded with considerable force, revealing that it was a hollow rectangular frame. It had been designed to fill the opening precisely, each corner wedging firmly in place. Noret pushed at it. The frame didn't move. 'It is secure!'

'Roger, Papillon,' said the man in the other jet. 'Commencing transfer.'

Noret rushed back to the controls. Any actions needed now

would be well beyond an autopilot's capabilities. He looked up again – and felt another shot of fear. Knowing what was going to happen had not prepared him for the reality.

A black-clad man leaned out of the Global 7000's open hatch. He wore a harness, which he clipped to the bucking steel line – then as Noret watched in amazement he rapidly lowered himself down the cable towards the 747, the hundred-knot wind tearing at his thick clothing. The dark figure grew larger and larger before disappearing above the windscreen. A moment later, thuds told the co-pilot that he had made contact with the hull.

He looked back at the hatch. The sunlight streaming in from outside was suddenly shadowed. Legs swung through the opening, the man smoothly dropping into the cockpit as if he carried out such stunts on a daily basis. The new arrival wore a breathing mask and tinted goggles, his features completely hidden. He detached himself from the cable and touched a microphone on his throat. 'I'm in.'

'Papillon, second transfer commencing,' said the filtered voice in Noret's headphones. A second figure climbed from the Bombardier. His descent and arrival in the cockpit was as rapid and assured as the first.

'They are both here,' Noret said, awed.

'Copy, Papillon. Begin phase four.'

The Frenchman switched on the intercom to address the passengers and crew directly. 'Ladies and gentlemen, this is the co-pilot. We have suffered a structural failure that has caused the cabin to decompress. The aircraft is now at an altitude low enough for the air to be breathable, and we are changing course for the nearest airport . . .'

Garrison listened to the announcement, one hand holding his oxygen mask in place. His sidearm was in the other. The first thought of all three marshals had been that an attempt was being made to free Mukobo, Garrison covering their prisoner while his comrades fixed their weapons upon the staircase. But the only person who had climbed it was a stewardess, ordering the marshals to return to their seats before disappearing again.

Whatever the situation, it was deteriorating. The draught escaping around the cockpit door warned that the hull had been compromised. The co-pilot's announcement of a structural failure seemed to rule out any connection to Mukobo – nobody trying to rescue him would risk not only the warlord's life but their own by sabotaging the plane – but Garrison still wasn't going to allow his charge to take advantage of it. 'You just keep still now,' he warned, pushing the gun's muzzle against the shackled man's side. 'Only way you're leaving this plane without me is through a hole in the hull.'

Mukobo, however, appeared genuinely surprised and afraid. Reassured, Garrison turned his attention back to the co-pilot's message: '… are aware of the situation, and emergency services will be waiting when we land . . .'

The two black-clad men moved to the cockpit door as Noret continued speaking, one lifting his goggles to peer through the peephole. 'Four men,' he muttered. 'Target is on our left, three rows back, window seat. One hostile next to him, aisle seat. Second hostile on our right, front row, aisle seat. Third hostile also on right, rear row, aisle seat.'

His comrade nodded. 'You take the right. Ready weapons.' Noret had been assured that their guns were non-lethal and incapable of penetrating the airliner's fuselage.

Noret had been told a lie.

Both men carried Glock 17s, fat cylindrical suppressors attached. They stepped back from the door, the first man slowly reaching for its lock. 'On three,' said the other. A silent, perfectly synchronised countdown—

The bolt clacked back – and both men burst out into the upper cabin.

A screaming wind rushed through with them, startling the four men within. The marshals quickly reacted to the unexpected new threat . . . but not quickly enough.

The first attacker's gun was already locked on to Szernow, sending two bullets slamming bloodily into the deputy's chest before snapping up to do the same to Radley. The second man fired three shots at Garrison with similar lethal efficiency. The grizzled man slumped dead against his prisoner.

Mukobo stared in shock as the two men approached, one covering the stairs as the other dumped Garrison uncaringly on the floor and retrieved his keys. 'Stand up,' the intruder ordered.

The warlord hesitated, but a flick of the gun told him that he had no choice. The man unlocked his shackles, then produced another harness. 'Put this on. Make sure it's secure if you want to live.'

Mukobo did as he was told. The gunman gestured towards the cockpit. 'In there. Move!'

Rescuer and prisoner scurried through the door, Mukobo recoiling from the blasting wind. Noret looked back. 'How long before the marshals wake up?'

The black-clad man ignored him, going to the hatch and securing a clip on the African's harness to the steel cable before repeating the action with one of his own. The second gunman backed into the cockpit, weapon raised to cover his retreat. Noret reacted with shock as he saw it was no Taser or dart gun. 'Wait, you said there would be no killing!'

The figure turned towards him – and fired.

Two bullets hit the Frenchman's head. A wet burst of blood and brain matter splattered the windscreen and instruments. The gunman closed and locked the cockpit door, then came to Noret's position and shoved his corpse aside to deactivate the autopilot. The 747's nose began to pitch downwards, slowly . . . but inexorably. He touched his throat mic. 'Dragonfly, this is Sparrow. Prepare for extraction.' He went to the hatch and attached himself to the line.

The first man climbed out into the gale. Mukobo, shivering in the wind, stared in disbelief. 'What are you doing? We will be killed!'

'Fold your arms and stay calm,' said the remaining man. He looked up through the opening. The Global 7000 had moved directly above the 747's nose. 'Stand under the hatch.'

Mukobo's eyes flicked to his gun, then he reluctantly obeyed. The man stood close beside him and peered upwards again. The other jet was now right overhead. 'Dragonfly, extraction *now*.'

The intruder braced himself, gripping Mukobo with one hand – and pushing a button on the folding frame with his other.

A sharp crack as an explosive bolt fired, breaking the frame apart – and all three men were hauled skywards as the Bombardier climbed. The slipstream immediately snatched them backwards, swinging them terrifyingly over the larger jet's fuselage, but the line was already being winched in. The 747 dropped away beneath them – with no one at the controls.

The dangling trio ascended towards the business jet. Mukobo cried out in fear, but his companions remained stoic and calm. Hands reached out from the hatch to grab them, a man pulling the first rescuer inside and detaching him from the cable before hauling Mukobo and the second intruder through the opening.

The warlord collapsed breathlessly on the deck as the arm was retracted and the hatch closed. The wind's roar abruptly cut out, the sudden silence almost disorienting. The men who had extracted him from the 747 carried him to a seat at the cabin's rear.

Panting, Mukobo focused on the man facing him – then jumped in alarm as recognition struck. 'You!'

He tensed as if to lunge at him, but his rescuers shoved him back down. The other man didn't even flinch. 'Mr Mukobo,' he said as the plane banked, turning back eastward. 'I have a proposition . . .'

The 747 thundered on, its descent gradually steepening. Desperate hammering sounded over the wind as the cabin crew beat uselessly on the cockpit door. A pause, then gunshots, bullets from the dead marshals' weapons smacking into the lock – but the armoured barrier remained secure.

The altimeter dropped below two thousand feet. The combination of altitude and descent angle triggered a warning, a whooping alarm sounding as a synthesised female voice spoke with inhuman calm. 'Pull up. Pull up. Pull up.'

Nobody could respond to it. Fifteen hundred feet. 'Pull up. Pull up.' The Boeing dropped towards the sea—

Watley stirred.

The cacophony finally overcame the remnants of the drug in his bloodstream. One thousand feet. The American groaned. 'What . . . Pierre, what the—'

He froze as he saw his co-pilot dead in his seat, half his skull missing. The computer's repetitive words finally sank in. Five hundred feet. Terror-induced adrenalin obliterated any lingering sedative and he grabbed the controls, pulling back the yoke and slamming the throttles to full power. Three hundred feet, two hundred, and the 747 responded, but too slowly—

One hundred feet, fifty, the airliner's bow hitting the water – and augering into it.

With the engines at maximum thrust, the results were catastrophic.

The 747's tail flipped upwards, the nose crumpling as it drove deeper into the sea. Watley had just enough time to scream before a broken structural spar sliced him in half. An engine tore loose from its mount as the plane rolled and punched through the hull, compressor blades disintegrating into razor shards that shredded everyone in their path. Fuel from a ruptured wing tank burst into a liquid inferno and sent a wave of flame crashing over the wreckage. Blazing chunks of mangled metal skipped across the water before finally being swallowed by the Atlantic.

Silence soon fell, drifting smoke and floating debris all that remained of Skyblue Airlines Flight 180.

2

Jerusalem, Israel

One year later

A hot and gritty wind blew across the Temple Mount, making Dr Nina Wilde narrow her eyes behind her sunglasses. Despite the discomfort, however, the archaeologist was still in awe of her surroundings. The hilltop was one of the holiest sites of three religions – Judaism, Christianity and Islam – with a history dating back over five thousand years, and the splendid buildings dominating the walled enclosure, the Dome of the Rock and the Al-Aqsa mosque, were two of the world's oldest Islamic structures.

It wasn't simply the air of history that excited her, though. Something new was about to be discovered. And she was not just involved with it; she was largely responsible for it.

Six years earlier, Nina had been kidnapped by a religious fanatic intent on uncovering a deadly secret encoded in the Book of Revelation. The trail led her to a cave in the desert of southern Israel, where she found a statue: one of the angels that would supposedly herald the apocalypse. It was the container in which it was hidden that had been the most amazing discovery, however.

The Ark of the Covenant.

The golden chest had waited undisturbed for millennia until she, her husband Eddie Chase and young Mossad agent Jared Zane found it. The Ark contained the items promised by biblical legend, including the tablets inscribed with the Ten Commandments – a world-shaking find.

That had only been the beginning, though. Once Israeli archaeologists secured the site, they unearthed more relics – including some leading back to the Temple Mount. Records from the era of the great King Solomon revealed the precise location of a place long thought lost: the First Temple, dedicated to Yahweh, god of the Israelites, by Solomon himself. The temple had been destroyed by the Babylonian king Nebuchadnezzar in 587 BC, its remains buried and forgotten as later places of worship were built over it . . . but now, thanks to her, the archaeologists knew exactly where to look.

And they had found it.

She gazed down the slope. Amongst the trees was a large tent covering a newly excavated entrance to the hidden ruins. Nina had been given a privilege rare for a Western archaeologist by being allowed to participate; the politics of the Temple Mount were tangled, riven by centuries of religious and national hostility, and it had taken a great deal of bargaining with the Israelis, who controlled access to the site, and the Jordanians, who controlled the site itself, for the work to be permitted at all. But her reputation as the world's most famous archaeologist held weight, and now she was here, to witness the opening of the First Temple.

An astounding discovery . . . for which she would have an audience.

Nina glanced up. A small drone was flying over the hill, getting aerial footage of the Temple Mount for later editing into a documentary series. *Her* series. Two years earlier, she had been offered a new challenge: to recount her discovery of the lost civilisation of Atlantis for television. Those who knew her had been surprised that she accepted, given that her prior appearances in the public eye were slightly begrudging, but a movie based on her first adventure had been – to her mind – a ludicrous collection of chases, gunfights and exploding helicopters, and she wanted to set the record straight about what *really* happened. (Even though it had indeed involved chases, gunfights and exploding helicopters.)

The series had been successful enough for the network to request a follow-up. The obvious choice was her biblical discoveries, bringing her to the Middle East along the trail of the Ark of the Covenant. There was also the bonus that with excavations ongoing, something amazing might be discovered on camera: an irresistible hook for any executive.

That was, she mused irritably, if the other archaeologists ever got their asses in gear . . .

Nina finished a bottle of water and went to the tent. The drone, a quadcopter fitted with a high-definition camera, tracked her. The clip might be used to bridge together scenes of her exploration of the Temple Mount, or not at all, but the production team wanted as much material to work with as possible. With filming now entirely digital, the only limitation on how much they could shoot was hard drive space, and the crew always had many terabytes available for original footage, with multiple backups.

Her team was waiting outside the tent, some relaxing in the shade of the olive trees while others made the most of the sun. 'Have I missed anything?' she asked.

Steven Fisher, his back against a tree, tipped up the peak of his baseball hat. 'Nope, not a thing. Don't know what Ziff's doing in there. Reciting all six hundred-thirteen *mitzvot*, or something.'

'If you weren't Jewish yourself, I'd swear you were anti-

Semitic,' said the woman beside the documentary's bearded director. Lydia Spur was a blonde New Zealander who still had the look of a tomboy despite being in her mid-thirties.

Fisher grinned at her. 'Self-loathing is what Judaism is all about.' She smiled back.

'I'll see what they're doing,' said Nina, going to the tent's entrance. She called to a chunky Hispanic man who was stretched out sunbathing. 'Jay? Get your camera ready, we might be shooting soon.'

'I'll get right on that, *boss*,' replied Jay Rivero, scarcely bothering to veil his sarcasm. He didn't move. Nina shot an annoyed look at Fisher.

'We'll go when we've got a reason to, okay?' the director told her. 'Howie's getting drone coverage' – he gestured towards the fourth member of the small documentary crew, who was operating the quadcopter from a slim laptop – 'and we've got nothing to shoot until they let us in there.'

'We'll be in there in five minutes,' Nina told him, irked by their attitude. It wasn't just that they had no particular excitement about what they were doing, treating it as just another job; it was also that as the shoot progressed, they had developed a personal animosity towards her. The same thing happened on the Atlantis documentary, none of her original crew returning. What the hell was their problem? 'Be ready.'

She entered the tent. Inside were four men, two Israeli and two Jordanian archaeologists, engaged in a discussion. She went to the oldest. 'David, what's the hold-up?'

Dr David Solomon Ziff turned to her. 'There isn't a hold-up, Nina,' he said. 'We are just proceeding with due attention, that's all.'

She looked past the balding, white-bearded man into a steeply sloping tunnel. Spotlights revealed stonework at the bottom – a section of the First Temple's outer wall. Only a cracked stone slab separated the scientists from what lay within.

And they had been vacillating over how, or even whether, to move that slab for most of the day. 'I think you've given it as much attention as humanly possible,' she said. 'All the potential risks have been taken into account – so let's just do it.'

'I'd remind you that you're not in charge here, Dr Wilde,' said Ziff pointedly. '*I* am. *I'll* decide when to open the temple.'

She folded her arms. 'All right, so when *are* you going to open the temple?'

'Soon.'

'Soon? Five minutes is soon. Ten minutes?'

Ziff shook his head. 'Why are you in such a rush, Nina? The First Temple has been buried for over two thousand years. It will still be here tomorrow. And the day after, and a week from now.'

'But my camera crew *won't* be,' she said. 'We're almost at the end of our schedule. But this gives us an ending, brings everything full circle. The Ark was once kept in the First Temple, and now what we found with the Ark has brought us back to it. It's perfect.'

'We are not here so you can have a happy ending on television,' said Mohammad Talal, one of the Jordanians. 'This is real archaeology.'

Nina gave the young man a chilly stare. 'Well y'know, Atlantis, the pyramid of Osiris, the vault of Shiva, El Dorado, Valhalla – oh, and the Tabernacle and the Ark of the Covenant – seemed pretty real too when *I found them all*.' Talal looked away, his expression a mixture of anger and humiliation. She turned back to Ziff. 'David, this isn't about satisfying my ego. This is my way of doing archaeology; it might be unconventional, but it *works*. It's about showing the world something remarkable – something that we've all dedicated our lives to finding.'

Ziff adjusted his wire-rimmed glasses. 'Finding Solomon's

temple is *my* lifelong ambition, not yours. But . . .' A long, slow exhalation. 'You are right. There's no reason to delay any longer.' He smiled at her for the first time since her entrance. 'After all, why have a lifelong ambition if you stop when you are about to reach it?'

'I know what you mean,' she said, returning the smile. 'Atlantis was my obsession. But there was still a lot more for me to find afterwards.'

He nodded. 'So much that you must wonder if there's anything left. But yes, we will open the temple. It is time.'

'Thank you,' said Nina, feeling a little unsettled by the first part of his reply. She shook off the feeling and went to the tent's door. 'Okay, we're going to open up the First Temple,' she told those outside. 'Five minutes, just like I said.' The redhead gave Fisher a smug smirk, then tied her hair into a ponytail. 'Everyone get ready.'

It actually took rather more than five minutes, but eventually all the preparations were made. The archaeologists took up position at the tunnel's end, two men carefully inserting long crowbars into cracks on each side of the obstructing slab while Talal positioned himself to take the block's weight should it tip forward. Nina and Ziff crouched expectantly before the opening, the Israeli holding a still camera to photograph the procedure.

Behind them were the film crew. Rivero was closest, his rugged Sony Handicam on his shoulder and the viewfinder fixed to his eye like a cybernetic attachment. The camera was such an integral part of the Californian that he looked odd to Nina without it. Beside him, Lydia held a microphone on a boom. The mic was connected to a pair of expensive but travel-scuffed headphones and a digital sound mixer in a padded bag hanging from her neck.

Fisher peered over their shoulders. 'We all set?' he asked.

'Good to go, man,' drawled Rivero. He switched on a light atop his camera.

Lydia adjusted a knob on her mixer. 'Audio is good. Ready when you are.'

'Okay, roll it,' said Fisher.

'David, can I have a few seconds?' said Nina. 'I want to do a piece to camera.'

Talal muttered impatiently in Arabic, but Ziff nodded. 'Of course.'

'Thanks.' She gathered her thoughts, then looked into the lens. 'Behind this doorway is a chamber of the First Temple, buried here on the Temple Mount for two and a half thousand years. What's inside, nobody knows. It may be nothing – or something wondrous that we hadn't even imagined. Either way, we'll know in a few moments.' She faced the entrance again.

Ziff took the cue, issuing an instruction. The two men strained at the crowbars. Metal rasped on stone, red dust spitting out from the cracks . . .

The slab moved.

With a deep crunch, it lurched forward by half an inch. The pair wielding the bars pushed harder. The great stone shifted again. 'It's coming,' Nina whispered as it crept from its resting place. 'It's tipping outwards at the top. Mohammad, get ready to catch it.'

The Jordanian reached up to the stone's upper edge. 'I can feel a gap!' he cried. 'A little more . . .'

A crackle of ancient, dusty cement – and the slab came loose.

Talal arrested its fall, the two other men hurriedly dropping the crowbars and gripping it. They carefully edged it aside.

Nina looked back at the camera. 'This is it,' she said, trying with little success to contain her excitement. 'The door is open – and now we'll be the first people to enter the First Temple in over two millennia.'

Ziff aimed a powerful flashlight inside, casting a disc of light on a plastered wall. Nina's own light joined it. 'It's some sort of antechamber,' she said, moving closer. 'Carvings on the walls, but . . . they look decorative rather than being inscriptions.'

The senior Israeli also advanced, subtly but firmly positioning himself in front of her. 'Yes, I've seen similar designs in the ruins at Gezer. The timescale would match the era of Solomon.'

'Almost three thousand years ago,' she said in an aside to camera. Carved stones were visible in places through the crumbling surface layer of plasterwork. 'Look at the workmanship, though. The stone blocks are cut far more precisely than anything at Gezer.'

'Solomon would have demanded that the First Temple be made to the highest standard,' Ziff mused. 'Equal to anything in Egypt, or better. This place was dedicated to God – it had to be worthy of Him.'

He stepped into the doorway and swept his light to take in the rest of the room. Nina joined him . . . and suppressed a feeling of disappointment. The whole chamber was just fifteen feet by twenty, the only other apparent exit choked by debris. She examined the floor, but if the room contained anything, it had been buried under rubble. Putting on a brave face, she signalled to Rivero. 'Can we get a shot of this before everyone comes in?'

She stepped back so the cameraman could film the interior. Ziff also retreated, his companions peering into the chamber past him. 'It is not the Holy of Holies,' said Raphael Yaron, the other Israeli, 'but still, it is amazing. The First Temple! Here for all this time, right underneath us.'

'What's in there?' Fisher asked.

'Not much, man,' Rivero replied. He slowly panned his camera around the room, then moved back to record the archaeologists' entrance.

'Huh. Disappointing,' said Lydia.

'What did you expect?' Nina re-entered the chamber, sniffing the air. Past experience had led her to expect a damp, musty atmosphere – water had a way of finding its way through to any open space – but this felt dry, even desiccated. Had it been deliberately sealed up before the temple was destroyed? 'I already found the Ark of the Covenant; there wasn't going to be a spare in here.'

Ziff went to the blocked exit and regarded a cracked section of plasterwork beside it. 'There is some Old Hebrew text here.'

The other members of his team joined him, Rivero filming over their shoulders. Nina watched as they puzzled over the inscription, shining her flashlight across the chamber . . . then her gaze went to the beam itself. The dust they had kicked up on entering was still in the air, drifting motes catching the bright light.

It was *where* they were drifting that caught her attention. She would have expected them to move away from the entrance as fresh air came in from outside. But they seemed to be moving perpendicular to it, towards one wall . . .

She turned to investigate. Fractured plasterwork greeted her, the temple's underlying stonework showing through. Again, the precision of the blocks stood out. The Solomonic-era ruins in Gezer, about twenty miles from Jerusalem, were much more irregular, gaps filled with copious amounts of mortar. The ones before her, cracks and chips of age notwithstanding, were so smooth-faced they could almost have been cut by a laser. Each block, each row, was perfectly aligned with the next—

Except where they weren't.

'Okay, weird,' Nina said to herself, gazing at the discrepancy.

'What's weird?' Lydia's voice. The redhead looked around in brief surprise before realising that the New Zealander's boom mic had picked up her whisper.

Rivero faced her; Nina addressed the camera as much as the

curious Ziff behind it. 'These bricks here,' she pointed at one of the gaps, 'don't line up with the ones on each side.'

'Not surprising,' said Ziff. 'The First Temple stood for over four hundred years, and Jerusalem has been hit by many earthquakes. It is probably just where damage was repaired.'

'I don't know,' Nina replied. 'I looked at this in the first place because I saw dust drifting in a breeze, but there's nowhere a breeze could be going. Unless . . .' She stared at the wall – then ducked through the entrance to collect one of the crowbars.

Ziff reacted in alarm. 'Nina, what are you doing?'

Fisher followed her back in. 'Keep filming,' he told Rivero. The cameraman moved to cover both Nina and the Israeli as they converged on the wall.

'I think there's another room behind here,' Nina announced, pointing the crowbar at the cracked plaster.

'You – you are not going to use that to break open the wall, are you?' asked Ziff, his eyes going wide.

'No,' she replied. 'I'm going to use it to move these stones on the floor to see if there's a threshold.'

'Good, that— No, wait!' he said, relief vaporising as he realised she was announcing an action rather than a plan, but by then she had already jammed the crowbar into the rubble. 'Stop! We haven't even photographed the chamber, never mind catalogued it!'

'David, there's nothing to catalogue,' said Nina, pushing at the crowbar. 'Not on the floor, anyway.'

'There could be valuable finds underneath it!'

'There won't be. Trust me, I *know*.' She realised that Rivero was filming the argument, but pressed on regardless. 'This rubble's just junk left over from when they blocked up that doorway. But the wall might be something a lot more interesting.'

Ziff scowled, glancing at the camera. For a moment he seemed about to demand that filming be stopped, but then he continued;

either he considered making his point a higher priority, Nina thought, or he wanted to ensure some screen time for himself. 'This is extremely unprofessional, Dr Wilde. You are rushing! Archaeology does not work to a shooting schedule.'

'You'd be surprised how often I've had a ticking clock,' Nina said. 'But it's got nothing to do with avoiding overtime. It's got to do with . . .' With a grunt, she levered up a gritty clod of debris. 'Being right. Look!'

She pointed at the newly exposed hole. 'There,' she went on, indicating a horizontal slab at the wall's base. 'I'd say that's the threshold of an entrance that was sealed up and plastered over. A secret chamber.' She looked at the camera, knowing that last would make a good dramatic moment.

'Why would they hide it?' asked Talal, unconvinced.

'Jerusalem was under siege by Nebuchadnezzar,' said Nina, carefully probing the wall above the slab. The plaster flaked at her touch. 'The priests of the First Temple knew he would loot and destroy the heart of their religion. They couldn't get out of the city without being seen by the Egyptian army, so anything they wanted to protect would have to be hidden. But they had to act in a hurry. See this?' She waited for Rivero to zoom in, then rubbed the crumbling plaster, more fragments breaking away. 'It's why there aren't any inscriptions here; it's much too coarse. It was applied in a rush. And like I said, the brickwork behind it isn't aligned with the other visible sections.' She stood. 'I think that if we clear away this plaster, we'll find another doorway behind it.'

Ziff took out a pouch of small tools and produced a brush, carefully swiping it across the plasterwork before blowing away dust. 'A draught . . .' he said, surprised, as the particles gently wafted past his face. 'You are right, there is a draught. Very small, but . . .'

'You think there *is* another room?' Yaron said.

'There could be, yes,' replied the bearded Israeli, deep in thought. 'There could be . . .'

'So what do we do about it?' said Nina. She tried not to sound too pointed, but it was clear to all that she had only one opinion on the proper course of action.

Ziff contemplated the cracked surface, then stepped back. 'Photograph this entire wall,' he ordered. 'A full record. Then we will remove a small piece of the plaster and investigate further.' He turned to Nina. 'Is that acceptable?'

'For now, absolutely,' she said. Ziff nodded, then issued more detailed instructions. Nina looked back at the watching camera, composing herself for another sound bite. 'If there really is a secret chamber behind that wall, then hopefully . . . we'll soon find out what's hidden inside.'

3

The process of photographing the wall was painstaking and, to Nina's mind, excessively prolonged. She decided not to call Ziff out on it, however. Having a debate with him based on her archaeological knowledge and experience was one thing; haranguing him for dragging his feet, on the other hand, was not something she wanted to do in front of a television camera.

Instead she went back outside. The crew had returned to the surface after Fisher decided the ongoing work was not interesting enough to film. The director was now on his phone – from the snippets of conversation she caught, she guessed to the production company's offices in Los Angeles – while the fourth member of the small crew lounged under an olive tree, the quadcopter beside him.

Howie Pinkett was tall, tanned and in his early twenties, wearing a corded wooden necklace and matching bangles. Nina had not been surprised to learn that the fast-talking Angeleno was a surfer. He did not lack ambition, though; while his official position in the crew was 'production assistant', a catch-all term that boiled down to 'gopher', the film school graduate also acted as a second cameraman, digital editor and archivist, and drone operator. Had Lydia ever let him touch her precious sound equipment, Nina was sure he would have taken on some of her role as well. But he most obviously had his eyes on an eventual director's job, usually staying as close to Fisher as his own shadow. 'So you really think there's a secret room down there?' he asked.

'I do, yeah,' Nina replied.

'That is so cool. Genuine Indiana Jones stuff, huh? Or Eden Crest stuff, I guess.' He flashed a perfect white smile.

'Uh-huh.' Her opinion of her sexed-up Hollywood avatar was not the highest.

'I guess you can visit the set of those movies whenever you want,' he went on, sitting up. 'Any way you could get me an invite? It'd be awesome to watch a big-budget blockbuster being filmed – especially when it's based on the life of someone I know.'

'*Very* loosely based,' she said. 'But I'm not really interested in that side of things.'

'Oh.' The single word conveyed his disappointment. 'But still . . . could you ask?'

To her relief, a distraction came when Ziff emerged from the tent. 'Nina!' he called. 'We're ready. Are you coming?'

'I wouldn't miss it,' she told him. 'Okay, everyone, let's go! Steven, hang up – it's time.'

Fisher frowned, saying something to his other party that she suspected was uncomplimentary, but ended the call. 'All right,' he told Lydia and Rivero, 'let's get down there. Howie, you coming?'

'Got all the drone footage we need, so I'm not gonna miss anything this time,' Howie replied, springing up. He collected an SLR camera – another of his roles was the team's still photographer – and strode to the tent with the others.

Nina and Ziff made their way back down underground, the camera crew following. The other archaeologists were waiting below. Lights had been positioned in the chamber to illuminate the wall. 'Okay,' she said, indicating one of the patches of missing plaster, 'I'd say that if we remove this corner here, it should reveal the doorway's edge. That'll confirm if there really is something here.'

'Or if there is not,' said Talal. 'Dr Ziff, we are moving too fast. Just because there are cameras here, we do not have to perform for them.'

'This is not a performance,' Ziff told him, a little defensively.

'Then why do this first when there is a real doorway?' He indicated the blocked exit.

'I have made my decision,' snapped the Israeli.

'So let's do it,' said Nina.

'All right.' Fisher waited for his crew to get in position, then retreated. 'Roll it.'

'I think you should do the honours, David,' Nina said to Ziff.

'Thank you,' he replied, taking a small chisel and carefully sliding its tip under the plaster's edge. 'We may be able to remove it in one piece if we are caref—'

A *snap* – and a chunk the size of a man's boot print fell away, smashing into gritty powder at the two archaeologists' feet.

Nina and Ziff stared mortified at the hole, the silence broken by a muffled snort. They both glared at Howie, who was struggling not to laugh. 'Sorry,' he said, holding a hand over his mouth.

The awkward moment was broken by a gasp from Yaron. 'Dr Ziff!' he cried. 'It *is* a doorway! Dr Wilde was right!'

She looked back at the broken section. A vertical line marking the division between the near-perfect brickwork and the misaligned section was clearly visible. 'Look at that!' she said, running her fingertip down it. 'Wow. That's almost *sharp*. I don't know what they used to cut it, but they did a hell of a job.'

Ziff glanced towards the blocked doorway. 'If this is like the other door, it would be . . . *this* wide,' he said, indicating a point four feet from the exposed edge. He poked the plaster with his chisel. A ragged crack opened in the surface. 'Yes! Here, I found it.' He flicked away the crumbled coating.

Nina leaned closer to the wall. 'I can feel the draught on my cheek,' she whispered. 'David, give me your chisel, please.'

He passed it to her. 'I can't see anything.'

'Nor can I, but I can definitely feel it . . .' She gently tapped the wall. Specks of grit dropped from a crack in the plaster – then she flinched from a puff of dust. 'Whoa! Okay, I think I found it.'

She eased away a piece of plasterwork. Behind it was a mortarless gap between two of the cruder bricks. 'It's a right bodge-job,' she said.

Ziff gave her a quizzical look. 'A what?'

'That's what my husband would call it. He's British, he says weird stuff,' she added. 'But this hole goes all the way through.' She poked the chisel into the gap. It penetrated easily.

'So what is inside?' asked Yaron.

'Only one way to find out,' Nina told him. 'David?'

The older archaeologist was caught between his innate caution and the prospect of unearthing something completely unexpected. 'Finding the First Temple alone is a major discovery,' he said at last, remembering he was being filmed and turning towards Rivero. 'Ordinarily, we would proceed slowly, searching one room at a time. But it is clear that this chamber is merely an entrance to something more important. We should open this hidden door, to find out what wonders of the Temple of Solomon are inside.'

Fisher nodded appreciatively; Nina was not the only one who had got the hang of playing to the camera. However, not everyone was as impressed. 'Dr Ziff, I protest!' said Talal. 'The Temple Mount is under the jurisdiction of Jordan, and I refuse to allow this . . . this *performance* to go any further.'

Ziff drew in an angry breath. 'This dig is a joint cooperation between Israel and Jordan. And *I* am in charge. That is what was agreed.'

'We are scientists, not television stars!' Talal protested. He jabbed a finger at Nina. 'We are not extras in her story!'

'You wouldn't even have found this place if it wasn't for me,' she reminded him. 'I told you, my way works.'

'But now we are rushing and causing damage so that she can . . . she can trend on Twitter!'

Ziff held up a hand. 'Mohammad, can you honestly say that if you were in charge, and the cameras were not here, you would not also want to open the secret door?'

'I – no, no, I would not,' he said, but his hesitation revealed his true feelings.

'Look,' Nina said to Talal, 'I'm not here to step on any-one's toes – and I'm grateful to both Israel and Jordan for being invited. But I know while we as professional archaeologists would all absolutely *love* to spend a week excavating each little corner of a site, I'm also a realist. I've run a major archaeo-logical agency. And I know for a fact that the big, exciting finds finance the smaller ones, the ones that sometimes we care about more.'

Talal frowned. 'What are you saying?'

'I'm saying that something I've learned from dealing with Hollywood is that if you start with a bang, you get people's attention. And the bigger your initial find is perceived to be, the more time and resources you'll get to follow it up.' A wry smile. 'And the better it reflects on you. You *personally*, Mohammad. One big find can make your career.'

The Jordanian was still unconvinced. 'That is how it works in America. We are not so . . . shallow.'

'That's how it works *everywhere*. You just haven't been doing this long enough to see it.'

Ziff nodded. 'That is the truth.'

Talal snorted. 'I hope that when I am as old as the two of you, I am not so cynical.'

'I'm not *old*!' said Nina, affronted – though her recent fortieth birthday was something she had tried to downplay as much as she could. Another muffled chuckle came from Howie's direction.

'We will open the door,' Ziff announced firmly. 'Let us see what the priests were hiding from Nebuchadnezzar.' He issued instructions to the other archaeologists. Talal scowled, but joined them.

She quietly sighed in relief. 'That was good, Nina,' said Fisher, giving her a thumbs-up. 'Drama, conflict – that's what people want to see. It creates a good narrative.'

'The only narrative I care about is the one that ends with us seeing what's behind that wall,' she replied.

'Yeah, sure. But if you can use a sledgehammer to make the first hole, that would be great. It's more exciting. Remember, start with a bang!'

She gave him an irritated look for echoing her own words, then went to assist Ziff and the others.

'Ready when you are,' said Fisher eagerly. 'Make it big!'

Nina tried not to let her exasperation show. The plaster covering the hidden doorway had been cleared away, the bricks blocking the entrance now fully exposed. More gaps were visible in the mortar, some of the roughly hewn stones actually loose to the touch. 'Okay,' she told Ziff and his team, 'I think if we pull this out first, it'll make it very easy to clear the rest.'

'I agree,' Ziff replied, prodding the brick she had indicated. It clunked against its neighbours. A long breath, then: 'Raphael, the pry bar.'

The other Israeli slid the crowbar into a gap, then pushed. The stone ground out of its space with very little effort. Talal lifted it clear, then Nina and Ziff shone lights through the hole.

'Definitely another room,' the redhead reported. 'A lot bigger than this one. I can see . . .' She frowned. 'A pit, but I can't tell what's in it.'

'If you open that hole a bit wider, I could fly the drone in for a look,' suggested Howie.

'I'd prefer to see for myself, thanks,' said Nina. She drew back to let Yaron continue his work.

The opening was soon wide enough for a person to traverse. 'Are we going in?' she asked Ziff, who nodded. 'You first.'

'No, you, Dr Wilde,' he replied. 'Without you, the First Temple would never have been found. It is only right that you should be first to see what is inside.'

She smiled. 'Thank you.' A quick aside to camera. 'Let's hope the priests didn't leave any booby traps.'

Talal shook his head. 'You have seen too many movies.'

'I've seen too many booby traps,' she retorted. 'You wanna go first instead?'

He hesitated. 'No. Dr Ziff is right. You should go.'

Her smile became more sardonic. 'Okay,' she told Rivero, 'follow me and Dr Ziff inside. Everyone else, come through after the camera. You ready?' The others acknowledged. 'All right. Let's see what we have.'

She stepped into the secret chamber.

The first thing that struck her was, to her relief, not some long-poised mechanism of death. Rather, it was the smell. The air felt much damper than in the outer room. But it was also stagnant, unpleasant.

Rivero entered behind Ziff, sweeping his light across the circular chamber. It was close to a hundred feet across, broad columns supporting a domed ceiling. A round pit occupied most of the floor. Its walls were stepped, forming an inverted ziggurat. She followed the beam as the cameraman tilted it downwards to reveal . . .

'Wow!' she cried, the exclamation echoing from the walls.

Ziff's reaction was of equal astonishment, though more reverential. He murmured in Hebrew, putting a hand to his chest in wonderment.

A city was exquisitely rendered in miniature on the pit's broad floor. The largest building – a temple or palace, Nina guessed – was an elaborate rectangular structure with twelve towers rising like battlements around its vaulted roof. Not just the city's structures had been modelled; its landscape was also present, the palace sitting atop a jutting promontory with a near-vertical cliff dropping down to a river curling around its foot. The latter explained the smell. The channel had once had water flowing through it, but now only sludge remained.

The sight overcame even Talal's dour mood. He exchanged excited words with his Jordanian colleague, then darted his flashlight beam over the model city. 'It must be ancient Jerusalem!'

Nina shook her head. 'The topography's wrong. There isn't a cliff like that on the Temple Mount.'

'But what else could it be?'

Ziff noticed something on one of the lower tiers. 'Look at this,' he said, hurrying down a steep flight of steps. 'There is text, all around the wall.'

'Is that Old Hebrew?' Nina asked as she followed.

'I think so – yes, it is,' he said as he reached the inscriptions. 'The language of King Solomon.'

'So what does it say?' demanded Fisher as he descended behind Rivero and Lydia. The cameraman positioned himself to watch Ziff.

'Wait, let me work.' The elderly archaeologist studied a prominent section of text enclosed in a rectangle. 'This is Solomon's name, here,' he pointed at a particular word, 'and these first lines say . . . "The farthest reach of King Solomon's realm." Then there is a word I don't recognise – it must be a name. *Zan, hhet, el, kaph* . . .' He fell silent for a moment, combining the individual

Hebrew letters into a word. '*Zhakana*, it says. "Zhakana, city of . . .'"

His eyes widened. 'What is it?' asked Nina.

Ziff turned towards her, Rivero's camera catching his unnerved expression. 'It says,' he announced, 'that this is Zhakana . . . City of the Damned.'

'Well, that's not ominous or anything,' muttered Lydia.

Nina cautiously went to the bottom of the pit as Ziff continued reading. Talal followed her, as did Rivero. The turgid river's outer bank marked the diorama's edge. She stopped at it, trying to get a sense of how big the city would be in the real world. The palace on the clifftop had no visible doors or windows, nothing she could relate to a human scale.

The smaller buildings did have them, however – as well as a surprise. 'They're ruins,' she realised. 'The whole city's in ruins, except for the palace.' The models themselves were not broken, but had been carefully built to replicate how their originals had succumbed to the ravages of time.

Assuming the doorways were six feet high . . . 'The whole city must be well over half a mile across,' she said after some rapid mental calculations. 'And I'm guessing from these trees around the outside,' she pointed out clusters of shrivelled twigs, 'that it was either in a forest or a jungle.'

'It was in the jungle,' said Ziff.

Nina looked up at him. 'You're sure?'

'I've translated more of the text. It describes Zhakana as being hidden in the jungle on the outer reaches of the territory of Sheba.'

'Sheba?' asked Howie, who had been taking photographs. 'As in, the Queen of?'

'No, the cat food,' Nina said sarcastically. 'Of course *that* Sheba. Or the kingdom of Seba or Saba, depending on the translation. There hasn't actually been much archaeological evidence found of it to date, but it seems that it covered both the Arabian and African sides of the Red Sea.'

'The queen, Bilqis, came to Solomon here in Jerusalem,' said Talal. 'Some say Solomon summoned her to pledge her kingdom to God, others say she came to test him, to see if he was truly the wisest man on the earth. But in each story, they married and had a son, Menelik – the first emperor of Ethiopia.'

'Bilqis is the Arabic name for the queen,' said Ziff, excitement in his voice. 'But I think we can now say that her traditional Ethiopian name, Makeda, is correct.'

'Why?' Nina asked.

'Because it is written here! After they married, the kingdoms of Israel and Sheba were united. Solomon visited his new lands with his wife – and she took him to Zhakana, City of the Damned, the greatest secret of Sheba.' He waved a hand towards the impressive miniature below. 'And this is it. Perfect in every detail, or so Solomon claims.'

'*Solomon* claims it?'

'If the text is correct,' Ziff continued, 'this chamber, this map room, was built on Solomon's orders to be an exact replica of Zhakana.'

Nina noticed more carvings on the lowest wall surrounding the city. These were not words, however. She pointed her flashlight at the nearest. 'Look at this.' The beam revealed a rolling relief chiselled into the stone. 'It's a landscape – hills and mountains.' She moved the light along the wall. The terrain rose and fell, sometimes with multiple planes to show where a more distant peak was visible beyond nearer features.

She looked back at the model, noting that one of the palace's towers was capped by a small bronze cylinder – the only metal in the city. 'I wonder . . .' she said to herself, crouching beside the cliff to peer more closely at it. Its top had several vertical slots cut across it at different angles. At a nudge from

Fisher, Rivero turned away from Ziff to film her.

Nina positioned herself to look through one slot as if it were a gunsight, aiming her torch at the target area of the wall. One of the carved mountains was highlighted.

Talal stood beside her. 'What have you found?'

'Hold on, let me try this . . .' She sidestepped to look through another slot. This led her gaze to a second peak. 'I think it's some sort of navigation aid, a way to—'

'Nina!' Ziff's cry this time was full-blown exhilaration. 'Mohammad! Come here, quick!'

She and Talal hurried back up the stairs to find Ziff reading a dense section of Hebrew text. 'What is it?'

'More about the city. The large building on the cliff – it is the Palace Without Entrance!'

'What, from the legend?' Nina asked dubiously.

'I know, it sounds unbelievable. But according to this, Solomon ordered the Palace Without Entrance to be built to contain a great, yet dangerous power. Only those with the wisdom to use it for good can enter, because Solomon's own riddles protect it.'

'How do you enter somewhere without an entrance?'

'I don't know. Perhaps the legend itself holds a clue?'

'What legend?' asked Fisher.

Ziff faced him. 'An ancient Hebrew story. Once, when Solomon was travelling, he discovered a magnificent palace, with no doors or windows. He spoke to some eagles guarding it—'

Lydia's eyebrows rose. 'He could talk to birds?'

'Solomon could do a lot of things, if you believe the legends,' said Nina, amused. 'He could summon and control demons, fly on a magical throne, talk to animals – all this and the whole "being the wisest man in the world" thing too.'

Ziff made an impatient sound, then continued. 'Solomon

spoke to the eagles until he found the oldest, who remembered an entrance now buried by sand. So Solomon's men dug, and found the way in.'

'I didn't see any eagles on the model,' said Nina. 'Or sand.'

'We will have to examine it in detail. But there is more in the text.' He went back to the wall. 'The power Solomon built the palace to contain is named here. He calls it *Imashamir* . . . "the Mother of the Shamir".'

'The Shamir?' she echoed, startled. 'The stone he supposedly used to build the First Temple?'

'Nina,' Fisher said quietly from behind the camera, 'explanation for the rubes?'

'The Shamir is . . . well, it's hard to describe,' Nina said. 'It's either a green stone or a living creature, like a worm, depending on how you interpret the stories. Either way, it was kept in a lead box that was only opened when it was needed, because its gaze could split stone and shatter metal.' The crew's impressed reactions told her that was exactly the kind of juicy legend they wanted to hear.

'It was given to Solomon by God,' Ziff went on, bowing his head slightly, 'so he could build the temple without using anything that could also be used as a weapon, which would defile it. It was only very small, the size of a peppercorn, but incredibly powerful. Solomon used it to cut the temple's stones.'

'Which might explain how they were so precisely made,' Nina mused. She regarded the model. 'The Mother of the Shamir . . . it could be where Solomon's Shamir originally came from. This city in Ethiopia.'

'Are there jungles in Ethiopia?' Howie asked.

'Actually, yes. But the borders of modern Ethiopia are much smaller than in the past – it used to cover a big chunk of the entire continent.'

Ziff was disappointed. 'Then there is very little chance of

finding it. A pity – finding the Temple of Solomon is remarkable, but an entire lost city? That would be incredible!'

'We still *can* find it,' Nina said, her excitement returning. 'That's what I was about to say.'

'What do you mean?' asked Talal.

She looked between the archaeologists and the omnipresent camera. 'The metal spire on the palace – if you look through the slots on it, they point to different mountains. It's a way to triangulate the city's exact position! If you can identify the mountains, you can use their relative positions to calculate the only place where you would see them from those bearings.'

Talal examined the carved landscape. 'But none of the mountains have names. We do not know which ones they are.'

'We don't *need* to,' Nina insisted. 'There are topographical databases of the whole of Africa, and we can use a computer to search for a particular configuration of mountains. I've done it before.' She gazed at the sprawling miniature below. 'Solomon left clues to Zhakana's location. We can follow them – and we can find the lost city!'

4

England

Eddie Chase stood before the gravestone, head bowed in respect. It was the final resting place of his former commanding officer, mentor, comrade – and friend – Colonel Jim McCrimmon, known to all close to him as 'Mac'. The Scot had taken the young Corporal Chase under his wing when he was first accepted into the SAS, teaching him both what it meant and what was necessary to be a member of the British army's elite force. Eddie had repaid the favour by carrying his badly wounded commander to safety while under intense fire in Afghanistan, the act for which he had received the Victoria Cross.

Mac had helped the Yorkshireman out on several occasions after he left the SAS, even joining him and Nina on some of their adventures. Until one of them cost him his life.

Eddie had thought he was long over the grief of Mac's murder, but the memory brought some unexpectedly raw emotions. He swallowed, but held a stoic expression, not wanting his daughter to realise he was upset. His eyes went to the headstone's inscription.

Fiducia integritatis honore
He served and protected his country

Latin was one of Nina's specialities, not his, but he had

checked the text's meaning after first visiting the grave some years before. *With courage, integrity and honour* was a near enough translation, and as far as he was concerned, completely accurate. Mac had given him standards to live up to, and he hoped he had done his commander proud.

'Was he your friend, Daddy?' Macy asked, drawing him out of his reverie.

'Yeah, love, he was,' Eddie told the red-haired five-year-old. 'He was . . . my boss when I was in the army. He taught me everything I know.'

'So he was like your mommy?'

He smiled. 'Not exactly. Come on, then. Shall we go and meet Auntie Lizzie and Grandad?'

'Daddy!' she chided. 'She told you to call her *Elizabeth*, not Lizzie.'

'Did she? Must have said it to my bad ear.' He faced the grave again. A last moment of contemplation, then he saluted. 'Wish you could have met my little girl, Mac,' he said quietly, again feeling emotion welling. He took her by the hand and walked away.

Eddie checked his watch as they headed for the nearest Underground station. They were due to meet his family in about thirty minutes; he knew from having once lived in London that they should make it on time.

Things had changed since calling the capital his home, though. Times were clearly harder: payday loan companies the only new businesses amongst boarded-up shops, cars jolting hard over crumbling potholes, refuse spilling from uncollected rubbish bags along the pavement, a general sense of *grime* that nobody had the money or inclination to scrub away. London's energy was still there, but compared to fifteen years earlier it felt as if people were keeping it to themselves, hoarding it. Heads were down, eyes fixed on the ground one step ahead so as not to bump into anyone while scurrying to the next appointment.

Eddie knew the vibe. He had felt it before, but in places he would never have expected to compare to London. He associated it with the fringes of war zones, a perpetual tension and worry that however bad things were now, they could get worse at any moment. Don't look anyone in the eye, don't attract trouble . . .

Rather than give in, he lifted his own head higher. 'What do you think of London, Macy?'

The little girl's reply was hesitant, as if not wanting to hurt his feelings. 'I . . . I don't like it as much as home, Daddy.'

Having lived in Manhattan for twelve years, and mainly associating London with his disastrous first marriage, he was inclined to agree. 'That's okay, love. I don't either.'

'It's very dirty,' she went on. 'And everybody looks really angry. Or scared.'

'That's London, baby,' he said with a smile, impressed by her astuteness. Although a raised voice had perhaps given her a clue. Ahead, a large man was shouting at someone he had cornered in a vacant shop's doorway. A few paces nearer, and Eddie realised the object of his ire was a much smaller woman with pale Slavic features, clutching shopping bags. Other pedestrians hurried past, unwilling to get involved. Not liking the look of the situation, he quickened his pace.

The man's words became clear as they approached. '. . . an' now we're out of Europe – so you lot are out too!' he bellowed, his accent a coarse Estuary English. 'This is our country, not yours, so fuck off home!'

'This – this *is* my home,' the woman stammered, terrified.

'No it fuckin' isn't! Fuckin' Poles, you came over here an' nicked all the best jobs! I 'ad ten years on the dole 'cause of you lot! Well, we're kickin' you all out now, so you can fuck off!'

'Oi!' Eddie said, ushering Macy behind him. 'There a problem?'

The red-faced man glowered at him. He was six inches taller than the Yorkshireman, and much broader, though fat rather than muscle stretched the fabric of his football shirt. 'What's your fuckin' problem?'

'You, if you don't stop swearing in front of my little girl.' He looked at the frightened woman, who was barely half her abuser's weight. 'Are you okay?'

'I – I was just shopping, he started shouting at me,' she said, almost in tears.

Eddie turned back to the man. 'I think you should leave her alone.'

'Fuck off, you bald ponce!'

'Macy,' Eddie said, 'go back by that other doorway, love.' His daughter hurriedly retreated.

The man wheeled on him, fists clenched into meaty balls. 'Who d'you fuckin' think you are?' One arm drew back—

Eddie's combat instincts had already kicked in. Killing, crippling or knocking out his opponent were all readily available options, but instead he chose forceful self-defence. He grabbed the other man's arm as it swung at his head, ducking and twisting sharply to shove it up behind his attacker's back. The man gasped in pain – then the sound was abruptly cut off as the former SAS soldier slammed his face against the shop window. 'I'm the bloke who's going to make you apologise to this lady.'

The man strained to peel his mouth off the glass. 'Fuck off, you – *aaaagh!*'

Eddie forced his arm even higher, making his shoulder joint crackle. 'Sorry begins with an "s", not an "f". You want to try again?' He increased the pressure.

'F— s— *sorry!*' the man screeched. 'Sorry, sorry!'

'Say it to *her*.'

He squinted at his victim. 'I'm sorry! Oh God, stop, let go! You're breakin' my arm!'

'Macy, cover your ears,' said Eddie. She did so. 'Okay,' he growled at the now-keening thug, 'you: fuck off. And if I see you again, a broken fucking arm'll be the least of it. You get me?' The other man nodded. 'Right. Now bugger off.'

He eased the pressure and stepped back. The sweating man gasped, lowering his arm as far as Eddie would allow. The Yorkshireman turned him away from the woman, then shoved him clear. The man made a hasty retreat, shouting abuse once he reached a safe distance.

Eddie ignored him. 'You all right?' he asked the woman.

She managed a faint smile of relief. 'Yes, thank you, thank you. I don't know why he did that – he just trapped me and started shouting. I'm not even Polish, I'm Estonian!'

'I think he was too thick to know the difference.' He returned to Macy, who was still covering her ears. 'Okay, love, you can let go now.'

She lowered her hands. 'Are you all right, Daddy?'

'Yeah, I'm fine. Are you okay?'

She nodded, looking worriedly after the retreating thug. 'He wasn't a nice man.'

'He wasn't, no.'

'Did he hurt that lady?'

'No, he just scared her.'

'Why?'

Eddie didn't feel the time was right for a discussion about racism and xenophobia. 'Some people are idiots, and bullies,' he said instead.

'But you stopped him. You're really brave, Daddy!'

He smiled. 'I did what was right, that's all. If everyone did that, the world'd be a much nicer place.'

'Is that why you joined the soldiers? To make the world nicer?'

He grinned. 'I don't think anyone's ever described it that way before, but . . . yeah, I suppose I did. There are nasty people who do bad things, and we tried to stop them and help the people they'd hurt.'

She hugged him. 'You *are* really brave, Daddy.'

'I do my best.' He picked up Macy and resumed their interrupted journey.

The encounter had made them late.

'And what time do you call this?' said his sister Elizabeth mockingly.

'Couldn't find a clock,' Eddie told the three people waiting for them in the small park across from the Houses of Parliament. 'You know where one is?' He pretended to squint at the Elizabeth Tower, the official name of the clock tower more commonly known as Big Ben. The Yorkshireman had arranged to meet his family there to show Macy the iconic symbol of Britain. 'Actually, we got held up on the way.'

'Daddy told a nasty man to leave a lady alone!' Macy said excitedly.

Larry Chase, Eddie's father, knelt to embrace the little girl. 'He did, did he?'

Elizabeth shook her head. 'Even when you're on holiday with your daughter, you can't stay out of trouble, can you?'

'Well, I could've just let some no-neck idiot keep on abusing a woman half his size, but hey,' he shrugged, 'I wanted to set a good example for my daughter. Mad, I know. Anyway, hi, Lizzie! And Dad, Julie.'

'Hi, Eddie,' said Julie Chase, his stepmother. Larry's second wife was actually younger than either of his children, a fact that Eddie still found disconcerting even after he had settled most of his differences with his once-estranged father. 'And hi, Macy! Gosh, you've got so big.'

'What happened, then?' Larry asked him. 'Was this just on the street?'

'Yeah, we were on our way to the Tube station when this moron started having a go. I had words with him, and he stopped.'

'Daddy beat him up!' Macy said proudly.

'I did *not* beat him up,' Eddie hurriedly clarified on seeing the trio's startled looks. 'I just made him apologise and then told him to get lost, that's all.'

'Why was he having a go at her?' said Larry.

'For not being English, far as I could tell.'

Elizabeth made a disgusted sound. 'There's been so much of that going on since Brexit, it's horrible. You're lucky to be out of it in the States.'

'Because nobody in America's said anything racist lately,' Eddie replied sarcastically. 'But yeah, things feel different.'

'Not as much money around, and what there is, is going to the people at the very top,' said Larry. 'Granted, 'twas ever thus, but it seems more so than usual. Pulling out of Europe's really hit my company, because more than half my business was with the EU. *Very* glad I'm about to retire.'

'He's pretty much retired already,' Julie said with a smile. 'He spends as much time playing golf as in the office now.'

'How's Holly?' Eddie asked Elizabeth of his niece. 'We haven't seen her since she was in the States two years back.'

'She's fine,' his sister replied. 'She finished her degree – with a first, so I'm very proud! – and is working for a media company in Bristol, but she's hoping to get a job in America. She would have come tonight, but couldn't get away.'

'Aw, shame.'

'I know, she would have loved to see Macy again. So what else have you two been doing? You've been in England for a couple of days, haven't you?'

Eddie nodded. 'Nina's filming her documentary in Israel, so I thought I'd show Macy her roots. Took her up to Yorkshire to see our old neck of the woods, visited the children's museum in Halifax, then went to Alton Towers before coming down here.'

'How is Nina?' Julie asked. 'I tried phoning her to wish her a happy birthday, but couldn't get hold of her. I suppose she was already in Israel.'

'Yeah, she spent her fortieth in the bloody desert. Even I didn't get to talk to her until the next day. Although to be honest, she wasn't exactly celebrating it anyway. The big four-oh's more when a lot of people start worrying about being middle-aged.'

'Did you worry about it?' Julie asked him.

He had passed the landmark five years earlier. 'Nah, only thing that bothered me was that I was halfway to going bald. So I thought, sod it, and went for the full Captain Picard.' He rubbed a hand over his shaven scalp. 'Got my retaliation in first.'

'Everything's war with you, isn't it?' said Elizabeth. 'It always has been.'

He didn't take her bait for two reasons: the first was that he had no intention of getting into an argument with her in front of Macy, and the second that his phone had started ringing. 'Speaking of Nina, that's her,' he said, recognising the ringtone. He answered. 'Ay up, love! I'm here with the rest of the family. How're you doing?'

'Great, thanks!' Nina replied. He instantly knew she was excited about some new discovery, the barely contained exhilaration in her voice as familiar as her ringtone. 'You won't believe what we found today. We opened up the First Temple, which was a big event in itself, but then once we were inside—'

'You want to say hi to everyone before you get into an archaeological frenzy?' he suggested. 'I'll put you on speaker. Macy, it's Mummy.'

'Mommy,' Macy corrected as he switched to speakerphone.

'Yeah, yeah. Say hello to her. Everyone else, an' all.'

A chorus of 'Hi, Nina!' followed. 'And a belated happy fortieth birthday!' added Julie. 'Sorry we missed it!'

'Thanks,' Nina said, sounding far from sorry herself. 'Is everyone okay?'

'We're all fine,' Julie told her. 'We're taking Macy to see *Starshine Stables* this evening.'

'I . . . don't know what that is.'

'It's a musical, love,' said Eddie, grinning. 'You know, with songs and dancing and stuff.'

Her reply had a light touch of frosting. 'Yes, I'm aware of the form, darling.'

'It's about magic horses!' Macy said enthusiastically.

'Sounds like you'll enjoy it, Macy. I hope everyone else does! Anyway, can you put Daddy back on? I need to tell him something.'

Hiding his exasperation, Eddie returned the phone to his ear. 'It'd better be "I love you". Or about that thing you don't want to do nearly often enough.'

'Funny man. No, I've got to tell you about what I found today, because I might need to stay out here a bit longer to examine it fully.'

'What?'

His disapproval was clear in the single word. Nina tempered her enthusiasm, slightly. 'We found a secret chamber, a map room. We think it gives the location of a lost city visited by King Solomon. I want to work with the team here to decipher it. We'll also be shooting extra material for the documentary to cover the new find.'

'And how long'll that take?'

'I don't know yet. A couple of days? Maybe.'

He moved a few steps away from the others for some modicum of privacy. '*Maybe?*'

'Look, it's a major discovery! I really don't know how long, okay?'

Now trying to conceal more than mere exasperation, Eddie glanced at their daughter. 'Macy was expecting to see you in two days.'

'If I can wrap everything up in time, I will. But I can't guarantee it at the moment.'

'Well, you could if you let someone else take care of this new thing you've found.' He considered what he had just said. 'You see? You were worried about turning forty 'cause you thought there wasn't anything else left for you to discover, but there you go. There's still loads of old buried junk out there.'

'It's hardly "junk", Eddie.' The frost became more icy.

'I'm joking, love. You should know what I'm like by now.'

'And you know what *I'm* like. So you know I really, really want to see this through. Okay?'

His promise to stop using obscenities entirely had been spectacularly blown on a Himalayan mountainside two years earlier, but he still dropped his voice so Macy wouldn't hear him swear. 'For fuck's sake, Nina. If it was just me, you know I'd complain, but let you do your thing. But what about Macy? What am I supposed to tell her, that her mum thinks some old ruin's more important than her daughter?'

'That's not fair! Of course I don't think that. But—'

'If you didn't, there wouldn't *be* a "but".'

'God *damn* it, Eddie!' A long pause as she calmed herself. 'Okay, look. I wasn't scheduled to leave Israel until the day after tomorrow anyway, so we'll talk about this again tomorrow evening. Is that all right?'

'Yeah. So long as you haven't already made up your mind.'

'I haven't, I promise.' She sighed. 'Can I talk to Macy?'

'Yeah, of course.' He put on a broad smile for the little girl's benefit. 'Hey, love. It's Mummy. *Mommy*, I know,' he added, pre-empting her inevitable correction.

'Everything okay?' Elizabeth asked him as Macy chatted to Nina.

'Yeah, yeah,' he replied.

'Archaeology?'

'Uh-huh.'

'Ah.' Knowing glances passed between his family members.

Macy said goodbye to her mother, then returned the phone. 'Eddie?' said Nina.

'Yeah, I'm here.'

'I'll talk to you tomorrow, then. Okay?'

'Okay.'

'Right. I love you. Hope you enjoy the show.'

'Love you too,' he replied, still annoyed at his wife – and himself, for letting himself *get* annoyed with her. 'Talk to you soon.' He faced the others with another fake smile. 'So. This horse thing'd better be good, then!'

5

Jerusalem

The alarm on Nina's iPhone warbled at 6 a.m., but she was already up, making her first coffee of the day before checking her laptop. She had left the computer running overnight, a program comparing a topographical database to a set of search parameters. Said parameters were vaguer than she would have liked, as there had been no indication of the heights of any of the mountains used to triangulate the lost city's position. She had instead been forced to input the relative bearings of each carved peak surrounding the model of Zhakana and hope there was enough data to produce a result, but had not predicted much success.

Which meant the message on the screen came as a true surprise.

She hurriedly reread it, almost expecting it to morph into something more disappointing. But it remained the same. *Location found*. A string of numbers followed – the longitude and latitude of the place the program had identified.

The numbers were not as long as she had hoped, though. The software was capable of deducing a location to within as little as fifty feet. The result here had only narrowed it down to an area of four square miles.

But that was more than close enough.

Nina quickly brought up the coordinates on a digital globe,

zooming in on Africa, central Africa, the Democratic Republic of Congo, the huge country's eastern region. The nearest sizeable settlement was over thirty miles away, which considering the terrain and dense jungle might as well have been a hundred. No roads were visible on the satellite imagery, only rivers winding languidly through the unbroken carpet of verdant green.

She switched to a three-dimensional view of the target zone. Terrain features sprang up. A river had curved around the base of the promontory upon which the model Palace Without Entrance stood; she used the trackpad to rotate the view, searching for places where waterways ran around cliffs.

It took several minutes to survey all the rivers. Two locations seemed promising. She zoomed in on the first.

Nothing unusual was visible on the ground, but she knew from experience that even large structures could be hidden from aerial observation by the jungle canopy. She moved the virtual camera in a full circle. The terrain didn't correspond to the model, not flat enough to contain the city.

The second site. She immediately saw that this was a much closer match. There was the promontory, the river wrapped around its foot like a constricting snake . . .

And peeking through the covering of green, tantalising hints of stone.

Nina felt a little kick of excitement. She zoomed in, but the image degenerated into pixelated splodges. The satellite photography was at the limit of its resolution; with nothing there but raw jungle, none of the commercial providers had felt the need to photograph it in higher detail. Government agencies would undoubtedly have better images, but she no longer had access to them.

'Dammit,' she muttered. She was sure there was more on the clifftop than just trees, but had no way to confirm it. Another click to mark the exact spot, then she returned to a map view.

The nearest major town with an airport was Butembo, close to the Ugandan border about a hundred miles to the north-east. Could she hire someone to make a photographic overflight?

Before she could ponder any more on the prospect, her phone rang. She was surprised; it was barely past dawn. 'Hello?'

'Nina, hello.' Ziff. 'Sorry to wake you.'

'No problem, I was already up. I'm surprised you are, though.'

'I had a phone call.' He sounded concerned. 'I've just been told about a news story. Are you at your computer?'

'Yes. David, what's going on?'

'You should see for yourself.' He gave her the web address of what she guessed was a Jordanian newspaper. 'The top story, you can't miss it.'

'Okay, let me see – oh my God!' she gasped as the page loaded.

The headline was in Arabic, the script unreadable . . . but the accompanying pictures told her everything. They showed the map room inside the First Temple, the largest image a wide shot of the model city. 'Where the hell did these come from?' Nina demanded, appalled. 'Nothing was supposed to be released until – wait, son of a bitch,' she said as a possibility occurred to her. 'Did Mohammad Talal take these?'

'I already spoke to him,' Ziff told her. 'He says he had nothing to do with it. The others deny it as well. What about your film crew?'

'I don't know, but I'm sure as hell going to find out.'

'It may not have been anyone on either of our teams, though. Some of the diggers still had access after we left, and the security guards on the Temple Mount could have simply walked in and taken pictures on their phones.'

'Great, so anyone could have leaked the biggest archaeological discovery of the year for fifty bucks a photo, and we've got no way of finding out who.' She scrolled through the pictures.

'Jesus, these are clear enough to read the text on the walls!'

'I know. The story has a partial translation,' the Israeli told her glumly. 'It names Zhakana, describes how Solomon visited the Palace Without Entrance—'

'There's a – a goddamn *panorama* here!' Nina cut in. Another picture showed a great swathe of the carved landscape surrouning the model city. 'They might as well have printed a treasure map!'

'What do you mean?' Ziff asked, surprised.

'I mean, I put the data from the model into a topographical analysis program. And it found Zhakana!'

He was shocked. 'Where?'

'Eastern Congo, the Democratic Republic. It's in the middle of the jungle, but it should be accessible by river. And these photos tell the whole world where it is! If I could find it, so can anyone else.'

'Just because they *can* find it doesn't mean that they *will*. Jungle exploration is hard work, as we both know. And DR Congo is not a country many people would choose to visit.'

'People will do a hell of a lot if they think there's something valuable at the end of it,' she countered. 'One of the reasons the International Heritage Agency was set up in the first place was to control this kind of information and stop tomb raiders from looting newly found sites. But this? Anyone with a map, a computer and patience will be able to use these pictures to find Zhakana. And there's nothing we can do to stop them.'

'I can contact the Jordanian government. They can put pressure on the newspaper to take down the pictures.'

'It's too late now. Once something's on the internet, you may as well put it on a billboard in Times Square.'

'So what should we do?'

'We need to have a full meeting, try to figure out damage control. Beyond that, though? I have no idea.'

'I'll call everyone to the site.'

'Great. I'll see you soon.'

Nina huffed in angry exasperation as she hung up. Finding whoever had leaked the pictures was now less important than trying to minimise the damage, both to the ongoing work at the First Temple and whatever might happen at Zhakana. But what could she do?

Contact the IHA was her first thought. But she had left the agency over half a decade ago, her last dealings two years previously, and Dr Lester Blumberg was still its director. She and Blumberg were not on each other's Christmas card lists, to put it mildly.

So how to protect the new discovery from looters?

She didn't know much about the Democratic Republic of Congo, other than that the first word of its name was practically ironic and that while it was rich in natural resources, it was also unstable and fraught with violence. Someone would have to locate the site on the ground, then arrange with the Congolese government to secure it.

But who could she trust to do that, and who had the contacts necessary to protect the site once it was found? And who would pay for it? She considered herself very comfortably off thanks to her television work, books and film deals, but not nearly enough to fund an expedition out of her own pocket, and she couldn't imagine Eddie being happy about her doing so even if she could. So who . . . ?

An idea took on form. She almost dismissed it out of hand, but then gave it greater consideration. Why not? At the very least, she had to try.

She scrolled through her phone's contacts. The number she found was American, the area code 323: Los Angeles. There was a ten-hour time difference between Jerusalem and LA, so it was evening in Hollywood. The person she needed to speak to might still be available.

Nina gathered her thoughts . . . then made the call.

Two hours later, she arrived at the Temple Mount and entered the dig's tent. Ziff and his team were there, as were Fisher and the film crew. 'What happened?' said the elderly Israeli. 'We expected you over an hour ago.'

'I know, I'm sorry,' she said. 'I had to make a call, which lasted a lot longer than I expected. But I've got some good news.'

'You have found out who sold the photographs of the First Temple?' asked Talal.

'No, I'm afraid not.'

'This leak's kinda destroyed one of our unique selling points,' said Fisher. 'We could have had a worldwide exclusive – the first time Joe Public saw the map room, it would have been on our show. But now, by the time we reach the air it'll be old hat.'

'Well, hopefully the rest of the documentary should still draw the crowds,' Nina said. 'But this call was about something else.' She addressed the whole film crew. 'A proposition – for you.'

'For us?' said Lydia, confused.

'Who did you call?' Rivero asked.

'Mike Konigsberg, in LA. And after he heard what I had to say, he got the network head on a conference call right away.'

Fisher was not happy. 'Wait, you called my boss behind my back?'

'This wasn't about the current show. This is something new. I told David this morning that the leak of the map room pictures means that sooner or later, and probably sooner, someone will use them to find Zhakana.'

'Because that'll be dead easy to do,' Lydia scoffed.

'I've already done it.'

That brought surprised reactions from the documentarians,

though not from the archaeologists. Ziff had been selective in sharing the news. 'It's in the jungle, in the Democratic Republic of Congo,' she went on. 'It'll be hard to reach – but not impossible. The site is two days' travel from the nearest airport. The problem is that now the images from the map room are out in the open, anyone else can get there too.'

'Only if they're crazy enough to go *Apocalypse Now* into the Congo,' said Rivero.

'Or *Heart of Darkness*, more accurately,' Nina said.

'Heart of what? Anyway, it sure as hell isn't somewhere I'm in any rush to visit.'

'That's a pity,' she replied. 'Because what I discussed with Mike and the network – what they've provisionally agreed to back – is a documentary expedition to *find* Zhakana. They want to follow up the current series with a journey into the unknown, literally. Whatever's out there, whatever we find, we'll be the first people to see it for thousands of years.'

'They already agreed to fund it?' asked Lydia.

Fisher looked thoughtful. 'It's a good hook. Documentary meets reality TV. Indiana Jones, live – or live-ish. It could work.'

'You said *we*,' noted Howie.

Nina nodded. 'That's right. You guys are already out here, and you've seen everything leading up to the map room's discovery, so you know the background. Plus you already work as a team, so Mike thought you'd be the obvious choice to do it.'

'Nice of him to ask us first,' Lydia objected. 'And you, too!'

'I did tell him you'd probably want to think about it,' Nina assured her.

'Aw, that's real good of you!' The sarcasm was biting.

'It's definitely worth considering,' Fisher said to her. She was not convinced.

'How long would this take?' asked Rivero. 'We've been out

here for almost three weeks already. I kinda want to see my girlfriend again.'

'I don't know,' Nina admitted. 'I'd guess we'd be on the ground for about two weeks.'

'You would be going as well?' asked Ziff.

'Well, yeah. I mean, it's my series, it's about the things I've discovered. And I found the map room.'

'We *all* found it!' Talal protested.

'You wouldn't even have *looked* at that wall if I hadn't been there. But the main reason the network was willing to consider this is because I proposed it, and it's conditional on my involvement.'

'So they won't do it without you, but they will do it without us?' said Lydia.

'Pretty much, yeah. Mike wants to know if you're interested. But we're kind of on the clock,' she warned. 'The main reason I proposed this is so we can find Zhakana before anyone else – looters, treasure hunters, even locals out for a quick buck. So don't take too long thinking about it, because if it goes ahead, it'll be soon.'

'How soon?' Fisher asked.

'As soon as everything can be arranged. We'll have to deal with the Congolese government, hire guides and porters. And we'll need security too. The DRC isn't super-safe right now.'

'No shit,' muttered Rivero.

'So decide whether or not you want to be involved as soon as you can,' Nina told them. 'If you want to stay together as a team, that's good. But if the network has to hire replacements, they need to know.'

A discussion began amongst the film crew. Lydia and Rivero appeared the least enthusiastic, Fisher undecided, while Howie was positively excited at the prospect. 'We get to explore an uncharted jungle?' he said, grinning. 'With a lost city in the middle of it? C'mon, that's awesome! Imagine seeing that model spread out ahead, only for real. That would be . . .' He struggled to find a suitably hyperbolic word, settling for one he had already used. 'Awesome!'

'It'd be a hell of a feather in our caps,' mused Fisher. 'If we actually did find the city, it could be Emmy material. This could really boost all our careers. What do you think, Lids?'

'I don't know,' said the New Zealander uncertainly. 'I get what you're saying, Steve, but it's another two weeks. And we'd be roughing it in the jungle too.'

'Come on!' Fisher said with a smile. 'Where's that Kiwi spirit?'

'In the bar of a nice comfortable hotel?'

Ziff came to Nina. 'Can I talk to you for a moment? Alone?'

'Sure. I'll let you discuss it,' she told the crew before following Ziff from the tent. 'What is it?' she asked him.

He twiddled his beard before replying. 'It seems you've made up your mind that you are going to search for Zhakana.'

'That depends on the Congolese government,' said the redhead. 'But if they give us the go-ahead, then yeah, I want to do it.'

He carefully considered his next words. 'Then . . . I would like to come with you.'

The request startled her. 'Really? If you did, that would mean handing over the First Temple dig to someone else.'

'I know. And it is not a sacrifice I would make lightly, believe me! My career – my *life* – has been dedicated to finding relics of King Solomon. His name is my middle name – I suppose it was my destiny!' He chuckled, but quickly became more serious. 'The First Temple is an incredible discovery. But you saw the other passage down there; it is completely blocked by rubble. It will take weeks to dig out.'

'So you're thinking that while the rest of your team are doing that, you could take a quick side-trip to find Zhakana?'

'I know that exploring the jungle will not be easy. But at my age, nor is bending down to lift heavy stones!' Ziff smiled. 'Delegation is part of being a good leader, wouldn't you agree?'

'I dunno, I still have trouble staying hands-off,' Nina replied.

'I had noticed.' He gazed over the sprawl of Jerusalem beyond the Temple Mount. 'This city is full of history, Nina. But . . . it is buried. Each new generation builds on top of what was there before, and it gets harder to see what is hidden below. Zhakana, though? It could still be there, exactly as Solomon left it. And I would like to see that.'

'You think it's stayed untouched?'

He nodded. 'I translated more of the inscriptions. Makeda's people never went to the City of the Damned unless they had to. They believed it was cursed. The people who built it died out thousands of years before.'

She was intrigued. 'How did they die?'

'Solomon said that according to the legends of Sheba . . . let me think of the exact words.' A brief frown of concentration. '"That which gave them their power as an empire, that which they used to conquer their enemies, brought their own walls crashing down and left them barren but for monsters and demons." Melodramatic, but I don't believe Solomon was exaggerating. He was reporting what he had been told.'

'"That which gave them their power,"' Nina echoed. 'The Shamir? Or the Mother of the Shamir, rather?'

'He built the Palace Without Entrance to hide the Imashamir, and to make sure that nobody without the wisdom to use it could ever reach it. So whatever it is . . .'

'Could still be there,' she finished for him.

He nodded. 'Solomon used the Shamir to build the First Temple. God granted him an incredible gift. The legend goes that it disappeared once its task was done, but perhaps Solomon returned it to its home.'

93

KING SOLOMON'S CURSE

'Or its mother.'

'I do not think that we will really find a great worm inside the Palace,' said Ziff with a wry smile. 'But we may find something even more amazing. That is . . . if you are willing to let me join you.'

She didn't reply at once. She didn't *dislike* the Israeli, but neither had he been the easiest person to work with. He was territorial, and she suspected was more than a little jealous of her fame. But he was intelligent, experienced, well-versed in ancient languages like Old Hebrew . . . and as he had pointed out, King Solomon *was* his area of expertise.

'It won't be easy,' she finally said. 'Do you really want to slog through the jungle looking for something that might not even be there any more?'

'Do you?'

'Well, yes,' she said, surprised by the question.

'Then you know why I do. You are not the only archaeologist with an obsession. Mine is Solomon, and if I discover another unknown wonder of his, then I can die happy!'

Nina smiled. 'I hope it doesn't come to that.'

'Ha! So do I. My grandchildren would be very sad.' He looked her in the eye. 'If you are still unsure if you want me to come on an expedition, I am sure I can persuade the Israel Antiquities Authority to provide additional funding. But . . . I hope you would want my help for more than mere money.'

'I would, yeah.' She cocked her head. 'Are you absolutely sure you want to come?'

'Yes.' There was no hesitation.

'Okay. Then . . . welcome aboard, I guess!' She extended her hand; he shook it.

'Thank you.'

'Don't thank me yet. We might spend two weeks in the jungle being eaten by mosquitoes and find absolutely nothing.'

'Let us hope we find something more worth our time.'

'Yeah. We should let the others know.'

Inside the tent, they found that the documentary crew had reached a decision. It was unanimous, though Lydia and Rivero's trepidation suggested both had come close to dissenting. 'I just got off the phone with Mike,' said Fisher. 'We're in – with certain provisos.'

'Which are?' Nina asked.

'You said two weeks. That's too long. We're saying eight days in-country. So if you're right and it takes two days to reach the place, and it takes another two to get back, that gives you four days to explore.'

Nina had wanted more time, but reluctantly nodded. 'Okay. Eight days in the DRC. What else?'

'Pay and conditions we've already agreed with Mike and the network. The issue I want addressed up front, right now, is: who's in charge.'

'Meaning?'

'Meaning I'm the director, and I call the shots. Off-screen as well as on. If I decide we need to pull out, for *any* reason, then we go. You don't get to make us wait because you've found a particularly interesting piece of pottery. We won't have hospitals just a phone call away – we'll be in the middle of nowhere in an unstable Third World country. Everyone in the team is my responsibility, so my top priority is keeping us all safe. Including you.'

'And including me too,' said Ziff, to much surprise from both the film crew and the other archaeologists.

'I know what I'm doing, Steven,' said Nina. 'I have done this before. A lot. You don't need to take on extra responsibilities.'

'That's the deal, Nina,' he insisted. 'Mike already okayed it. You want us, then you accept it. Otherwise you'll have to wait to find a new crew – and I know you're not the patient type.' He indicated the tunnel entrance. 'What we found down there isn't a secret any more, and like you said, if you can figure out how to find the lost city, so can someone else.'

She struggled to contain her irritation. The proposition felt more like blackmail, and she had often felt Fisher was more interested in using the series to boost his résumé than showcase her discoveries.

But he was right about her concerns; the longer it took to get the expedition moving, the greater the chance that Zhakana might be looted first . . . 'Okay,' she grumbled. 'We do it your way, Steven. But I still decide what's important archaeologically, okay? It *is* kinda my area of expertise.'

Lydia rolled her eyes, but Fisher nodded. 'If we're all in agreement . . .' He regarded his crew, who one by one gave their assent. 'I'll call Mike, get the lawyers to draw up contracts.'

'With danger money,' said Rivero.

'Hell *yes*, with danger money! We're not filming this on Malibu Beach.'

'More's the pity,' Lydia muttered.

'But yeah, we're good to go. So Nina, I think you need to make some calls yourself.'

'You're right,' Nina replied. 'I've got to contact the Congolese government and actually get permission to visit the country in the first place – although I won't tell them straight up that we're looking for a lost city housing a palace built by King Solomon. We don't want to draw *that* much attention. I'll also have to arrange the logistics, security . . .' She stopped as she realised that in her excitement and focus on one objective, she had overlooked something equally important. 'And . . . I *really* should tell my family.'

6

England

'You want to do bloody *what*?' Eddie barked.

He was in Larry and Julie's luxurious home outside Southampton, Macy reading a book with her grandparents while he took the phone call. 'What's Mommy doing?' she asked, worried. 'Is she okay?'

'Yeah, love, she's fine,' he assured her. 'At least, until I get hold of her!'

'I heard that,' said Nina.

'You were meant to!' He went into the adjoining room to continue what he knew would be a heated discussion in privacy. 'Okay, say that again, so I can be sure I didn't just have a massive brain fart. You want to go to . . .'

'The Democratic Republic of Congo.'

'Yeah, that's what I thought. You haven't got a talking gorilla or Tim Curry, so why the' – he lowered his voice – '*fuck* do you want to go there?'

'The map room I found in the First Temple? I figured out where it leads. There's a lost city, somewhere in the jungle in the eastern Congo. King Solomon visited it three thousand years ago and built a palace to protect a biblical relic. It might still be there.'

'And it might not! Three thousand years is a long time.'

'The Atlantean temple we found in Brazil had been there even longer, and it was still intact.'

'And it'd been looked after by a tribe who tried to kill us, remember?'

'I can hardly forget,' she said. 'But someone leaked photos of the map room online – with enough detail for anyone else to find the city the same way I did. If looters get there first, they'll destroy the site.'

'So? Tell the IHA where it is. I know you think Blumberg's a cock, but he's on the same side as you.'

'Lester's too by-the-book. He'd tell the Congolese govern-ment everything up front – and I'm not sure I'd trust them to protect the site. There's a high level of corruption – and right now, there's a lot of conflict with a secessionist movement in the east.'

'Uh-huh,' said Eddie, unimpressed. 'And whereabouts in the country is this place again?'

Her voice became almost apologetic. 'The . . . east?'

'Right. So you want to search for a lost city full of treasure during a civil war in a country that's famous for violence and corruption?'

'Well, when you put it like *that*, of course it makes me sound crazy,' she said sarcastically. 'But we won't be near the conflict zone, because we're going into the jungle.'

A humourless laugh. 'Where do you think rebels go and bloody hide? They're not working out of their bedrooms.'

'Eddie, I already checked all this,' she protested. 'Most of the secessionist violence is in the population centres along the eastern border. We're going much farther west, into an uninhabited part of the country.'

'Oh, "we" are, are we?'

'Not we-us, obviously. You'll stay with Macy, because I sure as hell don't want her coming to the Congo! But the network has already agreed to fund the expedition. The documentary crew is coming with me.'

'Great, so a bunch of rich Americans with expensive camera gear want to trek through one of the world's poorest countries, that's full of men with guns?'

Nina made an irritated sound. 'We're not all Americans, and that's not the point anyway! I certainly wasn't intending to go out there without help. That's actually something you can help with.'

'Me?'

'I can't think of a better person to arrange international security. You've got friends and contacts everywhere, and you've worked in the business – from behind a desk *and* on the front line. You must know people who can protect us.'

'Well, yeah,' he told her. 'There are people in Congo and the countries near it who I'd trust. Question is, whether any of 'em'd be available. Especially on short notice.' He thought for a moment. '*How* short notice?'

'I want to start as soon as possible.'

'Why am I not bloody surprised? And for how long?'

'Eight days in the DRC. Two days to reach the site from the nearest airport, two days back, and four to explore.'

'Uh-huh. And what about the time it'll take you to *get* to and from that airport? Airlines don't do direct international flights to piddly-shit little airstrips. What you're actually saying is that you want me to look after Macy on my own for another two weeks on top of the time you've already been away!'

'I thought you loved looking after her?'

'I do! But it's *her* I'm thinking about, not me. She hasn't seen her mum for three weeks, and now you want to extend that by another fortnight?'

'I know it's a long time, and I know it's not what we planned,' said Nina. 'But this is a big deal for me.'

'Why?' he demanded. 'I mean, you've just found the original Jewish temple – and you found that because you also found the bloody Ark of the Covenant! *And* you found Atlantis, *and* the Garden of Eden, *and* all the other stuff you got books and movies and TV shows out of. And you did all of that before you turned forty! So why's it so important that you find this city, right now?'

A long pause, enough that he wondered if they had lost the connection, then Nina spoke again. She sounded almost sad. 'It's *because* I did all that stuff before I turned forty, Eddie.'

'What do you mean?'

'I mean . . . I know when you turned forty, you didn't treat it as a big deal. But for me . . .' Another lengthy silence. 'Maybe this'll sound silly and petty. But I found Atlantis when I was twenty-eight. In academic terms, that's still practically just a kid. I hadn't even had my PhD for long. But then there was this mad rush, all these incredible discoveries, fame of a sort, running the IHA . . . and then it stopped.'

'But you did plenty even after you left the IHA,' he said, puzzled. 'You found the Ark of the Covenant, and then after that you found the Midas Cave. And while you were at it you saved a load of world leaders from being gassed and stopped North Korea from shipping out a plane full of nukes. That's not bad going.'

'I found the Ark five years ago, Eddie. The Midas Cave was two years ago. What have I done since then?'

'You made a TV series? Two, actually. And you wrote your books about everything you've done—'

'Exactly!' she cut in unhappily. 'That's all I've done – I've gone back over things I already did when I was younger, regurgitated my own work for a new audience. I haven't done anything *new*. And that's been making me think lately: what if I've already *done* everything I'm ever going to achieve? I'm not a wunderkind any more. I'm forty, and I've accomplished so much already that I'd wondered if there isn't anything left for me to find. But this city, Solomon's palace . . . *that's* something. And this time, it'll be documented on camera. Nobody'll be able to doubt it.'

He was puzzled. 'Nobody *does* doubt you.'

'Are you kidding? Do you know how many emails I get accusing me of being a fraud, an agent of the New World Order, the frickin' Antichrist? I got some abuse right to my face here in Jerusalem from some fundamentalist types who think that because I wasn't struck dead on the spot when I opened the Ark, I must have fabricated the whole thing.'

'They did, eh?' said Eddie, feeling a flash of anger that some-one had threatened his wife and he hadn't been there to force an apology. 'They really thought we'd blow Macy's college fund on a fake Ark?'

'People believe all kinds of things, and they get very angry when someone challenges them. But this is one discovery no-body will be able to deny. So that's one reason I want to do this. And another is . . . to prove that I've still got it, I guess. Yeah, I'm forty, I'm a mom, I did all these things when I was younger – but I can still do them now.'

'Who do you need to prove that to?'

'Myself, as much as anyone,' she admitted. 'Consider it my mid-life crisis.'

'Couldn't you just buy a sports car? Although wait, that's what men do. Women have boob jobs.'

'I know you'd rather I had a boob job – and you can stop smiling!' she added in faux outrage.

'I'm not,' said Eddie, smiling.

'This is what I want to do, though, Eddie,' she continued, serious again. 'I *need* to do it. Not just for myself, either – I really do think a major archaeological site will be looted if I don't get to it first.'

'You always have to do everything yourself, don't you?' he said. 'But I won't talk you out of it, will I? I can tell.'

'You know me.'

'Yeah, I do. And that's probably going to knock twenty years off my life . . .'

'Don't say things like that. You need to be around for Macy for a long time yet.'

'And so do you! Wandering around the Congo jungle isn't the best way to guarantee that, though.' Now it was his turn to fall silent, as he made a decision he suspected he would come to regret. 'Okay. You go and find your bloody lost city.'

She was delighted, but also surprised. 'Really? Are you fine with this?'

'No, but I'm going to do everything I can to keep you safe.'

'I wouldn't expect anything less.'

'Two things I want. First, I need to know what your plan is so I can figure out who to contact in Africa. So, start at the beginning. When are you going?'

'As soon as possible – in the next few days, if we can. I need to get permission from the Congolese government, but I can use my United Nations connections for that.'

'All right. How many in your team?'

'Me, a four-person film crew, and another archaeologist. An Israeli, David Ziff.'

'And where are you going?'

'I'll send you the city's GPS coordinates, but the nearest major town is a place called Butembo. It's on the eastern side of—'

'I know where Butembo is,' he interrupted. 'Worked over the border from it in Uganda and Rwanda back in the day.'

'Anyway, that's the nearest place with an airport. I think it should take two days to reach the city from there; a day overland to a village called Nakola, and then by boat upriver. Once we're there, we explore, film what we find, then head back. Do you think you'll be able to find people to help us?'

Eddie considered the matter. 'I can probably get TD – Tamara Defendé, you remember her?'

'Of course.'

'She's worked in DR Congo before, I can get her to fly you and your team in. People on the ground, though? I know some good blokes, but no idea if any of 'em are available right now. I'd have to check.'

'If you could, that would be fantastic. Thank you.' She hesitated. 'What's the second thing you wanted?'

'The second,' said Eddie, 'is that you can tell our lass yourself that she won't see you for an extra two weeks! I'm not dropping that one on her.'

'Oh. Yeah. I should, shouldn't I?'

'You really, really should. Macy?' he called. 'Your mum wants to talk to you.'

Macy hurried in and eagerly took his phone. 'Mommy? Hi!'

Eddie leaned in the doorway, turning away so she wouldn't see his dark expression. It was clearly visible to his father, though. 'Something up?' asked Larry.

'You could say that. Nina's decided that not only is she going to be filming for another couple of weeks, but she's going to the middle of the bloody African jungle.'

Larry shook his head in disapproval. 'Why didn't you just tell her that's unacceptable and not let her go?'

Eddie snorted. 'You've *met* my wife, haven't you? Red hair, green eyes, about five-five, makes the average mule look as stubborn as an easily persuaded jellyfish?'

'Then you haven't tried hard enough. I wouldn't just give in to something like that.'

'Of *course* you wouldn't, dear,' said Julie, with exaggerated sweetness. 'Now go and play with your toy trains.'

'They're scale models, not— Ah, very funny.'

103

Eddie smiled, but then heard a sound of dismay. He turned back to Macy. 'Are you okay, love?'

She looked stricken. 'Mommy said she's not coming back!'

'I don't think that's really what she said, is it?' He gently took the phone from her. 'Is it?' he asked his wife.

'Of course it's not!' cried Nina, almost as upset as her daughter. 'I just said I wouldn't be home for another two weeks.'

'She's five, love. To her, that's like three thousand years!' He hugged Macy, then switched the phone to speaker. 'Mummy is coming back, don't worry.'

'I absolutely will, honey,' Nina promised. 'I miss you so much, and I can't wait to see you again. I'll be home as soon as I can.'

Eddie decided not to remind her that could be the day after tomorrow if she chose; the last thing he wanted Macy to witness was a parental argument. Instead, he said: 'We'll talk to Mummy again later, okay? I need to make some phone calls for her. Is that all right?' Macy nodded, but did not look happy. 'Nina, I'll see who's around in that neck of the woods. But first, I need to cheer up our little girl!'

'I'm so sorry, Macy,' said his wife. 'I didn't mean to upset you. I'll be back with you real soon, I promise. I love you. Bye-bye.'

'Bye, Mommy,' Macy said, with a reluctant pout.

Eddie added his own farewells, then disconnected. 'Okay, love. Daddy's got to ring some people.'

It took a few hours to get answers from his contacts, and they were mostly not what he had hoped for.

'So what did your friends say?' Nina asked when he called her back. 'Did you find anyone who can provide security?'

'I did,' he replied, 'but literally *only* one. Everyone else was either already on a job, or out of contact. And I called everyone I know in central Africa. Flight's not a problem, TD said she can take you. But as far as security goes, the only guy who's free is a mate of mine, Fortune Bemba.'

'He's the only person you could get?'

'He's from DRC, so he knows the country, and he's got plenty of local contacts. He said he can round up some help. The thing is, I don't know 'em. I trust Fortune, but even though he says he'll vouch for anyone he brings aboard, I still want to check 'em out for myself. You made our little girl a promise that you'd be back. And I want to be absolutely sure it's going to be kept.'

Uncertainty entered her voice. 'Wait, so you're saying . . . you want to meet this Fortune's associates in person? You want to go to the Congo yourself?'

'There's no "want" about it. It's definitely not high on my holiday list! But I need to be sure that whoever else is helping out is up to the job. And I want to check out the situation on the ground, an' all. The news doesn't pay much attention to countries like that unless something really major happens, but just because it doesn't make headlines doesn't mean it isn't dangerous.'

'You're not suggesting that you bring Macy, are you?'

'Course I'm bloody not! No, she can stay here, either with my dad and Julie or with Lizzie. I'll fly into Butembo with you, meet Fortune and check out his mates, then come back. If I time the flights right I should be able to do the round trip in three days.'

'That's a long time to leave Macy with someone else, even if they are family.'

'We did it before, with the Midas Cave. And then North Korea.'

'And in hindsight I wish we hadn't. I know she's sometimes had a nanny at home, but one or both of us has always been there if she needed us. I don't think you should come.'

'Well, I don't think you should *go*, but hey. Look, Nina,' he went on, wanting to forestall the approaching argument, 'I just want to be sure you'll be safe. Okay? Once I know you've got reliable people watching out for you, I'll come back to Macy and let you get on with it. But there's no way I'm going to let you go out there without knowing what's what.'

'There isn't, is there?' she said, terse.

'You're not the only one who can be stubborn. God, I feel sorry for whoever marries Macy. She's going to be as bloody-minded as both of us combined.'

Her tone lightened. 'Afraid so. Have you told Macy yet?'

'No. And I haven't asked my dad or Lizzie if they can take her either. This should be fun.'

'Well, I already upset Macy today, so I think it should be your turn.'

'Gee, thanks!' They both laughed. 'Okay, love. I'd better go and do it, and then wipe up all the tears – probably from Dad as well as Macy!'

'Good luck,' she said. 'Love you.'

'Love you.' He went to find his daughter.

She was playing in the living room with Julie, Larry stretched out in a recliner reading the news on his phone. 'That's the face of someone with bad news,' he said as his son entered.

Eddie crouched beside Macy. 'Hey, love. I need to tell you something very important.'

She sat up. 'What is it?'

'You know how Mummy—'

'Mommy.'

'Yeah, yeah. Anyway, you remember she's going to be away for a bit longer?' She nodded. 'Well, Daddy needs to make sure that everything's all right for her. So that means I'll have to go away too. Just for a little while, and I'll be back as soon as I can,' he quickly added, seeing her sudden worry.

106

'Is Mommy going to be okay?'

'Yeah, of course she will! I'm going to talk to some of my friends in Africa who'll—'

Concern was instantly replaced by amazement. 'You're going to Africa? That's where they have elephants, and lions! Can I come?'

'Sorry, love, I'm afraid not.' She looked disappointed. 'I'll bring you back a toy elephant or lion, though. How about that?' She gave him a begrudging nod.

'Wait,' said Julie, confused. 'If you're going to Africa, who's going to look after Macy?'

Eddie put on his broadest smile. 'That's something I wanted to talk to you two about . . .'

Larry popped upright. 'Wait, what?'

'I'll only be gone a couple of days.'

'You want to leave your daughter with us for *two days*?'

'Well, more like three.'

Julie looked appalled, but at her husband rather than her stepson. 'Larry! She's your granddaughter! Of course we'll look after her, Eddie. We'd love to. Wouldn't we, Larry?'

Larry was far from thrilled. 'But I was going to play golf with Trevor and Michael and the boys this week.'

'Oh, you and your golf. The course'll still be there next week, but how often do we see Macy? You don't mind staying with us, do you, Macy?'

'*Can* I stay?' Macy asked, directing the question at her grandfather. 'We can go and see the magic horses again!'

'I think Macy's fine with it,' said Eddie, amused by Larry's attempt to mask his dismay. 'I guess that settles it, then.'

'It does,' Julie added firmly. Larry gave her a thin smile, before treating Macy to a more genuine one.

Eddie turned back to his daughter. 'I'll be back as soon as I can. Is that okay?'

Her enthusiasm had already faded. 'I . . . think so. Are you going right now?'

'No, we'll do some fun stuff together first. Us, and Julie, and your grandad. Whether he wants to or not.' That drew a giggle from Julie and a resigned sigh from Larry.

'And you and Mommy are coming back soon?'

'Definitely,' Eddie assured her. 'That's why I'm going to Africa. To make sure of it.'

7

The Democratic Republic of Congo

It was one of the world's more mean-spirited ironies, Nina mused as she gazed at the landscape below, that one of the countries richest in natural resources was also one of the poorest financially. The Democratic Republic of Congo held huge reserves of rare and valuable minerals, but the fortunes made from extracting them were far from equitably distributed amongst its people – if they went to its people at all. Almost a century of rapacious exploitation under the auspices first of King Leopold the Second of Belgium, then the brutal colonial administration of the Belgian state itself, had been followed by an independence marked by violence and corruption to an extent that the country's very name – at the time, Zaire – became international shorthand for shameless embezzlement.

The situation had improved over time, but only in relative terms. The modern DR Congo was still plagued by sectarian strife, wars both civil and national, drug smuggling and sex trafficking – and the old standbys of poverty, disease and graft. The secessionist movement in the east was merely the latest variety of civil unrest bringing misery to ordinary citizens.

And she was flying right into the middle of it.

Butembo, she had learned, was a hotspot for rebel activity.

That was worrying enough in itself, but she was leading others into a dangerous region. Fisher and the rest of his team were in the cramped seats behind her, Ziff reading on his own at the cabin's rear. Whatever the director had insisted in Jerusalem, Nina couldn't help but consider herself responsible for them. Now that she was actually in the country, her earlier enthusiasm was tempered by concern: maybe too little, too late.

But she knew Eddie would do everything he could to ensure the group's safety. Her husband sat beside her, unshaven and rumpled in his black leather jacket. 'You okay?' she asked as he rubbed his eyes.

'Yeah, just knackered,' he said. 'I had a much longer journey here than you did.' They had met in the Ugandan capital of Kampala: an eight-hour flight from Jerusalem, considerably more from London.

'Well, at least there's not much more of it left.' She leaned forward to address the pilot, a Botswanan woman in a baseball hat. 'Hey, TD. How long till we land?'

Tamara Defendé, known to close friends by her initials, glanced back. 'About twenty minutes.' Her trade as a bush pilot, roving over the vast continent, had been successful enough for her now to own three aircraft, but like most fliers she preferred to keep her hands on a set of controls rather than stay behind a desk. 'Eddie, you still want to fly back to Kampala tomorrow morning, yes?'

'Yeah,' the Englishman replied. 'My flight back isn't until the afternoon. That'll give me a chance to meet Fortune and whoever else he's rounded up, check 'em out, and hopefully get a night's sleep as well.'

'You really didn't need to come all the way out here,' Nina told him. 'I'm sure that if your buddy's vouched for these people, they're fine.'

'I just want to be sure,' Eddie insisted. 'Besides, it's a bit late to change my mind now!'

The elderly Antonov biplane flew on. The scenery was beautiful, verdant green over mineral-rich red soil, but the near-absence of vehicle traffic on the few weaving dirt roads was a clear sign of poverty even from several thousand feet up.

'That's Butembo,' Tamara said at last. Nina and Eddie looked ahead to see a brown sprawl across the surrounding jade. It was a large settlement, its population almost seven hundred thousand according to Nina's research, but she hesitated to qualify it with the honorific of being a city. It was obvious even from miles away that almost all the red-roofed houses were small, with very few buildings having more than a single storey.

Their pilot had an increasingly argumentative exchange with the control tower before winning some concession from the controller, then she lined the plane up with the runway and put it into final descent. 'What was that about?' asked Eddie.

'They wanted me to circle,' she replied. 'They're waiting for some VIP's helicopter. I told them I'm low on fuel, but if they want me to put down on the main street, I can. They got my point.'

'I'm glad,' said Nina, sharing a smile with her husband.

The landing on Rughenda airfield's dirt runway was bumpy, but the Antonov quickly slowed to taxi speed and pulled up near the modest terminal building. 'Thanks, Tamara,' said Nina as the Botswanan shut down the engines.

Eddie looked through a porthole. 'There's Fortune.' Nina saw a tall, broad-shouldered black man in a sleek three-piece suit waiting outside the terminal. A shorter, scruffier man with a wild frizz of hair stood beside him. 'That must be his mate.'

'Is he the guy you wanted to check out?'

'Yeah. I'd hoped he'd have more people, though.'

She laughed a little. 'How much security did you think we'd need?'

His expression displayed no humour. 'More than that.'

The passengers disembarked. The air outside was not as hot as Nina had expected, about seventy Fahrenheit, but it was uncomfortably humid. Fisher and the rest of the film crew retrieved their equipment while Eddie went to meet the welcoming committee. 'Fortune!' he called.

'Eddie, my man!' the tall man boomed in reply. French was the country's official language, and his English was rich with its almost musical cadences. 'Good to see you again!'

'You too, mate.' The two men embraced, the African more than a head taller than the Yorkshireman. 'Nina, this is Fortune Bemba. We go back a long way. Fortune, this is my wife, Nina Wilde.'

'The famous explorer, yes,' said Fortune as she joined her husband. He took her hand and kissed it, then gave her a broad smile that revealed two gold teeth in his otherwise perfect white set. 'An honour to meet you! Eddie tells me you are looking for something in the jungle. An ancient city?'

'That's what we're hoping for, yes,' she replied. 'You're Congolese, aren't you?' He nodded. 'Are there any legends of anything like that?'

'There are many legends about the jungle, including lost cities. I have never heard that any were true, though.'

'Me neither,' said the other man. He seemed about to burst with pent-up nervous energy, the words tumbling from his mouth. 'But I'm from Matadi, all the way out west, so jungle stories? Not so much my thing.' He had much less of a French inflection than Fortune, sounding almost American – or rather, Nina guessed, *trying* to sound that way, having picked up the accent from movies and TV.

'This is Paris Mbolo,' said Fortune, introducing him. 'He is very reliable, Eddie, very capable – I trust him completely. Even if,' a sniff, 'he has no dress sense at all.'

Paris gave his impeccably dressed partner a sarcastic look. 'Ha ha. Fuck you. Oh! *Excusez-moi*,' he said to Nina, almost embarrassed.

'Don't worry about it,' she said, amused. 'I'm married to Eddie – I hear much worse all the time!'

Eddie gave Paris a critical look. 'Fortune said you were in the Congolese army before going independent?'

He nodded. 'Six years, then two with the blue helmets' – the United Nations peacekeeping force that had worked to suppress rebel groups operating across the border – 'before I realised I'd get more money and less hatred in plain clothes.'

'If you can call those clothes,' said Fortune disdainfully.

Paris held back another obscenity for Nina's sake. 'So yes, Mr Chase – Eddie? Can I call you Eddie? Eddie, I know what I'm doing. I've been in tough situations, and I know the people. I'll take care of your wife and her friends.'

'He is very good,' Fortune assured the Englishman. 'I would not have asked him to join me if he was not.'

Eddie nodded. 'Although I'd hoped you'd drum up more people.'

'Private security is in very high demand. And that is why.' He looked up at the thrum of an approaching helicopter.

Nina and Eddie turned to see a gleaming white-and-blue Airbus AS355 descending towards the terminal. The name *Monardril* was emblazoned along its fuselage. 'Who's this?' Eddie asked.

'The big boss of a mining company,' said Paris. 'His people have been here for weeks, setting up some deal.'

'They have hired many mercenaries to protect them,' Fortune went on. 'Some of them you know. Scotty Roux, for one.'

'Scotty's working for this lot?' said Eddie. 'Wondered why I couldn't get hold of him.'

Another noise, that of ground vehicles, caught their attention. A convoy of new and expensive SUVs and pickup trucks rolled through the airport gate to stop nearby. Heavily tinted windows hid their occupants, but the men riding in the pickup beds wore dark paramilitary uniforms. No guns were immediately apparent, but from the way the security team were warily scanning the surroundings, Eddie guessed their weapons were stashed within easy reach.

A rangy, bearded man emerged from the lead SUV. 'Hey!' he called. 'Fortune, Eddie!'

'Speak of the devil,' Eddie said to Fortune before shouting back. 'Scotty, hi! I heard you were here.'

Roux jogged to them as other men spread out behind him. 'Yeah, working corporate security,' he said. 'What about you?'

'My wife's filming a documentary. I'm just making sure she's safe. Would have been easier if your guys hadn't poached everyone!'

The South African shrugged apologetically. 'Always up to do you a favour, Eddie, but Monardril got me first. Very good pay too, mate!' He squinted into the wind as the chopper touched down. 'Anyway, got to go. If you're staying around, give me a call.'

'Leaving first thing, but thanks anyway.'

'No problem. Catch you later. You too, Fortune.' He tipped them both a cheery salute, then hurried to the helicopter. 'Sir Robert! Your car is over here.' He led a tall, stone-faced man with expensively styled silver hair to his SUV.

'That's the mining boss?' Nina asked.

Fortune nodded. 'British. A very funny thing. Very few of the men he hired are Congolese, and none are black. If I did not know better,' a wink at Eddie, 'I would think all British are racist.'

'Doubt the big boss hired 'em all personally, but yeah, afraid some Brits are still arseholes. Had to have words with one in London just the other day.'

'You did?' said Nina. 'Wait, was Macy with you?'

'Yes, but don't worry, I didn't kill anyone in front of her. Just some light maiming.'

'Uh-*huh.*'

He grinned, then watched as the convoy swept away. 'All that for just one bloke?'

'There has been much violence recently,' Fortune told him. 'The rebel group, LEC – *Liberté pour l'Est du Congo* – has made many attacks.'

'How bad?'

'Mostly against the government and the police, but there have been some attacks on civilians, including foreigners. That is why the mining company has hired so many guards – they do not want their executives to be kidnapped or killed.'

'Oh, that's not scary at all,' said Nina.

'Nina!' called Ziff, approaching with the camera crew. 'We've unloaded everything. Are we ready to go?'

'Whenever you are,' she replied. 'I assume?'

'We are ready,' said Fortune, gesturing towards a pair of battered minibuses.

'Okay, cool.' Introductions were made, then the group had their passports checked by a bored official before going to the buses. Nina joined Fortune, Eddie and Ziff at the first, Paris taking the film crew to the second. 'Shall we go?'

Rughenda airfield was actually surrounded by the low-rise sprawl of Butembo, so they entered the town immediately upon leaving its grounds. Nina's observation from the air still held; it was not a place of great wealth, most houses mere shacks. She also noticed that while the road from the airfield towards the civic centre was blacktop, almost all those leading off it were mere dirt tracks. What money there was in the area was highly concentrated.

She saw a commotion ahead. 'What's going on?' A group of policemen had cornered some youths against a building, one of the cops tearing down posters from its wall.

Fortune glanced over. 'They were putting up posters for the LEC. Idiots. Why do that in the middle of the day? They know people will call the cops.'

'Maybe they want to get caught,' she mused. 'Make a political statement.'

'The only statement will be made by the police, and it will be in broken teeth and bones. The government is doing everything it can to stop Kabanda. They will not allow the east to break away without a war.'

'Who's Kabanda?' asked Ziff.

'The leader of Liberté pour l'Est du Congo, Fabrice Kabanda. That is him on the posters.'

Nina looked across as they passed the disruption. She had just enough time to see the image of a handsome, smiling man in his early thirties before the last poster was ripped down. 'He looks kinda young to be a revolutionary leader.'

'When better to be one?' said the Israeli rhetorically.

'He is only half the story,' said Fortune, driving on. 'Kabanda is the public face of the LEC. I personally do not agree with him, but he is very charismatic. He is the man who attracts new followers. But if he is the glove, Le Fauchet is the fist inside it.'

'Le Fauchet?' Nina asked. 'Doesn't that mean something like "the scythe"?'

'Yes. It is not his real name, I am not sure what is. But he has united many of the local militias behind Kabanda. When the LEC commit acts of violence, it is Le Fauchet who has ordered it.'

'The LEC – are they pros?' Eddie asked, concerned.

Fortune shook his head. 'Most are boys with Kalashnikovs,

high on drugs. The government soldiers usually deal with them easily. But they are becoming more dangerous now that Le Fauchet is training them and buying modern weapons.' He pointed. 'Look, there – that man. He is one of Le Fauchet's victims.'

Eddie and Nina saw a skinny man walking along the roadside, a transistor radio held to his ear in one hand – his *only* hand. All that remained past the elbow of his other arm was a diagonal stump. 'Oh, my God,' said Nina. 'What happened to him?'

'He must have opposed or offended Le Fauchet in some way,' Fortune said sombrely as they drove past. 'But that is his trademark, to cut off the right arm with a machete. It is what the Belgians did when they ruled the country. Le Fauchet has . . . *appropriated* it.'

'Poor bastard,' muttered Eddie.

'He is lucky,' Fortune countered. 'He is still alive. Most who have met Le Fauchet are not.'

'Then I really, really hope I never meet him,' said Nina.

'We will do everything we can to protect you, do not worry.'

'There's only two of you to do it, though,' said the Yorkshireman. 'What about porters? Did you find anyone?'

'Yes,' came the reply. 'Three local men. I have worked with one before, and the other two were recommended to me.'

Eddie was not reassured. 'Only three?'

'You wanted men with experience in the jungle. Such people are always in demand.'

'It'll be fine, Eddie,' said Nina. 'I'm sure they'll be enough.'

'We'll see,' he said, unconvinced.

Fortune brought them to one of Butembo's few major hotels. Both minibuses were checked at a security gate before being allowed through its high wall. They pulled up at the entrance. 'Everything has been prepared for you,' said Fortune as he got out.

Fisher came to them from the second bus, a pair of heavy bags slung from his shoulders. The other members of his team were equally laden with gear. 'Is this place safe?' he asked. 'I saw lower walls in Israel around the Palestinian territories!' Ziff shot him a disapproving look.

'The hotels are as safe as anywhere around here,' Paris assured him.

Lydia snorted. 'Now I'm *really* worried.'

'Do not worry,' Fortune intoned sonorously. 'I assure you, the dark hordes of Africa will not swarm over the walls in the dead of night to feast upon your precious white flesh.'

Fisher blanched. 'Uh – no, I didn't mean it that way. It wasn't a racial thing. Really!'

'No, nothing like that,' Lydia hurriedly added.

Eddie tried not to laugh. 'You're an arse,' he whispered to Fortune as he collected Nina's luggage. His friend regarded Fisher and Lydia sternly, then turned away and grinned. 'Come on then, love,' the Yorkshireman said to Nina. 'Let's check in.'

The hotel's interior was surprisingly anonymous, a bland refuge for the corporate traveller that could have been anywhere in the world; only its staff's accents provided any distinctive flavour. Nina led the way to the reception desk, Eddie surveying the lobby. 'Least we can get a drink,' he said, spotting the entrance to a bar. 'After that journey, I could really use a—'

He stopped, startled. Nina looked back at him. 'What is it?'

'Just . . . seen someone I know,' he said, disbelieving. 'Can you check us in? I need to . . .' In his distraction he didn't even finish the sentence as he headed for the doorway.

'If you're that desperate for a drink, do I need to book you an AA appointment?' she called after him, but he barely heard the joke.

The bar was as faceless as its parent hotel, a softly lit room of pale wooden furniture assembled to a standardised blueprint.

The man by the windows in the far corner was very distinctive, though.

Eddie approached his table. 'Ay up. Never expected to see you again.'

John Brice, a cigarette in one hand, slowly looked up at him. 'Well, well. Eddie Chase. I'd certainly *hoped* never to see you again.' In the almost three years since their meeting, he had let his standards of appearance slip. He was bestubbled, his hair greasy and untidy and his clothes crumpled enough to suggest he had recently slept in them.

'That's nice. What the fuck are you doing here? MI6 trying to start a coup?'

Brice sneered at him. 'I don't work for the British government any more, Chase. Your fuck-up in Tenerife destroyed my career.'

'Wasn't a fuck-up as far as I was concerned,' Eddie shot back, turning a seat around and sitting facing the other man over its back. 'A mass murderer got arrested – turned out okay in my book.'

'But that wasn't the mission objective, was it?' He took a swig from a glass of whisky. 'You botched it, just like your test at the Funhouse. And because of that, my promotion prospects went out of the window. So I resigned.'

'And you didn't end up like Patrick McGoohan in *The Prisoner*? Shame.'

'I ended up in this shithole country, which is arguably worse. Maybe I got out of Britain at the right time, though. Looks like the Opposition will win the election next month, and they've been making a lot of noise about gutting SIS and the other intelligence agencies. All in the name of *human rights*.' His disgust at the term was plain.

'Yeah, those damn humans,' said Eddie mockingly. 'But of all the places you could have gone, you came to the bloody Congo?'

'Hardly by choice, but it's where the work is.' Another drink.

'The kind of work you once did, ironically enough. Security for corporate bigwigs.'

'Like Sir Robert whatsisface from that mining company? I saw him at the airport.'

'Yes, he's one of mine. Which leads to the question: what are *you* doing here? You and your wife.'

The mention of Nina unsettled Eddie. 'How'd you know she was here too?'

'I didn't pick this spot by accident, Chase.' He gestured at the windows. 'I can see the main gate and the lobby entrance from here. I saw you both arriving.'

'I'd wondered why you didn't seem that surprised to see me.'

'The only surprise is that you wanted to talk to me.'

Eddie smiled sardonically. 'Just wanted to make sure you weren't up to something dodgy.'

'The days of state-sanctioned immunity are behind me, unfortunately. But the local authorities have bigger things on their plate than harassing every white man working on their turf.'

'This LEC lot?'

'You're in the loop, then. Yes, the east of the country's only one step from total chaos. Still, it's good for my business – and the government is probably itching for the LEC to make a major attack. Declaring a state of emergency is a very good way to suspend democracy and remove any troublesome elements. Cynical, but you do what you must.' He contemplated the glass for a moment before imbibing again. 'As for what you're doing . . . I can only assume that the celebrated Dr Nina Wilde has made some amazing archaeological discovery in the jungle, and is going to film it for television.'

Eddie's unease deepened. 'You know all that just from watching us arrive, do you?'

'Simple deduction. Your wife is famous, after all. She's had a documentary series on TV, and some of the people who arrived with you were carrying camera gear. I also know, because I keep my ears open, that Fortune Bemba has been recruiting bearers with jungle experience.'

'You know Fortune?'

'By reputation only; never met the man. Not the kind I'd normally hire.'

'Why? Because he's black?'

Brice gave him a mocking smirk. 'You're not going to give me a tedious lecture on the evils of racism, are you?'

'No, but I might give you one on the evils of being an arsehole.'

He chuckled. 'My hiring practices have nothing to do with race. They're more about culture. Specifically, I limit myself to people who actually have the self-reliance and willpower to make things happen for themselves, rather than wallow in misery and squalor waiting for handouts. I mean, look at this place!' He waved at the window again, this time to encompass the land beyond the security wall. 'This country is literally a treasure trove, with mineral resources the civilised world is desperate to secure, and what does it do to exploit them? Nothing. They do *nothing* without being told. For God's sake, it's a major national news story when they manage to lay down a stretch of tarmac road. The whole continent was better off when it was being run by the colonial powers.'

'Didn't they go around chopping people's arms off?' said Eddie, scathing.

'Better than heads. And that was mad King Leopold's method of maintaining order. We were much more civilised about it.' He straightened, as if filled with nostalgic pride. 'There's a reason we ruled half the world. The greatest empire in history. And then,' – a frown – 'we threw it all away, let the bloody Yanks and Krauts walk all over us. And now even the Chinks, for God's sake.' He sighed, then held up his glass in an imaginary toast before taking another drink. 'But that'll all change now we've got back our independence. I just hope we don't vote in the wrong lot next month and balls it up even more by grovelling to whoever's got the most money.'

'I know I've been out of touch by living in the States, but aren't the bunch in power right now the same ones who flogged everything off to China in the first place?'

Brice fixed him with a disapproving stare. 'Frankly, I don't think you deserve the right to criticise anything that goes on at home, Chase. You abandoned your country.'

Eddie was offended by the accusation. 'Like fuck I did.'

'No? You live in New York, you married a Yank – your daughter automatically has dual nationality, but I bet you haven't even got her a British passport.' Eddie's silence was all the confirmation the other man needed. 'I thought so. You know, I'm . . . I'm *disgusted*. Your country educated you, kept you healthy, kept you safe, made you who you are. And how did you repay that? By running off somewhere else the first chance you got.' He shook his head. 'Britain's never needed its people to work to build a new future more than now, but where are you?'

Eddie stood. 'I'm leaving before some bell-end gets punched in the face.'

Brice's expression was halfway between a smile and a sneer. 'You're welcome to try. Squaddies always overestimate their chances.'

'I'm tempted, but to be honest, I'd rather spend the evening on the phone with my daughter than down at the local police station explaining why I knocked some drunken arsehole's teeth out.' He glanced at the whisky glass; while Brice had raised it to his lips several times, the level of the brown liquid within didn't seem much lower than when he had first arrived. *Lightweight*, he thought. 'And I've got a plane to catch tomorrow morning, so think yourself lucky. Be better for you if I don't see you again, though.'

'I assure you, I don't spend all day hanging around in hotel bars. I've got business to attend to. Enjoy your stay, though, Chase. Try not to catch anything.' Another sarcastic toast.

'Twat,' was Eddie's parting shot as he walked out. Nina was waiting at the reception desk, the expedition's other members having joined her. 'Hi, love. We all booked in?'

'Yeah, but who was that in there?' she asked. 'You looked like you were having an argument.'

'Just someone I had a run-in with once.'

'Small world.'

'Not bloody big enough. Still, won't be seeing him again. Thank God.'

Paris glanced into the bar. 'Is that John Brice?'

'You know him?' Eddie asked.

'I know *of* him. Not a man I want to drink with. He's been dealing with some bad people, is what I hear.'

'Doesn't surprise me.'

Fisher approached from the desk, holding up his room key. It was an actual piece of metal rather than a swipe card, attached to a large block of wood. 'Welcome to the nineteenth century! I suppose this is one way to stop people from stealing them.'

Fortune grinned at him. 'Would you prefer to be locked out of your room when the electricity fails?'

'The power goes off?' asked Lydia.

'Most nights, yes. The hotel has a generator, but not always enough gasoline to run it.'

'Sometimes the old brute force approach is best,' said the amused Nina, holding up her own equally bulky key fob. 'You'd agree with that, wouldn't you, Eddie?'

He was looking distractedly back into the bar. 'Hmm? Oh, yeah.'

'You okay?'

'Yeah, I'm fine.' He composed himself, then retrieved their bags. 'Come on, then. Let's check out our pad.'

By the time they were installed in their third-floor room, sunset had arrived with equatorial swiftness. They sat on the small balcony to watch. Butembo became more visually appealing in inverse proportion to the amount of remaining daylight, shadows hiding the squalor.

'So, that guy downstairs,' Nina asked, 'who was he? Paris said he'd heard of him . . .'

'His name's Brice. Used to work for the British government.'

She picked up the disdain in his voice. 'You mean MI6?'

'Yeah.'

She smiled. 'You really don't like spies, do you?'

'Nope. Bunch of sneaky, lying bastards. Doesn't matter which side they're on, they're as bad as each other.'

'Well, Peter Alderley's okay.'

'Alderley! That tosser.' But he said it with a crooked smile.

'How did you meet this Brice, then?'

'Job I did a while back,' he said, being deliberately vague. 'Ended okay from my point of view, but not his, which he was pretty pissed off about. He wound up quitting because of it, and now he's out here as a private contractor.'

'Not someone I want to get to know, then.'

'Nope. Alderley's a bell-end, but he's a relatively good guy. Brice is just an arsehole, though. Anyway, let's not—'

He broke off as the lights scattered across the darkening town flickered, then vanished. The hotel's own lights briefly dimmed before returning. 'Whoa. Fortune wasn't kidding about the power,' said Nina. The sun was now gone, the sky turning a bruised purple in its wake.

Eddie shook his head. 'Happens a lot in this part of the

world, even in pretty big cities. The only places you can guarantee the lights'll stay on are the ones with lots of tourists . . . or the country's rulers.'

'Where the money is, in other words.'

'Yeah. I got cynical about that a long time ago. Even back home in England.'

'You still think of it as home? Even after living in New York for twelve years?'

'Always will, because, well, it *is* home. It's where I grew up, it's what made me who I am . . .'

He trailed off with a small frown. Nina caught his change of expression. 'What's wrong?'

'Something Brice said, that's all. Made me wonder where I actually belong.'

'You've got a wife and a little girl! You should *know* where you belong.'

He smiled, then regarded his watch. 'We should call Macy soon.'

'It won't be her bedtime for a couple of hours.'

'I'm thinking more about *our* bedtime. It'll be a long day tomorrow, for both of—'

Eddie stopped mid-sentence again, but this time at the sound of gunfire. He jumped from his seat to shield Nina as he scanned the dark streets below. The shots, he could tell, were from a rifle rather than a handgun, probably a Kalashnikov set on single shot. Shouts reached him from a few hundred metres away, but he couldn't pick out any activity at ground level. 'Think we should go inside.'

'Yup,' Nina quickly agreed. Even before Eddie had closed the French windows behind them, they heard another gunshot. 'Who do you think it is?'

'Militia, probably – maybe this lot Fortune told us about.'

'I'm glad the hotel's behind that wall.'

'Won't keep 'em out if they really want to come in.'

'Thanks, honey. You know how to make a woman feel safe.'

Someone knocked on the door. The Englishman cautiously opened it. Ziff was outside, eyes wide. 'Did you hear those shots?'

'Yeah,' Nina told him. 'Eddie thinks it's the militia.'

'They didn't sound far away! I hope the hotel is safe.'

She looked at her husband. 'You want to tell him, or shall I?' He gave her a grim smile.

'I assume you think the whole town is unsafe, then?' asked the Israeli. 'At least we're leaving in the morning.'

'The countryside won't be any safer,' Eddie told him.

'Wonderful.' Ziff put a hand to his head. 'Still, I suppose it will make your television show more exciting. If we make it back alive, that is.'

'I'm sure Fortune and Paris will make sure we do,' said Nina, trying to sound reassuring – both for Ziff's benefit and her own.

A door opened down the hallway. 'Did you just hear shooting?' asked Lydia in alarm. The New Zealander was clad in an oversized T-shirt, clutching it protectively around herself.

'It'll be okay,' said Eddie. 'If you've got earplugs, you might want to put 'em in, though.'

'Oh, great. We're in a war zone.' She retreated and closed the door.

Ziff regarded the doorway curiously. 'Isn't that Mr Fisher's room?'

'I'm sure they're just sharing to save the production company some money,' said Nina, holding in a smile. The director and sound woman weren't a couple, but it had become clear that they were at the very least friends with benefits.

The bearded archaeologist gave her a wry look, then returned to his own room. 'I'll see you in the morning, Nina.'

'See you then,' she replied. Eddie closed the door. She saw

when he turned that he was deep in thought. 'What?'

'I don't think Fortune and Paris will be enough to look after you all,' he said. 'Not with these militia twats running around.'

'It won't just be them. Fortune said he'd hired three other guys.'

'They're porters, not bodyguards. And I don't know anything about them.' A pause, then: 'I'm coming with you to the river.'

'What?' she protested. 'Eddie, it's a full day's drive away – that's a two-day round trip for you. And it'll take at least another day before you can get back to Macy.'

'My dad and Julie can look after her for a bit longer.'

'That's . . . kind of an imposition. Are you serious?'

'Bloody right I'm serious. Fortune's a good man, and Paris seems on the ball, but they're just two guys. And two guys aren't enough to protect a nice juicy party of rich foreigners.'

'And you think having *three* guys will make all the difference?'

'You know what the third guy can do. Especially when it comes to keeping you safe.'

She couldn't dispute that after everything they had been through together. 'Yeah, but . . . Eddie, you can't leave Macy with her grandparents for an extra two days. It's not fair on them, and it's not fair on her.'

His attitude did not change. 'I'll tell you what else wouldn't be fair on her: her mum not coming back at all because some militia scumbag decided to steal some camera gear. Once you're safely on the boats I'll head back, but I'm not leaving you until then. And that's that.'

'It is, is it?' Nina said, defiant – but knowing that on this occasion, there was no way he would back down. Nevertheless, she refused to retreat herself. 'Then I think you should be the one to explain to Macy why her daddy isn't going to see her for at least another three days. And also explain to *your* daddy.'

'I will, don't worry. And I know Macy'll be upset, but there are things that'd upset her a lot more. As for Dad, pfft.' A dismissive sound. 'He always preferred playing golf to being with his kids, so he can bloody well make up for it with his *grand*kid.'

Nina had more to say, but another couple of gunshots outside – more distant, but still clear – held back the words. 'Hope that doesn't go on all night,' she said instead, with false levity.

'We'll see,' Eddie replied. 'I'll let Fortune know about the change in plans, then we'll ring Macy. After that, we'd better get some food and then some shut-eye. 'Cause tomorrow's going to be a long day.'

'Yeah,' she said, still frustrated with him. 'I get the feeling it will.'

8

If there were any further incidents in the night, Nina had been too tired to hear them. But she awoke before dawn, filled with renewed energy. Reaching Butembo was merely the overture; the expedition proper was about to begin.

Knowing they had a long journey ahead, the team had a full breakfast before assembling outside the hotel. The two minibuses awaited them, along with a well-worn Toyota pickup truck. Joining the explorers were three Congolese men. 'Our porters,' Fortune announced. 'Masson Kimba, Lenard Chumbo and Cretien Wemba.'

'Morning,' said Eddie, shaking hands with each in turn. Kimba was broad and muscular, his smiling round face shaded by a ragged red baseball hat bearing the incongruous logo of Manchester United football club. Chumbo, in contrast, had a wiry build and prominent cheekbones, but his expression was equally cheerful. The last man, Wemba, fell unremarkably between the others' extremes. His eyes were hidden behind a pair of knock-off designer sunglasses with reflective blue lenses. 'Nice to meet everyone.' He turned back to Fortune. 'They know how to handle themselves?'

His Congolese friend – his suit from the previous day replaced by a more practical but equally stylish safari outfit – nodded. 'They will not panic if there is trouble. You can count on that.'

Eddie stepped back as Nina and Ziff introduced themselves to the newcomers, noticing that Rivero was recording events with a professional Handicam. 'You putting this on Facebook?'

'I'm always shooting, man,' Rivero replied. 'The more footage you got, the easier things are in the edit. Besides, you never know when something's gonna happen.'

'Make sure you get my good side,' Eddie joked.

Fisher shook hands with the porters, then straightened imperiously to address all the Africans. 'Just so you all know, I'm the director, which means I'm in charge,' he told them. 'I call the shots. If I say something needs to be a certain way, then that's how it gets done. I'm not really a bad guy, so if everyone does what I say, I won't have to act like one. Okay?'

The porters exchanged looks, Wemba frowning behind his glasses – then Paris exaggeratedly bowed to the director. 'Oh, yassa, yassa, massa. We all do what the great white man say, yassa.' Fortune laughed.

Fisher's cheeks flushed. 'That's – that's not how I meant it. It wasn't!' He turned to his crew for support, only to find them trying to hide smirks. 'Really, it wasn't.'

Eddie nudged Rivero. 'Did you get *that*?' The cameraman nodded.

The three chuckling porters responded to an instruction from Fortune and began to load the baggage into the waiting vehicles. Rivero conspicuously refused to surrender his Sony, while Lydia hurriedly retrieved a padded bag that Eddie guessed contained her sound equipment. Just as soldiers were fiercely protective of their gear, so too were the documentary crew.

It did not take long for everything to be secured. Fortune addressed the group. 'It will take eleven, twelve hours to reach Nakola – if we are lucky. The road is bad, so we cannot go fast, and we may be stopped along the way. If that happens, stay in your seat and let Paris and me handle it.'

'That sounds kinda ominous,' said Fisher.

'Why do you think we've got three bags of US dollars?' Nina said. 'It's not for snacks at gas stations.'

'Huh. So we're gonna get shaken down?'

'Just tell 'em you're the director and you call the shots,' Eddie told him, grinning. Fisher huffed.

They boarded the three vehicles. Fortune started the lead bus, Paris following suit in the second and Wemba bringing the pickup to rattling life at the rear of the little convoy. *'D'accord, tout le monde est prêt?'* Fortune asked over a walkie-talkie. Both replies were in the affirmative. 'Okay,' he told his passengers. 'We are go.'

He pulled away, the other vehicles following. They waited for the security gate to open, then rolled into the streets of Butembo, heading out of the dusty town.

'You weren't kidding about the roads,' Nina complained. Three hours into the journey, and any tarmac surfaces were a long way behind them. The scenery was beautiful, rippling hills dotted with increasingly dense stands of trees and bushes, but once they left the main route between Butembo and Goma far to the south to head west towards the Congo basin, hard-packed red earth was the best surface they could hope for. Unfortunately, even that was an infrequent luxury, the track mostly suspension-punishing ruts, potholes and stones. 'I'm starting to feel seasick.'

'Starting?' said Fisher queasily. He had chosen to ride with Nina, Eddie and Ziff in the lead bus, his crew in the second.

'This is the *good* part of the road,' Fortune assured them cheerily.

Nina sighed. 'Eddie, the next time I decide to head into the jungle to look for a lost city, remind me to bring a big-ass cushion.'

'Or you could, y'know, not go at all,' suggested her grumpy husband from the seat behind. He had endured plenty of hard rides in his military career and beyond, but now he was in his mid-forties he was realising to his annoyance that his tolerance for discomfort had lowered considerably.

131

'You didn't have to come with me,' she said pointedly. 'You were *supposed* to be going back to Macy.' She turned away to watch the landscape roll by.

Eddie sat back, glowering. Fisher glanced between the couple, then leaned closer to him. 'Can I ask you something?' he whispered.

'What?' said the Englishman.

'Nina. So she's always like that, then?'

'Like what?'

'You know. Ah . . . *pushy*. Okay, rude.'

Eddie almost told him to mind his own business, but was irked enough by Nina's attitude to reply. 'Yeah, she is,' he said quietly. 'About anything archaeological, anyway. Once she decides to go after something, that's it. That's all she cares about.'

He paused, about to correct himself for being unfair, but Fisher spoke first. 'Yeah, I'd noticed. But you seem like a pretty determined guy – you're ex-military, right?' Eddie nodded. 'So why do you put up with that crap?'

Eddie stared at the American. 'Because I love her. Why do you think?'

Fisher shifted uncomfortably in his seat. 'Just . . . just making conversation, you know. No offence.'

The convoy continued along the ragged road for another thirty minutes – then Fortune sat bolt upright. 'Eddie,' he said in a warning tone before delivering a terse radio message to the drivers behind.

'What is it?' asked Ziff.

'Think we're about to stop,' Eddie cautioned. Ahead, the road weaved through a narrow pass between two humped hills – where a couple of vehicles blocked the road. As they drew closer, he saw men lounging in the shade of nearby trees scramble upright.

'Military checkpoint?' asked Fisher hopefully.

'Nope.' The waiting men were armed, but none wore uniforms. 'Militia.' Fisher swallowed and shrank in his seat.

'Call themselves Insekt Posse,' said Fortune, slowing as a man stepped into the road and held up one hand, an AK in his other. 'You can tell by the armbands.'

Eddie saw that the group all wore strips of red material around their arms. 'They dangerous?'

'They can be. They will probably take a bribe, though.'

'So long as they don't take our gear,' said the nervous Fisher. 'Not sure the network would pay for a documentary shot entirely on someone's phone.'

'If they take your cameras, they will take your phones too,' Fortune told him. 'But we will handle this.'

He stopped thirty feet short of the man, the two other vehicles pulling up behind. Eddie assessed the four militia members as they approached. All were barely into adulthood, the oldest at most in his early twenties, and had the macho swagger common to undisciplined young men with guns facing those without. He also saw they had red, watery eyes and almost woozy movements; they were high on something. That would slow their reactions, but he didn't know what it would do to their tempers . . .

'You got guns in here?' he asked Fortune.

'Yes,' replied the African as he opened his door, 'but you won't need one.' He gestured to Paris, who joined him, then they went to meet the gunmen.

'I don't like this,' said Nina, watching warily as Fortune spoke in French to the oldest of the group.

'If anyone can handle them, it's Fortune,' said Eddie. All the same, he wished his friend had told him where he had stashed his weapons. He deliberately avoided direct eye contact as one of the militia rounded the bus, staring menacingly at each passenger in turn. The young man was pungent with the odour of both tobacco and whatever narcotic had laced it.

To the relief of the travellers, negotiations were quickly concluded. The leader called out to the others, then came with the expedition's bodyguards back to the lead bus. 'They wanted everything we have as a toll,' Fortune announced, 'but I have bargained them down to one thousand American dollars.'

'What!' snapped Fisher, before hurriedly falling silent as the militia man glared at him.

'Trust me, it is a bargain. The money?'

'Outside pocket on the grey-and-blue backpack,' Nina told him. Fortune found it and produced a wad of hundred-dollar bills, which he counted off into the leader's hand. The man stuffed the money into a pocket, then said something doubtless meant to sound threatening but which came out under Fortune's level stare as a reedy stammer. He retreated and shouted to his comrades to move their vehicles off the road.

'How did you make a deal?' Nina asked as Fortune returned to the driver's seat.

He grinned, gold flashing in the sun. 'I told them my name.'

'That's all?' said Fisher, agog. 'They backed down just because you told them who you are?'

'Fortune's got quite a reputation,' Eddie said with a smile. 'Lucky for us, he's on our side.'

The well-dressed man laughed. 'You might even say I am your good *fortune*, eh?' He signalled to Paris, who had returned to his own bus, and the convoy set off again. The members of the Insekt Posse watched with evident hostility as they passed, but took no action against them.

Ziff sighed in relief. 'That was close.'

'There may be more before we reach Nakola,' said Fortune. 'Insekt Posse is one of the largest militia groups supporting the LEC, but it is not the only one.'

'Any of 'em operate out past Nakola?' Eddie asked.

'There is no way to know for sure, but I have heard of them

hiding in the jungle in the past. Some may be there now.'

'They use the rivers to get around?'

'Sometimes, yes.'

'Right.' He sat back, thinking.

Nina turned to speak to him, but on seeing his pensive expression held her tongue. His questions to Fortune gave her the feeling that another argument was brewing, and after escaping one tense situation she had no desire to drop immediately into another.

Despite Fortune's concerns, the rest of the journey to the small village of Nakola was completed without any further militia interference. The rough road, however, had not been so cooperative, a puncture on Paris's minibus adding almost two hours to the predicted travel time. 'Oh, my God,' gasped Rivero as he clambered exhaustedly from his ride. 'I never want to do *that* again!'

'You'll have to on the way back,' Howie reminded him.

'Maybe I'll just stay here. There's a hotel, it's got a bar – what more do I need?'

'I don't think it'll win any Michelin stars,' said Nina. Even at night, lit only by the headlights of the three vehicles and scattered lamps, Nakola's wretched poverty made Butembo look like Dubai.

'It's not bouncing around over potholes, so that's good as far as I'm concerned,' Eddie grunted as he collected their belongings.

'I know,' she agreed. 'It'll be great to get into a room for the night.'

Five minutes later, she had changed her mind. 'Okay. Maybe we'll just sleep in the bus,' she said in disgust on seeing their squalid chamber. The bed linen not only hadn't been changed since the previous occupant, but it seemed entirely possible that said occupant had died in their sleep and not been discovered for days.

Eddie shrugged. 'I've slept in worse places.'

'Oh yeah? Where?'

'Well, I was in a Zimbabwean prison once. And you've camped in the jungle before, you know what it's like with all the insects and stuff.'

She pointed at a thumb-width crack in one wall, through which a creeper was protruding. 'Yeah, but it's different when the jungle's trying to get indoors with you!'

'We'll stick a groundsheet over the bed and kip in our sleeping bags. It'll be fine.'

'I'm not convinced,' she said as he opened a pack. 'And . . . there's something else I'm not convinced about.'

'What's that?'

'That you're going back to Butembo tomorrow. You're going to insist that you come all the way to Zhakana, aren't you?'

Eddie briefly paused in his search. 'What makes you think that?'

'Because I know you? You were determined to see me this far, and after that business at the roadblock I can't imagine you waving goodbye in the morning and letting me head upriver into a jungle where more of those assholes might be hiding out.'

He tugged out the groundsheet. 'That pretty much covers all the arguments I was going to use, so yeah.'

Nina rubbed her temple. 'For God's sake, Eddie. What about Macy? Do you really want to leave our daughter with her grandparents for an extra week or more, without even seeing her in person to explain why? Let's be honest – you don't even especially *like* your dad! But you're happy to dump Macy on him for that time?'

'Of course I'm not bloody happy about it,' he protested, spreading the waterproof sheet over the stained bedding. 'But what else can I do? You heard Fortune. The militia might be in the jungle—'

'*Might* be.'

'You willing to take the chance? 'Cause I'm not, not when it's your life on the line. And everyone else's too. Those Insekt Posse dickheads wanted to strip us of everything at gunpoint – and who knows what else they would have done?'

Nina regarded him with disapproval. 'You mean to me and Lydia.'

'*Yes*, to you and Lydia. This isn't some sexist thing either,' he added, cutting off her impending objection. 'This is what these bastards do. Rape's as much a weapon as an AK in this part of the world. I've seen it – Rwanda, Sudan. And if—' He broke off, briefly affected by a surge of emotion. 'And if something happened to you out here and I could've been with you to stop it, but wasn't . . .'

'Eddie . . .' she said, realising the depths of his feelings. 'I – I know what you're saying, and I appreciate it, you know I do. But I'm sure we'll be okay.'

'You might be. But I'm not. That lot at the roadblock were trying their luck. If you run into a bigger bunch in the jungle, though . . . that's their territory. Fortune's reputation won't scare 'em off.'

'You said yourself that Fortune and Paris should be able to handle them.'

'Fortune's good. But I'm better. And you know it.' He finished covering the bed. 'There's a satphone in the gear, so I'll call Dad. And we'll talk to Macy too. I know she'll be upset, but like I said yesterday, there are much worse things that could happen.'

'God damn it, Eddie,' she said, but she knew he would not change his mind. Resigned, she took out the sleeping bags to prepare for what she was sure would be an uncomfortable night in more ways than one.

9

Nina did not sleep well. The night had come alive with the chirps and rattles of countless nocturnal creatures, and the cracks in the hotel's walls let many of them pay her a personal visit. But it was Eddie's presence that had kept her awake the most, still angry about their argument. She understood full well why he had insisted on staying, and even saw his point to a degree – which only made her mood worse.

Her husband was still asleep. Brushing away several creepy-crawlies, she rose and quietly left the room. 'Morning,' said Howie from a wicker chair as she entered the run-down lobby. 'You're up early.'

'Doing my yoga.' He munched an energy bar. 'You might want to skip the breakfast buffet. I saw a bug the size of a phone checking it out.'

'Maybe just a coffee, then,' she replied. 'Who else is awake?'

'The local guys are all outside. I think they're loading the boats.'

She went to see what Fortune and his men were doing. It was past dawn, but heavy clouds blocked out the sun, the gloom rendering Nakola even more miserable than she had imagined. She saw their vehicles had been moved to the bank of a sluggish river. 'Good morning!' called Fortune from the water's edge.

'Hi,' she replied. He, Paris and the three porters were indeed loading the crew's gear into a pair of boats. Both craft were eight-seaters powered by outboard motors, the free spaces crammed with cargo. 'You sure everything will fit?'

'Yeah, yeah,' Paris assured her. 'No problem.'

'I should probably tell you that Eddie's decided he's coming with us.'

He regarded the boats. 'Huh. Okay. Problem.' He started to haul items back ashore.

Fortune raised his eyebrows. 'He is?'

'Yeah, thanks to those guys at the checkpoint. I told him we'd be fine with you guys watching out for us, but he wouldn't listen.'

She had half-expected the African to be offended by her husband's lack of faith in him, but it was not the case. 'Do you trust Eddie?' he asked.

'Yeah, of course I do,' she answered, surprised.

'So do I. He is a very good man to have at your side when there is danger.'

'You think there'll be danger?'

He smiled. 'We are going into unexplored jungle. There is *always* danger!'

By the time Paris had repositioned enough items to free an extra seat, the other expedition members had arrived – along with several interested villagers. Rivero recorded the proceedings with his Handicam. 'Ay up,' said Eddie, greeting his Congolese companions. 'You got room for an extra one?'

'You are always welcome,' Fortune told him. 'And we will get paid whether or not you are here!'

'Wait, now *he's* coming into the jungle too?' Fisher complained to Nina. 'Don't you think you should have asked me first?'

'You're welcome to tell him he can't come,' she replied.

The director turned to Eddie as if to do just that, but the Yorkshireman's folded arms and unblinking stare deterred him. 'Well, he's . . . not eating our food,' he said instead, rejoining the camera crew.

The group's remaining items were placed aboard. While Paris

and the three porters checked that everything was secured, one of the villagers, an elderly man with a straggly grey beard, approached and spoke in French. Nina had some fluency in the language, but his heavy accent made it hard to understand. 'What did he say?' she asked Fortune.

He gave her a look of both intrigue and mild concern. 'He wants to know if we are looking for the City of the Damned.'

She was shocked. 'He's heard of it? Ask him what he knows!'

Rivero hurriedly moved in to record the discussion. 'He says it is a legend,' Fortune reported at last. 'He does not know where it is, only that it is supposed to be out there in the jungle.' He glanced upriver. 'But nobody ever goes to look for it.'

'Why not?' Fisher demanded.

Another exchange, the villager shaking his hands as if to disassociate himself from the very idea. 'He says there is a curse,' said Fortune. 'A sickness, a . . . a "bad feeling", that poisons even the trees.'

Lydia responded with alarm. 'A sickness? Great, I hope all those shots I had will cover it.'

Fisher was much more enthused. 'A curse? That's great, it's a good hook. *The Curse of Solomon*, there's our series title.'

'I think that's a Clive Cussler book,' Eddie noted.

Nina irritably shushed him as Fortune recounted the old man's words. 'He says that no one who has ever gone to search for the city has returned.'

'Sounds about par for the course,' said Eddie.

'You still sure you want to come?' Nina asked him.

'If soldiers turned back every time they had a bad feeling, they'd never leave the barracks. So yeah, I'm still coming with you.'

'Just checking. Fortune, does he know anything else?'

The Congolese questioned the villager further. 'Sadly, no.

But he wishes us good luck.' The old man gave her a smile that was not especially reassuring.

She noticed that Rivero was holding his camera on her, hoping for a quotable line. 'Let's hope we're the first to come back, then,' was the best she could manage as she tied her hair into a ponytail, ready to begin.

Half an hour later, the expedition set out.

Nina sat at the lead vessel's bow, watching the jungle rise around them. Nakola was on the edge of the Congo basin, and from here on the region became much wetter. The river was unusual in that it eventually drained into Lake Edward to the east rather than the mighty Congo itself, which suggested it could have been used both by Solomon and the empire of Sheba to reach Zhakana, but it also meant they were travelling against the current. With both boats fully loaded, they wouldn't make much speed on the outward journey.

Fortunately, the waters were placid and slow-moving. She took out a GPS handset to check their position. 'If the lost city's where the map room said, then it's thirty-two kilometres in that direction.' She pointed ahead, slightly off the present path of the river.

Eddie looked across at the nearest shore to judge their speed. 'We're doing maybe five kph. That's, er . . .'

'Six and a half hours to get there,' she told him, doing the mental arithmetic in a blink.

'If the river's straight. Which it isn't. And if there aren't any waterfalls. Which there probably are. We'll be lucky to get there before nightfall.'

Lydia and Fisher were on the row behind. 'Only thirty-two kays?' said the former. 'Can't believe it hasn't been found if it's so close.'

'You can pass thirty-two *feet* from something in jungle like this and never see it,' Nina replied. 'There's a reason the Atlantean temple in Brazil and the city of Paititi in Venezuela were lost for so long.'

Fisher took out a laminated chart. 'I had a satellite map made before we left Israel,' he said, unfolding it. Wemba, sitting on the next row back, peered at it with interest. A bright yellow line showed the route to take at each of the numerous forks where tributaries merged. 'The river definitely isn't straight, but it looks pretty easy to navigate.'

Eddie glanced back. 'Were the satellite photos taken at the same time of year as now?'

'I don't know, but we're almost at the equator, aren't we? It shouldn't make a difference.'

'You still get seasons at the equator. If you're in the jungle, they're basically wet, and *really* wet. What's a river on your map might be a lake now – or it might be dry land.'

'At least if we get lost, Howie can send up the drone to see which way to go,' said Lydia, swatting in irritation at insects.

'How long do its batteries last?' Eddie asked.

'We've got plenty of spares and everything we need to keep it charged up, don't worry,' Fisher said. 'Same for all our gear. Cameras, mics, laptops – they won't run out of juice.'

'You brought bloody *laptops* into the jungle? We're not at Starbucks.'

'Actually, we do our preliminary editing and sound mixing on them in the field,' said the director, becoming defensive. 'The drone's even controlled from one. Plus, we need them to back up all our media every day. If a camera gets damaged or, God forbid, lost out here, we can't exactly go back and reshoot anything.'

Eddie shrugged. 'That's a lot of stuff that might go wrong or break.' He turned away, shaking his head. 'Bet it's not even bloody waterproofed,' he whispered to Nina.

'They do know what they're doing,' she said with a little smile. 'Believe it or not.'

Fortune guided the boat onwards, Paris at the tiller of the second behind them. The vegetation grew thicker, drooping branches dipping into the water like grasping hands. Before long, it became impossible to make out the surrounding terrain beyond the dense green curtains. The air filled with the rich, cloying scent of rot, dead flora and fauna alike rapidly decaying in the warm, humid environment. 'Ah. There's a smell I haven't missed,' said Nina, wrinkling her nose.

'Easy to see who's in the jungle for the first time,' Eddie remarked, checking on the documentary crew. Most were reacting far more expressively to the scent, Howie the only one who appeared unperturbed. 'The kid doesn't seem to mind it.'

'Maybe it smells like his dorm room.' They both grinned.

The boats continued on up the snaking river. An hour passed, two, more, the unchanging view and the plodding chug of the outboards as wearing as the incessant attention of insects. Nina checked the GPS again. 'Halfway there,' she announced.

'We should stop for a break soon,' said Eddie. 'Dunno about you, but I could use a piss.'

'Charming,' Lydia muttered behind him.

Nina looked at her watch. 'It's past noon, so we should eat too.' She searched the banks for somewhere to put ashore. 'If you see any—'

'Hold it,' Eddie interrupted, raising a hand.

Fortune immediately dropped the outboard's throttle to idle, Paris following suit in the other boat. 'What is it?' the Congolese asked.

'Rough water ahead. You see it?'

'Yes, I do. Waterfall?'

'Probably. Stop the engines so we can hear.'

Fortune shut down his outboard, as did Paris. With the boats silenced, a new sound became audible over the chitterings of bugs and birds: a deep, hissing rumble. 'Definitely a waterfall,' said Nina.

'Going up or down?' asked Rivero from the other boat.

The question drew him mocking looks. 'We're going *up*river, and water flows *down*hill – what do you think?' said Fisher, smirking.

The tubby cameraman huffed. 'All right, Jeez. I'm not a hydrologist.'

'Fortune, we'd better take a look and hope there's an easy way we can get to the top of it,' said Eddie.

'When you say, "get to the top",' Fisher said uncertainly, 'I'm assuming you mean on land.'

'No, we're going to flip up it like a salmon. Course I bloody do!'

'You've seen the movie *Fitzcarraldo*, right?' Nina asked. With every member of the documentary crew either a film school graduate or having ambitions of working in Hollywood, she was not surprised that they had, or at least pretended to have done so. 'We'll have to pull the boats up to the top of the waterfall.'

'Sure, that'll be easy,' said Lydia, unimpressed.

'Six to a boat, should be doable,' Eddie told her. 'So long as we can find a slope that's not too steep.'

The engines started up again, Paris and Fortune bringing the boats side by side. It did not take long before the rumble of falling water became audible even over the outboards. Rounding a bend, the source of the noise came into sight. Fisher shouted across to the other boat. 'Jay! You getting that?'

Rivero already had his camera rolling. 'You bet,' he replied. He stood for a better view, only for Paris to yell for him to sit again as the boat rocked.

The waterfall was not especially high, around forty feet, but was near-vertical where the upper river cascaded over a cliff. A white mist masked the churning waters at its base. 'Okay,' said Nina, 'it's very pretty, but how are we going to get up it?'

Eddie was already searching the shores, Fortune and Paris doing the same. 'Over there!' the latter shouted, pointing to the right.

Treetops beyond the bank swept up to meet the canopy on the cliff. 'It's shallow enough to climb,' the Englishman decided.

'We can land there,' said Fortune, indicating a small muddy cove. He turned the tiller, Paris swinging his own craft to follow.

The water downriver of the falls was choppy, but both boats made it to land without being swamped, to the camera crew's great relief. Fortune deliberately ran the bow aground, Eddie jumping out and grabbing a rope to hitch it to a tree. The second boat pulled up alongside. 'Okay, unload everything, then we'll drag it out of the river,' said Eddie. The cargo was extracted, then he, Nina, Fortune, Wemba and – with a little reluctance – Fisher pulled the vessel on to the shore. Lydia eventually offered half-hearted assistance under Nina's pointed gaze. Those aboard Paris's boat followed suit, both vessels soon sitting beached on the bank.

'Well, that was the easy part,' said the Yorkshireman, surveying the waterfall. 'Now we've got to get them up there!'

While the others ate, Eddie and Fortune scouted ahead, finding a relatively easy route up the slope to a stretch of riverbank safely clear of the waterfall's quickening current. With six people carrying each boat, it took a little more than an hour to heave them up the hill.

'Fitzcarraldo would be proud,' said the sweating Nina as the craft were laid down beside the river. She took a GPS reading. 'Only fifteen kilometres to go.'

'Sunset is in less than four hours,' Fortune cautioned. 'We may not make it before dark.'

'Let's hope there aren't any more waterfalls, then.'

'Yeah, let's,' griped Lydia.

Everyone returned to the lower river to retrieve their cargo. Another half-hour passed before they returned and everything was reloaded. 'Okay, where's Jay?' asked Fisher, looking around.

'Oh, for fuck's sake,' Eddie said in dismay as he spotted the cameraman balancing precariously on a large boulder in the rushing river, filming the waterfall. 'Why do people with cameras always have a death wish?'

'That's how they win awards – if they survive,' the director joked. 'Jay! We're leaving!' Rivero turned, wobbling alarmingly before catching himself and hopping back to shore.

This time there was little ceremony as the boats finally set out, just a tired desire to reach their destination. Once clear of the falls, their passage became as monotonous as before, the unbroken walls of trees along the flat, swampy land on each side almost claustrophobic. Conversation dried up in the muggy heat. Nina eventually broke the silence as she checked the GPS. 'Three kilometres. Will we get there before sunset?'

'I am not sure,' Fortune replied.

'I've got an idea,' said Fisher, wiping sweat from his face. 'We can send up the drone and see what's ahead.'

'How high can it go?' Eddie asked.

'In theory, over half a mile. I don't think Howie's ever taken it that high, though. But it'll easily clear the trees.'

Everyone looked to Nina. 'Sounds good to me,' she said.

'I almost thought you'd consider that cheating,' said Lydia.

'Why? I used technology to work out Zhakana's location, so I've got no problem with using it in the field. Just because I like to be hands-on at a site doesn't mean I have to grope around in the dark.'

'We can land at that bank,' said Fortune, pointing to a flat, marshy area within one of the river's meanders.

'Then let's do it,' said Fisher. He called to the second boat. 'Howie! We're going to stop. Get the drone ready.' The production assistant gave him a thumbs-up.

They made landfall, mooring the boats. While Howie prepared the drone, everyone else gratefully took the opportunity to stretch their legs. 'Don't go too far,' Paris cautioned as the group dispersed.

Nina went with Fisher to the second boat to speak to Howie, but saw Kimba having trouble getting out of the craft. 'You okay, Masson?' she asked, helping him on to land.

'Yes, thank you,' he replied. He was obviously experiencing discomfort, but trying to hide it behind a smile. 'My leg.' He patted his left thigh just below the hip. 'I was beaten by a soldier when I was a boy. If I move, it is okay. If I am still for too long . . . it hurts.'

'I'm sorry.'

'Why? You did not beat me!' Another smile, but this one was genuine. He rolled his hips, then took a few steps. 'Already it is better. Thank you again, Dr Wilde.'

'Call me Nina,' she said, smiling back.

'Okay, dudes, the drone's ready,' Howie announced. He placed the little aircraft on level ground, then opened one of the team's slim laptops and plugged in a compact antenna dongle. After a few seconds, a window appeared showing the feed from the drone's main camera – which from its current low angle was a comical view of Rivero standing nearby. 'There's a shot for the gag reel.'

'Gag is right,' offered Lydia as the unwitting cameraman tugged at his cargo shorts to adjust his underwear. 'Can you change the channel?'

Howie snickered, then waggled his fingers. 'Okay. Fly, my pretty!'

Rather than use a joystick, he worked the keyboard with the

skill of a lifelong videogamer. The quadcopter's rotors buzzed, lifting it into the air with hummingbird speed. 'Where are we going?' he asked.

'West,' said Nina. 'There should be higher ground three kilometres away.'

He nodded. 'Let's see what we got.' The drone jinked through gaps in the trees before soaring into open sky.

Nina and her companions watched the screen intently. A superimposed heads-up display told them the quadcopter's altitude and bearing; it quickly rose to five hundred feet, turning west. 'There's your higher ground,' Howie announced. With the lowering sun behind them, the hills and cliffs the drone revealed were mostly silhouetted, looming ominously over the jungle.

'I can't make out much detail,' Nina said. 'How much closer can you get?'

'The camera's got a five-times zoom, so that'll help,' the young man replied. 'And the drone's got a full charge, so over a mile before having to RTB. Return to base,' he added, seeing her confusion.

'Go for it,' she told him. 'But head south-west rather than due west – that way, the sun won't be right behind the hills.' The drone changed course, the jungle crabbing diagonally past below as it kept its camera fixed on the highlands.

Details appeared in the shadows. 'That cliff, there,' said Nina, pointing at a feature on the range's edge. 'Can you zoom in on it?'

'Sure can.' The image enlarged.

'It *could* be the cliff from the map room . . .' said Fisher, though with uncertainty.

Nina was more confident. 'It looks a *lot* like it,' she said. 'There's too much tree cover to see if there's anything on top, though.' The view gradually enlarged over the following minutes, but the jungle remained frustratingly opaque. 'Dammit, we won't spot anything from the air,' she finally had to admit. 'Not unless we get a lot closer.'

'Not enough battery left for that,' Howie said apologetically. 'Gotta turn back soon.'

Fisher made a frustrated sound. 'So near, yet so far.'

'We can reach it in person,' Nina reminded him. 'Let's get back in the boats. We might still make it before sundown.'

She called to Fortune, who in turn shouted for everyone to return. 'You find it?' Eddie asked as he reached her.

'I think we've found the right place,' she said. 'As for whether there's anything still there . . .'

He did a headcount, coming up short. 'Someone's missing. Where's Cretien?'

Paris gestured towards a clump of trees a hundred feet away. 'He went that way.'

'I'll get him. Maybe he's constipated and stuck mid-dump.'

'Gross, Eddie,' Nina said, smiling. Lydia was also disgusted, but without humour.

He grinned, then picked his way across the wet ground towards the trees. 'Cretien?' No response. He rounded a trunk – and found the porter hurriedly stuffing something into a pocket. 'What're you doing?'

'I, I . . .' Wemba stammered, before a flash of what Eddie could only interpret as cunning crossed his face. 'I came to smoke, I did not want anyone to see,' he said, delving back into his pocket and producing a packet of cigarettes. 'They are not mine, I took them from the baggage.'

'You stole them, is what you're saying.'

He nodded, looking down at his feet. 'Yes, yes. I am sorry.'

Eddie regarded him dubiously. He couldn't smell cigarette smoke, but there was enough of a breeze to have carried it away, and the Congolese might have flicked the butt into the river when he realised someone was coming. 'It's a bad habit, you should give it up,' he said at last. There was no proof that Wemba had been up to anything worse, and at this early stage of the expedition he didn't want to rouse any antagonism – especially as Fortune had vouched for him. 'Just don't do it again.'

Wemba nodded with vigour. 'You are right. I am sorry.'

'Anyway, we're going. Better get back to the boats.' He retraced his steps, the other man following.

The drone buzzed back down to a landing as they arrived. While Howie collected it, Fisher flicked through its recorded footage on the laptop, comparing a still frame of the distant cliff to one of the model in the First Temple's map room. 'You know, Nina, it actually could be the same place.'

'We'll find out soon,' she said. Eddie reached her. 'Everything okay?'

'No problem,' he said, glancing at Wemba, who avoided his gaze. 'We ready to go?'

'Yeah.' She waited for Howie to return the drone to its case and get back into the boat, then boarded her own. The sun had dropped lower behind the trees, but with so little distance still to go she was sure they could reach their destination before nightfall. 'Let's see what's waiting for us.'

10

The atmosphere changed the closer the team got to the journey's end.

It took a while for Nina to realise exactly *why*. Rising anticipation, sure; but there was something else, beyond the boats. It took a swat of her hand at an insect buzzing around her face to realise what it was. 'Is it just me, or aren't there as many bugs?' Now that she thought about it, she had not been bothered by flying critters for several minutes.

'I think you're right,' said Eddie. He regarded the sluggish river's surface. It had previously been alive with countless low-flying insects and water skaters, but now, while there was still no shortage of bugs, they were no longer swarming. 'Not as many birds either.'

Fortune shrugged. 'If there are not as many insects, there will not be as many birds to eat them. And the sun is setting. They will be going to sleep.'

'I know, but I've spent a lot of time in jungles before. Something's not right.'

'That's it exactly,' said Nina. 'Something doesn't *feel* right. Anyone else getting that?'

'Nothing's felt right since we started down this bloody river,' Lydia complained.

'No, I know what she means,' said Fisher. She gave him a curious look. 'It's hard to describe, but I feel kind of . . . *unsettled*? Like the back of my mind's saying we shouldn't be here.'

'Maybe it's the curse,' suggested Eddie with dark humour.

'I'm not saying I *believe* it. But yeah, there's definitely a weird feeling.'

Nina consulted the GPS. 'Just over a kilometre to go, so if it gets weirder, we're probably in the right place.' She looked at the riverbank to starboard. The ground rose on that side, exposed rock peeking through the vegetation. 'We're coming up to the cliffs.'

A wall of stone lay ahead. Fisher called to Rivero to ready his camera. The inexplicable feeling of unease grew stronger. 'Look,' said Eddie, pointing at the left bank. 'There's something wrong with the trees.'

'It's definitely a tulgey wood,' Nina replied. The jungle vegetation was as dense as before, but appeared oddly sickly, twisted and gnarled.

He lowered his voice. 'We're not going into another bloody dead zone, are we? A pool of eitr, or a radioactive cave . . .'

'I hope not.' The couple's previous adventures had brought them dangerously close to deadly secrets from within the earth itself, the lethal effects of which had been worked into the mythology of ancient civilisations as diverse as the Vikings, the Greeks and even the Atlanteans. 'But Zhakana's linked to the Hebrew legend of King Solomon's Shamir, which had great powers, so maybe this is some side effect.'

'Great. And we didn't bring any hazmat suits.'

They passed into the cliff's shadow. Nina checked the GPS again, then looked ahead, excitement overcoming nervousness. 'We're close. I think that when the river comes around this promontory, we'll be there.'

Fisher shouted to the second boat. 'Jay, start filming. I'll use the SLR for reaction shots of Nina.' He took out a Nikon digital still camera and switched it to its video mode.

'Quick, put on some make-up,' said Eddie. Nina gave him a mocking smile.

The river curved around the cliff. As they emerged from its shade, light from the setting sun caught the streams of several small waterfalls gushing from halfway up it, sending a sparkling cascade down at them. 'Wow, look at that,' she said, entranced – until her peripheral vision caught Fisher's camera lens edging ever closer to her face. She resisted the urge to turn and glower at it, instead holding position long enough for him to get his shot – *then* turning and glowering. Fisher retreated without apology.

A giant rock came into view on the right bank. 'That was on the model in the map room!' she said. 'There should be a slope on the other side leading to the city.'

Fortune angled the boat towards the shore, Paris following. Beyond the rock were more trees, more disturbingly warped than those downriver. A slope rose towards the top of the promontory beyond them – steep, but climbable. 'We can land there,' said Eddie, indicating a stretch of bank.

'I think someone already did!' cried Rivero.

'What do you mean?' asked Nina.

'I've zoomed in – and I can see stones along the side. I don't mean fallen rocks either. I'm talking actual carved blocks!'

Fisher's camera snapped up to capture Nina's reaction. This time, she was too thrilled to be annoyed. 'Okay, let's go take a look!'

The boats manoeuvred to the shore. The broken blocks were entangled in roots and reeds, but there was no doubt that they were man-made. Nina climbed on to the base of a twisted tree for a closer look. 'Look at this! I'd say it was a quay, so whoever built it could land without having to drag their boats out of the river.'

Her husband followed her, tying up the boat. 'So who *did* build it?'

'A civilisation that's been completely lost to us – until now.'

'Good trailer line,' said Fisher as he awkwardly climbed

ashore. 'You're getting the hang of this, Nina. Now if you can say it again when there's a camera on you . . .'

She didn't reply, absorbed in her findings. 'These blocks are all damaged, but they were originally very precisely cut. Just like the stones in the First Temple.'

Ziff joined her. 'Very similar workmanship. But according to the inscriptions in the map room, this place pre-dates Solomon by centuries.'

Nina looked up the slope. Any path from the river to the plateau above was now completely overgrown. 'The answers will be up there.' A glance at the reddening western sky. 'We don't have much time before it gets dark.' She started for the incline.

'Wouldn't it be better to make camp and see what's up there in the morning?' asked Lydia.

'It might, but I'm not going to wait now that we're this close,' the redhead replied. 'Steven, you'll want to film all this.' She pushed aside a bush and started to climb, then paused to look back. 'Well, come on! This is why we're here!' She continued upwards, branches cracking as she bulldozed through the undergrowth.

'I do love her, really,' Eddie said to Fisher with a grin before starting after her. 'Fortune, chuck me a machete – although the way she's going, we might not need it!'

The climb to the top took several minutes, the combination of dense vegetation and the steep slope making it an arduous ascent. But Nina still made another discovery along the way: beneath the topsoil, her boots found a firmer surface. The route between the river and whatever lay above had once been paved.

By the time she and Eddie hacked their way to the summit, the documentary team had caught up. Lydia carried the boom microphone, her sound equipment hanging from her neck. The New Zealander had an aggrieved expression, but it was from more than the strain of the climb. 'This is weird,' she said, adjusting dials. 'There's some sort of interference on the audio, but I can't figure out what it is.'

Rivero glanced at his camera's mic. 'I'm not getting anything.'

She pushed one of her headphone cups more firmly against her ear. 'It's really low-frequency, but . . . there's definitely something. Kind of a background hum.'

Eddie stopped to listen. 'I can't hear anything either, but I know what you mean. Like when you go past an electricity substation and there's that buzz you can *feel*.'

'There's something else I can't hear,' said Nina. '*Anything*. No birds, no insects. Listen.' Everyone halted, silence falling unnervingly around them. 'Maybe this place really is a dead zone. The only living things here are plants, and even they don't look too healthy.'

'Yeah, they're definitely Tim Burton-y,' Eddie noted, regarding a spindly and twisted tree. He whispered to Nina: 'If there's another source of eitr here, remember that we gave away most of the cure . . .'

'I don't think that's what it is,' she replied. 'Eitr would have killed *everything*, including the vegetation. But it's more like the animals and insects have been driven off. Maybe that hum Lydia's picked up is scaring them away, like an ultrasonic repeller.' She pressed onwards. 'But we don't scare that easily. Right?'

'You get that?' Fisher asked Rivero below. The cameraman nodded.

The ground levelled out. Eddie swept a machete through obstructing branches, then held them aside so Nina could pass through. She pushed clear – and stopped in amazement. 'Okay, guys?' she called. 'You'll *definitely* want to have the cameras rolling.'

'What've you found?' asked Fisher as the others reached the summit.

Nina looked into Rivero's lens. 'Welcome,' she announced, 'to Zhakana . . . City of the Damned.'

They had emerged on to a field of ruins.

There were dozens of structures, hundreds, disappearing into the shadows beneath the overhanging trees. The buildings were ancient, but even in a state of collapse there was something almost *triumphal* about them, a sense that they had been built to celebrate their civilisation. Even after being eroded by rain and cracked by creepers for multiple millennia, traces of elaborate carvings were still discernible on the walls.

Ziff gasped. 'Magnificent! Oh, this is glorious.'

'You're not kidding,' said Nina. 'And I bet that if we compared each building to the model in the map room, they'd match perfectly.'

'So Solomon was a model train nerd like my dad?' Eddie chipped in. He held the bushes aside so Howie, Paris and finally Wemba could reach the top of the hill, the other Congolese having remained below to unload the boats. It occurred to him that Wemba should have helped them, but he forgot about the porter's lax attitude when he glanced back at the top of the promontory – and saw something new. 'Er, Nina?'

His wife was examining the carvings on one of the ruins. 'Hold on, I just want to see this.'

'I think you'd rather see *this*.'

His tone prompted her to look around – and her eyes went wide. 'Yeah, you're right!'

A building sat upon the jutting clifftop. Unlike the others, this was almost completely intact. It was a stout rectangular block, the sheer outer walls some thirty feet high and capped with ranks of square towers. Its bricks had the same precise, almost laser-cut appearance as those inside the First Temple in Jerusalem. The canopy of trees provided almost total cover, explaining how it had remained hidden from aerial observation

– but these were the most sickly specimens yet, their deformed trunks seeming barely able to support their own weight.

Nina was not interested in the flora, though. She hurried towards the building. 'No doors or windows,' she said. 'It really is the Palace Without Entrance!'

Ziff broke into a jog to catch up. 'So the legend of Solomon is true! And according to the story, the way in is buried in sand on the west side.'

Nina glanced in the direction of the setting sun as she cleared the ruins. 'We're by the north wall, so . . . around that corner.' She pointed.

'Hey, can you wait for us?' said Rivero, breathing heavily as he and the others caught up. 'People running away from the camera only makes good TV on *Cops*.'

'Sorry, sorry,' she said. 'But according to the legends of King Solomon, the way in to the Palace Without Entrance should be over there.'

'Wouldn't that make it the Palace *With* Entrance?' joked Eddie.

'It's hidden. In the legend, Solomon had to follow a trail of eagles to find one that told him where to find it. But the story already gave us the location.' She approached the corner. 'Around here.'

'According to the legend, they had to dig in the sand,' said Ziff. 'Should we get a shovel from the boats?'

'Let's see what's here first,' Nina replied with rising excitement. 'Which is . . .' She stopped as she cleared the corner. 'Oh.'

Rivero was right behind her. 'Hey, cool,' he said, with no little sarcasm. 'Trees!'

Warped vegetation formed a dense wall along the palace's western side. There was no sand on the ground, no convenient pits to be excavated. 'Maybe the legend's wrong,' said Eddie.

With the camera fixed upon her, Nina tried not to let her

frustration show. 'But it corresponds to what we discovered in the First Temple. This *is* Zhakana, this *is* the Palace Without Entrance, it has to be. The legend is a clue telling us how to get in, so there must be a way!'

'Nina, it will still be here in the morning,' said Ziff gently. 'We should make camp and start work again at first light.'

'I know, I know. But it's so *annoying*! We found the city exactly where the map room said, the palace is right here . . . but we can't get in.'

'Yet,' the older archaeologist added. He smiled. 'For someone who has found so many ancient wonders, you are very impatient to find more!'

'Tell me about it,' Eddie said, smirking. 'Now I know where our little girl gets it from. It's not enough that she's got a great Christmas present waiting for her – she's got to open it now, now, *now*!'

'Thanks for sharing that with the world, Eddie,' Nina told him huffily, seeing the film crew smile at what she was sure would be a quotable line.

'Dr Ziff's right, though,' said Fisher. 'We won't get anything else done before dark, so we should set up camp.'

'I will tell the others to bring your gear,' said Wemba. He started back towards the river path.

'Yeah, come on,' said Eddie. 'We'll get the tents, sort out some nosh, then kick off first thing tomorrow.'

'Okay, okay,' Nina sighed. She gave the palace a last look, then reluctantly turned away.

It was long past nightfall by the time everything had been brought to the hilltop. Luckily, the film crew's array of portable lamps made it easier for everyone to see what they were doing as they set up camp.

It also made the strange absence of wildlife more obvious.

'We'd normally have every bug within five miles coming to look at those lights,' Eddie noted as he ate. Insects were flitting around the bulbs, but only a fraction of the number he would have expected.

'Yeah, it's weird,' Nina agreed absently. Something else was dominating her thoughts. They had set up their tents amongst the ruins near the top of the slope. The Palace Without Entrance loomed like a huge spectre over the encampment, its pale stone walls soaking up the spill from the lights. 'What's inside?' she said, almost to herself. 'What did Solomon consider so dangerous that he built *that* to hide it?'

Ziff nodded. 'And hide in such a way that only he could get back in. Or someone as wise as him. I hope we are up to the task.'

'I'm sure we'll get in one way or another,' said Fisher. 'We've got a three-thousand-year technological advantage.'

'At the risk of sounding like Yoda,' Nina replied, putting on a growly voice, 'technology not make one wise.'

Eddie looked askance at her. 'Was that meant to be Yoda? Sounded more like Jar Jar Binks!'

'Says the man who can't do an accent to save his life! Go on, do your American voice. Give us all a laugh.'

He adopted a mock-offended look. 'Ah'm show-ah ah dowan knur what yer-wah tarkin' abart.'

Fisher chuckled. 'It's as if John Wayne himself was here.' Laughter from the crew – with one exception. 'Of course, a Kiwi wouldn't know the difference.'

'Uh-huh,' said Lydia, engrossed by the playback in her headphones.

'What're you doing, Lydia?' Rivero asked. 'I thought Howie'd backed everything up already.'

'I did,' Howie insisted. While the others made camp, the young man had spent half an hour copying files from the team's various devices.

'I'm just checking something,' Lydia said, tapping at her own laptop. 'That humming noise? I've been trying to isolate it – and I found it.' She turned the computer towards the others. Its screen displayed an audio waveform, a stuttering green line showing various sound frequencies. 'This is a composite of twenty seconds of ambient noise.' She pointed out several peaks. 'It's got the wind in the trees, the river, the odd bug or bird – all natural stuff.'

'But you filtered that all out and found . . .?' Nina prompted.

'Nothing – at first. But that's because the defaults on the software clip out anything beyond the range of human hearing. If you aren't going to use it, no point having it – it just wastes processing power and bandwidth. But,' she continued triumphantly, 'the raw recordings are made at the full spectrum. So I went back to *them* and filtered out the higher-frequency stuff. And here's what I found.'

She clicked the trackpad to bring up a new waveform. This was flat – except for a sharp spike at the extreme left-hand end. '*This* is the hum,' Lydia went on. 'The frequency's well below anything we can hear.'

'But we can still feel it,' said Eddie.

'Absolutely. It's not loud, but it's definitely there.'

'So where is it coming from?' asked Nina. 'And what's causing it?'

'The second, I don't know, but the first?' She pointed at the Palace Without Entrance. 'It's coming from in there. Or more likely, *under* there. I think the source is underground.'

Ziff and Nina exchanged looks. 'The Mother of the Shamir?' said the Israeli.

'It could be,' she agreed. 'And now I want to get in there to find out more than ever.'

11

Dawn broke over the thick jungle of the Congo basin, but Nina was already up.

'Thought I'd find you here,' said Eddie, pushing through twisted undergrowth along the palace's west wall to find her kneeling at its base. 'You shouldn't wander off without letting anyone know, mind.'

'I told Paris where I was going,' she replied, not looking up.

'He says you just went "hi" as you walked past and went into the trees with a torch. Not quite the same thing.'

'I'm okay, aren't I? Anyway, I wanted to see if I could find any sand that might hide an entrance.'

'And?'

'Nope.' She retrieved a small shovel and straightened. 'It's either topsoil or rock all the way along. So maybe you were right about the legend last night. The Palace Without Entrance exists, but the part about how to get in could be as much a fantasy as the talking eagles.'

'You mean they weren't a pretty obvious clue?' he said, smiling.

'I know, I know. But it wouldn't be the first time an ancient story that sounds impossible on the surface turned out to have a truth beneath it.'

'Not this one, though. So how are you going to get inside?'

They started back towards the camp. 'I know what I said to Steven last night, but three thousand years of technological progress *can* be useful. We can use the drone to check the roof for entrances. For all we know, it collapsed centuries ago and the whole thing's open to the sky.'

'If it is, climbing up there'll be a pain in the arse,' he said. 'We've got those folding ladders, but we'll probably need ropes too.'

'We'll worry about that if we have to.' They saw activity through the trees and ruins. 'Looks like everyone else is awake.'

'Don't think people got much sleep. That weird hum's not exactly relaxing. I know I wasn't the only one who kept waking up. Heard Lydia whingeing at about three o'clock.'

'Good morning, Eddie!' boomed Fortune as the couple approached. 'You have made an early start, I see.'

'Yeah,' the Yorkshireman replied. 'If there's archaeological stuff to be had, she'll drag me up before dawn's even had a chance to crack.'

'Where's Howie?' Nina asked. 'I want to use the drone to check the palace roof.'

'Way ahead of you,' said Rivero, yawning. 'He's been getting some aerial shots.'

'Sunrise over a lost city in the jungle,' added Fisher. 'It should look spectacular.' The director picked up a walkie-talkie. 'Howie, how's it going?'

'Looking good,' came the crackling reply. 'I'm flying orbits of the cliff so the drone can see under the treetops. Real nice shots.'

Nina gestured for Fisher to hand her the radio; he did so, with territorial reluctance. 'Howie, it's Nina. How much charge does the drone have left?'

'Five minutes, maybe.'

'I know Steven wants his beauty shots, but it would be a huge help archaeologically if you could get a closer look at the palace's roof for any potential ways inside.'

'I can do it, sure,' said Howie. 'Boss, do you want me to?'

Fisher gestured impatiently for Nina to return the walkie-

162

talkie. 'Yeah, go ahead,' he said. 'Once you've got your current shot.'

'No problemo.'

'Where is he?' Eddie asked.

'Over by the cliff,' said Lydia, pointing. 'He wanted clear space for the drone to take off.'

Nina started in that direction. 'Let's see what he's got, then.'

Eddie and the documentary crew followed, Ziff joining them. Fortune and Paris stayed with the porters at the camp. 'You not coming?' Eddie called back to them.

'Sure we'll know soon enough if you find anything interesting,' said Paris, stretching out on Fisher's newly vacated chair.

Fortune gave the Englishman a shrug of exaggerated apology. 'He is good at his job when it counts, I assure you!' Paris threw a plastic fork at him, the smartly dressed man easily catching it.

Eddie smiled. 'So what do you think of Paris?' Nina asked him. '*Is* he good at his job?'

'Fortune wouldn't let him piss about like that if he wasn't,' he replied, nodding. 'He trusts him, so . . . I trust him, yeah.'

'Fortune's a tough boss? He seems so laid back.'

'Remember how he scared those militia arseholes? He doesn't need to make a scene to stay on top of a situation.'

They rounded a ruin to find Howie perched cross-legged on a fallen stone block, controlling the quadcopter from his laptop. 'Hey, there you are,' he said, glancing around. 'I'm bringing the drone through the trees now. We'll see the roof in a sec.'

'I'll let you concentrate, then,' said Nina. 'I don't want you to crash!'

'Won't happen, I'm a good pilot. Although,' he admitted, 'I *did* have a hairy moment when the drone went around the palace's far side. Started to get a load of interference from something.'

'What would cause that?' asked Fisher. 'If it gets broken, we've got no way to fix it out here.'

'Dunno. It was like the signal was being blocked. She dipped a little low, and boom! Huge dropout, and I almost lost control. Good thing is that if there's a major glitch, the drone's programmed to retrace its route until it gets a solid signal again. Only took a few seconds, so after that I kept her higher.' Howie nodded at the screen. 'Anyway, here we go.'

The view from the drone showed it descending beneath the tree cover over the palace's southern end. Nina saw that the roof was not flat. Between the ranks of towers on each side it was vaulted, curving up to a line of keystones running the building's length. 'Solomon knew how to build 'em,' she said, impressed. 'It's survived this long, and I don't see any signs of damage.'

Ziff nodded. 'A roof like that would be self-supporting as long as the lower walls remained intact. How large are the individual blocks?'

'Probably a couple of feet long . . .' She frowned, leaning closer. 'What's that? Howie, hold position.'

The production assistant set the drone to hover. 'There's something on that block,' said Ziff, pointing out a detail. 'A carving?'

'Hard to tell with all the crap on the stonework.' The palace's upper aspect was covered in detritus that had fallen from the overhanging trees. 'Howie, can you get closer?'

'Sure can.' The young man's fingers played over the keyboard. The drone descended. Features upon the block became clearer.

'It *is* a carving,' Ziff said, entranced. 'I can't tell what it is, though.'

'You know what it looks like to me?' said Eddie, tilting his head. 'A bird.'

Nina gasped as she saw what he meant. 'My God. It really is!

Howie, turn the drone ninety degrees to the right.'

Howie did so. The image on the screen rotated through a quarter-turn – and what had seemed abstract took on form. Enough of the carving was visible through the decaying leaves to show its true nature: a stylised bird, wings spread wide. 'It's not just any bird,' the redhead went on. 'It's an eagle!'

'Then that means—' stammered Ziff.

'The legend is true!' she cut in.

Fisher hurriedly checked that Rivero was filming the discussion. 'Okay, hold on,' he said. 'Quick recap for the benefit of everyone who isn't an archaeologist?'

'The Hebrew legend of the Palace Without Entrance,' Nina said, addressing the camera. 'It said that to find the way in, Solomon questioned eagles that lived on its roof. Well, there are the eagles!'

'Are they going to do "Hotel California"?' asked Eddie.

'Shush! And the other blocks around it have eagle carvings as well.' She looked more closely. 'And . . . see that? They're not the same.'

She darted a fingertip between details of the two carvings. 'You're right,' exclaimed Ziff. One eagle had its left claw raised higher than the right and its beak tilted downwards, but both its neighbour's feet were level while it was looking up. 'What about the others? Are they all different?'

Howie moved the drone to examine other blocks. There were indeed more subtle variations between each bird; heads looking left or right, wings extended or drawn up, claws open or closed. 'So what does that mean?' said Eddie.

'It means,' Nina said with delight, 'it's a puzzle. A puzzle that tells you how to find the entrance!'

'According to the legend,' continued Ziff, 'Solomon first spoke to one eagle, who directed him to his older brother, who then directed him to *its* older brother, and so on until they found the oldest of them all – the only one who knew the location of the entrance.'

Nina nodded. 'My guess is that certain eagles point to other similar ones. You look for—'

'Sorry to butt in, but the drone's almost out of power,' said Howie with sudden urgency. He quickly swept the little aircraft off the roof. 'I need to land it.'

'Oh . . .' – Nina was about to swear until she realised Rivero's camera was still focused on her – '. . . dammit. How long to recharge?'

'Just gotta swap in a new battery. Then we'll have another twenty minutes of flight time.'

'Is that all? *Really?* We're a fifth of the way through the twenty-first century and batteries still suck?' She glowered at the drone as it buzzed down to land, then turned to regard the looming palace. 'I'll need to look at the carvings for much longer than that.'

'How?' asked Fisher.

She addressed the camera. 'Isn't it obvious? We've got to get up there ourselves!'

As Eddie had thought, the folding ladders the team had brought did not reach all the way to the roof. The Yorkshireman reluctantly ended up climbing as high as he could, then tossed a grappling hook on a rope over the edge above. It took a couple of attempts, but finally held firm. 'Sorted!' he called down to the others before ascending the final stretch. 'I'll fix the rope so everyone else can climb up.'

Fisher was not enthusiastic. 'I haven't climbed a rope since gym class. And I wasn't good at it even then.'

'We can push you up if we have to, Mr Fisher,' Fortune told him.

Rivero grinned. 'Can't wait to get *that* on camera.'

Nina inevitably was the first to follow her husband. Eddie helped her on to the roof. 'Ay up. Fancy meeting you here.'

'Hi,' she said, grinning, before hurrying to the arched section. She brushed dirt from one of the blocks to reveal the eagle carved into it, then did the same to its neighbours.

By the time she had cleared the images, Howie, Rivero, Ziff and Lydia had also made the climb. 'Wait, don't do anything until I've got the camera running,' puffed the sweating Rivero. He turned to receive it from Paris, who had carried it up behind him. 'Okay, what we got?'

'What we've got,' said Nina, 'is a puzzle involving these eagle carvings.' She wiped another block. 'So far, I've seen eleven different points of variation: the position and direction of the heads, the feet, wings outstretched or bent, these feather details on the chest, and so on. That's two thousand and forty-eight possible combinations, and while there are a lot of blocks in this roof, I don't think there are that many.'

More panting and scrabbling signalled Fisher's arrival as Paris and Eddie pulled him on to the roof. 'So . . . so what are we looking for?' the director asked as Fortune climbed effortlessly up behind him.

'Based on the legend, I'd say we need to find the eagles that match – that are family, so to speak.' She indicated smaller markings on one of the slabs, Rivero moving in to film them. 'I'm not sure what these mean yet, but they're probably some kind of directional clue. Three rows up and eight blocks over, something like that. Find the first eagle, and it points you towards the next.'

'The obvious question,' said Ziff, joining her, 'is: which is the first eagle?'

'I don't know, is the answer.'

'First time for everything,' said Lydia under her breath.

Nina ignored her. 'We'll need to check the whole roof.'

'Do we have any high-resolution pictures of the model in the First Temple?' Ziff asked. 'Perhaps there is a clue on *its* roof?'

'My God, you're right,' she realised. 'Why didn't we think of that before? It's a perfect replica – so its roof should be an exact copy of this one! Steven, Howie; do we have backups of everything from Jerusalem?'

'Yeah, but I'll have to dig 'em out from the hard drives,' Howie told her.

'Okay, do it! It'll be a much faster way of finding the entrance than cleaning this entire roof.'

'I know an even *quicker* way,' said Eddie.

Nina knew from his tone that he had discovered something important. 'What is it?'

'See that tower? It's got a little tree growing on top of it.' He pointed. A spindly plant stood upon the flat top of one of the towers along the palace's western side, stretching hungrily towards a gap in the overhanging canopy. 'None of the others have got anything more than creepers on them – so how's it taken root?'

'I don't know,' she said, curious. 'It'd need soil, but not much would accumulate up there. It's not even that thick here, and it's a much bigger surface.' She dug her boot's toe into the dirt on the rooftop, easily scraping through to the stone beneath.

'I'll tell you how it could, though,' Eddie said. 'If there's a hole in the roof for it to build up in!'

'A hole?' said Ziff. 'Or – an entrance?'

'Maybe. It could be! We've got to look.' Nina hugged her husband. 'I know there was a reason I married you.'

Eddie grinned. 'What, my enormous cock?'

'*Eddie!*' Blushing, Nina punched his arm. 'We're being filmed!'

'Oh, are we?' he asked innocently, winking at Rivero's lens.

'We could just bleep that,' suggested Fisher with a chuckle.

Wemba brought up another ladder, which was taken to the tower and extended. It fell short of the top, but this time only by a few feet – enough for someone on the top rung to pull themselves up.

Eddie was about to scale it, but Nina pushed in front of him. 'No, no. I want to do this.'

'You don't know if it's safe,' he objected.

'We're on the roof of a three-thousand-year-old temple on top of a cliff in the middle of the jungle. How safe is *anything*?' She started to climb.

Eddie sighed and looked into the camera again. 'Some day, our daughter's going to watch this and use it as an excuse for why she should be allowed to ride her bike down Fifth Avenue without a helmet.'

'Yeah, yeah,' Nina said dismissively. She quickly reached the ladder's top and peered over the edge of the new roof.

Even from her low angle, she saw at once that the tree had taken root in more than a thin layer of dirt. The platform was square, about twenty feet along each edge – but set into its centre was a recess some six feet by six, full of dark, moist soil.

She pulled herself up. 'What can you see?' Ziff called.

'There's a pit in the middle of the roof. Enough dirt's built up in it for the tree to grow.' She scooped out some soil. While it seemed rich at the surface, it was gritty not far below. 'There's sand underneath it!'

'Sand? Do you think—'

'Yeah, I *do* think,' she said. None of the other towers had any features resembling the one at her feet. 'Eddie was right. This is the Palace *With* Entrance!'

12

With a crackle of tearing roots, the little tree toppled over the tower's side and plunged to the ground over fifty feet below in an explosion of leaves and dust. Those watching from the roof whooped and cheered.

Eddie, who along with Fortune, Paris and Wemba had dug the tree out from the pit, was less vocal but equally exuberant. 'Bye, you bugger,' he said, shaking off sweat.

'Nice work!' Nina shouted from below. 'Was anything underneath?'

'God, give us a chance!' He turned to the ragged hole where the tree had stood. 'More sand, but . . .' He jabbed a shovel into the newly excavated space. Muffled thuds as the blade cut into the soil – then came a harsh clank as it struck stone beneath. 'The bottom's about a foot down.'

'How long will it take you to clear it?'

'The four of us? Twenty minutes, if that.'

'More digging?' said Fortune. 'I am glad I took off my jacket.'

Eddie regarded him sidelong. 'Yeah, and there's still not a speck of dirt on you. How do you do that?'

The African gave him a gold-toothed smile. 'I am just lucky.'

'If you were that lucky, you wouldn't be up here digging a bloody hole in eighty-degree heat.'

Fortune laughed, then picked up another shovel. With the four men working in concert, it did not take long to clear the pit. 'Okay, we're done,' Eddie finally announced. 'The people with an archaeology degree can get their lazy arses up here now.'

'We will get out of the way,' said Fortune. He and the two other Congolese descended the ladder.

They were soon replaced by Nina, Ziff and the documentary crew. Nina stepped into the pit to examine its floor. 'This,' she said, running a finger along a narrow gap surrounding a block at its centre, 'looks like it might lift out.'

Ziff probed the crack with a fingernail. 'It will be heavy.'

'I came prepared.' She unslung a backpack, metal clanking inside it.

'Bollocks,' said Eddie as she produced some crowbars. 'No prizes for guessing who'll be hoiking big stone blocks out of the floor. I should've gone back down with Fortune when I had the chance. He *is* bloody lucky.'

'Oh, stop moaning,' Nina said, smiling. 'You sound like . . .' She realised her eyes had gone to Lydia. 'Mona the moaner,' she hurriedly concluded.

'Who?' Eddie asked, puzzled. Rivero snickered.

'Nobody, never mind.' She picked up a crowbar to cover her embarrassment as the New Zealander's look of suspicion grew. 'Help me get this thing open.'

Both bars were jammed into the gaps on each side of the block. The couple readied themselves, then pulled. The slab inched upwards as they repositioned the tips of their crowbars in turn. 'Nearly – got it,' Nina grunted. 'Just a little—' The stone slab jerked upwards. 'Whoa, wedge it, wedge it!'

'I've got it,' said Eddie, holding it in place. Nina tugged again. The thick flagstone lifted higher – and dust blew out from beneath it as a dark crack opened up. 'It's coming out!' More effort, and he managed to slide the slab out of its resting place. Once freed, it did not take long to move clear.

Nina peered into the revealed opening. A vertical shaft dropped into darkness below, holes cut into one wall acting as a ladder. 'This is it!' she announced in awe. 'We found the way into the Palace Without Entrance. Or rather,' she went on, looking up at her husband, 'you did, Eddie. You bypassed the puzzle – which means you actually out-thought King Solomon!'

Eddie grinned. 'I always thought I was really wise. It's just no one ever agreed with me!'

'It's very possible that nobody has been inside the palace since Solomon built it!' said Ziff excitedly. 'We have to get down there and see.'

'Your attitude's changed since we opened up the First Temple,' Nina said, lightly teasing. 'You weren't in such a rush back then.'

'What can I say? You have shown me the benefits of your . . . unique approach.' The old man grinned. 'But this is an incredible find. The First Temple had been lost, yes, but its existence was never in doubt. This, though? It is a legend brought to life!'

'We'd better get some more gear, then,' said Eddie. 'Lights, for a start.' He was about to call down to Fortune when he noticed something odd about the slab they had removed. 'Hold on, look at this.'

He indicated the bottom of the square flag. Beneath the inches of pale stone was a layer of a dull grey material. 'Is that lead?' Nina asked. She tapped it with a crowbar. The soft metal dented with the contact. 'It is.'

Ziff pointed into the entrance. 'There is more here, on the inside.' Beneath its lip was another line of grey, close to an inch thick. 'It goes all the way around.'

Eddie drew back in alarm. 'The place is *lead-lined*? It *is* fucking radioactive!' Several of the others pulled away from the opening. 'No wonder all the bloody trees are sick! We need to get out of here.'

Lydia shook her head. 'A radiation source wouldn't make that low-frequency noise.'

'What are you, a nuclear physicist?'

She looked offended. 'As a matter of fact, I *did* study physics at university.'

'Oh, well, then I wholeheartedly apologise,' he said with a sarcastic lack of contrition. 'But King Solomon bricked up whatever's down there inside a lead-lined palace because it killed off the people who lived around it! This whole place was called the City of the Damned, remember?'

'There's a way we can check,' Lydia insisted. 'Jay, put the camera's lens cap on and point it down the hole, then shoot some footage.'

Rivero shot her a bewildered frown. 'What good'll that do?'

'If there's any dangerous radiation down there, the camera's CCD will still pick it up even through the cap – it'll show on the recording as static. We did an experiment using an old phone camera where we put tape over the lens and filmed a radiation source. It looks like snow.'

The cameraman was still unconvinced. 'Wait, so you want me to poke my face into Chernobyl?'

'If it really is radioactive down there, we've already been exposed to it,' Nina pointed out. 'And David and I have been closer to it than anyone else.'

'Okay, then *you* shoot the footage!'

She impatiently held out her hands. 'Give me the camera, then.'

The prospect of surrendering what was practically an inseparable appendage gave Rivero second thoughts. 'No, no, it's okay, I can do it,' he muttered, sulkily attaching the lens cap and moving to the shaft. All the same, he held the camera at arm's length as he pointed it into the darkness. 'All right, five seconds – that better be long enough,' he said, rapidly retreating.

The Sony had a small fold-out monitor. Everyone clustered around it as he reviewed the recording. 'It just looks black,' said Fisher, relieved.

Rivero paused playback, zooming in on the frame. Blocky digital artefacts became vaguely visible, but there was no sign of the snow Lydia had described. 'I think it's safe,' she announced.

Expressions of relief echoed around the group. 'Second kid's still an option, then,' Eddie said to Nina.

'As if the first isn't enough of a handful?' she replied. 'So why would Solomon have lined the roof with lead if not to keep radiation in?'

'It would protect whatever is inside from water,' suggested Ziff.

'Only one way to find out.' Nina went to the top of the shaft. 'We have to go inside.'

With the help of the three porters, the team brought all the equipment needed to explore the palace's interior to its entrance. 'Okay,' said Nina, 'I think we're ready. We should limit the number of people going inside to start with, though. Sorry,' she added to her Congolese companions.

'We don't get to see the treasure?' said Wemba, disappointed.

'We don't even know if there *is* any treasure,' Ziff told him. 'For all we know, the shaft could be blocked at the bottom.'

'I could send the drone down to look,' Howie suggested, patting the quadcopter's case.

'I'd rather get the first look with my own eyes, thanks,' said Nina. 'And why did you bring it with you at all? A drone won't be much use indoors.'

'You'd be surprised,' Fisher said. He indicated the vaulted roof. 'There could be a big open space underneath that. If there is, then the drone can fly up to the ceiling and get some great shots of the whole interior.'

'Just remember that this is an archaeological expedition first and a photo opportunity second,' Nina insisted. She donned a backpack, then shone a powerful flashlight into the darkness.

The holes cut into the wall descended all the way to the bottom, which she estimated was at least twenty feet below the level of the palace's main roof. 'Long climb, but doesn't look too hard.'

'Someone should stay up here while we're inside, just in case,' Eddie said to Fortune.

'You are expecting trouble?' his friend asked.

'No, but I want to be ready for it. If anybody gets hurt, we'll need to get them out quickly – and our radios won't work through walls this thick even if they weren't lined with bloody lead. So we might have to shout up to you.'

'Somebody will always be here on watch,' Fortune assured him. He issued instructions to Paris and the porters, who descended the ladder.

Rivero had by now switched on his camera. 'Nina, if you could give us a speech to camera about descending into the unknown?' said Fisher as she put on a head-mounted light and prepared to enter the shaft.

The redhead gave him an impatient look. 'I'm about to descend into the unknown,' she said, before starting down the ladder. Eddie laughed as the director sighed in annoyance. 'Okay, here I go.'

The initial climb was easy, boosting her confidence. She paused a few feet down to examine the underside of the entrance. There was no accumulated dirt or evidence of water damage; the slab had been tightly sealed. As Ziff had suggested, it was entirely plausible that it had not been opened since Solomon's time.

She continued down the stone ladder until darkness surrounded her, then switched on her head torch. The beam followed her gaze, revealing that the stonework was cut with incredible precision. Again, she was reminded of the interior of the First Temple in Jerusalem.

The remainder of the descent was straightforward. Nina finally stepped down at the bottom. Fine dust crunched under her soles. More had accumulated within the lowest stone rungs, as if it had been blown from somewhere below. She turned to see a passageway with a thin layer of the same residue on its floor. Were there openings beyond to let in air from outside? None had been visible on the palace's exterior . . .

'Nina!' Ziff, his voice echoing down the shaft. 'What do you see?'

She looked up to the little square of light above. 'There's a passage leading into the palace. Everything looks safe. Come on down.'

Some jockeying for position took place at the ladder's top, Eddie reluctantly ceding his place to let Ziff start down before him. Nina moved clear of the shaft, unable to resist the temptation to explore further. She took out her flashlight to complement her head torch and advanced down the tunnel.

A chamber opened out ahead. She entered the new space – and stopped, both in awe and a suspicion born of painful experience. Eight stone slabs resembling doors were set into the walls around the room, but the only open way out was a narrow passage. A prominent inscription in Old Hebrew had been carved above its entrance, and as she moved closer she spotted horizontal slots set into both walls of the tunnel. At the far end, some fifty feet away, was another chamber. All she could see inside it was a squat statue of a male figure, its mouth gaping open. Her torch beam picked out silver glinting within.

The wall slots were what had triggered her sense of lurking danger. She had encountered more than enough booby traps in the past to guess that something would sweep out of them at anyone trying to pass. Checking the floor, she saw that the individual flagstones forming its first half gave way to a single large slab at the other end. A channel of the same width was set into the floor of the room beyond.

Deciding to hold off on investigating the passage for now, Nina instead examined the doors. They seemed to be relics of the lost civilisation, inscriptions in an unknown language set into their surfaces. She cautiously touched one, but it didn't move. Moving to the next, she was about to test it when a thump of feet on stone told her that someone had reached the bottom of the ladder. 'David?' she called.

'Yes, I'm here,' Ziff replied, switching on a flashlight. 'Have you found anything?'

'You could say that.'

The Israeli made his way to her as Eddie dropped down behind him. 'Oh . . .' gasped Ziff as he entered. 'I see what you mean.' He shone his light at the inscription above the narrow passageway, then moved for a closer look.

'Don't go in there,' Nina warned. 'I'm getting a nasty feeling of "booby trap" from it.' He stopped sharply.

Eddie entered. 'What was that about a booby trap, and why am I not even the slightest bit surprised?'

'That would fit with the inscription,' Ziff said as he gazed at the text on the wall. 'It says . . . "The great King Solomon has decreed that those who wish to reach the Mother of the Shamir must prove their worth. This test of wisdom is the first of three. Only the dead shall pass alive; the living who enter shall die."' A rough translation, admittedly.'

'It gets the point across.' Nina went as close to the entrance as she was willing. 'Have you seen what's at the far end?'

Ziff directed his torch beam down the tunnel. 'Ah! Another part of the legend! Solomon found an idol with a silver tablet in its mouth bearing a message from the former ruler Shaddad, son of 'Ad.'

'So dad 'Ad 'ad Shaddad?' said Eddie. Both archaeologists shot him stony stares. 'I've 'ad that look before. What was the message?'

'A reminder of man's mortality,' Ziff continued. 'For all his achievements, all his conquests, Shaddad couldn't escape death in the end.'

177

'Nope, not ominous at all,' said Nina ruefully.

'Wait, whatever you're doing, wait,' said Fisher as he hurried into the chamber. 'We need to film whatever you find as you find it, that's kind of the point of the show. Oh, wow.' He looked around. 'This is impressive. What's behind all these doors?'

'I don't know,' Nina answered. 'I haven't tried opening them yet.'

'Okay, you can have a go once Jay and Howie get here with the cameras.' He saw the idol in the beam of Ziff's flashlight. 'Hel-lo! Who do we have here?'

'Don't go down there,' said Eddie. 'Nina thinks it's booby-trapped.'

Fisher regarded the corridor dubiously. 'Is that likely?'

'You did actually *watch* my first series, didn't you?' Nina said. 'But yeah, the Hebrew text above the entrance is a pretty big warning sign. So we're not going down there until we know what we're dealing with.'

Fisher held up his hands. 'Okay, okay. This is the part where you're the expert.'

Rivero and Lydia entered, Howie trailing behind them carrying the drone's case and a bag of equipment. 'What'd we miss?' asked the cameraman.

'Dire warnings of death, the usual,' Fisher replied dismissively. 'Howie, let's set up some lights. Flashlight beams are cool if you're making *The X-Files*, but we need more visibility.' The crew started to take out lighting gear.

'What do we do while we're waiting?' Eddie asked Nina. 'Try the doors?'

'We could, although I'm a lot more wary about touching *any-thing* after David read that little note from King Solomon,' she replied.

'It does seem to refer specifically to that exit, though,' said

Ziff. 'Which door did you try?' She pointed. He tested it as well, with no better result.

Eddie examined it. 'Want me to have a go?'

'I don't think it would help.' Ziff aimed his light at the door's edge. 'I'm not even sure if there is anything behind this. It looks as if . . .' He flinched in annoyance as Rivero switched on his camera's spotlight and shone it at his face. 'As if it has been fixed directly to the wall.'

'I did wonder if they were more like exhibits, or prizes, from Zhakana,' said Nina, nodding. 'Solomon might have rescued them from some important building in the ruins.'

'The design definitely doesn't match the rest of the palace,' the Israeli noted. 'And as for this text . . .' He peered at the inscriptions over his glasses. 'I thought at first it was a completely unknown language, but actually . . .'

'Proto-Ge'ez?' Nina offered. 'Some of the characters are similar.'

'Very close, yes. Perhaps with Sabaic influences, they both have South Semitic roots . . .' Rivero retreated, clearly bored, as the two archaeologists continued talking, turning to film other parts of the room.

Eddie went to the neighbouring door. 'We could try the others. They might not all be fake.'

'Maybe, but not just yet,' said Nina, still intrigued by the ancient writing. 'I'm wondering if this . . .' She stopped, registering on the edge of her vision that Rivero was continuing away from her—

Into the passage.

She whirled in alarm. The Hispanic cameraman had gone through the opening, regarding the slots in the wall with indifference before fixing his gaze upon something more attention-grabbing – the idol. He quickened his pace towards it. 'Hey, you guys seen this?'

'Jay!' Nina cried, rushing after him. 'Stop, get out of there! It's a—'

Rivero reached the large floor slab – which shifted under his weight, sending him stumbling.

A deep, crunching rumble came from behind the ancient stonework. The others stared in shock as the walls at the passage's far end began to *move*, closing in on each other.

The slab beneath Rivero dropped farther into the floor. He regained his balance, regarding the narrowing space around him in disbelief before his fear response kicked in. He turned to flee, vaulting up over the deepening step and charging back towards the first chamber.

A new sound, a dry metallic rattle. Chains scraped over each other, catching for a moment on the accumulated dirt of three millennia – then jerking free.

The brief pause gave Rivero enough respite to run farther along the passage . . . but not enough to clear it. Metal poles with savage hooks at their ends whipped out from the wall slots, lashing at him as he passed—

And tearing into his body.

13

'Jay!' Nina screamed as Rivero crashed to the floor, blood spurting from ragged wounds across his back. His camera skidded across the stones, spinning to a stop with its spotlight glaring back at his anguished face.

The hooked poles hit the limit of their movement with a clang, then swung back into their slots. Behind, the closing walls reversed direction and retreated to their original position. The stone slab rumbled back upwards until it was again flush with the rest of the floor. It stopped with an echoing crunch.

Eddie ran to join Nina, the couple dragging Rivero clear. He cried out in pain. 'Oh my God!' Lydia cried in horror as she saw the red trail behind him.

'Get me some more fucking light!' Eddie barked. Fisher hurriedly raised a torch as Nina snatched up the camera and shone its spot over its fallen owner. Rivero's clothing had been ripped open. The Yorkshireman lifted away the bloody material to see the extent of his injuries. The cameraman's lower back had been slashed in three places as if by a giant claw.

'How bad is it?' Nina asked fearfully.

'It got him pretty deep here,' he said of the largest wound. 'The other two probably look worse than they are. I'm more worried about tetanus or some other infection. I dunno how rusty those hooks were, but we're in the middle of the jungle as well. We've got to get him cleaned, closed and covered before any fucking bugs start making a meal of him.'

'I thought there weren't many insects here,' said the stunned

Howie, trying to overcome his shock by fixing on something mundane.

'Only needs one fucking botfly to lay eggs in a wound and you're in deep shit. Where's the first-aid kit?'

'I've got one.' Nina shrugged off her pack.

'I'll get started. Someone shout to Fortune, tell him to radio the others and bring more rope. We might have to lift him out if he can't climb.'

'I'll do it,' said Fisher. He ran back towards the entrance as Nina gave the medical kit to her husband.

'Will he be okay?' Lydia asked.

'I'll do what I can,' Eddie told her. 'I need some water.' Nina put down the camera and passed him a canteen. He cleaned his hands as best he could, then carefully washed the wounds before unrolling a length of sterile gauze and laying it over the deepest laceration. Rivero gasped. 'Jay, can you hear me?'

'Yeah . . .' the cameraman said, voice strained.

'I can't tell how deep you've been cut around your spine. Can you move your legs?'

Another gasp as Rivero shifted position, his toes scraping on the dusty floor. 'Thank God,' Nina said in relief.

Eddie nodded. 'That's something, at least. Fucking hell, that could have been *really* nasty if that trap'd worked a bit quicker.'

Fisher hurried back in. 'They're on their way.'

'Good.' He applied more gauze. 'Normally I wouldn't move you until you've been bandaged up,' he told Rivero, 'but I really don't want to stay down here.'

'No arguments from me,' Rivero replied through clenched teeth.

Nina was not so sure. 'I don't think we're in any immediate danger. Taking him up too soon might do more harm than good.'

'No, I . . . I think we should get him outside too,' said Fisher.

'We came here to film you finding a lost city, not get caught in killer traps! I've got to put the crew's safety first. As soon as we're out, I'll call for a medevac on the satphone.'

'How long will that take?' asked Ziff.

'It'll have to go via the company's offices in LA, but I'd hope they can get a chopper to us pretty fast. I was once on a shoot where someone broke their leg in a fall, and he was airlifted out in less than ninety minutes.'

'Where was that, though?' Eddie asked.

'The Arizona desert.'

The Yorkshireman shook his head. 'I wouldn't be surprised if the only chopper within two hundred miles is that mining company one in Butembo – and I bet they won't be too keen on loaning it out.'

'We've got to get him out of here, though,' said Lydia. She swapped her sound gear for a torch.

Rivero moved again, trying to bring himself up. 'No, stay still!' Nina warned.

'It's . . . it's okay,' he rasped. 'I wanna . . . get out of here. My camera, someone get the camera.'

'Forget the fucking camera,' Eddie snapped, but too late as Howie picked it up. 'God. Archaeologists, photographers – you're as bloody obsessive as each other!'

'Wouldn't be . . . here if we weren't,' said Rivero. With great effort, he levered himself to a kneeling position. 'Ah! Jesus fuck, that hurts!'

'What did you expect?' complained Nina. 'You just got slashed by a death trap.' She glanced back at the passage. 'Although . . .'

'What is it?' said Ziff, picking up on her change of tone from concern to curiosity.

Eddie heard it too. 'Oh, for fuck's sake. We've got an injured man here, and you're already thinking about how to get past the trap that whacked him!'

'I know what my priorities are, thank you,' she said, annoyed. 'It's just that . . . it *is* a death trap. If you go forward, you get squashed when the walls close in – but if you turn back, the hooks get you. The only reason Jay wasn't killed was because the mechanism was jammed by dirt and didn't spring fast enough. If someone else tries it now, I expect they'd be torn apart.'

'Saved by . . . bad housekeeping, then,' Rivero said, attempting a smile as he tried to straighten. It faded almost instantly.

'Just keep still,' Eddie ordered. He examined the cameraman's back.

'Solomon's inscription suggests that there *is* a way through, though,' Nina pressed on, directing her light at the ancient Hebrew text. 'It says, "Only the dead shall pass alive." That's got to be significant.'

'Maybe it is, but it doesn't matter, because we're not going to try again,' Eddie said with irritation. 'Jay, I'm going to lift the gauze. It'll probably hurt, so be ready for it.'

'If it's gonna hurt, any chance you could, you know, not do it?' replied Rivero. The Englishman ignored him. 'Ah, aah! Oh, you – you *fucker*! God damn.'

'Sorry.' Eddie gently replaced the bloodied gauze. 'It hasn't stopped yet, but it's bleeding less than I thought it would be. I think it's 'cause you've got a lot of fat down there.'

Fisher laughed, a release of nervous tension more than actual humour. 'Wow, Jay. Who would've thought that all those burgers and burritos would end up saving your life?'

'Ha ha ha,' Rivero responded with an equal lack of amusement, before giving the director the finger. 'Fuck you.' This time, Fisher's laugh was genuine.

'He'll be okay?' Lydia asked hopefully.

'He won't bleed to death,' Eddie told her. 'Still needs treatment, though. Got to sterilise it, then he'll need stitches, antibiotics, all of that. I can do it in the field, but it'd be a lot better to get him to a hospital and let the professionals handle it.'

Rivero nodded in agreement. 'Yeah, yeah. I definitely want it done by a guy in a white coat rather than a guy in a leather jacket!'

A shout from the entrance shaft: Fortune. 'Eddie! The others are coming.'

'Great,' said Rivero. 'Let's go.' He tried again to stand, this time – with the help of Howie and Fisher – managing to push through the pain and bring himself upright.

The Yorkshireman acknowledged Fortune, then looked back at Rivero. 'We should carry you – walking might make things worse,' he warned. 'You really want to risk it?'

Another nod. 'I don't wanna spend another minute in this hole.'

'Then let's go. You got a good hold on him, Steve?'

'Yeah, I've got him,' Fisher replied.

'All right. Howie, use that light so we can see where we're going. Nina, make sure none of the gauze comes off.'

'Actually,' said Nina, 'I think it'd be better if David and I stay down here.'

Eddie stared at her. 'You what?'

'We can keep working while you get Jay outside, see if we can figure out how to get through the trap—'

An incredulous snort. 'Are you out of your bloody mind? We're not leaving *anybody* down here – especially not to poke around at a death trap in the dark!'

'I know what I'm doing. I'm sure we can work out the solution and find the way through.'

'I guess we really do know what your priorities are,' said Lydia, voice dripping with disdain.

'Nina, they're right,' said Ziff. 'It's too dangerous.'

'But look what we've found already! I know we can—'

'What would you tell your daughter if you got hurt? Or what would your *husband* tell her if something worse happened?'

Nina had no answer to that – at least, none that she wanted to think about. 'I . . . okay, okay,' she said, with reluctance. 'We'll get Jay outside. And *then* I'll decide what to do about investigating this,' she went on, unwilling to surrender completely.

'Yeah, wouldn't want someone getting Freddy Kruegered to interfere with work,' Eddie growled. She shot him a hurt look. 'Come on, let's go.'

'What about the gear?' asked Howie, regarding the team's equipment.

'Leave it for now. You'll have plenty of time to bring it out before a chopper arrives.'

With Howie using the camera to light the way, Eddie and Fisher began to carry Rivero down the passage. The others filed after them. Nina was last to leave, giving the booby-trapped hallway a final frustrated glance before following.

Climbing the stone ladder was beyond Rivero in his injured state. Eddie had to fashion a sling, fastening ropes around him in a way that would cause the minimum pain as he was lifted up the shaft. That done, he climbed to the top so he, Fortune, Paris and the three porters could laboriously haul the big man to the top of the tower, then lower him to the palace roof.

The Yorkshireman loosened the lines to check the cameraman's wounds. 'Shit, it's bleeding again.' The gauze was wet with oozing crimson. Whatever it was about the ruined city that deterred insects from swarming couldn't overcome the lure of fresh blood, bugs already flitting hopefully around Rivero's back. 'We need to get this cleaned up, pronto. Where's the satphone?'

'Still at the camp,' Fortune told him.

'You didn't bring it?'

'Mr Fisher did not ask for it. I have many talents, my friend, but I am not a mind reader.'

'Fuck's sake.' Eddie glowered at Fisher as he descended from the tower, but knew he was as much to blame as the director for the omission. 'Jay, how're you feeling?'

'Not great,' Rivero replied. His face was pale and slick with sweat. 'Those painkillers you gave me? They kinda suck. Sorry, man.'

'Not your fault.' The tablets in the medical kit were prescription-strength, but only intended to dull the pain of minor cuts and contusions, not open wounds. 'Okay, we're gonna lower you to the ground and carry you to the camp, and then I'll have another look at your back while someone calls for an evac.' He resecured the sling.

Ten minutes later, all the expedition's members were reunited at the base of the wall. 'Seriously?' Eddie groused, seeing that Fisher had taken over the Sony to record proceedings. 'You're filming this?'

'We're a documentary crew, and I'm documenting,' Fisher replied. 'If nothing else, the insurance company will want to see what happened.'

'Hey, I'd do the same thing,' Rivero feebly told Eddie. 'It's more than just a job to me, man. It's what I *do*.'

'Sounds familiar,' the Englishman replied, looking at his wife. 'Okay, Fortune, help me carry him.'

The two men took Rivero's weight and set off towards the ruins. They soon reached the encampment. 'Get him in there,' said Eddie, indicating the largest tent. Paris cleared a space on the groundsheet for the American. 'If we close the zip it should keep out most of the insects. Someone get me water and the medical kit. Steve, find the satphone.'

'On it,' said Fisher, going to one of the backpacks.

'All right, Jay, we'll . . .' Eddie trailed off, suddenly on alert. Something had changed.

No, worse. Something was *wrong*.

'What is it?' Nina asked as he and Fortune looked around in

alarm. Paris also sensed that the situation had changed, dropping to a crouch behind a tree trunk.

'I can smell fucking *smoke!*' Eddie snapped. 'Everyone down – there's someone else here!'

He and Fortune ducked, bringing Rivero with them – as a gunshot cracked from the jungle.

14

More bullets lanced through the air, sending the other expedition members scrambling for cover. 'What the hell's going on?' Nina cried.

'Militia!' Eddie shouted back. 'The smoke – it's the same shit they were smoking at the checkpoint!'

'They *followed* us?' said Fisher from behind a tree. He was still clutching the camera, out of instinct rather than any conscious intent to film the ambush. 'All the way here? How?'

'I don't fucking care! Fortune! Guns?'

Fortune drew a gleaming nickel-plated automatic from a concealed holster. Paris did the same, though his weapon was considerably less polished. 'There are more in my bag.' He pointed at his tent. 'We will cover you.'

Eddie nodded. 'How many?'

'Two nine-millimetres. They are fully loaded, and there are spare magazines.'

The shooting stopped. The Yorkshireman remained still, assessing their unseen attackers. At least three men armed with rifles. Not professional soldiers; the firing had been too indiscriminate. He could handle them – if he could get to a weapon. 'Okay, I'm moving. Cover!'

Fortune and Paris both unleashed several shots in the direction of the intruders as he scurried for the tent. Someone yelled, but in fright at a near miss rather than pain. The cry told Eddie that the militia were amongst the ruins at the top of the path to the river. The expedition was cut off from the boats . . .

He put the thought aside. They were currently outgunned, needing to redress the balance before thinking of escape. He ducked into Fortune's tent. The interior was as neat as its owner, bedroll carefully folded beside a bag. Eddie tugged it open, quickly finding cold metal—

The militia opened up again, single shots giving way to furious bursts of automatic fire. Ringing ricochets screamed off stone, wood splintering. Eddie dropped flat as the nylon wall flapped and puckered with multiple impacts.

He yanked out the guns, a pair of Browning Hi-Powers, and grabbed the spare magazines before crawling back into the open. Howie was nearest to him, but the young man was curled up behind a stump, terrified. Farther away he saw Wemba crouching at a wall, Chumbo beyond him. The latter saw his two guns. 'Mr Chase! Here!'

'No, me!' called Wemba. Eddie was about to throw him a pistol – then on some subconscious reassessment lobbed it the extra distance to Chumbo. Wemba's face flashed with anger.

Eddie ignored him, certain he had made the right decision when Chumbo caught the weapon and immediately ejected the magazine to check its load before slotting it back into place. He knew what he was doing. 'We're armed!' he called to Paris and Fortune.

'Good, 'cause we could use some help!' Paris shouted back. The incoming fire was now concentrated on the two bodyguards, forcing them into cover.

Eddie peeked out from behind a tree. Muzzle flash and flailing undergrowth told him the position of one attacker, about a hundred feet away. He aimed at a point behind the stuttering flower of flame and snapped off two rapid shots. The hidden gunman fell backwards, his AK blazing uselessly at the sky before going silent.

The other attackers rounded on the new threat, but Eddie had already jerked back behind the twisted trunk. Fortune opened fire again, Paris darting into a new position in a half-collapsed doorway and following suit. Chumbo joined in the assault from Eddie's other side. A man let out a shrill scream. 'Two down!' Paris shouted in triumph.

'More coming,' warned Fortune. A moment later new rifles spat fire from the direction of the river path.

Eddie held firm behind the tree as rounds cracked past. The new arrivals were blazing away on full auto as they charged through the vegetation. It was the action of the rank amateur or the suicidally overconfident – and the latter turned out to be the case for one of the militia as the Yorkshireman downed him with a headshot. The others with him scattered, aggression instantly turning into panic as they sprayed bullets in all directions.

The defenders maintained their more controlled fire. Another militia man went down with a gargling shriek as Fortune put two bullets into his chest. 'Whatever they are smoking, they have had too much of it!' he called to Eddie.

'I know,' Eddie replied, running to new cover against the remains of a wall. He had glimpsed a red band around a gunman's arm, confirming them as members of the Insekt Posse – and they seemed just as stoned as the group at the checkpoint, an unco-ordinated rabble learning the hard way what it was like to face professionals. 'You two go left, me an' Lenard'll move right. We'll create a kill zone, take 'em all down.'

Fortune signalled his agreement, quick hand gestures com-municating the plan to Paris. The two men angled away to the left. 'With me,' Eddie told Chumbo, going the other way towards the roofless shell of a small building. 'That hut, get inside and wait for my signal.' The Congolese hurried in, Eddie continuing past to another broken wall.

The surviving Insekt Posse had found cover of their own, spurts of gunfire cutting through the shadow-shrouded city –

but their shots were aimed at where Eddie's team had been, not their new locations. The Englishman looked over the wall. Three, four, *five* shooters, and from this angle he could see two of them clearly enough to target.

'Lenard,' he called quietly to Chumbo. 'Can you see any of 'em?' A nod in reply. 'Okay, aim at him and get ready.'

Guessing that Chumbo would have a bead on the most exposed enemy, he locked on to the man with more cover. Another militia member raised his head—

'Now!' Eddie yelled. He pulled the trigger, a pinkish burst of brain matter exploding from his target's skull. No need to double-tap that one. He instantly switched his aim to the other man as his comrades released their own shots. Chumbo's quarry ducked – only to spin and fall in a spray of blood as Eddie's next shot tore a ragged wound in his neck.

'Target down!' Fortune shouted; he had eliminated another of the militia. Paris only scored a wound rather than a kill, but the animalistic scream that followed told them the man would not be getting back up to fight, or probably anything else. 'I think there is only one left.'

'Make that two,' Eddie replied as a new rifle opened up, full-auto fire spraying wildly across the ruins. A voice bellowed incoherent obscenities. He waited for the attacker's magazine to run dry, then snapped off two more rapid shots. A pained yell, then the obscenities returned, though now fearful rather than furious. 'Okay, let's move in and finish 'em. We'll—'

He broke off at new voices, farther away – but closing. 'Oh, shit!' gasped Fisher. 'There's more of them!'

One voice in particular stood out. It was deeper than the others, older, more commanding. Eddie couldn't make out the unseen man's orders, but when Fortune spoke again it was with a rare edge of worry. 'They have a leader,' he warned. 'He is telling his men to spread out and pin us down.'

Eddie glanced at the looming structure behind them. 'If they push us back to the palace, we'll be trapped on the cliff.'

'What do we do?' asked Chumbo.

The Yorkshireman ran through their options – and realised they were desperately limited. Staying low, he crossed first to Chumbo's position to tell him to follow, then back to the camp. 'Fortune, Paris – over here.'

'What's happening?' Nina asked as the two mercenaries returned.

'We've got one shot at getting out of here,' her husband told her. 'Take out the leader.'

'What do you mean?' asked Wemba.

Eddie listened. The man in charge of the militia was still shouting orders in French. 'Sounds like he's the only one who knows what he's doing. Get rid of him, and we might be able to make a break for the boats while they're confused.'

'*Might* be?' said Fisher unhappily.

'It's better than sitting here waiting for them to surround us.'

'What – what if we surrender?' The director pointed at the group's packs. 'We've still got those dollars. We could try to pay them off?'

Fortune shook his head grimly. 'They will be angry now we have killed some of them. They will want revenge more than money.'

'Then maybe you shouldn't have shot at them!' Lydia cried.

'They shot at us first!' Nina reminded her.

Eddie listened again. The leader had reached a ruined building a hundred and fifty feet away, still issuing commands. Scattered movement amongst the underbrush revealed that his men had not yet reached their positions. 'If we're doing it, it'll have to be now. Fortune, Paris, Lenard – you up for it?'

'I think we can do it if we are fast,' Fortune replied. 'If we go to the left of that building,' he pointed out a ruin, 'it will give cover from everyone on the right.'

'Just what I was thinking.' He reloaded. 'Okay, everybody with a gun makes a run for the boss. You see anyone ahead of you, shoot 'em. If it's the guy in charge, shoot him more! The rest of you, split off and get to the river. Masson, Cretien, carry Jay.' He glanced at Fisher, who was still bearing the camera, a red light telling him it was recording. 'Leave that fucking thing, will you? An Emmy won't do you any good if you're dead.'

Fisher reluctantly put down the Sony. Paris checked the overgrown ruins. 'They're still moving.'

'Now or never,' said Eddie. He went to the end of a wall and raised his gun, the other armed men following. 'Okay, on three.' He took a deep breath. 'One, two—'

A gunshot – from *behind* him. 'Drop your guns!'

Wemba shoved Rivero into Kimba, sending both men staggering, as he brought the small revolver he had just fired into the air to bear on the rest of the group. 'Drop them!' Wemba repeated. 'Or I shoot!'

Eddie knew he couldn't turn quickly enough to outgun the treacherous porter. But nor was he willing to give up his weapon so easily. He held position, waiting to see if any of the others would give him the moment's distraction he needed to take a shot . . .

Chumbo made a move – but it was the wrong one. He charged at Wemba, bringing up his gun—

Wemba fired first.

A wet rosette burst open above Chumbo's heart. He staggered, managing one final step before collapsing into the dirt.

Behind him, Fortune's own gleaming gun rose—

Another shot erupted from the revolver. The round tore through Fortune's sleeve, the tall man lurching backwards as he clutched at the wound. 'I – I said, drop them!' shouted Wemba.

His aim flicked between Eddie and Paris, challenging them to make a move.

The Englishman reluctantly let his Browning fall. Paris regarded the injured Fortune with dismay, then did the same. 'Kick them away!' Wemba ordered.

'Cretien,' said Fortune, jaw tight with pain. 'What is this? I trusted you!'

'I know, I – I am sorry,' Wemba replied. 'But I need money, and they . . . they paid much more than you.' He called out to the militia. '*C'est moi, c'est Cretien! Je les ai capturés! Ne tirez pas!*'

'You son of a bitch!' Nina growled.

Lydia stared in horror at Chumbo's still-twitching body. 'Don't . . . don't make things worse,' she whimpered.

Eddie glanced into the ruins. The Insekt Posse cautiously emerged from cover at a command from their leader, AKs raised. 'I think it's about to *get* worse, whatever we do.'

The militia surrounded their prisoners, forcing them at gunpoint to kneel with their hands behind their heads. Fortune gasped as he lifted his palm from his injury. Eddie quickly assessed the wound, seeing that his friend had lived up to his name: while his clothing was ruined, he had suffered only a flesh wound, the bullet's heat even cauterising it.

Wemba spoke nervously to the new arrivals. None replied, regarding him with deep suspicion. But nor did they threaten him directly, apparently awaiting further orders.

They soon came. The deep voice that had organised the rabble drew closer, in conversation with another man. The encircling militia parted to let their commander through. Eddie risked turning his head, wanting to see his opponents.

He got a double shock when he did.

One was John Brice, the dishevelled Englishman giving him a mocking smile as he passed. He went to Wemba and held out a hand, the porter reaching into a pocket – the one into which he had thrust something when Eddie startled him the day before – and handing over a small metal tube.

The other was someone Eddie thought was dead.

'Mukobo . . .' he said, shocked. The reaction from the expedition's other Congolese members was equally horrified.

Philippe Mukobo regarded each of them in turn with a threatening stare. The documentary team responded with uncertain fear, no one holding his gaze for more than a moment. Kimba didn't even dare look him in the eye. Paris and Fortune both held out for just long enough to establish that they were the defenders of the others before following suit.

Mukobo's hostility, however, was concentrated on one man. 'Chase,' he growled to Eddie. One hand went to his holstered gold-plated automatic. 'I remember you. You captured me . . . twice. But now . . . I have captured *you*.'

He drew the gun – and placed its muzzle against Eddie's forehead.

15

Eddie tensed, about to lunge at Mukobo, but knew he would not survive—

'Philippe. Don't.' The command from Brice froze the warlord's finger on the trigger.

Fury rose in Mukobo's eyes. 'Are you telling me what to do, Brice? This is *my* land. *I* rule here!'

'And I'm here to make sure of it. But I only meant for you not to kill him *yet*.' He indicated Nina. 'They're married – and she's the archaeologist who found this place. As long as we've got Chase, she'll tell us everything we need to know.'

'She will tell me anyway,' growled Mukobo. But after a nerve-racking moment he lowered the gun and faced Nina. 'You are in charge?'

Nina was about to reply, but Fisher beat her to it. 'No, I – I am,' he said, forced bravado cracking at the edges. 'I'm the director – I tell the others how to make the film?' He glanced at the camera. 'You know, the movie?'

'I know what a director is,' Mukobo replied coldly. 'We do have movies, even here in the Congo. So. You are in charge here?'

'I – no, *you* are in charge,' said Fisher, spotting the trap just in time. 'You are. Very definitely.'

'Yes. I am,' he said with cruel amusement. Holstering the gun, he addressed his captives. 'I am known as Le Fauchet, but my real name is Philippe Mukobo. It is a name some of you already know well, but soon, everyone in the world will know me. When I say this is my land, it is not an idle boast. This corrupt nation will soon be divided – and this half will be *mine*.'

'What about Kabanda?' said Paris. 'Won't he be in charge?'

Mukobo's eyes narrowed at the mention of the secessionist leader. 'Without me to unite the militias, he would be nothing! He does not know how to fight.' A sly smile. 'But we will give him a demonstration once we have our country.'

'Great, so you're going to follow your civil war with a civil war,' said Eddie sarcastically. 'What happens then, you keep civil warring until there's only you left?'

The warlord did not reply, instead nodding to a muscular giant with a long machete strapped across his back. 'Luaba.' The man punched the Yorkshireman hard in the stomach. Eddie collapsed, gasping.

'Eddie!' Nina cried. She tried to help him, but another man shoved her back.

'He is already dead,' said Mukobo ominously, 'his heart has just not yet stopped beating. But you may still have a chance to stay alive.' He surveyed the ruins. 'The lost City of the Damned. It is real.'

'You've heard of it?'

'In stories, as a boy. The city in the jungle, where a great treasure was hidden. I never believed they were true, but now . . .' He stared at the Palace Without Entrance. 'Tell me what you know. All of it.'

She gave Eddie a worried look before speaking. 'This place is called Zhakana – it was the centre of a civilisation that existed thousands of years ago.'

'How did it end?' Brice's question was posed with genuine interest.

'I don't know. According to legend, the people died out because of a curse – something here that they revered ended up killing them.'

'If this place was lost,' said Mukobo, 'how did you find it?'

'The records of King Solomon of Israel – we discovered them recently. They described how the empire of Sheba knew of Zhakana. When Queen Makeda married Solomon, she brought him here to see it for himself.'

'Solomon built the palace,' Ziff added.

'I have heard of King Solomon, of course,' Mukobo said, though the boast seemed directed more at his men to show his intellectual superiority than at the archaeologists. 'What is inside?'

'We don't know,' Nina replied.

His voice became threatening. 'But my scouts saw you come out.'

'We only got as far as the first room – one of us was hurt.' She glanced at Rivero. The kneeling cameraman was barely able to hold himself upright, ashen-faced and sweating. 'We needed to call for a medical evacuation.'

'They must have a satellite phone,' said Brice, suddenly concerned. 'Did you make the call?'

'Not yet.'

'Where's the phone?'

'That bag,' said Fisher, pointing.

Brice found the satphone and checked its screen. 'They hadn't called for help,' he confirmed. 'The last call was yesterday.'

'That is lucky for you,' Mukobo told Nina and Fisher. 'So. You have not been far inside – but you must know what is in there.'

'Something valuable,' said Brice thoughtfully. 'It would have to be, to bring the world's most famous archaeologist and a documentary team to the Congolese jungle. It isn't somewhere you come on a whim.'

'So what're you doing here?' Eddie demanded. Luaba made ready to kick him, but when his boss said nothing, stood down.

'Thought your business was looking after mining company guys, not crawling through the jungle with warlords.'

'They're both my business,' Brice replied. 'The best way to ensure visiting VIPs need bodyguards is to have something to guard their bodies against. A civil war does that quite nicely.'

The Yorkshireman frowned at him. 'Bollocks. There's more to it than that – you wouldn't be allying yourself with this lot otherwise. You want them to win.'

'Independence for eastern Congo would benefit a lot of people, yes.'

'Including the mining companies,' Fortune said.

'There's a lot of money to be made out here – if you deal with the right people. At the moment, those people aren't in power. That will change if the LEC takes control, though.' Brice nodded at Mukobo, who smiled smugly. 'All the deals for mining rights made with the current government will have to be renegotiated. I'm here to facilitate that.'

'For a cut,' Nina said acidly.

'Well, naturally. As for why I'm *here*, specifically . . .' He took out the small tube he had taken from Wemba. 'Tracking device. Wemba has certain financial difficulties, so he was good enough to make it possible for us to follow you.'

'Why?'

'As I said, it would take something very special to bring you into the back end of beyond. And here it is.' He spread his hands wide to encompass the surrounding ruins. 'No matter what's here, it's in the LEC's interests to control it. Even if it was looted a thousand years ago, it's still an astounding archaeological find – and anyone wanting to study it will have to pay for the privilege. But if there really *is* a great treasure hidden here, well . . .'

'It will be mine,' said Mukobo firmly. 'It *is* mine. If it is gold, or jewels, they can be sold to buy weapons. And you will help me find them.' He issued a command in French. Some of his

200

men moved to stand behind the prisoners. 'Take me to the treasure, now.' Another order, and the expedition members were yanked roughly to their feet. Rivero screeched as a blood-drenched length of gauze pulled free of the wound beneath.

'For God's sake!' cried Fisher. 'He's hurt, you bastards! Leave him alone!' He tried to break loose from the man holding him—

'Mr Fisher, no!' Fortune barked, but it was too late. Fisher was clubbed to the ground, another militia man grabbing him.

Mukobo had frozen at the American's shout. He seemed almost expressionless, but rage was burning beneath the surface. 'Did you,' he said, voice low and angry, '*dare* to challenge me?'

'No, he didn't,' Paris said quickly. 'He's just a dumb American, he doesn't know about Le Fauchet. It's our fault, we should have told him to respect you. Please, he didn't know any better.'

The warlord's searing gaze turned upon him. 'It is *your* fault?'

Horror rose on the bodyguard's face as he realised there was no good answer. 'It . . . yes,' he said, mouth dry. 'Please, I am sorry.'

For the normally ebullient Congolese to become so fearful told Nina that something terrible was about to happen. But there was nothing she could do to intervene, except—

'Okay, okay!' she gabbled. 'Any treasure that's here, it's yours. You can have it all. Nobody meant any disrespect, nobody has to get hurt. Okay?'

Silence. The Insekt Posse exchanged looks of nervous anticipation. Then Mukobo advanced on her. Now it was Nina's turn to feel fear. Somehow, she knew that his pitiless face was the last seen by too many people to count. He stopped just two feet from her, regarding her unblinkingly . . .

Then, unexpectedly, he smiled.

'Okay,' he said.

She hardly dared breathe. 'Okay?'

'Okay. You will let me take all the treasure. Yes?'

'Yes,' she said, nodding repeatedly. 'Yes, I will.'

'Good.' He stepped back.

Heart thudding, Nina finally managed to exhale. She gave Paris and Fisher relieved looks. The moment of terrifying tension had passed—

Mukobo whirled, stabbing a finger at the two men. 'It is not yours to give! *Tenez-les!*'

Several militia swarmed upon Fisher and Paris, holding them immobile. The rifles of the other Insekt Posse snapped up to force the others back. 'No – no! What're you doing?' Fisher gasped.

'Do you know why my men wear red bands on their arms?' Mukobo said. 'To show that I own their blood – that I own *them*. I demand it from all who follow me. From those who do *not* follow me, from those who oppose me in any way . . . I also demand blood. They too have a red band upon their arms – and now you will see it. *Luaba!*'

Two of the militia grabbed Paris's right arm and forced it straight across a tree stump. The big man drew the machete from his back – and in a single savage strike chopped it through the bodyguard's forearm to bury the blade in the rotten wood beneath.

Paris fell backwards – as the men gripping his wrist lurched in the other direction, the two halves of his arm separating with a gushing crimson burst. Nina stared in shocked disbelief, her mind unwilling to accept what it had just seen . . . until Paris's scream drove home the appalling reality. Blood gushed from the stump of his arm, white bone glistening amidst the gore.

But the horror was not over. Mukobo shouted another order. The men holding Paris swung him around, sending a bloody spray over the other militia as they whooped and chanted in demented glee. '*Le Fauchet! Le Fauchet! Le Fauchet!*'

'Oh my God!' Nina wailed. She stumbled back, falling to the ground. 'Oh my *God*!'

Mukobo was not finished. *'Encore!'* he roared, pointing at Fisher.

Luaba yanked up the machete as the militia dragged the director to the blood-covered root. Fisher snapped out of his stunned paralysis. 'No!' he screamed, struggling to break free – to no avail. 'No, don't do it! Please! Don't—'

Two cackling young men slammed his arm down on the stump. Luaba swung the machete again. It hacked through the American's forearm with a crack of bone. Fisher shrieked, eyes wide in shock as his captors pulled him back.

'Steven!' wailed Lydia as the two men flung his severed hand over their comrades. The awful chorus echoed through the jungle again.

Paris was thrown to the ground at Fortune's feet, Fisher following. 'This is what happens to anyone who challenges me!' bellowed Mukobo. 'This is what happens to my enemies!'

He rounded on Eddie. 'And you,' the warlord snarled, 'you are most definitely my enemy. You captured me – you *humiliated* me. Now, you will pay! I will take your blood, from both your arms – and both your legs! *Amenez-le!*'

Men dragged Eddie, kicking and thrashing, to the tree. 'You sick fucker!' the Yorkshireman shouted at Mukobo.

'No!' screamed Nina. 'No, don't!' But her desperate pleas only roused the militia's frenzy, the sadistic chanting starting again as her husband was slammed down on the stump. Luaba grinned as he hefted the machete. He looked to Mukobo.

The leader smiled, about to issue a command—

'The treasure!' Nina cried. 'Wait, wait! The treasure in the palace, I know what it is!'

Mukobo turned back towards her. The chants of *'Le Fauchet!'* petered out in confusion at the stay of execution. 'You told me,' said the warlord, unnervingly calm, 'that you did not know what is in there.'

'I – I said I wasn't *sure*,' she replied. It was her only chance to save Eddie, but she was all too aware that Mukobo might still carry out his threat . . . and if she said the wrong thing she would be next to face the blade. 'But – but the ancient texts in Solomon's temple, they talked about a thing called the Shamir – something of great power, sent to him by God. It came from here! Solomon built the palace to protect it!'

The mention of power visibly caught his interest. 'What is this . . . Shamir?'

'I don't know – really, I don't!' she begged as he frowned. 'It's mentioned in ancient Hebrew texts. According to Solomon, the people who lived in Zhakana used it to build their empire.'

'The Shamir is how they built this place – how they conquered their enemies,' Ziff added. The older archaeologist was pale with horror at the atrocities he had just witnessed, voice tremulous. 'Inside the palace is what Solomon called the "Mother of the Shamir". We don't know what it is – but it's here.'

'We can take you to it,' Nina pressed on. 'But please, please, don't hurt him. I'll do whatever you say, I'll take you to the Shamir – if you let him go.'

'Sounds like nonsense to me,' said Brice. 'She's just trying to save Chase's life – and limb. It's only a legend, Philippe.'

'So was Atlantis until I found it,' Nina told him, defiance cutting through her fear. 'So was the tomb of King Arthur. You think I'd come all the way out here if I didn't believe it?'

'I think these ruins are reason enough. Anything else is just icing on the cake—'

'No,' said Mukobo firmly, to the Englishman's surprise. 'The stories of this place – they do tell of a great power hidden here. I believe that *she* believes. And you told me on the journey here that she has been right about such legends, many times before.'

He addressed Nina again. 'Convince me that I *need* you to find this treasure. If you do, Chase will keep his hands and feet – for now. If you do not . . .' He cast his malevolent gaze over the other prisoners. Lydia was weeping uncontrollably, Kimba shivering as he whispered a prayer over and over. The two mutilated men had both gone into shock, barely moving. 'I will kill them all in front of you, one by one. Then your husband will watch as I *take* you, before you both die.'

'You touch her,' Eddie growled, 'and I will tear off your fucking balls.'

Mukobo's face darkened, but a distraction came from an unexpected source: Brice. 'I always thought there was a fine line between bravery and stupidity, Chase,' he scoffed. 'But you're so far towards the latter that you almost go all the way around to the other side. Your wife is desperately trying to save your life, and you insult the man with whom she's bargaining? How were you not beaten to death by bullies as a child?'

'Maybe I *was* the bully,' said Eddie. That brought a small twitch of humour to the former spy's face.

'Mr Mukobo,' Nina said, trying to take advantage of the interruption, 'you need us because King Solomon didn't want anyone to get into the palace unless they could prove they were worthy. He set tests that have to be passed; tests of wisdom. The first one was to find the hidden entrance.' She gestured towards the palace's roof. 'Which we did. But once we got inside, we only got as far as the first room – where our cameraman got hurt.'

Mukobo's eyes narrowed. 'You think I am not wise enough to pass these tests, *Dr* Wilde?'

'I'm saying that maybe *none* of us are – not individually. But the more of us there are, the better our chances. And wisdom isn't about whether or not you have a doctorate. Eddie found the secret entrance, not me.'

Both the warlord and Brice gave Eddie dubious looks. 'I did,' said the Yorkshireman. 'I actually out-thought King Solomon. Didn't expect that, did you?'

'I genuinely did not,' said Brice, though with sarcasm rather than praise.

'We can get through the tests,' Nina went on. 'It'll take all of us, working together, but we can do it. But if you hurt my husband,' she added forcefully, 'then you might as well kill me right now, because . . . I'd sooner go to hell than help you.'

Mukobo stared at her, expression unreadable . . . then finally nodded. 'You are brave, Dr Wilde. As my friend Mr Brice said, that can be very close to stupid. But for now, I will not hurt you, or Chase.' He stepped back. 'Or the rest of your people. I have decided they will be useful.' He snapped his fingers, then pointed at the camera. One of his men picked up the Sony. 'They will film me.'

Lydia looked up at him. 'What?'

He gave the documentary crew a crocodile smile. 'You will film my discovery of the treasures of King Solomon. Such wonders will increase my reputation, and win me more followers.'

'After all you've done to keep Le Fauchet's true identity secret,' said Brice, far from approvingly, 'now you want to be *filmed*?'

'I will not put it on YouTube,' Mukobo replied with a mocking snort. 'It will be kept for when the time is right. But such a film will serve my *legend*. It will prove that I am the true ruler of the Congo. And if there really is a source of great power hidden here, then the world will see me take control of it.'

He gestured at the injured team members. 'See to their wounds. Bring the others – and their camera. Dr Wilde, take us inside.'

16

With Rivero's injuries making it impossible for him to scale the ladders, Howie took over camera duties. The three wounded men remained under guard at ground level as the others climbed to the palace roof.

'Now, Dr Wilde,' said Mukobo. 'What do we do next?'

'There's a shaft at the top of that tower,' said Nina, pointing. 'The first chamber is at the bottom – that's as far as we got.'

'For your sake, we had better go farther.' He turned to Howie. 'Are you ready to start?'

Howie checked the camera. 'Yeah, yeah. It'll need a new battery in a while, but there are spares with the rest of our gear inside.'

'Good. Then begin.' The young man gave him a confused look. 'Film me, idiot! Or do you want to lose your arm too?'

'Okay, rolling,' Howie hurriedly responded. Mukobo composed himself, then began a self-congratulatory speech in French.

'So what are we gonna do?' Nina muttered to Eddie as the militia listened.

'What do you mean?' he replied.

'I mean, how are we going to get out of this?'

'Fucked if I know, love.'

'I'd . . . kinda hoped you had something more than that.'

'I'd happily chuck that bastard off the roof and take my chances if it was just me, but I've got everyone else to think about. Maybe once we're inside—'

Luaba stabbed his Kalashnikov's muzzle against the Yorkshireman's back. 'Hey! Shut up. No talk.'

Eddie glared at him. 'I remember you. You were with Mukobo in Rwanda.'

The huge man nodded. 'I been with Philippe a long time.'

'Surprised he kept you around after you fucked up and let me capture him.'

Luaba's face twitched at the reminder of his failure. 'Shut up!' he repeated, giving Eddie a harder jab with the rifle.

Mukobo finished his address. 'Dr Wilde! It is time. Lead the way inside.'

'You're not going first? I thought you wanted the world to see *your* great discovery,' she said with sarcastic emphasis.

'Your cameraman was wounded. If anyone else is hurt, it will not be me!'

The denuded expedition, now outnumbered more than two-to-one by the Insekt Posse, headed up the tower and clambered down the stone shaft to the first chamber. The documentary crew's equipment was where they had left it. Nina switched on a tripod-mounted lamp. Luaba seemingly lacked the imagination to be impressed by what it revealed, but Mukobo's reaction was more awed. 'Ah!' he exclaimed. 'Most magnificent.' He spotted the blood on the floor. 'Where your man was hurt, yes?'

'In there.' She indicated the passage beneath the Hebrew inscription. Mukobo looked, but with the lamp being angled away from the opening saw only darkness within.

More of the group entered, Eddie and Howie amongst them. 'You all right?' her husband asked.

'So far,' she assured him. Fortune and Lydia arrived behind them. 'How about you two?'

'Oh, absolutely fine,' Lydia said shakily. Her eyes were still red-rimmed from crying. 'Surrounded by drug-crazed psychopaths who want to – to chop our f-fucking arms off! Just fine, yeah.'

Fortune picked up her audio gear and gave it to her. 'Here.'

'W-what am I supposed to do with this?' she demanded.

'Your job, of course.'

'He's right,' Nina told her. 'Focus on what you do best. It'll take your mind off the . . . other stuff. Trust me,' she went on as Lydia was about to object. 'It helps. It really does.' The New Zealander still looked anything except happy, but donned her mixing box and headphones.

Brice was one of the last to arrive. 'Must admit, I expected something a little more spectacular.'

'This is only the first room,' said Nina as she switched on a lantern. With more people now in the chamber, the first light was partially obscured. 'There are probably more down there—'

She broke off as she saw one of the militia making his way down the dark passage towards the glint of silver at its far end. She was about to warn him to come back – but then held her tongue. 'If we get more lights working,' she quickly said instead, 'we'll be able to see what we're dealing with.'

'I'll help you,' said Howie. He lowered the camera – then saw the man in the passage. 'Whoa, whoa, that won't end well!'

His cry alerted Mukobo and Brice that something was wrong. Both men whirled, the warlord shouting a warning—

Too late.

The militia man reached the large floor block farther down the passage – and staggered as it dropped under his weight. The rasp of stone against stone echoed down the hallway as the walls began to close in.

Mukobo rushed to the opening. '*Sortez!*' he yelled. '*Sortez d'ici!*' Behind him, Howie whipped the Sony back up to capture events.

The man regained his footing and looked around in shock.

Unlike Rivero, rather than retreat he ran for the chamber containing the silver idol.

The slab continued to descend until it halted with a thud about a foot below floor level – then started to slide towards the next room. The jolt made him stumble again, but he recovered, racing down the rapidly narrowing passageway—

One arm banged against an approaching wall. He reeled, unbalanced – and hit the other. By the time he straightened, both sides were upon him. He turned sideways, but now couldn't move fast enough to get clear. A shriek of fear suddenly became a strangled croak as the passageway relentlessly closed in. A hideous crack as his ribcage was crushed – then the two walls met with a harsh and final bang.

Mukobo yelled for a flashlight. One was hurriedly found and shone down the hallway. He stared in horror as the trap completed its cycle and reset, the mashed remains of the young man splattering messily down as the walls pulled apart. The viscera-covered slab rolled back towards the first chamber, then returned to floor level.

The stunned silence was broken by Eddie. 'I've heard of runners hitting the wall, but not the other way around . . .'

Mukobo whirled, jabbing a finger. 'Another word! Say another word, Chase, and I will kill you!' He rounded on Nina. 'You knew that would happen! You knew – and you said nothing!'

'I told you our cameraman was hurt in here!' Nina replied. 'There was blood all over the floor – that should have been a goddamn clue not to go in!'

'You should still have warned him,' snapped Brice.

'I didn't see him,' she lied. The former MI6 agent's icy gaze didn't flicker, as probing as a polygraph. 'There were too many people in here!' She looked back at Mukobo. Her split-second decision to keep silent had been, she was forced to admit to herself, both in the hope of causing a distraction that Eddie or Fortune might use – and a desire to obtain more data on the trap's workings. She was proud of neither, and was afraid Brice would realise that . . .

Mukobo glared at her – then turned away, shouting in French at his men. All hurriedly retreated from the passage. 'So what do we do now?' Brice asked.

'If there is a trap, it is to protect something valuable,' said Mukobo. 'So we will find a way through it.' He addressed Nina again. '*You* will find a way through it.'

'The trap worked differently this time,' she said, 'but I saw more of how it operates. Hopefully I'll be able to figure out how to get someone through safely.'

'I don't think that's quite what he meant,' said Brice, with a serpentine smile.

'No?'

'No,' Mukobo told her firmly. '*You* will go through the trap!'

'No she fucking won't,' Eddie growled. He was about to step towards the warlord when Luaba raised his gun to deter him.

'Because of your *negligence*, one of my men is dead,' Mukobo went on. 'You are responsible – so you must make things right.'

'She's an archaeologist,' protested the Yorkshireman. 'If there are any more traps after this one, you'll need her to work out how to beat 'em. If she gets killed, then you're fucked!'

'But she isn't the only archaeologist, is she?' said Brice, indicating Ziff. 'Sorry, but we haven't been formally introduced. You are?'

'Uh – Ziff,' the older scientist replied. 'Dr David Solomon Ziff.'

'And what's your area of archaeological expertise, Dr David Solomon Ziff?'

Ziff gave Nina a worried glance before answering. 'The, ah, the life and works of King Solomon.'

Brice's voice became patronising. 'And who built the palace in which we're standing, Dr Ziff?'

'That would be . . . King Solomon.' The name emerged with resignation.

'You see?' Brice said to Eddie. 'We have an expert in the subject. Having a generalist as well feels somewhat redundant.'

Fortune stood beside Eddie. 'No, please. I shall do it. I am their guide – I should lead the way.'

'She will go!' barked Mukobo, stabbing a finger at Nina. 'That is an end to it. I will shoot the next one who argues with me!'

'Yeah, let her go,' muttered Lydia bitterly. 'She got us into all this, let her do it.'

'You can fucking shut up,' Eddie growled at her.

Mukobo started to draw his weapon. 'Okay, I'll do it,' Nina hurriedly said. 'I'll find a way through.'

'How?' asked Ziff. 'It really is a death trap!'

'If we get a load of big stones from outside,' Eddie suggested, 'we could block the walls so they can't close.'

'I am not a patient man, Chase,' said Mukobo with a malevolent smile. 'She has five minutes. That is all.' Brice held up his left wrist and tapped his expensive Omega watch for emphasis.

'Nothing like a deadline to focus the mind,' said Nina nervously. 'Okay. You reach the trigger point, and if you go forward, the walls close and crush you. You go back, the blades pop out and chop you up. Either way, you're dead. And I'm dead if I don't figure this out,' she added, as much to herself as to the others – including Howie, who was filming her again. She regarded the inscription above the passage. '"Only the dead shall enter alive . . ."'

'What does that *mean*?' wondered Ziff. '"The living who enter shall die" – that part is obvious. But how can the dead be alive?'

'I don't know. It *has* to be a clue, though. One of Solomon's riddles.' She went to the opening. 'I need a light.'

A flashlight was procured for her. She shone it down the corridor, grimacing as the beam passed over the bloody mess on its walls and floor. 'That section of floor drops downwards when you step on it,' she mused. 'And when that guy made a run for the far end . . . it *kept* dropping. But when Jay turned around and ran back this way . . .'

'It came back up,' Eddie recalled.

'Yeah. Like his stepping *off* of it stopped the walls from closing in – but at the same time it triggered the other half of the trap, the blades. You can't back out; once you go in, you're committed.'

'And then you end up as the jam in a wall sandwich.'

'There has to be a way through, though. There has to be.' She turned the light upon other parts of the passage, but found nothing.

Brice made a performance of looking at his watch. 'Tick-tock, Dr Wilde. Time is running out.'

'So's my patience,' she snapped. 'So shut up.' The ex-spy smirked. 'It's the only way through – you *have* to run the gauntlet and face Solomon's test, play his game. So if only the dead can get through, then how . . .?' Her eyes went wide. 'Of course. Duh! Of course!'

'What is it?' asked Ziff.

'I just cracked Solomon's riddle!' she said, unable to hold back a smile despite the dangerous situation. '"Only the dead will enter alive", right?'

'Yes?' said Mukobo, covering his lack of understanding with menace. 'Tell us, woman! Now!'

'Solomon tells you how to get through, if you're brave enough,' she explained. 'What do the dead do?'

The warlord shook his head, puzzled. 'They do nothing.'

'Smell after a while,' Eddie added, 'but mostly just lie there.'

'That's right!' said Nina excitedly. 'They do nothing, they just lie there. Or specifically, lie *there*!' She pointed at the large floor block. 'That drops downwards before the walls close in. When they meet, there's a gap underneath them!'

Ziff gave her an owlish look of surprise. 'You're saying that to get through, you have to lie down?'

'Exactly – you play dead! You do nothing. I think that if you're lying flat, you'll be carried underneath the walls.'

'You *think*,' Lydia said.

'I'm as sure as I can be, yes,' Nina fired back.

Brice tapped his watch. 'That's good. Because your time's up.'

'That was never five bloody minutes,' rumbled Eddie.

'Time flies when you're having fun. Well, I'm enjoying myself, at least.'

Mukobo gestured towards the passage. 'Go through,' he ordered Nina. 'If you are right, all is good. If you are not, then' – a cruel smile – 'you will die.'

'No pressure, then.' She went to the entrance.

'Nina,' said Eddie. She looked back, seeing fear and worry on his face despite his best efforts to show no weakness. 'You sure about this?'

'Not one hundred per cent, no, but . . . I don't really have much choice, do I? If I'm wrong, just . . . take good care of Macy.'

Eddie nodded. 'I will. But . . . don't be wrong, okay? Let's all get out of here.'

'Who is Macy?' demanded the warlord.

The Yorkshireman glared at him. 'Our dog,' he said, unwilling to provide any more ammunition that could be used against them.

Mukobo regarded him suspiciously, then turned back to Nina. 'It is time. Go.'

'Good luck,' said Ziff fearfully.

'Thanks,' Nina replied, exchanging a last look with Eddie – then she stepped into the passage.

Her light picked out the wall slots concealing the hooked blades. They were not an immediate worry, though. If she was right, they would only be triggered if she fled back into the first chamber. She moved on, stopping as she reached the passage's second half.

Her light passed over the floor slab, finding footprints in the dust of ages, Rivero's and the militia man's – then, close to the far end, the latter's gruesome remains. Even his rifle had been crushed flat.

'Go through, Dr Wilde,' said Mukobo impatiently. 'Now.'

Nina took a deep breath . . . then stepped on to the slab.

It sank under her weight. The ancient mechanism beneath rattled and thumped once more—

And the walls began to close in.

Even knowing what to expect, Nina still felt a jolt of fear. Every instinct told her to run. But she knew her instincts were wrong – or rather, she was *sure* they were. That was not the same thing.

She quickly stepped forward before lying on her back; if she was going to die, some defiant part of her mind had decided it wouldn't be on her belly with her face in the ancient dirt. The walls rumbled inwards as the slab kept dropping—

It jolted to a halt. Nina tried to judge if the looming walls would pass above her. From her worm's-eye viewpoint, it was hard to be sure . . .

Another jolt – and the slab moved again, sliding forward with a nerve-shredding scrape of stone. Nina held her breath as the undersides of the walls drew level with her arms, then brushed her chest – and she closed her eyes, fear finally taking over.

The walls slammed together—

But she was still alive.

Rough stone plucked at her clothing as she was carried onwards. A moment of utter revulsion as she felt the dead man's

215

blood drip on to her stomach, then the sound of grinding stone changed, echoing. She had reached the next chamber.

Nina opened her eyes and hurriedly scrambled from the moving slab. The walls behind her were clamped shut so tightly that she doubted a playing card could have been slipped between them. She checked the rest of the room. It was smaller than the first chamber, dominated by the statue at the end of the passage.

Silver sparkled in the torchlight. She examined the palm-sized metal tablet resting inside the figure's gaping mouth. Old Hebrew text was visible upon it.

A distant, muffled voice reached her. 'Nina! Are you okay? Nina!'

She scurried back to her point of entry. 'Eddie, I'm all right!'

His relief was palpable even through the stonework. 'Thank God! Okay, so now how do the rest of us get through?'

'That's a very good question.' Another passageway led to parts unknown, but apart from the statue the room was empty. She returned to the carved figure for a closer look at the silver tablet.

A rod was attached to the metal plate's underside, angling downwards into the statue's throat. Probably part of a mechanism – but what was its purpose?

'Only one way to find out,' she announced to an imaginary camera, pulling it upwards.

Metal scraped – then the clunk of something weighty being released reverberated through the room.

The trap rumbled back into motion, this time in reverse. The walls pulled apart, the floor slab trundling back into the passage before rising to floor level.

Lights shone at her from the other end. 'Is it safe?' demanded Mukobo.

'I think so,' Nina replied. 'I pulled a lever to reset the trap, and it probably locks everything so that other people can come through.'

'Probably?' said Brice scathingly. 'I think someone should test that. And I know the very man.'

Eddie laughed mirthlessly. 'Let me guess: he's British, ruggedly handsome, and *isn't* a smarmy clag-nut from MI6.'

'Go through, Chase,' the Congolese ordered. 'And do not try to escape at the other end, or I will kill your friends.'

'I'll wait for you, don't worry,' Eddie growled as he headed into the passage. He hesitated before putting a foot on the slab. The walls and floor remained stationary. He quickly strode through to Nina, who embraced him. 'Christ, love. For a minute there, I thought you'd been squished.'

'So did I,' she replied with relief. They looked back. Mukobo listened to Brice as the former intelligence agent whispered something, both men regarding the couple with unwelcome interest, then the warlord issued an order. The rest of the group began to traverse the defanged trap.

'Was that it, then?' Eddie asked his wife.

Nina's gaze turned to the new tunnel. 'No. The inscription said Solomon set *three* challenges . . .'

17

L uaba was next through the trap, holding Eddie and Nina at gunpoint while the others followed. Mukobo gave the silver tablet a greedy look. 'I wouldn't,' Nina told him as he reached for it. 'It's the only thing stopping the rest of your men from becoming chunky salsa.' He withdrew his hand.

Brice peered down the next passage. 'Is there another trap down there?'

Ziff, regarding the statue with wonderment, shook his head. 'I would imagine there's an inscription before each test of Solomon. A clue as to how you can pass it.'

'If you're smart enough,' added Nina.

'Well, we have two PhDs, a master's,' Brice put a hand to his heart with false modesty before indicating Lydia and Howie, 'I assume a couple of graduates, the future leader of Eastern Congo, and . . . well, the rest.' He gave the members of the Insekt Posse a disdainful look, which finished on Eddie.

'*You've* got an MA?' scoffed the Yorkshireman. 'What in, applied arseholery?'

'International relations, actually. But I'd hope that amount of brainpower would be a match for someone from the Bronze Age.'

'We will soon find out,' said Mukobo, pointing imperiously down the new tunnel. 'Follow me. And you, boy,' he added to Howie, 'keep filming.'

'Yeah, I will,' the young man nervously assured him.

The warlord raised a torch and strode into the darkness, the others filing after him. The new passage turned after a short distance, angling downwards. 'There is another room,' Mukobo soon announced. 'Dr Wilde, Dr Ziff – what is this?'

He stepped aside to let the archaeologists past. Nina lifted her flashlight – to see a large and elaborate frieze covering the wall ahead. Four distinct panels each bore a carved scene. 'Oh, wow,' she said, impressed.

Every relief was different, but all displayed the same exquisite workmanship. The first was an image of a dead animal lying on a desert plain, insects buzzing around it. The second was a tree in an equally desolate landscape; the third, a muscular bald man holding the carcass of a goat above his head. The final picture showed a field of wheat with more insects – locusts – swarming above. The only thing all four had in common was a circular hole about six inches across set into each.

Ziff hurried to examine the frieze. 'If this is from the era of Solomon, the style is very advanced for the time.'

Nina joined him. 'Egyptian or Assyrian influence, maybe?'

'Perhaps. Or it could be that Sheba had developed similar techniques, but we simply haven't found any examples yet.'

'I do not care who made it,' said Mukobo impatiently. 'What does it *mean*? Is this another test – and is it a trap?'

Nina checked the rest of the chamber. On a side wall was another inscription in Old Hebrew, one word in particular given great emphasis by being contained in a block of its own. 'David, over here.'

Ziff joined her, reading the text. 'It is another test, yes,' he confirmed. 'The first line says, "The Riddle of Samson". Samson's name is this word here.' He pointed out the distinct block.

'Samson as in, "and Delilah", right?' asked Eddie.

'Unless there's another Samson I missed in my theology lessons, then I'd imagine so,' Brice replied. He looked into one of the holes. 'This slopes downwards into the wall. There's something at the bottom, but I can't tell what it is.'

'I wouldn't try to find out until we know what we're doing,' Nina warned.

'No, no,' Eddie countered. 'Go right ahead, Brice!'

'I'll leave it to the experts,' said the former agent with a sneering smile.

Ziff had continued to translate the text. 'It's another message from Solomon,' he said. 'He says that Samson has the answer to the riddle that will allow visitors to pass, but only the wise will know where to find it.'

Nina looked back at the carved wall: specifically, the first panel. 'Well, that's obvious enough.'

Ziff nodded. 'Judges, 14:14.'

'"Out of the eater, something to eat; out of the strong, something sweet."'

Eddie gave them a bewildered look. 'Okay, *what*?'

Mukobo was no more enlightened. 'Explain.'

'It's a riddle Samson set for the Philistines,' Nina told him, going to the picture of the dead animal. 'If they solved it, he would give them a reward of thirty expensive garments, and if they didn't they'd give him the same reward.'

'They couldn't answer it,' Ziff continued, 'so they forced Samson's wife to tell them. When Samson realised what they'd done, he went to another town and killed thirty Philistines, then took their clothes to settle his debt.'

'What, just thirty random people?' Eddie shook his head. 'Why is it that all historical figures are actually dicks?'

'Typical bleeding-heart double standards,' scoffed Brice. 'You can't judge the actions of great men of the past through a politically correct lens. Alexander, Julius Caesar . . .'

'You were about to say bloody Hitler as well, weren't you? Go on, admit it.'

'So what is the answer to the riddle?' demanded Mukobo.

'This,' said Nina of the carved panel. 'It's a lion that Samson killed with his bare hands. When he came back to it some time later, he found that bees had made a nest in its corpse, and there was honey inside it. The lion is the "eater" and the "strong", and the honey is the sweet thing to eat.'

The warlord nodded. 'Then to find the way through, we reach into here?' He pointed at the hole set in the dead lion's mouth.

Nina and Ziff exchanged glances. 'I am . . . not sure,' said the Israeli.

'Why? What other answer could it be if it is written in the Bible?'

'The thing is,' Nina explained, 'it's – well, as a riddle it's bullshit. It's impossible to work out the answer based on the clues given, because it's something that only Samson ever saw in person. It's the biblical equivalent of asking "What's in my pocket?" and demanding someone guesses right first time when you've got . . . a clockwork mouse and a pencil sharpener in it, say. It's a cheat.'

Brice regarded the other panels of the quadriptych as Howie panned the camera's light along them. 'So could the real answer be any of these?'

Ziff examined the three pictures. 'The tree seems to be a fig tree. The man holding up the dead goat, I would say is not Samson – he doesn't have any hair. I don't know who he might be, though. And the last panel is a plague of locusts devouring a wheat crop. I can't see how any of those would relate to Samson's riddle.'

'Then it must be the lion,' Mukobo said firmly. 'Dr Wilde, reach into the hole.'

'Wait, wait,' she protested. 'There might be something else we haven't spotted.'

'There is nothing else!' The African swept his light around the room. Other than the frieze and the Hebrew inscription, the walls were blank. 'You have the answer. We must find the treasure. Do it!'

'It might be another fucking trap!' Eddie objected. 'Give her time to—' He folded in breathless pain as Luaba drove his Kalashnikov into his stomach.

'I grow tired of your voice, Chase,' the warlord said, his suddenly affectless tone somehow more threatening than any angry shout. 'I do not want to hear it any more.' Luaba readied his rifle, finger on the trigger. The wheezing Yorkshireman looked up into the gun's muzzle and opted to remain silent.

Nina was not about to do the same, however. 'The lion's much too obvious an answer. It's the only one it could be – which means it *can't* be. Solomon meant this as a challenge that only someone as wise as him could solve, but a passing know-ledge of the Old Testament is all you'd need to reach this solution.' She jabbed a finger at the image of the dead predator. 'That's not wisdom, it's just having paid attention to the stories of your own people.'

'Some would say that's the very definition of wisdom,' Brice observed smugly.

'And some would say that it's not falling for an obvious trap!'

'Enough,' Mukobo snapped. 'Put your hand in there. Now!' He shoved her to the carved lion. 'If you do not do it, then I will make one of your friends do it instead – and anything that happens to them will be on your head!'

Nina stared with rising panic at the waiting hole. She was absolutely convinced that the obvious answer to the riddle was also wrong, and the first challenge had proved that Solomon was lethally unforgiving of mistakes. But despite her fear, she was unwilling to let someone else take the risk in her place. She looked back at her companions.

Lydia's feelings were clear, her wide eyes pleading with the American: *you do it. Not me. Don't choose me!* Howie's sense of self-preservation was less blatant, but just as real. Ziff had the same misgivings as Nina about the puzzle, his expression almost apologetic for his failure to come up with a solution.

Eddie and Fortune, though, were both coiled springs waiting to unleash. She could see their eyes scrutinising their captors, searching for advantage, for weakness. And she knew Eddie would make a desperate strike rather than let her put her hand into the ominous opening – which would get him killed.

Her breath quickened, pulse pounding. A tiny shake of her head to Eddie, silently pleading with him not to sacrifice his life, but his determined expression warned her that he was not going to listen . . .

'You are out of time, Dr Wilde!' Mukobo barked. 'Put her—'

'Please – wait, please!' A new voice, one that had not been heard for some time: Masson Kimba. The porter's fear of Mukobo and his men had rendered him mute and passive, meekly going wherever he was pushed, but now he finally spoke again. 'Do not hurt her. Please.'

The warlord rounded on him. 'Do you want to take her place?'

'I do not *want* to, but . . . but I will.'

'Masson, no!' Nina protested. 'I can't let you!'

Kimba gave her a weak smile. 'You have to. I am to blame for all this.' He shot a disgusted glare at Wemba, who looked away in discomfort. 'I knew Cretien had money problems, that he had talked to the Englishman. I should have told Fortune that he could not be trusted.'

'It was not your fault,' said Fortune. 'It was mine.'

'I should have known,' the porter insisted. 'And Dr Wilde will be more likely to get you out of this place alive than me.' He faced Nina again. 'You were kind to me on the boat . . . Nina. Let me be kind to you. Please.'

She shook her head. 'But I can't—'

'Enough,' snapped Mukobo. 'He has chosen. Think yourself lucky, Dr Wilde. And hope you are wrong if you want him to live.'

He gestured, and his men pushed Nina back before clearing a space around the first panel. Kimba gave Nina a last worried look, then cautiously slid his arm into the dark circle, reaching down at an angle. 'It is . . . it is like a pipe,' he reported. 'There is a hole in the top, but . . . I cannot feel anything inside.'

'Keep going,' ordered the glowering Mukobo.

The porter leaned closer to the wall as his outstretched hand continued deeper. 'I found something! It is metal.'

'Careful,' warned Nina. 'Don't push or pull it, just tell me what it feels like.'

Kimba's face scrunched with deep concentration as his fingertips probed the unseen object. 'It is like . . . a handle?'

'A release for a hidden door?' suggested Ziff, nervously fingering his beard.

'Or it could be the release for a trap,' Nina countered. 'Masson, don't pull it until you're sure there's nothing else there.'

The Congolese felt around the space's entire circumference. 'There is only the metal thing.'

Mukobo folded his arms. 'Then pull it!'

Kimba glanced beseechingly at Nina for advice or salvation, but she had neither. He licked his lips, then turned back to the frieze. 'Okay. I am holding it.' A pause for breath, then: 'And . . . pull.'

A faint metallic *clunk* came from behind the wall. Everyone flinched – but nothing happened.

Kimba gasped in relief—

Another sound, harsher – and the African screamed as

something inside the hole slammed downwards with a crunch of tearing flesh and bone. 'Oh my God!' Nina cried. 'Get him out of there!'

The porter shrieked, unable to pull free of whatever had caught him. 'My arm! It has my arm, it—'

Another frightening noise, this time from the ceiling. Some instinct made Nina jump back – as a long metal spear lanced out of a hole overhead and stabbed diagonally downwards. Its prong plunged through Kimba's back, impaling him against the frieze.

He flailed, letting out one final anguished, gargling cry before falling limp. Lydia screamed. His body remained pinned to the wall for a moment before the spear jerkily retracted into its hiding place, blood drizzling from the shaft.

Kimba slumped, hanging briefly by his trapped arm before whatever was holding it also withdrew. The dead porter flopped to the floor, a gaping wound in his forearm revealing how another spear had plunged through it to transfix him.

Fortune held the shivering Lydia as she stared at the corpse. 'Is . . . is he . . .' she stammered.

Brice completed her sentence. 'Dead? Quite decisively, I'd say.'

'You can fucking shut up,' Eddie growled at him.

Mukobo directed his torch at the ceiling. He found first the hole from which the spear had fallen, then identical openings in line with each of the other three panels. 'You were right, Dr Wilde. The lion was not the right answer. So what is?'

Nina's voice was as shaky as her hands. 'None of them.'

'One must be. And you *will* find it.'

Anger overcame shock. 'None of them are right, damn it! I told you, the Riddle of Samson is bullshit. If we try those other holes, the same thing'll happen!'

'Three more holes,' said Brice, 'and by my count, one, two, three supernumeraries.' He indicated Lydia, Fortune and finally

Eddie. 'Archaeologists and a cameraman, we need, for now. Anyone else, well . . . a phrase involving coal mines and canaries comes to mind.'

'A phrase involving my boot and your arse comes to *my* mind,' said Eddie, glaring angrily at his countryman.

'That is a very good idea, Mr Brice,' said Mukobo. He pointed at Lydia. 'Begin with her. I grow tired of her whining.'

The sound woman tried to flee, but barely made a single step before being grabbed by the militia. 'No!' she screamed. 'No, *no*!'

'Wait, wait!' Nina cried. She aimed her own light back at the inscription. 'The answer's here, it's got to be! Just give me time, I can find it!'

There was no pity in Mukobo's gaze. 'Find it quickly,' he said, gesturing towards the panel bearing the fig tree. Three leering members of the Insekt Posse hauled the New Zealander to it, her protestations becoming a shrill, incoherent cry of terror. 'Put her arm inside.'

'Nina!' yelled Eddie, Luaba's gun locked upon him. 'Whatever the real answer is, you need to find it right fucking now!'

'I'm trying, I'm trying!' She stared helplessly at the inscription, struggling to remember Ziff's translation. The only word she knew for sure was the name sitting alone on its own block, *Samson*—

'Wait!' she gasped – not in panic, but sudden hope. 'David, the line with Samson's name in it – what does it say? What's the *exact* translation?'

The militia forced Lydia's arm into the second hole. Ziff regarded her fearfully before turning his gaze to the ancient text. 'It – it says, ah . . . "Samson has the—" no, "holds" would be more accurate. "Samson *holds* the answer that . . . that will allow, permit, those who enter this place to pass, but the wise—"'

'"—will know how to find it,"' she finished for him, recalling his earlier words. 'That's not the important part, it's the part about Samson. Samson holds the answer!' She ran to the inscription – and dug her fingernails around each side of the lettered block, clawing at the precisely cut stone.

Mukobo signalled for his men to pause. 'What have you found?'

'The answer – the real answer!' She finally found purchase and pulled. A nail broke as the block edged out, but she ignored the pain in the rush of discovery. 'Solomon gave the answer to the first challenge in a riddle. But the second one,' she tugged it free, 'was *literal*! Here, it's here!'

Mukobo and Brice came to look. 'What is it?' demanded the African.

'The switch that opens the exit!' The new hole in the wall contained a bronze lever. She reached for it.

'Are you sure?' Ziff cautioned.

'I'm sure,' she replied as she wrapped her fingers around the handle, lifting the inscribed block in her other hand. 'Samson really did hold the answer. It's so obvious in hindsight, but just like Samson's riddle, you'd only know the answer if someone had already told you. Which Solomon *did*. The test was to see if you were paying attention to exactly what he said, rather than jumping to the obvious conclusion.'

She pulled the lever. Metal creaked – then the section of wall bearing the inscription moved slightly, one edge inching outwards.

'*Ouvrez-le*,' Mukobo ordered. His men pulled it wider. Another passage was revealed beyond. 'Ah! We are getting closer to the treasure!' Almost as an afterthought, he signalled for Lydia to be released. Her captors let go, the New Zealander dropping to her knees in tears. Fortune went to help her, daring any of the Insekt Posse to stop him. None were willing to try.

'Well done, Nina,' said Ziff, relieved. 'Well done. I would never have thought of that. It seems that Solomon liked to play word games.'

'Perhaps his next challenge will be a Sudoku puzzle,' Brice remarked snidely. 'Well, you've got us this far, so let's hope your luck doesn't run out.'

'It already did,' said Nina, looking sadly at Kimba's body. She closed her eyes in silent tribute to his bravery and sacrifice, then – at Mukobo's menacing urging – led the way through the door.

18

The passageway descended deeper into the palace. Nina was sure they were nearing the mysterious 'Mother of the Shamir' that Solomon had constructed the great building to conceal. A huge structure with only one, hidden entrance; lead-lined walls; death traps guarding the way – whatever it was, the king had taken extreme measures to keep it from the world. Yet the fact that there was a way through all these hazards suggested that he still wanted it to be accessible if necessary. What could it be?

A new chamber opened out ahead. 'There's something else here,' she reported, surveying it with her flashlight.

More Old Hebrew inscriptions told her that Solomon had set another challenge. She would have to wait for Ziff's translation to get its full meaning, but another frieze offered a strong clue. This showed what she guessed was Solomon himself, seated upon a throne. Before him stood two women – and directly between them, a small child.

'The Judgement of Solomon,' she whispered.

Mukobo stopped beside her. 'What does it mean?'

'It's his most famous parable,' said Brice, before Nina could answer. 'Two women came before him, each claiming to be the boy's mother. Nobody could tell which was telling the truth – until Solomon found a way.'

'He decreed that since neither woman would give up the boy,' Ziff continued, 'he should be cut in two and one half given to each woman. One of them immediately surrendered her claim, so Solomon knew *she* was the real mother. She would rather lose her child than let him be harmed.'

Mukobo nodded, though he seemed unimpressed by the tale's moral. 'Then what is the test?'

'Something to do with *that*, would be my guess.' Nina directed her light across the room. Set into the far wall was what appeared to be an exit – but simply walking out of the chamber was not an option. Immediately beyond the opening was a small circular antechamber with a cage-like wall of hefty metal bars running around its perimeter. There was a way in . . . but no apparent way out. She guessed that once Solomon's challenge had been successfully completed, the cage would rotate through a half-turn so that anyone inside could leave via another doorway on the far side.

That challenge somehow concerned what sat beside the entrance. A round dais about a foot high and six across stood proud of the floor. Directly above it hung a huge cylinder of stone, suspended from the ceiling by thick chains. 'David, what does the text say?'

'It's another message from Solomon.' A pause as Ziff digested the ancient words. 'It says, "The Judgement of Solomon stands as an example. Heed the lesson of the mother, and you shall reach the heart of the Palace Without Entrance."'

'Another fucking riddle,' muttered Eddie. 'Where's Batman when you need him?'

'If we figure out what the lesson of the mother actually is, we should be able to get through,' Nina assured him. 'So . . . what *is* it?'

'Always follow the better judgement of men, perhaps?' offered the smirking Brice. Mukobo laughed.

Nina shot the Briton a look of disgust. 'Not helping. Asshole,' she added.

The rest of the group advanced into the chamber, though

none of the Insekt Posse were willing to go too far. Fortune risked a look through the exit. 'I cannot see anything on the far side. But there is another big stone hanging above the cage.'

'So they're both booby traps?' said Lydia. She sounded numbed, having passed beyond horror to resigned surrender. 'How are you supposed to get through?'

'Solomon must have left a way,' said Nina. 'Something to do with "the lesson of the mother". It's about a mother giving up her child in order to protect it. There are two traps there, the cage and the column, so maybe it's about . . . sacrifice.' A grim possibility dawned. 'For somebody to get through the cage, someone else has to stand under that pillar as it falls.'

'There's nothing stopping them from just stepping out of the way, though,' said Eddie.

'I know – and that's the worst part. Whoever does it has to *voluntarily* sacrifice themself to save the other.'

A nasty smile spread across Mukobo's face. 'If this is the last test before we reach the treasure . . . then I know who will take that test.'

Eddie jerked a thumb at Brice and Luaba. 'Cockface and Tooler here, maybe?'

'No.' The warlord pointed at the cage. 'Put Chase in there!'

Guns came up at the Yorkshireman. 'All right, I'm fucking moving,' he said as Luaba shoved him towards the cage.

'You come with me,' Mukobo said to Nina, forcing her to the dais. 'If one of you dies, or both of you, I do not care . . . but you *will* open that door.'

Luaba pushed Eddie into the enclosure. His weight tripped something – and with a shrill screech the cage made a quarter-turn, its open section grinding around to face the antechamber's blank inner wall. He tried to push it back to its original position, and then towards the opening opposite, but it wouldn't move. He was trapped.

There were no bars around Nina, but she felt trapped too as Mukobo brought her to the circular dais. It was not flat; a raised lip a few inches deep surrounded a recessed slab. She looked up at the stone cylinder. It was the same width as the recess rather than the whole rostrum, but whether that was significant she had no idea.

She had no time to think about it either. 'Get on,' ordered the Congolese.

'Please, don't,' she begged. 'I might be wrong about what we're supposed to do.'

'Then you will both die. Get on!' He aimed his gun at her, driving her on to the dais with his other arm.

As with Eddie, her weight triggered a mechanism. Dust showered her as the suspended column jolted. Mukobo hastily stepped back. The deep grumble of a giant cog reluctantly waking from its three-thousand-year slumber filled the room – and the pillar started to descend.

As did the ceiling above her husband.

Eddie pressed back against the bars, but the gap between the cage and the steadily lowering block was barely an inch. 'Nina!' he yelled. 'Get off that thing, save yourself!'

She held her ground despite her fear. 'If I do, you'll be killed! That's the whole point of Solomon's story – it's about sacrificing yourself to protect someone else!'

He angrily shook the cage. 'No, that's bollocks! She *offered* to make the sacrifice, but in the end she *and* her little boy stayed alive – and stayed together! There's got to be another option.'

'Maybe, but I don't know what!' The column above her was still rumbling downwards – slightly faster than Eddie's. It would reach her first. Solomon would have designed the test to work that way on purpose – but why?

'Then get off it! There's no point both of us dying!'

Nina's heart raced, but her mind was working even faster,

desperately trying to find an answer – the *right* answer. She was convinced that Solomon had not set an impossible challenge. The map room in the First Temple, the eagle puzzle on the palace's roof, both the previous traps – all had a solution.

So what was *this* solution?

Heed the lesson of the mother. Solomon's own words, his instruction to those accepting his final test. What was the lesson?

The column's base was less than a foot above her head. In a moment it would reach her, and she would either have to duck – or step off the dais. Doing the latter, she was sure, would doom Eddie.

The lesson of the mother. The phrase rolled around in her head. She had given up the most precious thing in her life to keep it safe—

No. Eddie was right. She had been *willing* to give it up. Intent, not action. They were not the same thing . . .

The answer came to her – she hoped.

If she was wrong, she would be dead in seconds. 'I love you, Eddie!' she cried . . . then closed her eyes.

'Nina!' he shouted, but she didn't respond, instead using every scrap of willpower not to jump clear as the pillar finally touched her head. She flinched, but stayed in place. It ground relentlessly downwards, forcing her to bend, then crouch.

Eddie was still pleading for her to move and save herself, his voice becoming more strained as he too was forced down by the descending ceiling. But she could barely hear his words over her panicked breathing as she was pushed lower and lower, pain rising as she was squeezed between the unyielding stones—

Fear finally overcame her. The terrified animal part of her brain tried to break free – but too late. She couldn't escape, the falling column squeezing the air from her lungs, crushing her bones . . .

Something moved.

For a moment she thought the pillar had stopped. But the agonising pressure didn't lessen—

Realisation hit her. The *dais* was moving, the recessed disc being driven into the floor. Her own body was acting as a shock absorber, painfully taking the weight of the stone piston above – and transmitting it to the platform beneath her.

A waft of cool air blew around her. She was being pushed into another chamber below!

The column shuddered, then stopped with a crunch – and rose slightly. Nina slithered sideways, falling off the platform to flop on to a solid floor. Panting, she brought up her flashlight.

A tunnel led out of the new room. Off to one side, a flight of steps led upwards – to the antechamber in which her husband was trapped. 'Eddie?' she gasped.

'Nina?' His relieved and bewildered voice came from the top of the stairs. 'Where are you? I thought you'd been fucking squashed!'

'There's another room underneath the chamber.' She staggered up the stairs to emerge behind the circular antechamber. The pillar above Eddie was rising back to its original position, the Yorkshireman straightening beneath it. 'The platform I was standing on got pushed down into it. You were right.'

'About what?' He took hold of the bars, which to his surprise moved. The lock had been released, allowing the metal cage to rotate freely.

'About the mother. It was her *offer* of a sacrifice that mattered, not the sacrifice itself,' she said as he hauled the open section of the cage around. 'Her willingness to give up her son to save him ended up bringing them back together.'

'Just like this.' He stepped out and embraced her.

'Ow, ow,' she protested. 'Don't squeeze so hard! I just had a couple of tons of stone pressing down on my back!'

'It wasn't pressing down on your mouth, was it?'

'No, why?'

He kissed her. 'That's why.'

Relief flooded through her, though tempered by the knowledge that they were still in danger. 'There's an exit down there,' she told him. 'It must lead to the Mother of the Shamir.'

'Whatever that is.' Raised voices from the other side of the cage warned that their survival had been noticed. 'If they didn't still have Fortune and the others, I'd say we run on ahead and make sure Mukobo and those other bastards never get their hands on it. But . . .'

She nodded, grim. 'I know.'

'Chase!' the warlord shouted, directing his light through the bars. 'Dr Wilde! How did you get out?'

'Long story,' Nina said. 'But everyone can come through now. I think that once someone proves willing to sacrifice themself for someone else, the trap stops.'

Mukobo pulled at the bars, turning the cage. 'And the treasure?'

'At the end of the next tunnel, I guess.'

'Good. At last!' He entered the antechamber, keeping his gun on the couple. 'Where is that boy with the camera? I want him to film me as I find it!' Howie was pushed to the front of the group as Mukobo rotated the cage again and emerged from the enclosure. 'So, Dr Wilde, we have overcome the tests of King Solomon. And now, it is time to claim my reward!'

Eddie and Nina exchanged looks of despair, then started down the steps, the gloating warlord behind them.

19

The final tunnel was not long. 'Do you feel that?' said Ziff. 'There is a breeze.'

'Yeah,' Nina replied. 'But we must be almost in the heart of the palace, so I don't know where it's coming from.'

'We'll find out in a second,' said Eddie as they reached an elaborately carved archway. 'Doc, there's some more text. What does it say?'

Mukobo halted impatiently as Ziff read the inscriptions. 'Another message from Solomon,' he reported. 'No, actually . . . a *welcome*. "In reaching here, you have proven you possess the wisdom of Solomon. The Imashamir awaits you. Those who wish to use it, do so with the same wisdom."'

'Wisdom, *wisdom*,' scoffed Mukobo. 'A true leader knows that power is worth more than wisdom! And whatever Solomon hid here, I will now have its power!' He snapped his fingers at Howie, ordering the young man to film him, then marched through the entrance.

The others followed, torch beams sweeping outwards to probe the huge new chamber – and finding more than they had imagined. 'All right,' said Eddie, trying to hide his amazement. 'Wasn't expecting *this*.'

High above was the underside of the palace's vaulted roof, the dull expanse of lead camouflaged by a sweeping decorative filigree in gold leaf. The walls bore ornate pillars that Nina imagined were designed to evoke the original architecture of Zhakana before its fall.

But it was not what lay above that drew everyone's attention.

The pathway continued downwards – into a gaping chasm. Steeply sloping bridges criss-crossed the abyss, linked by equally precipitous stairways carved into the cliff faces on each side. Nina went to the edge and peered down. Structures were dimly visible on terraces far below. Whatever lay at the bottom was beyond the range of her flashlight, however.

There was something else too: not seen, but heard. Or *felt*. An unsettling vibration, just below the limit of hearing, but undeniably *there* . . .

She turned to Lydia. 'Do you hear that? Is it the same noise you picked up outside?'

The chance to focus upon something technical drew the other woman out of her shell-shocked lethargy. She donned her headphones, adjusting her equipment's controls. 'Yeah, I hear it,' she said. 'It's definitely the same sound – but it's much louder here.' She aimed her microphone into the chasm. 'It's coming from down there.'

'Then that is where we will go.' Mukobo went to the first bridge, then had second thoughts as he saw that not only was it very steep, but also lacked any kind of safety barriers. The only thing between a person traversing it and a very long fall was an ankle-high parapet with a deep groove carved into it. 'Dr Wilde!' he said. 'You are the archaeologist – go first and tell me what you see.'

'Gee, thanks,' she said, but the odd architectural feature had already caught her attention. There was a large stone bowl at its top, a small hole in the base feeding into the channel. Stacked near it were several pottery casks, narrow necks sealed with dark wax or tallow. She went to investigate them.

'Ah, Dr Wilde? The bridge is *that* way,' said Brice, pointing.

'You said you wanted me to tell you what I see,' she told the frowning Mukobo. 'And I want to see if this is another trap.' She examined the casks. One was cracked, stained where its contents had drained out. She cautiously probed inside, finding a sludgy residue. 'It's oil.'

'What is it for?' asked Fortune.

'I think it's how they illuminated this place. They poured oil into this big bowl here and let it drain down the gutters, then set it alight.'

'Ingenious,' said Brice, not sounding remotely impressed. 'Fortunately, lighting technology has advanced since Solomon's day.'

Mukobo shone an example at the bridge. 'You are wasting time. Now go.'

Nina reluctantly started over the crossing. With no guardrails, she quickly felt a dizzying sense of vertigo. She fixed her gaze upon its far end, taking the descent step by step. As she neared the chasm's other side, she realised it was not a natural feature – at least, not in its present form. There were patches of raw rock, but most of it seemed to have been carved out of the ground. By the natives of Zhakana, or those who came after them?

She stepped on to the ledge at the bridge's foot with great relief. 'It's safe.'

Mukobo led the others after her. She moved down the steps cut into the cliff to make room, looking back up at the bridge. It was an elegant arch, the stone blocks supporting their own weight just like the roof high above. Each piece had the same precision-cut appearance as those in the Palace Without Entrance and the First Temple – a level of accuracy far beyond what archaeologists had previously thought the people of that era capable of. The chasm had been excavated in the same way. Maybe there *was* something to the legend of the Shamir being able to split stone . . .

The rest of the group arrived. 'That noise is louder down here,' Lydia reported.

'I can tell,' said Eddie. 'Still can't really hear it, but it's putting my teeth on edge. Like when some arsehole in the downstairs apartment's got their bass turned right up.'

'But he didn't do it again after you spoke to him, did he?' Nina said with a half-smile. 'Well, I say "spoke", but I could hear you from *our* apartment!'

Brice peered into the rift, his expression thoughtful. 'Feels almost like an LRAD.'

'A what?'

'A sonic weapon – Long Range Acoustic Device. Ships use them to ward off pirates, but police and military use them as well for crowd control. They're non-lethal, but nobody stays around when one's pointed at them.'

Eddie nodded. 'I've heard 'em. The high-frequency ones give you a banging headache. The low-frequency ones . . . well, if you've got constipation, they'll shake you loose.'

The last Insekt Posse stragglers finally crossed the bridge. At Mukobo's urging, Nina again led the way downwards to another arched crossing. She shone her flashlight back into the abyss. There was water below, a shimmering dark pool occupying part of the chasm's foot. More structures were now also discernible, the largest overlooking the body of water and what appeared to be mine workings above its edge.

Another careful traversal of the next bridge was followed by a stretch of winding pathway, then a third crossing. They were now over a hundred feet below ground level, deep inside the rocky promontory on which the Palace Without Entrance stood. Despite that, the air felt fresh. There was ventilation even down here.

They continued downwards, reaching the first of the terraces running the cavern's width. It seemed like a village, dozens of small buildings packed tightly together. They had the feel of barracks, or dormitories; basic living quarters for those who worked at the bottom of the mine. Another flight of steps descended to the next relatively flat area. The structures here were larger, but squeezed just as closely together.

Nina wanted to explore the buildings, but suspected Solomon's treasure would be in the grandest edifice below – and that Mukobo would not indulge her professional urges. Instead, she pressed on. A broad staircase led to the lowest terrace.

The large structure she had seen from above took on form ahead. It was semicircular, the flat wall facing her and the curved one overlooking the bottom of the chasm. A wide doorway had Old Hebrew text above. 'David,' said Nina, pointing it out.

Ziff went to translate it. 'This is it,' said the Israeli. Despite the tense situation, he couldn't keep excitement from his voice. 'Whatever Solomon was protecting, it's in here. This is the Chamber of the Shamir.'

'What's that noise like now?' Eddie asked Lydia.

'Very strong,' the New Zealander replied. She crouched and put a hand to the stone floor. 'I mean, you can actually *feel* it through the rock now.'

'She's right,' said Brice. 'Philippe, I'd recommend caution. We don't know what we're dealing with.'

'Scared, are you?' said Eddie.

'Pragmatic,' the former agent shot back. 'I never get into a situation without having a way out. And since we don't know what's in there . . .'

'We will see now,' Mukobo said firmly. 'Boy! Come with me. Film everything.' He signalled for Howie to follow him into the building. The expedition members went with him, Luaba summoning some of the Insekt Posse as extra guards while the others remained outside.

Within was a large chamber. Openings in the curved wall provided a panoramic view over the bottom of the cavern. But all attention went to the room's contents, not what lay in the darkness beyond. 'Look at this!' gasped Ziff. 'This Hebrew word, it's a name – Makeda! This is the Queen of Sheba!'

Nina joined him to examine a statue, a tall, athletic African woman with her hair in long braids down her back. 'Wow. After three thousand years, we finally find out what she looked like . . .'

'Impressive – and I don't only mean the quality of the workmanship,' said the old man with a small but cheeky smile as he admired the figure.

'It is just stone,' said Mukobo dismissively. 'But this – *this* is real treasure!' He went to a pedestal across the chamber. On it sat a bust, the head and shoulders of an unknown man cast in gold and inset with threads of silver and precious stones.

Nina gave it an analytical look. 'It's probably a relic of the city's original inhabitants. The art style is a lot like the statue at the end of the first challenge.'

'I do not care about that. But it must be worth millions of dollars. And it is mine!' He indicated other wonders nearby. 'And so is this – so is everything here!' He turned to Brice. 'They will give the LEC the money to buy more weapons, *powerful* weapons. You and your people can provide them?'

The Englishman nodded. 'Of course. I can arrange for someone with the right contacts to appraise these.' One of the Insekt Posse poked at a ruby, seeing if it was loose; Brice clicked his fingers to draw his attention, then shook his head. 'There are collectors who will pay much more for ancient relics than you could get for the raw gold and gems,' he told Mukobo. 'A little patience will get you a lot more money.'

The warlord seemed conflicted, but greed won out over expediency. '*Laissez-nous seuls*,' he barked. The man hurriedly withdrew.

Nina went to one of the windows. The pool lay beyond the mine workings, its surface rippling. Numerous streams trickled down the rock walls into it, but its level was holding constant rather than rising with the flow. 'This must be what's feeding the waterfalls,' she said, remembering the cascades falling from the promontory. She aimed her light around the water's edge, spotting openings in the walls. 'Looks like they dug flood-control shafts so this place always stayed above water level.'

'The fresh air must be coming through them,' said Ziff, joining her. He redirected his beam to the excavations. 'What were they mining?'

'I don't know.' Their lights picked out a dense vein of some glinting greenish mineral in the exposed stone. 'Jade, maybe? Or malachite?'

'Jade would be valuable, but so valuable that Solomon built all this to protect it?' He shook his head.

Eddie, meanwhile, had gone to the room's centre. A broad stone plinth was home to a dull grey box, easily overlooked amongst the glinting treasures around it. 'What's in this?' he asked.

Nina followed him. The box was about two feet long and a foot wide and high, its top held in place by bronze clasps. 'There's nothing on the box itself, but it's been given pride of place . . . and it's made of lead,' she said with sudden realisation. 'David – a lead box. What does that sound like?'

Ziff hurried over. 'This is the Chamber of the Shamir, so – could it be?' He reached for the container – then hesitated. 'If it is, then opening it could be dangerous.'

'What do you mean?' demanded Mukobo.

'According to Hebrew mythology,' Nina told him, 'King Solomon kept the Shamir in a lead box, because it was the only thing that could contain its power.'

'Let's not forget that the Hebrew mythology about King Solomon also features talking eagles and magic carpets,' said Brice, scathing. 'I doubt we have to worry about the wrath of God if we open it. After all,' he added to Nina, 'you yourself opened the Ark of the Covenant without being struck dead.'

'Yeah, but lead?' said Eddie. 'I know we did that test with the camera, but it still says one thing to me, and that's radiation. I wouldn't want to be the bugger who opens it.'

'That's a shame,' said the ex-MI6 man. 'Because it's an excellent suggestion.'

Mukobo exposed his teeth in a humourless grin as he raised his gun. 'Open it, Chase. When the rest of us are outside, of course.'

Eddie sighed. 'Me and my big fucking mouth!'

The others hastened to the entrance, Mukobo keeping his weapon aimed at the Yorkshireman as he retreated. 'Do it now, Chase,' he ordered.

Nina watched over the warlord's shoulder. Eddie gave her a look that was part-way between reassurance and resignation, then released the clasps and opened the lid.

To his relief, he didn't instantly vaporise or explode into flame. He raised the lead slab higher.

'What is it?' Mukobo demanded. 'Chase! What have you found?'

'If your idea of treasure is big green pointy stone things,' Eddie replied, 'then it's your lucky day!'

Puzzled, the Congolese returned to the chamber, Nina and the others behind him. The metal casket was lined with the desiccated remnants of a rough fabric. Laid amongst them was exactly what Eddie had described: a horn-shaped piece of glittering greenish mineral about eighteen inches in length. 'It's the same stuff they were mining,' she said.

'It's more than that,' said Ziff, awed. 'It's the Shamir! The lead box, the wool – it's exactly as described in the Babylonian Talmud.'

'I thought the Shamir was a little worm,' said Eddie.

'That was Solomon's Shamir. But there were supposedly

others – Moses used one to engrave the names of the high priests of the twelve tribes of Israel into gemstones. This one, though . . . it is much bigger. Maybe it is the "Mother of the Shamir"?'

'No,' Nina said thoughtfully, going to the windows and playing her torch beam over the open mine. '*That's* the Mother of the Shamir, down there.' She pointed at the exposed green vein in the rock. 'It gave birth to the others.'

Ziff nodded. 'That would make sense, yes. But what *is* it?'

'I don't know.' She turned – and her light caught something on the plinth's side that had previously been hidden in shadow. 'But that might tell us!'

Both archaeologists hurried to it. Their flashlights played over more Hebrew inscriptions. 'Ah!' exclaimed Ziff. 'Another message from Solomon!'

Mukobo came to see. 'What does it say?'

'Just a moment, let me read . . .' The Israeli fell silent as he absorbed the lengthy passage. 'This is one of several Shamirs, yes – the largest of them all. Solomon says it was the source of the lost empire's power, and they used it to destroy their enemies.'

'How?' asked Brice.

'I'm not sure. This line here,' he tapped the stone, 'says "its gaze fell upon them, and their walls broke and fell, and their weapons burst asunder".'

'Not seeing any eyes on it to gaze with,' noted Eddie. 'Unless it once had some googly ones stuck on.'

'It's the same way the Shamir's power was described in Hebrew mythology, though,' said Nina. 'Solomon built the First Temple by using its gaze to cut the stones.'

'There's more,' said Ziff, still reading. 'There's a name here, a place: Jericho.'

Surprise from his audience. 'As in, famous for its walls?' asked Eddie.

'It could be. This says the people of Zhakana took the

Shamir as far as Jericho, and used it to bring down their walls.'
He frowned. 'Although there's no archaeological evidence that
Jericho had any major defensive structures at the time of the
Battle of Jericho – or even that the Battle of Jericho ever really
took place.'

'There wasn't any solid evidence of the empire of Sheba until
we found it,' Nina pointed out, glancing at the statue of Makeda.
'And considering how old Zhakana is, it might not even be the
same Jericho. Names and events get muddled over time.'

'This is all absolutely fascinating,' said Brice dismissively, 'but
it still doesn't explain what this thing is, or how it could be a
weapon. It's just a stone.'

'And a ruby's just a ruby, until you focus a laser beam through
it,' she replied. 'I've seen previously unknown substances with
weird properties before.'

'Quite a few times,' added Eddie.

'If it is a weapon,' Ziff went on, 'then it destroyed its creators
as well as their enemies. Solomon said that according to the
legends of Sheba, "their greed for more Shamirs caused their
own walls to fall, and then their people. Those who were not
turned barren gave birth to accursed monsters, twisted and vile.
And so ended the great empire of Zhakana, reduced to the City
of the Damned. To those who wish to use the Shamir: heed the
wisdom of Solomon lest the same happen to you."'

Eddie regarded the mysterious stone unhappily. 'Okay,
seriously: that thing sounds like some kind of neutron bomb. It's
probably as radioactive as a Chernobyl meat pie.'

'Radiation can't cut stones,' said Brice firmly. 'If it was some
kind of weapon, then that's not how it worked.'

'Then we shall find out!' declared Mukobo. 'We can buy guns
and rocket launchers with the treasure here. But if this stone
really is a weapon, then I will use it on my enemies. *Their* walls
will fall – and their heads!' He shouted a command, and the rest

of the Insekt Posse came in. 'Take everything to the boats. They will help carry it,' he said of the prisoners.

Luaba gestured for Eddie and Fortune to pick up the Shamir's casket. 'No, no,' said the warlord. 'I do not trust them. Especially not Chase!' He pointed at two of the militia. '*Vous, amenez-le.*'

The pair went to the plinth and tried to pick up the box, only to strain in surprise at its weight. Grunting, they hauled it off the plinth. 'That'll be tricky to get up the ladder to the surface,' said Brice.

'Then we leave the box,' Mukobo replied. Another instruction, and the men gratefully returned the case to its original position before removing the Shamir. Both looked unsettled at its touch.

'What did he say?' asked Nina as one of the men expressed his discomfort.

'He thought it was . . . electric,' said the warlord, himself perturbed. 'But now it has stopped.'

The chamber's valuables were gathered. 'We will come back to see if there is more,' Mukobo proclaimed. 'Now, go! *Allez, vite!*'

The journey to the surface was laborious, the weight of Mukobo's prizes slowing progress. The Insekt Posse were elated by the riches they had found, but the limited conversation amongst the captives was far more muted. 'I do not know how we can get out of this,' Fortune murmured to Eddie as the group bunched up at a bridge.

'Me neither,' the Yorkshireman replied. 'Even if we had a big enough distraction to grab some guns, they've still got hostages.'

'Then we need to get our people away from them.'

'I know. But how? I don't—'

Luaba struck his rifle's butt against Eddie's back. 'Shut up! Move away from him.' Shooting the hulking bodyguard an angry glare, Eddie retreated from his friend.

They continued upwards, at last reaching the top of the chasm and re-entering the palace's tunnels. The three traps were still inactive, everyone passing through safely. Finally, they arrived at the shaft to the roof. 'Go up and get rope,' Mukobo ordered. 'We will use it to lift the treasure.' The more weighty items were gratefully set down, then some of the Insekt Posse scurried towards daylight.

Nina felt a sick tension, knowing that her usefulness to the warlord would soon be over. But there was something else adding to her nervousness – and it was growing stronger. 'Lydia,' she whispered. 'Is your mic on?'

The New Zealander still had her sound equipment. 'Yeah,' she said sullenly. 'Why?'

'That weird noise – is it still there?'

The other woman reluctantly donned her headphones. Her expression became one of wary curiosity. 'Yeah – but it's changed,' she said, adjusting dials. 'The frequency's different . . . it's rising. And so's the intensity.'

'It's getting louder?' Nina's eyes went to the Shamir. The horn-shaped stone rested at the bottom of the shaft, light from high above reflecting faintly from its green surface. She surreptitiously put her palm against the wall beside her. The sensation was almost *disturbing*, as if the rock was buzzing, squirming under her touch.

'You feel it too?' Eddie quietly asked.

'Yeah. I don't know what's causing it . . . but I can take a pretty good guess.' She eyed the Shamir again. 'It started when they put it in the light. Maybe it's reacting to it?'

'Maybe, but then why would Solomon need to line the place with lead? If he'd wanted to keep it in the dark, just wrapping it in a blanket would've done the job.'

They were not the only ones feeling the unsettling effect. The Insekt Posse shifted with growing restlessness. There was considerable relief when ropes eventually dropped from above. 'Take up the treasure – start with that one,' ordered Mukobo, pointing at the golden bust before turning to two of his men. 'You and you, go up and help from the top. Take them with you,' he added, indicating Ziff and Lydia.

'What about us?' Eddie demanded.

'You, Chase? You are not leaving my sight. Until I am finished with you.' He smiled, but there was no mistaking the threat.

Militia above and below them, Lydia and Ziff ascended while the bust was secured. Luaba and his other men guarded Nina and Eddie as Mukobo triumphantly watched its journey towards the light.

Brice, meanwhile, had turned his attention to the Shamir. He cautiously touched it, then looked at Nina. 'As a rule, rocks don't hum, so clearly this is no ordinary rock. You said you'd seen similar things before – what were they?'

'Where to start?' she replied. 'A crystal that transforms mercury to gold; a meteorite fragment that pumps out enormous amounts of deadly gas when it's exposed to air; an underground lake of poison that mutates DNA. I've even seen stones levitated by the earth's magnetic field. I've done a lot of research into how they could have worked, and the impact they had on ancient cultures. They've all become part of myth and legend – just like the Shamir.'

'So you think this really is a weapon?'

'I don't know *what* it is. And to be honest, I think it would be better for the world if we didn't try to find out.'

He chuckled. 'Your entire career has been based on unearthing things that would have been better left buried. I know that the IHA's real purpose wasn't to protect archaeological finds – it was to *control* them, make sure your discoveries never fell into the wrong hands. But wouldn't the world have been safer if you'd never found them at all?'

'Wouldn't the world be safer without you selling guns to people like him?' Eddie countered, nodding towards Mukobo.

'That's always been your problem, hasn't it, Chase?' Brice's voice oozed condescension. 'You really do want to save the entire world, when frankly there are large parts of it that don't deserve to be "saved". We need forest fires every so often to clear the rotten wood.' He regarded the warlord, though his expression was more calculating than admiring. 'I'm just giving Philippe a match.'

'Or a flamethrower,' said Nina.

One by one the treasures were removed, Howie and Fortune also climbing, until only the Shamir remained. 'Bring it up behind us,' ordered Mukobo. 'We will climb out now. It will be good,' he told Brice, 'to be in the light again. There is something about this place that is . . . *wrong.*' He started to climb the stone ladder, Brice behind him. Luaba waited until they were clear before gesturing with his gun for Nina and Eddie to ascend. Resigned, they followed their captors to the top of the tower.

They finally emerged into daylight. Shafts of sun penetrated the leafy canopy overhead, but the atmosphere was still oppressive – all the more so as they saw Mukobo's look of malevolent expectancy. The only thing keeping the warlord from killing them both on the spot was the prospect of making the York-shireman suffer first. 'Go down,' he told them.

Nina looked over the tower's side. Some of the Insekt Posse were on the palace roof, lowering the stolen treasures to the ground. Her companions were already below, reunited with Fisher, Rivero and Paris under armed guard. She started to climb down as the men at the top of the shaft began to haul up the Shamir. Eddie followed once she reached the roof, then the couple descended to the foot of the wall.

'You are still alive,' said Paris, relieved, as they reached the other prisoners.

'For now,' Eddie replied. 'Probably not for much longer unless we can do something, though.'

'Are you okay?' Nina asked Paris and Fisher. Both men's severed arms had been crudely bandaged, spots of blood soaking through.

The director listlessly raised his head. 'Yeah. Great. As good as can be expected considering I had my goddamn hand chopped off.' A flicker of anger broke through his numbed mask, directed not at Nina but Luaba as he climbed down behind her.

Lydia was with the American, trembling as she held him. 'What's going to happen now?'

'I would imagine nothing good,' said Fortune. 'Unless you have any ideas, Eddie?'

'I've got loads,' he said with a bleak smile. 'Problem is, they all start with me having an AK.' He eyed their guards' weapons.

'We think alike, my friend.' Fortune too managed a small grin, which vanished as Mukobo and Brice reached the ground. Above them, the men on the roof readied the Shamir for the final stage of its descent.

'How can you make jokes?' demanded Lydia, starting to cry again. 'We're – we're going to die!'

'We're not dead yet,' Nina reminded her. 'There's always a chance, we just have to be ready for it.'

'Fight to the end,' Eddie added.

The sound woman was not cheered. 'Oh, stupid platitudes, that's just what we need!'

'Better than just giving up,' snapped Nina – before something made her pause.

She wasn't sure what it was at first. But then she caught the confusion of the men lowering the Shamir. She was not the only one to have felt it . . .

'Lydia,' she hurriedly said, 'your sound gear – check it, quick.'

'What good's that going to do?' asked the New Zealander.

'Just do it! That weird noise – what's it doing?'

Lydia reluctantly regarded her sound mixer . . . then reacted in surprise. She hurriedly donned her headphones. 'It's – it's getting stronger,' she announced. 'A *lot* stronger.'

Rivero cautiously pressed a hand against the palace. 'I can feel it! The wall's . . . *humming.*'

Nina looked back at the descending stone. 'It's the Shamir, it must be!'

The same thought had occurred to others. Mukobo regarded it with alarm, then marched to his prisoners, stabbing an angry finger at the redhead. 'What is happening? If you have tricked me—'

'I don't know!' Nina protested.

A noise became audible, an almost impossibly deep rumbling. 'It's really spiking!' said Lydia. 'The intensity's climbing, it's shooting through the roof!'

A moment later, her words became literal – as an entire section of the palace exploded.

20

The Shamir's wider end had scraped down the palace wall while it was lowered, cracks appearing in the pale blocks as the strange sound reached a crescendo – then stone shattered as if blasted by tons of dynamite.

Debris bombarded those below. The prisoners, against the wall to one side, were the least exposed – but the Insekt Posse nearer the treasures took the full force. One man was smashed flat by a flying hunk of rock as others were pummelled by smaller pieces.

Brice took a blow to the shoulder that knocked him down – and a lump the size of a fist struck Mukobo's head. He fell.

Part of the roof collapsed into the widening hole. The men above plunged screaming after it. The Shamir tumbled out of the swelling dust cloud to land in the rubble not far from the prisoners. It stopped with its blunt end pointing towards the jungle. A militia man staggered upright in front of it, raising his gun—

A shrill buzz, the man reacting as if his rifle had been electrified – then the weapon *shattered*, metal shredding his arms and chest in a storm of razor-sharp shrapnel. Behind him, the ancient bricks of a ruined wall burst apart.

'Jesus!' Eddie gasped. How, he had no idea, but the Shamir was shooting out some invisible force with catastrophic effects on steel and stone.

It didn't seem to affect people – but he saw something that *would*. One of the fallen guards had dropped his Kalashnikov.

Eddie dived for it. He snatched up the rifle just as the man lunged to reclaim his weapon—

Too slow. The bullet punched through the guard's outstretched palm and hit him in the face, blowing a bloody chunk out of his cheekbone.

Eddie jumped up. 'Fortune!'

The Congolese was already moving, delivering a crushing karate chop to another reeling militia man's throat. The youth staggered back, choking. Fortune kicked his rifle out of his hands, snatching it from the air in a single smooth movement and whipping it around to shoot him.

'Nice!' Eddie shouted. He was about to tell his companions to run for the river when he saw some of the Insekt Posse who had taken loot to the boats hurrying back uphill. 'Get inside!' he ordered instead.

'Inside where?' Nina yelled back – then she saw what he meant. The dust was clearing, revealing a gash in the palace's wall.

Eddie gunned down another militia man, then pointed at the hole. 'Everyone *go*!'

Nina started towards what she fervently hoped was sanctuary. The other expedition members followed – with one exception. 'David!' she cried, seeing the Israeli running not for the opening but the nearest dead enemy. 'Come on!'

Ziff didn't waver, snatching up the fallen man's Kalashnikov – *then* he changed direction, arcing towards the hole as he loosed a couple of shots. One of the Insekt Posse scrambled for cover as a round narrowly missed his head.

Eddie started after Nina as Mukobo sat up with a hand to his bleeding head. The warlord spotted the former SAS man and groped for his golden revolver—

The Yorkshireman snapped the AK around at him and pulled the trigger, making Mukobo flinch – but nothing happened. 'Shit!'

Kalashnikovs were famed for their ability to keep working under the most extreme conditions, but they were not infallible, and this one was both old and ill-kept by someone more concerned with looking tough than proper maintenance. By the time he cleared the jam, Mukobo would have shot him—

Instead he charged, swinging the rifle like a club.

The Congolese had just drawn his revolver when the AK smacked against his head. He yelled in pain, falling again. Eddie grabbed the Magnum, jamming its muzzle against Mukobo's cheek. 'Fortune! Grab this arsehole!'

Fortune didn't need to ask why, knowing that the militia leader was more valuable as a hostage than a corpse. He let off several more rounds to force the Insekt Posse into cover, then he and Eddie dragged the stunned Mukobo after the others.

The Yorkshireman glanced back, seeing Brice dart towards the remains of a building. Eddie raised the revolver, but his target had disappeared before he could draw a bead on him.

Out of sight – but not out of hearing. The ex-MI6 agent shouted in rapid-fire French. Eddie only understood a few words, but one was perfectly clear: *Mukobo*. He was warning the Insekt Posse that their leader had been taken . . . and preparing a counter-attack.

The others were now inside the new opening, Nina waiting anxiously at the threshold. Eddie was sure the gap was defensible – if he and his comrades had enough time to secure their positions. But Brice was not going to give them that time, already barking more instructions over the Shamir's basso growl—

The Shamir. It was only yards away . . .

'Get him inside,' he told Fortune – before letting go of Mukobo and running for the glinting green stone.

He shoved the revolver into his waistband as he reached the bizarre artefact. Its destructive effect was confined to a fairly tight beam, the now-crumbled wall the only hard object that had been in its path—

That changed as he hauled up the Shamir and swept it across the ruins.

The sensation was like holding a pounding jackhammer multiplied a hundredfold, nausea filling him as his bones shuddered and his teeth seemed about to shatter in his skull. But the effect on everything before him was far more severe. Stones detonated like grenades, a wall sheltering one of the militia flying apart as if swept away by a giant's invisible hand – and the man behind it falling with a horrible scream as his rifle exploded into jagged shrapnel.

Eddie forced the Shamir around like a fire hose. The Insekt Posse scattered, another man dying in a shower of blood and ripped flesh as his rifle blew apart in his hands. Others realised the danger and flung away their weapons as they fled, the Shamir's otherwise devastating effect causing them no apparent harm. Some of the discarded guns disintegrated as the beam caught them.

He was hunting for one particular target, though. Fighting the urge to throw down the Shamir before his bones shook apart, Eddie swung it towards the ruin where Brice was hiding.

Stonework shattered, the entire front wall collapsing with a pounding crash. The other sides survived mere moments before they too fell, the strange stone's relentless power tearing them apart—

Brice sprang out from his toppling cover and ran for the palace's corner. Eddie tracked him, blasting a low wall to pieces in the other Englishman's wake. The spy's gun was in his hand – but he flung it ahead as the disruptive effect caught up. The pistol spun out of sight.

Eddie stopped as Brice reached the palace wall, not wanting to further damage the building in which his companions were sheltering. Instead he resumed his sweep over the ruins, forcing the remaining members of the militia to retreat as he backed towards the broken opening.

Fortune was waiting just inside it, covering him with his AK while Ziff held Mukobo at gunpoint. Nina was behind them. 'Eddie, don't bring it in here!' she cried. 'The whole place'll collapse on top of us!' The remains of the roof were hanging precariously atop sagging sheets of lead.

'Long as I don't point it upwards, we should be okay!' he replied. 'It's like a torch beam, it only comes out of one end.'

'That is no torch,' objected Fortune. He searched for targets, but the militia had fled in panic. 'You should leave it out there to keep them away.'

Eddie ignored him, stepping awkwardly up the piled rubble. He passed under the drooping lead canopy – and to everyone's surprise, the noise from the Shamir noticeably lessened. He retreated still farther. The vibration eased with each step. 'It's stopping!'

He realised he was in the passage leading to the first chamber. Debris had blocked the stone ladder, but Paris and the others had already safely reached the room at the other end. The Shamir's sound faded away. It was still humming, but at a much lower level. He cautiously aimed the end of the horn at the strewn debris outside the entrance. Nothing happened. 'Okay, whatever powers this thing, it's not getting enough of it any more.'

'The light?' Fortune wondered.

'Maybe some sort of radiation, if the lead's blocking it,' said Nina. She warily touched the stone. 'It's still getting *something*, or it wouldn't be buzzing like that.' She saw an exposed layer of torn lead inside the broken wall. 'If it's completely surrounded by lead, maybe it'll stop.'

'Doc, if he moves, shoot him,' Eddie told Ziff, who was still guarding Mukobo. 'Nice work out there, by the way.'

'I did my military service like every Israeli,' Ziff replied with a small but proud smile. 'I remember how to use a gun.'

'Glad to hear it.'

The warlord lay on the floor, a hand to his head. 'You will die for this, Chase,' he growled. 'All of you will die! I will gut you, I will—'

Eddie kicked him hard in the stomach. 'Shut up. We got anything we can tie this shithead up with?'

Nina looked towards the first chamber. 'All the crew's gear is still in there. There might be something we can use.'

'Great.' He checked outside to make sure the Insekt Posse were not returning, then assessed his surroundings. The ragged opening was about six feet above ground level. It was a choke point; at most two people could fit through at once, and fallen stones would provide good cover for the defenders. Fortune had already taken up position in one well-protected spot, with a clear line of fire over the ruins. 'Fortune, Doc, keep an eye on things here. We've only got limited ammo so don't shoot unless you have to, but don't let any of those bastards get too close.'

Fortune nodded. 'If any raise their heads too high, they will not live long enough to regret it.'

Eddie put down the Shamir, then unslung his AK and ejected the magazine, tugging the charging handle until the jammed round finally spat free. He retrieved it and examined the cartridge. It wasn't damaged, so he thumbed it back into the mag and reloaded. 'Spare if you need it,' he told Fortune, leaning it against the wall and drawing Mukobo's revolver. 'I'll go and tie up this arsehole.' He pointed the golden gun at its former owner. 'All right, move.' When the warlord didn't rise at once, he added: 'I had two chances to kill you before, in Rwanda and Tenerife, but I didn't take 'em. That was a mistake. So I *will* fucking shoot you dead if you piss me off.'

Mukobo glared angrily at him, but eventually looked away

under the former soldier's stony gaze. 'This is not over, Chase,' he muttered as he stood.

Eddie didn't reply, instead directing his prisoner down the passage. Nina collected the Shamir and followed them. 'So the bad guys can't get in here, that's good,' she said quietly, 'but how do we get *out*?'

Again, he did not answer.

'Luaba!' Brice shouted, finding the big man in frantic discussion with some of the Insekt Posse. 'Over here!'

The militia had retreated to a position in the ruins beyond the expedition's camp, but it had not been an orderly withdrawal. Luaba had been forced to fire a few shots over the heads of his panicked men to stop them from fleeing to the boats. He gave the Englishman an angry look, but after a moment reluctantly joined him. 'What do you want?' he demanded in French.

Brice replied fluently in kind. 'They've got Philippe – Chase took him inside.'

'And what are we supposed to do about it? That thing, that stone – it's like a tank gun!'

'So you're just going to *abandon* him? Without Philippe, the LEC and the Insekt Posse will be crushed. Any chance of independence for eastern Congo will be gone.'

'I know,' said Luaba, frustrated. 'But we can't help him without reinforcements! There's an LEC camp in the jungle about fifteen kilometres south-east of here; we can reach it by river, but it'll take most of the day to get there and back. Even if we leave guards here, they might still escape. Especially if they use that thing again.'

Brice contemplated the situation. 'This camp – do they have a radio?'

'Yes. But we don't, not any more. Philippe had it!'

'I can take care of that. Chase's people had a satellite phone.

All I need is your people's radio frequency, and I can reach them.'

'How?'

'I have friends,' was the smug reply. 'Bring me the phone, and I'll get you through.' Luaba was dubious, even suspicious, but still called to one of his men to retrieve the satphone. 'Oh, and if they have grenades and explosives?' he added with a sly smile. 'Tell them to bring them. All of them.'

21

'Okay,' announced Howie, 'that's everything backed up.' He disconnected a solid-state hard drive from one of the team's laptops and returned it to a waterproof bag.

'Oh, that's great,' said Lydia sarcastically. 'We're going to die, but at least all our data'll be intact!'

'We're not going to die,' said Eddie wearily. They had been inside the palace for some hours now, and the New Zealander's negativity was like a wet cloud filling the first chamber, fraying already strained tempers still further.

But if she was fraying them, Mukobo was actively tearing. 'Oh, but you are,' he intoned. Eddie had tied his hands behind his back and dumped him in a corner with a promise that if he tried to leave it, he would be shot. The warlord had taken him at his word – but that hadn't stopped him from making the occasional threat. 'My people will come for me, and when they do, you will *beg* for—'

He broke off with a pained gasp as Eddie delivered another savage kick to his stomach. 'I'm getting pretty fucking tired of this, Mucky. Another word, and I *will* just shoot you.'

Even winded, Mukobo still managed to strain out a retort. 'You would kill me for talking, Chase? And I thought you believed yourself a good man, a man of honour. Where is your honour if you are afraid of mere words?'

'I'm not bothered about words,' Eddie snapped. 'I'm bothered that you actually *mean* them.'

The warlord's lips curled into a mocking smile. 'Ah. You *are*

260

afraid. So afraid that you do not dare even use the word.' He raised his voice to address the others. 'And this is your protector? A coward who is scared of the words of a bound and helpless man?'

'Yeah, whatever.' The Yorkshireman turned away, fuming inwardly that Mukobo had called his bluff. Both men knew that for the team to have any hope of leaving the City of the Damned alive, they would need to use the militia leader as a bargaining chip.

'Hey, Howie,' said Rivero. The cameraman's wounds had been cleaned and rebandaged as best as the team could manage. 'You got my camera there?'

Howie brought the Sony to him. 'What do you want that for?' asked Fisher. The director was huddled with Lydia, his left arm folded over the stump of the right as if hiding it could negate what had happened.

'I'm gonna do my job,' Rivero told him. 'I want the world to know what happened to us. If I die here, then maybe the footage'll still get back to civilisation. And if we *do* get out . . .'

'You've got something that might win you an award,' Lydia noted, voice cutting.

'Not what's at the front of my mind, but hey, if it does that'd be cool.'

Fisher chuckled, without any humour. 'Well, if an opportunity comes, I guess you've got to grab it with both hands.' A long sigh. 'Get it?'

'Jesus, Steven,' said Lydia quietly.

'If you let me go,' said Mukobo, 'that hand will be the last thing you all lose. You will go free.'

The blonde raised her head. 'Really?'

'All I ask is that you give Chase to me. The rest of you can leave.'

'Don't listen to him,' said Eddie. 'This twat doesn't know mercy. He probably doesn't even know *merci*.'

'Think about it,' Mukobo went on. 'You would return safely to your homes, to your families. You would even have your television show. Perhaps you really will win awards, no? You would be famous, even rich.'

'Enough of this bollocks,' said Eddie, not liking that some of the documentary crew – Lydia foremost, but even Rivero – seemed to be considering the warlord's proposal. He pointed the revolver at Mukobo. 'Get your arse up.'

'Where am I going?' asked the Congolese.

'Long term? Hell. Short term, somewhere you can't stir the shit.' Keeping his gun trained on Mukobo, the Yorkshireman went to the passage. 'How are things out there?' he called.

Fortune had remained on guard at the entrance, though Paris had taken over from Ziff. Despite the loss of his hand, the mercenary had assured Eddie he could still use a gun, resting the Kalashnikov's wooden foregrip in the crook of his right elbow. 'Quiet here,' the scruffy man replied.

'I have seen a couple of scouts in the ruins,' Fortune added, 'but nobody has dared come close. They probably still think we have the Shamir with us.'

'Maybe we should've kept it up here,' suggested Howie. 'Guns are one thing, but that was like a death ray.'

'Nina thought it was best to put it back in its box, and considering what it can do, she's probably right,' Eddie told him. He did not entirely agree with her – his own opinion could have been decided by a coin toss – but had decided that presenting a united front was the only way to hold the already fragile group together. 'If we need it, we can get it.'

'Sure, so long as we don't need it in a hurry,' sniped Lydia. 'Since it's all the way down in the damn basement!'

Mukobo was now standing. 'You see? If you trust in Chase, he will get you all killed. He cannot save you. Only I can. Let me go, and—'

Eddie pointed the Magnum at his head and thumbed back the hammer. 'Move it. Through there.' He nodded towards the booby-trapped tunnel. 'Don't tempt me to turn that thing back on while you're inside it.'

Mukobo reluctantly set off, giving the other expedition members a last meaningful look. 'Remember what I said.'

Eddie collected a torch and followed him. 'Fortune, Paris?' he shouted. 'Keep an eye on things here.' He hoped it was clear that he meant inside the palace as well as out.

'We will, Eddie,' Fortune assured him.

Keeping Mukobo at gunpoint, he headed deeper into the building. 'Do you really think you will get out of here alive, Chase?' said the warlord as they crossed through the second chamber. 'You are a man of violence, as am I. We both know how this will end for you. Whether your friends meet the same end is your choice.'

'Yeah, maybe I *am* a man of violence,' Eddie replied, angered, 'but the difference is that I only use it if I have to. You use it because you fucking get off on it, you sick bastard.'

Mukobo shrugged. 'I use it because it achieves what I desire. As does every true ruler. That you do not understand this is why you were always a follower, and not a leader. Even in the SAS, you were only a common soldier, *Corporal* Chase. And when you became a mercenary, you again worked for other men, to achieve their goals. And now . . . ha! Your wife gives the commands. Where she goes, you follow.'

'You can shut the fuck up about my wife,' Eddie growled. 'And I was a sergeant, actually.'

'Until you were demoted.'

He frowned. 'Brice been telling you about me, has he?'

They reached the third of Solomon's challenges, Eddie ushering the Congolese into the cage before entering and rotating it so they could pass through. 'Mr Brice has been very informative,' said Mukobo. 'I know all about you, Chase.'

The Yorkshireman tried to conceal his discomfort at the revelation. 'Great, can you tell me my Facebook password? I forgot it ages ago. Now shut up, or you'll go down to the bottom of the cave the quick way.'

Mukobo fell silent, though he clearly considered himself the victor in their little war of words. They entered the great cavern and picked their way down the steep steps. Lights were visible at the bottom, voices becoming audible as they neared the Chamber of the Shamir. 'Nina?' Eddie called as he approached.

Nina came to the doorway, concern on her face as she saw who was with him. 'What's going on? Is everything okay upstairs?'

'Brought him down here before he offers Lydia thirty pieces of silver,' he replied, pushing Mukobo inside. Ziff looked up in surprise from an inscription.

'I don't think she'd take it. Not after what he did to Steven.'

'Well, I wasn't going to give her the chance.' He flicked the gun towards a high-backed stone seat. 'Sit down, dickhead. No, arms over the top,' he added as the warlord sat. 'I'm going to tie you to it.'

Mukobo grimaced as he forced his bound arms over its unyielding back, then awkwardly lowered himself. 'You really are afraid of me, aren't you, Chase?' he sneered as Eddie took a strap from one of the tripod lamps that had been set up in the room and used it to secure him to the throne-like chair. 'I am already bound – what could I possibly do?'

'More than you can now,' said the Yorkshireman as he pulled the restraint tight. Mukobo held in a grunt of pain. 'Hurts? Tough shit.'

Ziff regarded the new arrival with unease. 'Isn't there anywhere else you could keep him? We were working in here. And making good progress too.'

'Oh, sorry, Doc,' Eddie said with pointed sarcasm. 'Is the civil war interfering with your archaeology?'

The Israeli scowled at him over his glasses. 'That was uncalled for.'

'So was this fucking maniac chopping off people's hands.'

'Eddie,' Nina chided. 'I'm sorry, David.'

The older archaeologist shook his head, then headed for the exit. 'I need a rest anyway. Let me know when I can get back to work without any . . . distractions.'

The redhead watched him leave, then turned to her husband with an exasperated breath. 'Dammit, Eddie.'

'Well, I'm right. We've got more important things to worry about than reading Solomon's blog.'

'Actually, I'm not sure if that's true,' she told him. 'David managed to translate quite a lot of the text in here. We found out *why* Solomon built the Palace Without Entrance, for a start.' She went to one of the inscriptions on the rear wall.

Eddie joined her, positioning himself so he could still observe the African. 'To piss off door-to-door salesmen?'

'Not exactly.' She indicated a particular passage. 'This describes what he was told by Makeda and the historians of Sheba about the people who once lived here. The mine down there' – a glance towards the excavations below – 'was literally the source of the empire's power. The Mother of the Shamir is a vein of . . . well, they didn't know exactly what it was, and nor do we. I've been wondering if it's related to the Sky Stone from Atlantis, or the meteoric material that became part of the prophecy in the Book of Revelation: an arrival from the wider universe. Or maybe it's produced by the earth itself, like eitr or the water from the Spring of Immortality. Either way, it's something beyond conventional science that we don't fully understand yet.'

'We seem to find a lot of stuff like that,' Eddie noted wryly.

'But even if they didn't know what the Shamir *was*, they knew what it could *do*. Blow shit up, in this case.'

'Yeah – and extremely well. The bigger the piece, the more extreme the effect. The Shamir that Solomon used to build the First Temple was tiny, but it could still split stone and metal. That one, though?' She turned towards the altar, where the Shamir had been returned to its lead box. 'Well, you saw for yourself. The story of the Battle of Jericho from the Bible, where Joshua used a horn to blow down the city's walls? I think that's what we've found.'

'I thought you two said this place was much older than that.'

'The stories were probably conflated over time, one mythology absorbed into another. Like the way the story of the Great Flood long pre-dates Hebrew lore. But once the people here found the mineral vein, the Mother of the Shamir, they used the pieces they were able to break off against their enemies. They got greedy, though.' She gestured at the mine beyond the windows. 'They wanted more Shamirs, bigger – and more powerful – ones. So they dug out this whole place to make the mineral vein easier to reach, built all the bridges and passages down to it. But something went wrong.'

'What happened?'

She went to another section of the inscriptions. 'They used the Shamirs they already had to cut away the rock down to here. When it was fully opened, though, when the Mother of the Shamir was exposed to daylight for the first time . . . it had the same effect as when Mukobo's men brought that one,' a glance at the lead box, 'outside. Only hundreds of times more powerful.'

'What, it blew up the city?'

'Not quite – but it caused an earthquake. Most of the city was flattened, thousands of people killed. And parts of the new cave they'd dug out collapsed. According to what the historians of

Sheba told Solomon, as soon as the Mother of the Shamir was covered again, the destruction stopped.'

Eddie regarded the box thoughtfully. 'So it really does only work in daylight? Cut it off and it stops?'

She shook her head. 'There was a mention somewhere that the Shamirs still had their power at night, so I don't think it's light that activates them. But they do seem to have to be outside to work, or at least not under too much cover. Lead blocks, or at least reduces, the effect, so maybe it's cosmic radiation or neutrinos, something that can penetrate solid matter more deeply.'

He smiled. 'Didn't think particle physics was your thing.'

'Kind of a hobby after all the weird science artefacts I've found. But even after their city had been destroyed, the first thing they did was go back down and clear the rubble so they could reach the Mother of the Shamir again.'

'And let me guess, they got another earthquake?'

'Smaller, but yes. This time, it stopped when the bottom of the cave flooded. Water blocking the effect is something else that makes me think the cause might be some sort of radiation. We saw it in Nepal with the Midas Cave, where the water in the natural reactor stopped the radiation from reaching us.' She went to the altar, staring at the dark grey casket. 'The thing is, once they opened this place up, the genie was out of the bottle. Enough cosmic rays or whatever could now reach the mineral seam to keep the effect constantly active at a low level. Obviously Solomon's texts put it in terms of curses and God's wrath, but the results were pretty clear in modern terms.'

'What were they?'

'You saw the jungle outside. The vegetation has been ... twisted, mutated. Long-term exposure to the effect caused genetic damage, which got worse over time. And the same thing happened to the people. Remember what Solomon said about the people who didn't become sterile giving birth to monsters? That's why they died out. They weren't willing to give up the source of the Shamirs, and it ended up making them extinct.'

'Holding on to their ultimate weapon even though it's killing them?' said Eddie. 'There's a metaphor there somewhere.'

She smiled. 'Once the empire of Sheba found the lost city and discovered the secret of the Shamirs, they tried to reopen the mine for themselves, but the same thing happened again. They were smart enough to learn from their mistake, though. They kept the small Shamirs they'd found, but left their source alone. When they learned that Solomon had somehow gotten hold of one and was using it to build the First Temple, Makeda travelled to see him to determine if he could be trusted to use it properly. If he couldn't, she apparently had an army ready to take it by force.'

'I guess he passed the test, seeing as they got married.'

Nina nodded. 'The marriage was as much to unite and strengthen their two powers as out of love. After the wedding, Solomon went with her to Sheba to see his new domain – but he also wanted to see the source of the Shamir itself. Once he learned what had happened to Zhakana and its people, he ordered the Palace Without Entrance to be built to contain it – like the sarcophagus that's been built over Chernobyl. He also put in the challenges so that only the wisest visitors, or those to whom he'd already entrusted the knowledge, would be able to get inside. This Shamir,' she tapped the box, 'is basically a weapon of last resort, one that's only supposed to be used when all else fails. Solomon realised that any empire which used it as a *first* resort would eventually bring about its own downfall. History repeating itself.'

'Solomon was wrong.' Nina had almost forgotten about Mukobo's presence, his words taking her by surprise. 'Whoever used such a weapon would win a war very quickly.'

268

Eddie put a hand to his chin in exaggerated deep thought. 'Hmm, who should I listen to? The bloke who was so wise he actually has a saying about wisdom named after him, or a murderous rapist arsehole who's going to get his head kicked in if he keeps talking?'

The warlord sneered at him. 'Here is some wisdom for you, Chase. We are in the jungle. Only power matters here. If you do not use force, use *violence*, to protect your power, it will be taken by others.'

'That's not true,' Nina insisted. 'There are other ways to transfer power – peacefully.'

'Democracy?' It sounded like a mocking insult coming from Mukobo's lips. 'This country claims to be democratic, so much so that the word is even in its name, but it is a joke! Men with guns control the vote, control the country.'

Eddie shook his head. 'Don't let him drag you into some political debate,' he told Nina. 'He's not a politician. He's just a psycho.'

'You think that because you come from a rich country, the rest of the world is the same?' Mukobo nodded towards the revolver in Eddie's hand. 'You are using force to hold power over me, Chase. You are proving that I am right, but you are afraid to admit it. When the situation changes, I will have no such fears.' A hint of anticipation turned up the corners of his mouth.

'The situation isn't going to change,' said the Yorkshireman firmly. 'Now shut up.' The African fell silent, but his expression did not alter.

'How do you even *know* this guy?' Nina asked her husband. 'You said you'd met him before – where?'

'First time was in 2006, before I met you,' he said. 'I was working as a troubleshooter across the border in Rwanda, body-guarding aid workers and refugees. There was a war going on between Rwanda and the DRC, and Mukobo was leading one of the militia groups running around the place killing people. The convoy I was protecting ran into him, totally by fluke. We outgunned him, so he didn't have any choice but to surrender.'

Nina looked at Mukobo, whose face revealed clear anger at the memory. 'So what happened?'

'We didn't realise who he was, 'cause he'd been very good at keeping his picture out of the news. Thought he was just some mercenary. So we confiscated his guns and let him go.' A small sigh. 'That was a big fucking mistake. Not long after, he massacred another aid convoy. And that was on top of all the local people he murdered or chopped the arms off. They'd still be alive if I'd stopped him.'

'By "stopped", you mean . . .'

'Killed? Yeah. I could have done it – one of the guys with me was all for it, because even while we had him at gunpoint he was threatening us, saying he'd hunt us down and find our families, lots of nasty shit. But I didn't, because it was . . . against the rules of war.'

'There is only one rule in war,' said Mukobo. 'Do what you must to win. If you pretend there are more, then you have already lost.'

'I didn't find out who he was or what he'd done until later,' Eddie went on, deliberately not responding to the warlord. 'So, when I had a chance to put things right, I took it.'

'When was that?' Nina asked.

'When I went to Tenerife. Peter Alderley said MI6 had tracked him down, but they needed someone who'd seen him before to confirm his ID before they moved in. So I helped out. Things got a bit out of hand, but eventually we caught him.'

She frowned. 'So *that's* what you were doing there? Hunting down a war criminal? Why the hell didn't you tell me?'

'Because first of all, you would probably have thrown a fit. And second, because . . .' He hesitated before making the admission. 'Because I didn't want you to know that I'd fucked up by letting him go in the first place.'

Nina was taken aback by both reasons, though her offence at the former took second place to her dismay at the latter. 'But . . . you couldn't possibly have known. I wouldn't have blamed you for it – it wasn't your fault!'

Eddie shook his head. 'Mac taught me in the SAS that if something goes wrong, someone's got to take responsibility – so they can set it right. It took eleven years, but I finally got the chance to do that. I caught Mukobo, and turned him over to the cops so Interpol could deal with him.' He looked across at the Congolese, who stared back with disdain. 'He was supposed to be going to the States on trial for killing the aid workers. But somehow, he ended up back here.' He returned to his prisoner. 'How the fuck did you manage that, "Le Fauchet"?'

Mukobo let out a nasty laugh. 'You were afraid of your wife? That little woman? You are no man, Chase!'

Eddie smashed his boot heel on to the other man's kneecap, making him thrash in pain. 'Answer the fucking question. You should be dead! You were on the 747 that went down in the Atlantic last year – I saw a news story about it. Everyone else on the plane died, so how come you're still shitting up the world?'

Breathing heavily, Mukobo glared at him. 'I had help. From Mr Brice.'

The Yorkshireman was startled. 'Brice? How did he help?' There was no reply beyond a look of smug defiance. 'How the fuck did Brice get you off a plane at thirty thousand feet?'

'When my people rescue me, you can ask him yourself,' said Mukobo. 'Before I kill you, I will let him tell you how completely you have *failed*, Chase. Not just here, now, but ever since we first met.' He leaned as close to Eddie as he could. 'All the people who have died since then, at my hand or those of my followers,

271

every single one is on *your* head – because you were too weak to kill me when you had the chance!'

Eddie brought up the gun. 'I've still *got* the chance.'

Mukobo made a spitting sound. 'Which you will not take. I am unarmed, I am tied to a chair – I am a helpless prisoner! To you, it would be murder. And you do not believe that you are a murderer, do you, Chase? You believe in your laws, your rules of war. Your conscience cowers behind them. But even though I am the one who is tied, I am stronger than you – because the only rules I follow are my own. In the jungle, the law is for me to *make*, not obey.' He drew back. 'And this whole country will be my jungle.'

'What about your friend who runs the LEC?' Nina asked, sensing that Eddie was too furious to speak. 'Won't he have his own ideas?'

'Kabanda?' The name emerged as a sarcastic snort. 'I tolerate him, that is all. As I do Mr Brice. He thinks I am some tin-pot warlord he can control, but I am ahead of him. They are both useful to me now, but when the time is right, I shall sweep them away.' He looked back at Eddie. 'You know that time is coming, Chase. It is inevitable. One way or another, I will rule this country.'

'Thought you just wanted to rule the eastern half,' Eddie growled. The gun lowered, but did not move away from the warlord.

'To begin with. But unlike you, I see no reason to limit myself.' Mukobo sat as straight as he could, a small smile appearing. 'And as the future ruler of the Congo, I am prepared to make you a most magnanimous offer, Dr Wilde.'

'And what would that be?' Nina asked suspiciously.

'It is very simple. Let me go, and return my gun. I promise you that the only person I kill will be Chase. I have no interest in the others. You can all go free.'

'You'll forgive me if I don't believe you.'

The warlord shrugged. 'Whether you do or not, the offer is real.'

'Yeah, right,' Eddie muttered.

Nina was more vocal. 'You're seriously suggesting I let you go so that you can murder my husband?'

'Is one life not worth it to save more?' asked Mukobo. 'You, Dr Ziff, the others in your team will all live to return home. I am sure the other woman, the one who complains so much, would certainly take my offer.'

'Maybe *she* would, but I wouldn't. It's not going to happen.'

His expression became darker. 'Then you are condemning yourself to death, Dr Wilde. All of you. When the militia come for me, they will kill everyone they find. Should any of you survive, I myself will remove you from this world. After I have had my way with you, and all of my men have done the same.' Nina felt a sickening chill at the threat, but tried not to let her fear show.

'You should probably stop talking now,' said Eddie with an unnerving calmness. 'Before you say something you'll really regret.'

'I *have* no regrets,' Mukobo replied, getting louder. 'For nothing I have ever done, nothing I will ever do. I have killed men, women, children – burned babies in their beds! And I will do it all again, I promise you. Anyone who opposes me will be slaughtered like pigs. If you do not let me go, *now*, then your friends in this place will not be the only ones who will be killed. Your little girl, your precious Macy, will die too!'

Shock hit the couple at his use of their daughter's name, Eddie as still as a statue while Nina went pale. *Now* fear entered her voice. 'How – how do you know about her?'

'Why, from Mr Brice, of course,' said the warlord, cruelly pleased at her reaction. 'He has told me much about you. Your family, where you live – New York, 78th Street, yes?' Nausea roiled in Nina's stomach at the revelation that he knew how to find their home. 'He has powerful friends in the world of spies. They will bring your girl to me. She is five, yes?' He closed his eyes, drawing back his head as if smelling a delicious meal. 'So fresh, so innocent. So . . . *undefiled.*' The last word was drawn out, savoured, before he opened his eyes again. 'She will be most popular with my men. And the last thing she sees before I let her die will be your severed heads! Unless,' he said, fixing them firmly with his unblinking gaze, 'you let me go, right now.'

Nina was too horrified to speak. She tried to retreat, but almost stumbled as her legs shook.

Eddie, in contrast, remained utterly still, looking back at Mukobo with equal intensity. Finally, he spoke. 'You're right. Yeah, you're right. It *is* worth one life to save more.'

The warlord smiled. 'I knew you would agree with me in the end, Chase. Now. Give me my gun.'

The Yorkshireman nodded. 'Here.'

He lifted the revolver again – and fired it at Mukobo's groin.

The Magnum's echoing boom was like cannon fire. Nina jumped in shock – first at the near-deafening noise, then at what her husband had done.

Mukobo himself was no less stunned. He stared at Eddie for a moment, wide-eyed as blood gushed over the seat . . . then the pain hit him. He screamed, thrashing against his bonds and howling French obscenities.

Eddie was unmoved. 'You're not going to touch my daughter. Or anyone else. Ever.'

Mukobo looked back up at him, realising what he meant—

Five more Magnum rounds erupted from the gun as the Englishman emptied its cylinder into the warlord's chest. The bullets ripped right through him, cracking bloody craters in the chair's stone back. Mukobo shuddered, then slumped forward, dead.

The rolling thunder of the gunshots faded. Nina slowly lowered her hands from her ears as she gaped at the quivering corpse. 'Oh . . . oh my God, Eddie. Jesus *Christ*! What did you do?'

'What I should've done back in 2006,' he replied, opening the revolver's cylinder and tipping out the spent brass.

'But – but holy *shit*, Eddie! He was tied up! You *murdered* him!'

'And how many people's *he* murdered?' he demanded. 'Hundreds, probably thousands if you count all the people he ordered killed. And he would have gone on to kill a load more.'

'That – that's not the point!' she stammered. 'We captured him, he should've gone on trial—'

'You see any judges around here?' Eddie snapped. 'Any cops? You heard what he said – the only law he follows is the law of the fucking jungle. Well, I played by his law. And in case you weren't listening, *he threatened to rape and kill our daughter*. Fuck him!'

Nina had felt the same horror and rage as her husband when Mukobo made his threat, her natural instinct as a parent being to protect her child by any means – but was still unwilling to justify a cold-blooded execution. 'If he'd been about to hurt Macy for real, I'd have blown the bastard away myself. But he wasn't, he was tied to a goddamn chair on a different continent! Yes, it was a threat, but it was an empty one!'

'You think? Brice told him where we *live*! And Mukobo was the kind of sadistic fucking maniac who'd follow up on a threat like that. The aid workers he murdered, the ones he was going to the States to be put on trial for killing – you know *why* he went after them? Because their leader called him a "dangerous man" in a newspaper interview. That was all, but it was enough. And if I'd known who he was when I first met him, I could have saved their lives.' He flicked the empty cylinder, sending it spinning. 'I could have saved hundreds of lives . . . but I didn't.'

'That wasn't your fault,' she insisted. 'You can't blame yourself for that!'

'Yeah, I can, and I have. But he won't be killing anyone else now.' He stared down at the slumped figure. 'Fourteen years late, but I stopped him. And if you think I did the wrong thing, if that's changed the way you look at me . . . then I'll just have to live with it, because I don't regret it.' He faced Nina again. 'I did it to save Macy, *and* you. And everyone else in this place. And fuck knows how many more people in the rest of the country, because without Mukobo, this revolution'll go nowhere. He was the one holding it together. So by killing him, I've just stopped a civil war.'

'Maybe you have,' said Nina. 'And maybe you did do the right thing—'

'There's no maybe about it.'

'—but we can debate that later.'

'And I'm sure we will,' he said sardonically. 'But I'm not going to apologise for it. The world's better off with this bastard dead.'

Her shock was replaced by anger and exasperation. 'That might be true. But you just shot our only bargaining chip! Without Mukobo as a hostage, there's nothing to stop the militia from killing us.'

Eddie gestured towards the lead casket. 'There's that.'

'Yes, if we want to risk bringing the rest of the palace down on top of us. Look, Eddie, I – I understand why you did what you did to Mukobo. But with him dead, our situation's just got worse, because now there's no way out of here. What are we going to do?'

Any answer the Yorkshireman might have had remained unspoken as Ziff shouted from outside. 'Nina! Eddie! Are you okay?'

Nina hurried to meet him, not wanting anyone else to see the grisly scene. 'We're okay, we're fine,' she assured the Israeli as he scuttled down the last flight of steps. 'Nothing to worry about.'

'We heard shots!' shouted Howie from a bridge higher up. 'We thought Mukobo'd escaped!'

'He's not going anywhere,' Eddie replied as he emerged. 'Go back up. Fortune and Paris might need your help if the militia make any moves.'

The young man hesitated, then started back up the chasm. Ziff was less easily persuaded, though. 'Is there any chance you could take Mukobo somewhere else so I can get back to translating the inscriptions?' he asked hopefully.

Eddie shook his head. 'Definitely best if he stays put for now.'

Ziff's eyes went to the revolver in his hand, its empty cylinder still open. 'I'm . . . getting the feeling there's something I should know about.'

'Everything's fine, really!' said Nina with forced brightness. 'You could always explore the other buildings instead?'

Ziff gave the couple a look of concerned suspicion, but before he could question them further another voice echoed down the rift. 'Eddie!' cried Paris. Even at the top of his lungs, his words were barely audible by the time they reached the mine. 'We have a situation!'

The older archaeologist looked up in alarm. 'The militia – are they attacking?'

'Paris wouldn't have left Fortune to face 'em on his own,' said Eddie, taking out a box of Magnum rounds he had confiscated from the warlord earlier and reloading the golden gun. 'It's something else. We need to get back up there.'

He and Nina ran for the stairs. 'What about Mukobo?' Ziff asked.

'Like I said, he's not going anywhere. Come on.' With the confused Israeli trailing them, they began a hurried trek back to ground level.

22

Even hurrying, it took several minutes to make the ascent. There had been no gunfire, so the Insekt Posse hadn't attempted an assault, but the documentary crew's concerned expressions told them that something was going on.

'Where's Paris?' said Eddie. 'And Howie?'

'They're with Fortune, at the entrance,' Fisher told him.

'So what's happening?' asked Nina, breathless.

Rivero raised his camera to record her and Eddie as they headed for the passage. 'Probably easiest if you see for yourself.'

'This isn't a movie,' she sniped. 'You don't have to keep things from us for dramatic tension!'

Fortune and Paris were maintaining their watch over the ruins, Howie nervously holding the third Kalashnikov behind them. 'What've we got?' Eddie asked.

'A visitor,' the tall Congolese replied. 'Your friend Mr Brice.'

'And you haven't shot the fucker?'

'He has a white flag,' Paris clarified.

'So? He can use it as a bandage.' The Yorkshireman peered into the daylight. There was indeed a white flag, a piece of material on a branch being waved from behind a broken wall.

Nina looked cautiously past her husband. 'Somehow, I don't think he's here to surrender.'

'Flag of truce,' Eddie rumbled. 'He wants to talk. It's definitely him?' he asked the defenders.

'Yes. He came alone,' Fortune confirmed.

'Great, so the others could be anywhere . . .' With their

278

ANDY MCDERMOTT

position set back inside the palace's thick wall, there was no way to see if anyone was stealthily creeping up from either side – unless the defenders exposed themselves to fire from the jungle. 'All right, better see what he wants.' He took the AK from Howie. 'Brice! I'm here!'

The other Englishman cautiously raised his head. 'About time, Chase. I just want to talk to you.'

'Go on, then.'

'I meant talk, not shout. I'd rather do this face to face. Preferably not with a gun pointed at me.'

'I'm sure you would,' said Eddie, who had fixed the rifle's sights unwaveringly upon the ex-MI6 officer. 'Convince me. And start by convincing me not to blow your head off.'

'I'm offering a deal,' Brice replied. 'One that will get all of you out of here safely. But it's an offer I can only make to you, Chase – because you're the only person there who'll understand why I'm making it.'

The shouted exchange had drawn the attention of those in the first chamber, Fisher leading them to the entrance to hear more. 'Wait, now you're in charge of negotiations?' the director asked Eddie. 'You're not even an official part of the team!'

'You're not making any deals behind closed doors,' Lydia said forcefully. 'We should all be there. It's our lives you're bargaining with!'

'Dissent in the ranks?' called Brice. 'I'll make this clear for everyone – your only chance of staying alive is by dealing with me, and the only person I'll talk to is Chase. I'm not going to explain myself; that's just how it will work. Either I deal with Chase, in private, or I leave and let the militia handle things their own way. Believe me, theirs will be a lot more bloody.'

Worried looks were exchanged. 'So what do we do?' asked Rivero. 'Do we trust him?'

'Course we bloody don't,' Eddie muttered, before addressing

279

his countryman again. 'Brice! I'm assuming you want Mukobo back.'

'That should go without saying,' Brice answered. 'It's *why* you should do it that I want to discuss. Other than the obvious incentive of not being brutally slaughtered by a group of drug-addled barbarians, of course.'

'Hope they can't hear you calling them that.'

'I honestly don't care. They know the LEC is relying on me to supply weapons, so they wouldn't dare touch me even if they understood English. Which very few of them do.' He rounded the wall into the open. 'So what will it be, Chase? You should at least hear me out. I'm sure your friends would want to know that an offer was made, even if you didn't accept it.'

All eyes turned to Eddie. 'What are you going to do?' asked Fortune.

'We can't let him make a deal on his own!' protested Lydia. 'For all we know, he might sell the rest of us out!'

'Oh, shut *up*, for God's sake,' snapped Nina. 'But we know we can't trust Brice, Eddie. As soon as he gets Mukobo back, we're all dead.'

'We still have the Shamir,' Ziff pointed out. 'That could give us something to bargain with.'

Eddie made a decision. 'Let's find out what he's offering.' He shouted to Brice. 'All right! Come over!'

'You sure about this?' asked Fisher.

'Nope. Fortune, Paris, keep him covered. Howie, quick word.' He took the young man aside and whispered to him. Howie looked surprised, then nodded and hurried back to the first chamber.

'Where's *he* going?' asked Lydia.

'I just want him to check something.' He returned his attention to the entrance as Brice, hands raised, picked his way over the fallen rubble. 'Right, everyone without a gun, get out of the way. Fortune, watch the ruins; Paris, watch *him*. I'll frisk him.'

'I'm not armed,' said Brice as he arrived.

'If you've got a fucking paper clip on you, I'd consider that armed. Hands high, against the wall.'

The former agent took up his awkward position as Eddie conducted a thorough search of his clothing. Apart from a cigarette pack and lighter, his pockets were empty. 'Travelling light, aren't you?'

'I thought you might take a perverse pleasure in breaking anything valuable, so I left everything else outside,' Brice replied. 'I have every intention of returning to collect them, though.'

'That depends on you, doesn't it?' Eddie finished the search. 'He's clean.'

'As promised.' Brice turned towards him. 'My cigarettes?'

'Filthy habit. You should give up.' Eddie tossed the pack and lighter outside. 'Maybe I've seen too many James Bond movies, but I just have a funny feeling about the lighter being a bomb or the fags shooting poison darts.'

'James Bond isn't real. If SIS had the budget for gadgets like that in real life, the British Empire would never have faltered.'

'Yeah, I always thought Alderley having that crappy old Ford Capri instead of some fancy Aston Martin spy car was a bit of a giveaway.'

Brice gave him a half-smile. 'Poor old Peter never did have the drive to reach the top, did he? Anyway, to business. First, I'd like to see Mukobo before we start negotiations.'

'You can see him, sure,' said Eddie flatly. 'Okay, move.' As Brice started down the passage, he spoke to Paris and Fortune. 'Watch things here – if anything happens outside, shout. I'll be up as quick as I can.' He followed Brice. 'If the militia try anything, this bell-end'll be the first to get shot.'

'I'm here in good faith,' said Brice patronisingly. 'I hope that when you hear me out, you won't just accept my offer, you'll do so willingly.'

'We'll see.' They entered the first chamber. Eddie drew the revolver and handed the Kalashnikov to Ziff. 'Doc, take this and help Fortune and Paris if they need you – or me if *I* do.'

'Where are you going?' asked Fisher.

'He wants to see Mukobo, and he's at the bottom of the mine, so we're going down there. Howie, did you check the batteries like I asked?'

Howie held up one of the torches. 'Fully charged, man.'

'Thanks.' Eddie took it. 'Nina, I want you to come with me.'

She was surprised. 'What? Why?'

Brice had his own objections. 'That's not the deal, Chase. I talk to you, and you alone.'

'She's my wife. What I know, she knows. I found out the hard way that it's not good to keep secrets from her.' He gave her a small but genuine smile, which she returned in kind. '*That's* the deal. And you're going to accept it.' He twitched the revolver at the ex-spy for emphasis.

'Very well,' said Brice with clear displeasure. 'Just take me to Mukobo, and let's get started.'

Eddie indicated the booby-trapped tunnel. 'You know the way. Lead on.'

Leaving the others behind, he and Nina escorted Brice through the palace and down into the chasm. They descended the last flight of steps to the Chamber of the Shamir. The lanterns were still lit within. 'Philippe!' called Brice. 'It's me, John. Are you okay?' There was no answer. 'What have you done to him?' he demanded. 'Did you knock him out?'

'Ah . . . no,' said Nina, truthfully.

'He's inside,' Eddie told him. 'Go on in.'

Brice strode into the ancient room – and halted at the sight of the warlord's corpse. 'What – oh. Really, Chase?' He shook his head. 'This complicates matters.'

'You're not kidding,' Nina muttered.

ANDY MCDERMOTT

'You don't know how much.' He went to examine the body. 'Six shots at close range – including one to the balls? Rather a case of overkill.'

'Well, when someone says they're going to rape and kill my little girl, I kind of take offence,' Eddie told him thinly. He fixed the gun upon Brice's back, thumbing the hammer. The other man froze at the click. 'And he said *you* were going to help him do it. Any reason I shouldn't put the next six into you?'

'You'll need the bullets, for a start.' Brice very slowly and carefully turned to face the other Englishman. 'If I'm not back within the hour, nothing will stop the Insekt Posse from making an all-out assault.'

'It won't go well for 'em.'

'It will go even less well for you. And you know that, for all your bravado. You may not have been an SAS officer, but you're fully capable of making a tactical assessment.'

Eddie scowled, but knew he was right: with their limited ammunition, the defenders would be unable to hold back a concerted attack. 'Okay, then. What's this deal of yours?'

Brice regarded the lead case. 'I assume you put the Shamir back in there.'

'It's the safest place for it,' said Nina.

'Perhaps. But it's not *fully* safe, is it? I can still feel that . . . *vibration* in the air.' He tipped his head as if listening to the omnipresent hum. 'Solomon may have built the palace to shield the Mother of the Shamir from whatever activates it, but even with an inch of lead inside every wall, something's still getting through. I'd assume that only some kind of high-energy particle or radiation could penetrate this deeply.'

She nodded. 'Whatever it is, exposure charges up the Shamir until it reaches a critical level. I've seen something similar before. Although this is much more destructive. It seems to produce ultra-low-frequency sound waves to shake apart – *smash* apart – solid objects.'

'A sonic weapon,' said Brice, almost admiringly. 'The Horn of Joshua, for real. The Americans and Russians spent years working on similar ideas, but never managed to make them useable in the field. This, though? A man-portable weapon that can obliterate a building using nothing but focused sound, and do so from a distance – it's an extremely valuable find.' His expression became more calculating. 'The perfect tool for regime change. Just wait for a country's leaders to be in the same place at the same time, then open the box. Take them all out in one go, and make sure your preferred replacements are ready to step up in the ensuing state of emergency. And there's no defence, because nobody even knows it exists . . .'

'Is that your deal?' Eddie asked, scathing. 'You going to offer us a cut of what you get from selling the Shamir to the highest bidder?'

'Actually, no. That wasn't why I wanted to speak to you. My business here in the Congo is more important. Or rather, it was until you put a spanner and six Magnum rounds in the works.' A small sigh. 'And after everything I did to rescue him from the Yanks . . .'

'How *did* you rescue him? He was on a bloody plane!'

'A pilot with some large debts, and a mid-air interception and transfer,' Brice told him, as if it was no big deal. 'Members of GB63 – the Removal Men – pulled Mukobo out through the 747's cockpit escape hatch and winched him up.'

'But . . . then the plane crashed,' said Nina. 'What went wrong?'

There was no regret or apology in his reply. 'Nothing. The plan went exactly as intended.'

'You what?' said Eddie in disbelief. '"As intended"? Over three hundred people fucking *died*!'

'You crashed a plane full of civilians just to cover up that you'd rescued one man?' she cried, appalled. 'My God!'

'Over half a million Iraqis died to secure American interests in the Middle East,' Brice replied patronisingly. 'A few hundred deaths to secure British interests in Africa is a rounding error by comparison.'

'What do you mean, British interests?' demanded Eddie. 'What's Britain got to do with the Congo?'

The other Englishman laughed. 'Why do you think I'm here, Chase? I never really left SIS – that was all part of my cover. I'm here on a mission, a very important one.'

Eddie was stunned. 'What – the British government *knows* you're trying to start a civil war?'

'They *authorised* it! Do you think I ended up in this hellhole on a whim? I'm working on the orders of C, and with complete immunity from prosecution for any and all actions I take in the course of my mission. We *want* secession for eastern Congo. My job is to make sure it happens. Although,' he glanced at Mukobo's body, 'you've complicated things quite considerably.'

'Oh no, I heartily fucking apologise,' said Eddie, though his sarcasm was blunted by shock. His *own country* was behind everything?

'You destroyed an airliner!' Nina added. 'You killed hundreds of civilians – how can you possibly have immunity?'

'Section 7 of the 1994 Intelligence Services Act,' Brice replied in a smug, lecturing tone. 'Otherwise known as the "James Bond clause". SIS officers are protected from prosecution for any actions taken in service of Her Majesty's Government anywhere in the world, as long as they have written authorisation from the Secretary of State. And I assure you, I have full authorisation.'

'You were *ordered* to take down a plane to rescue Mukobo?' asked Eddie, horrified.

'No, no. There are very few politicians willing to get their hands that dirty. I was simply given an objective – "to bring about the independence of eastern Congo and secure any and all British interests therein" was, I believe, the exact wording. *How* I achieved it was entirely my decision. Mukobo was by far the best strongman to unite the various political groups and militias, so I had to arrange his removal from American custody. Which,' he gave Eddie a sharp look, 'I would never have had to if you hadn't turned him over to the police in Tenerife. If the Removal Men had bagged him as planned, we would have brought him back to DRC and set things in motion three years sooner. You cost us a lot of time, effort and money. And lives.'

'Don't you fucking try to put *any* of that on me!' Eddie shouted. 'You set up the plane crash, you let that fucking maniac Mukobo run loose and kill God knows how many people. *You're* the one responsible, not me.'

'And why are you doing all this?' Nina demanded. 'Why would Britain want to split this country in two? What's in it for them?'

Again, Brice became distinctly lecturing. 'The Democratic Republic of Congo has some of the world's largest deposits of rare minerals. Unfortunately, the mining rights have been handed to other countries of late – China and even Russia have been taking control. I'm not saying the current government is utterly corrupt, but . . . money talks. However, if the east becomes an independent state—'

'You get to negotiate new deals,' she realised. 'And the new rulers will be very grateful to the people who put them in power.'

He nodded. 'You're brighter than your husband. Although I never really doubted that.'

'And you're only as bright as Mukobo if you're going to insult a man pointing a gun at your head,' the Yorkshireman rumbled.

Brice ignored him. 'But yes, you're right,' he told Nina. 'We may have won our freedom with Brexit, but because it's taken us out of the European Union, we're losing out on a lot of deals that were signed with the EU as a bloc. This way, we get to secure vital access to rare minerals with exclusive mining concessions for Monardril – a British company.'

'All this is about fucking *mining*?' Eddie said with disgust. 'MI6 has killed Christ-knows how many people, just so some silver-haired twat in a helicopter can make more money?'

'It's about securing the future of my country!' Brice replied, for the first time revealing a hint of defensive anger. 'Of *your* country too. Never forget that, Chase. We both took an oath to protect it against all enemies. And any nation that denies us a resource we *need* is an enemy. There are plenty who are rushing to sabotage us now that we're going it alone.'

'So your allies suddenly become your enemies because they've got a contract to mine coltan or whatever, and you haven't?' said Nina.

Eddie rolled his eyes. 'Great, like we need more people who hate us. So is this how MI6 protects us from enemies – by making sure we've always got plenty of enemies we need protecting *from*?'

'Oh, grow up, Chase!' Brice snapped. 'The job of SIS isn't to chase spies or fight terrorists. We have far more important things to do. We were founded to help the British Empire play the Great Game against the other imperial powers of the day; the players may have changed since then, but the game is still going on. We've lost some pawns, but we still have powerful pieces on the board. Our purpose is to keep them there, and make the best use of them.'

'But whenever you move your fucking chess pieces around, real people get killed. And it's the poor buggers in the forces who take the brunt of it. Let me guess: if eastern Congo became independent, the army and SAS would be sent here to "help"

Monardril take over from the mining companies who were already there?'

'The armed forces exist to secure and maintain British interests by force, whether the threat thereof or actual. That's their sole purpose.'

'Bollocks!' Eddie protested. 'I didn't join the army or the SAS to fight for some rich bastard's business plan. Or to start coups that'll leave a lot of innocent people dead. I did it to serve my country and make a difference to the world.'

To his anger, his heartfelt assertion produced only a mocking smirk from Brice. 'If you really believe that the SAS and our other special forces are there to preserve world peace and protect the innocent, you're even more naive and stupid than I thought. You know, you were actually lucky to join the SAS when you did, just as there was a genuine war against a clear enemy.'

Eddie snorted. 'Yeah, I felt really lucky while I was being shot at by the Taliban and al-Qaeda.'

'I mean that you had the fortuitous timing to be able to take the moral high ground and be a soldier with a good cause: a rescuer, a hero,' the MI6 officer went on. 'Rather than being an enforcer, muscle for Britain's friendly despots and warlords. A few years earlier, and you would have been in the islands of the Far East burning farmers' villages and shooting their livestock to clear their land for rubber plantations, or executing dissidents who challenged the authority of our allies.'

'That's bullshit. We don't do things like that.'

'Things like murdering an unarmed prisoner?' A sly smirk curled his lips at the Yorkshireman's discomfiture. 'You do what you're told to do! Your purpose was to kill whoever we pointed you at, Chase. Nothing more, nothing less. SIS determines the targets, and you eliminate them. It doesn't matter if they're ISIS or the IRA, or civilians in some backwater country most people back home couldn't even find on a map. If we decide their deaths serve British interests, then you make them dead.' Another dismissive laugh. 'Don't give me any airy-fairy nonsense about making the world a better place.'

'So it's "My country, right or wrong?"' Eddie said, appalled. 'Wrong is wrong, whichever fucking side it is!'

'You serve your country by putting it first, above everything else,' Brice replied. 'Your own opinions, your own morals, even your own family – and your own life.'

Nina regarded him contemptuously. 'Sorry, but you don't seem the kind to sacrifice your own life for your country. Everyone else's lives, maybe—'

'You don't know *what* I've sacrificed for my country, Dr Wilde,' Brice cut in, again with a flash of anger. 'But you, Chase – I said once that your country had given you everything, and you repaid her by walking away. Well, now it's time to settle your debts. Your turning Mukobo into Swiss cheese affects things, but I didn't intend to let him stay around after independence anyway.'

'You were going to kill him?' Eddie asked.

'He was far too unstable to allow to run a country, even by the standards of some of the despots we've supported in the past. Fabrice Kabanda is much more ... civilised. And easier to control. Which brings me back to my offer, or at least an amended version.' He straightened his clothing as if about to make a sales presentation. 'With Mukobo dead, the chances of the secessionists winning have decreased considerably. Kabanda just doesn't have the necessary capacity for violence. But *that* would redress the balance in their favour.' He indicated the box containing the Shamir.

Nina was not impressed. 'You want to give it to those lunatics outside?'

'Since you murdered their leader, the only way you and your friends will get past the Insekt Posse alive is under my protection. The Shamir for your lives seems like quite a good deal.'

'At the cost of a lot *more* lives.'

'Obviously they wouldn't get to keep it. A weapon that powerful needs to be held by the right hands.'

She cocked her head. 'By which you mean yours.'

'It would absolutely be in Britain's best interests to control it, so yes. And you're going to help me do so, Chase. You took the oath of allegiance when you joined the army, and I don't believe that a man like you would let it slide after you left.'

Eddie frowned at him. 'What's my oath got to do with this?'

'The last clause, specifically. Your promise to "obey all orders of Her Majesty, her heirs and successors and of the generals and officers set over me." As a senior officer of the Secret Intelligence Service on an operation fully authorised by Her Majesty's Government, I *am* such an officer. Whether you dislike me personally or consider what I'm doing repugnant is irrelevant. My mission has been deemed vital to the national interest – so you *will* help me accomplish it. That's an order, Chase.'

Eddie was still and silent for a moment . . . then brought up his free hand in a mocking salute. 'Yes sir, sir, lickety-split, sir!' he said with exaggerated enthusiasm, before snorting. 'Fuck off, Brice. I'm not a soldier any more.'

'Nor was your friend Colonel McCrimmon after he retired from the SAS. But he still served his country by working for us – and obeying our orders.'

The mention of Mac served only to anger Eddie still further. 'Mac would never have followed orders to do what you're doing here. And you're not a real officer, whatever MI6 calls you. I'm not going to help you start a war.'

The spy narrowed his eyes. 'Then you're a traitor,' he said, the words oozing venom. 'An enemy of the state. And I can assure you that if by some miracle you get out of this place alive, you'll be treated as such. You'll never see your daughter again.'

Eddie snapped up the gun, his face turning to stone. 'Last time someone threatened my little girl, I killed him.'

'I'm not threatening her. I'm making a promise to *you*. Obviously I'll deny everything I've told you both, but I still have no intention of letting you spread any rumours about SIS's involvement in DR Congo. The Removal Men will be called in – and their targets will be you. I doubt you'd even make it past the border.'

The Yorkshireman's expression remained cold . . . then, to both Nina's and Brice's surprise, he smiled. 'Funny thing about rumours. They stop being rumours if they become fact.'

'Meaning what?' the agent asked suspiciously.

'Meaning . . . smile! You're on *Candid Camera*.' Eddie tipped his head towards one of the windows.

Brice and Nina turned to look. Nothing was visible in the darkness – until a small red light flashed. Brice stiffened as he realised what it was. 'You little *shit*,' he muttered.

'While you were droning on,' Eddie continued, his grin widening, 'we were just *drone*-ing. I thought it'd be a good idea to get whatever dodgy crap you had to say on tape, and I was right.'

The other man whirled back to him. 'You're bluffing. That thing won't have a microphone.'

'Howie? If you can hear me, come a bit closer and give us a dance.'

A pale shape took on form outside as it approached the spill of illumination from the lanterns. Rotors whispering, the quad-copter stopped outside the chamber, wagging from side to side before retreating again. 'Modern technology,' said Eddie. 'Innit great? Everything you said's been recorded on a laptop. Soon as we get somewhere with an internet connection, boop – it'll be in the inbox of every news service in the world. It's not the first time I've done something like this.'

'That recording would be a hell of a thing to show to the

291

United Nations,' said Nina. 'Or the US! You just confessed to destroying an American airliner, with the approval of the British government. That's an act of terrorism – an act of *war*.'

Brice tried to conceal his concern, eyes flicking upwards as if seeking help from on high. 'They wouldn't believe it,' he said. 'And even if they did, they wouldn't act upon it. It would wreck the special relationship between Britain and the US.'

'I think you already did that when you wrecked a fucking *plane*,' Eddie told him sarcastically. 'But anyway, how about we make *you* an offer? You said you could get us out of here without the militia killing us. Do that, for all of us, and we'll make sure that video doesn't pop up on everyone's Facebook feed. Obviously we'll keep a copy, or twenty. Just in case anyone really does think about sending some boys from the Increment after us.'

'The what?' asked Nina.

'MI6 crossed with SAS. You don't want to meet 'em if you're not on their side. But we're not *going* to meet 'em. Are we, Brice?'

'The Increment are the least of your worries at the moment,' said the other Englishman. He now seemed tense, almost anxious, again glancing up at the ceiling. 'I may not be able to hold the Insekt Posse back once they find out you killed Mukobo.'

'Well, you'd better try, hadn't you? 'Cause I doubt they'd be too happy to see the guy who let their leader get shot by another Brit. They might even think we were working together.'

'I highly doubt that.'

'Oh, I'll make sure to tell 'em.'

Brice said nothing for several seconds, thinking. 'Okay. There's another option,' he said at last. 'Even with Mukobo gone, the secession still has a chance of success as long as they have a supply of weapons. The militia outside know I was going to provide them. I can use that as leverage to keep us all alive long enough to get out of the jungle. Once we're clear, I'll arrange for my contacts to extract us on the sly.'

Nina had stood back while the two men had their discussion, but now started to feel uneasy. It wasn't until Brice yet again flicked his gaze upwards – unconsciously, it seemed – that she realised why. 'Eddie, something's wrong,' she said. 'He's *waiting* for something.'

'The only thing I'm waiting for is your accepting the one chance we all have of escaping from here,' said Brice curtly.

She shook her head. 'No, there's something else. I mean, you know you're still being filmed, right?' She waved at the windows. Beyond them, the drone dipped in response. 'You just said you're going to screw over the militia the first chance you get. Why would you do that if you know they might find out? For that matter . . .' She paused, worried.

Eddie stepped back to join his wife, keeping the revolver fixed upon Brice. 'Uh-oh. What is it?'

'He's a spy. More than that, he's deep undercover to give his bosses plausible deniability. So . . . why would he tell us *anything* about the true nature of his mission? I mean, isn't the first rule of spy craft that you never talk about what you're doing?'

'I think that's Fight Club.'

'Yeah, you just keep on quippin', Roger Moore,' she snipped. 'But either everything he's told us is another lie, or . . .' Dread rose as the only other possibility became clear. 'Or he felt safe telling us the truth, because he doesn't think we'll live long enough to pass it on.'

'I'm here to offer a deal that's mutually beneficial, that's all,' insisted Brice. 'I want to get away as much as you do.'

'No, she's right,' said Eddie. 'All you care about is completing your mission – which means we have to be dead so we can't fuck it up by telling anyone.' He glanced at the drone. 'And everyone else with us has to be dead too, so that recording can't ever get out. What're you waiting for, then? You keeping us occupied so the militia can set up an attack?'

'Your men are in a well-defended position with a clear line of fire. A direct assault on that entrance would be suicide without grenades and explosives – which the rabble who came with me don't have.'

Eddie knew Brice was right – but was now as convinced as Nina that he had come to them as a distraction from some larger plan. 'I think we should get back to the others,' he told her. 'Brice, get moving.'

The spy's hesitation told him that Brice was exactly where he wanted to be. 'I'm telling you, the only way out of here is with my help. I—'

The Yorkshireman stepped closer. 'Move. Now. Or you can stay down here with Mukobo, permanently.'

'All right, all right.' Brice raised his hands higher and started towards the exit. 'But you really should take my offer.' He looked at his watch. 'Because if it expires, then so will you—'

A thunderous explosion shook the chasm – and daylight streamed in from above.

23

Nina and Eddie reacted in shock at the detonation. Brice, however, had clearly expected it to happen, but not known exactly *when*. He flinched – then recovered and ran for the windows.

Eddie's revolver tracked him—

Something smashed down on the building with such force that the ceiling split apart. Brice dived behind the altar, Eddie whirling to shield Nina from flying debris. More impacts came from outside as falling stones hit the bottom of the cavern.

The Yorkshireman looked up – to see Brice vault through a window. 'Nina, you okay?'

'Yeah,' she gasped. There was a gaping hole in the ceiling, broken stone scattered beneath it. She saw the remnants of a carved eagle on one piece of rubble. 'Oh my God, they blew open the palace roof!'

Eddie ran to the window. The darkness outside had been pierced by an eerie shaft of grey light – picking out Brice running for the mine. He raised his gun, but the other Briton leapt into the excavations as he fired. The bullet shattered against the vein of greenish stone with an almost musical clang. 'Shit!'

Nina hurried to him, but the escaping spy was not her greatest concern. 'Eddie, listen!' The Mother of the Shamir glinted in the first natural light to reach it for thousands of years – and its constant, unsettling hum changed.

Growing louder.

'We should get the hell out of here,' she said, alarmed.

'Remember what happened to Zhakana when they dug this place out? I think it's going to happen again!'

'Brice is still down there,' Eddie snapped.

'Yeah, and we'll be stuck here with him if we don't move. That thing's charging up, just like the Shamir – only it's *way* bigger!'

He got her point, reluctantly retreating. A voice reached them as they emerged into the chasm. 'Nina! Eddie!' shouted Howie.

Nina looked up to find the young man on a bridge. 'Get up to the surface!' she cried. High above him, she saw an elongated hole had been blasted in the palace's vaulted roof.

'Those rocks took out my drone!' Howie told her.

'You've got the recording, haven't you?' demanded Eddie.

The American held up his laptop. 'Yeah, but—'

'Guard it with your fucking life! It's the only proof of what's been going on here! Now move!'

Clutching the computer, Howie ran up the bridge. 'We've got to get up there fast,' Eddie told Nina as they hared up the stairway. 'If they rope down from that hole, they'll be able to attack from both sides – shit!' The sharp retort of an explosion echoed down from above. 'That was a grenade! They must've called in reinforcements.'

'What, so now we're even *more* outnumbered?' Nina said unhappily. 'Great!'

The sound of gunfire reached them – Kalashnikovs on single shot against similar rifles on full auto. Another grenade exploded, the detonation ringing through the tunnels. Now the militia had explosives, it would take more than a few boulders to form a defensible position – and Eddie wasn't even sure if there was anywhere inside the palace that *could* be defended.

They had to try, though. He and Nina hurried across the lowest bridge. He glanced down – and saw Brice climbing from the mine. He couldn't spare the time to take a shot at him, though. 'Buggeration and fuckery!'

Nina looked to see what had drawn his ire. She spotted the British agent – but then saw something else, newly revealed in the light from on high. A faint mark on the rock, perfectly level, ran all the way around the chasm's walls just above the upper tier of buildings. Water, she realised; the residue of flooding, long-drained. But had it escaped naturally over time, or . . .

The thought was interrupted by another gunshot – from overhead. Howie yelped in fright as a bullet struck the cliff near him.

Silhouettes appeared in the hole in the roof. More shots cracked downwards. 'Whoa!' Nina gasped as a round whipped past. '*Now* what do we do?'

'Get into cover,' Eddie said. They reached the next ascending ledge cut into the rock face, the overhang partially shielding them. He flattened himself against the wall and sidestepped upwards, Nina following. 'Dunno how the fuck we'll—'

He broke off as a rope dropped from the hole and uncoiled into the buildings below. It fell still – then juddered as someone began to climb down it.

Eddie leaned out to see a militia man with an AK slung over his back making a clumsy descent. A second rope made the long fall from the hole's other end. 'That bastard Brice,' he growled as he continued upwards. 'He was just buying time for them to plant the explosives and get ready for an assault!'

A shout came from the uppermost ledge. 'Eddie!' cried Ziff. 'Nina! They've broken in!'

'Yeah, I noticed!' the Yorkshireman shouted back. 'You got ammo left?'

'Yes!'

'So bloody use it!'

The Israeli took the hint, aiming at the first of the descending men. He hesitated when he found his target, the Congolese completely defenceless as he lowered himself, but the sight of both the Kalashnikov on his back and a savage machete hanging from his belt brought home the threat. Ziff fired, sending the man screaming to the rocky ground far below.

The second man hurriedly wound his rope around one wrist before fumbling for a pistol with the other. Ziff took aim – only to duck behind a wall as someone on the roof sprayed shots at him.

One shattered a cask of oil, splashing its contents across the ledge – and igniting them. The archaeologist gasped, scrambling out of cover to escape the flaming liquid.

The man on the rope brought up his handgun—

Two bullet holes burst open in his chest as Paris rushed from the passageway, his rifle propped in the crook of his right arm. The militia man tumbled after his late comrade, smacking on to the roof of a building below.

Ziff found less fiery cover. 'Good shot,' he told his rescuer.

The scruffy little man gave him a dark smile. 'I'm left-handed.'

Fortune emerged from the passage, firing two shots at the ruptured roof. One struck a sagging block at the hole's edge – and the other a man lying on top of it, smashing his shoulder. He shrieked, flopping face down as his arm gave way – and the jolt caused the lead sheet supporting the stone to split. The carved block fell away, the wounded man following it into the darkness below.

The other Insekt Posse around the opening hurriedly withdrew as more stones ground ominously against each other. 'They're pulling back!' Fortune shouted.

The documentary team arrived behind him. Rivero was still filming, Lydia equally unwilling to abandon her own equipment. 'That's not gonna help us!' the cameraman objected. 'There's no way out of here!'

Eddie halted at the end of a bridge, assessing the situation. The militia above had retreated, but would come back the moment they realised the remaining blocks were holding in place. 'Fortune! How many behind you?'

'At least ten,' the African replied.

'How long before they catch up?'

Even from a distance, he could see Fortune's gold-tinted smile. 'It could be some time. We reset the traps.'

'At least two guys got squashed in the first one,' Paris added.

'Best thing to do to an Insekt,' said Eddie. 'But if we can't go back that way, I don't have a fucking clue how we're going to get out. Short of climbing those ropes,' he gestured at the two dangling lines, 'and it's a long-arse climb!'

'Eddie, wait,' Nina said urgently. 'There might be another way out!' She pointed at the bottom of the chasm. 'The drainage tunnels come out on the cliff, above the river – the waterfalls are fed by them.'

'Maybe, but there's one little problem – they're full of water! And the waterfalls are fifty, sixty feet high. The fall'd kill us.'

'I think there are more tunnels, higher up.' She indicated the tide mark. 'There, you see?'

Eddie peered down. Beyond the upper tier of buildings was a patch of blackness that could have been a tunnel entrance – or nothing more than a shadowed recess. 'If it's higher up in the cave, it'll come out even higher on the cliff.'

'I know, it's a risk. But if we stay in here, sooner or later we'll run out of bullets – and then they'll massacre us.'

'Okay, we'll try it,' he reluctantly said, before shouting: 'Get down to the village! There might be a way out through the drainage tunnels!'

'*Might* be?' wailed Lydia.

'You can bloody stay here if you want! But it's the only chance we've got.'

'He is right,' Fortune said firmly. 'Everyone, across the bridge. Quickly!'

Panting, Howie reversed direction. 'Great, just . . . ran all the way up here, now gotta . . . run all the way back down!'

'What about Brice?' Nina asked Eddie as they hurried back. 'He's still down there.'

Her husband hefted the revolver. 'If I see him, I'll shoot him. Pretty simple.'

Fortune took up the rearguard position as his group headed downwards. 'I can hear them in the tunnels,' he warned. 'They must have made it through the traps – if any were with Mukobo when we first came down, they would know how to beat them.'

'If we got a couple of 'em, that's still a help,' Eddie called back to him as they crossed another bridge. 'The less we have—'

Another explosion ripped through the palace's roof.

Everyone ducked as gritty debris showered them, stone blocks plummeting past to explode on the cavern floor. Eddie looked up at the new rent overhead. The Insekt Posse reinforcements had this time planted their explosives with considerably less precision. The hole was bigger and more ragged than its predecessor, a loose block slowly bending the lead beneath it before falling away.

But this did not deter the militia. Ropes were hurled through the second opening. A third line also dropped from the original hole, armed figures crouching at its edge to cover those about to descend. 'There's more coming – go, go!' cried Eddie.

Nina looked down at the terraces as they hurried deeper. 'I think there's more than one drainage tunnel,' she said. 'So which do we take?'

Gunfire above. Eddie glanced up to see Paris return fire at an attacker on the roof as the militia started to descend from the second hole. 'The nearest sounds good!' More men lowered themselves from the first set of ropes. 'Fortune, hurry up or they'll cut you off!'

Fortune fired at the rappellers, one falling with a scream that was abruptly truncated as he hit the cave floor. 'Running low on ammo!'

'Me too!' added Paris as he sent a couple of shots at the other opening.

'Some extra mags down here!' Eddie shouted, pointing at the bodies below. He and Nina crossed the last bridge and headed as quickly as they could for the first tier of buildings.

Movement below it: Brice, at the Shamir chamber's entrance. The Yorkshireman halted sharply to take aim—

Nina, unprepared for his sudden stop, ran into him as he pulled the trigger. The Magnum round blasted a chunk of stone from the wall beside the British agent. His countryman reacquired his target and fired again, but Brice had already darted into the opening. 'Bollocks! Not your fault,' Eddie quickly reassured her as he moved again.

'Are you going to go after him?' she asked.

'No time.' It would be touch and go whether everyone reached the terrace before the rappelling militia touched down.

He jumped the last few stairs to the cavern floor. The village spread out before them, a ghostly maze in the shafts of half-light. 'Where's the nearest drain?'

Nina had hoped the drainage tunnels – if that was what they were – would be evenly distributed, but the closest she could see was above the next tier down, unreachable without scaling the rock face. 'Dammit! It's on the other side of the village.'

'Come on.' He ran for one of the narrow alleys between the little structures.

'That one's closer!' said Nina of another.

'A guy fell over here,' Eddie countered. They raced along the confined street. It zigzagged, the dwellings seemingly not constructed to any orderly plan, but he soon saw what he had hoped for. 'There!'

The broken corpse of one of the Insekt Posse was slumped over a roof, his lower jaw mashed grotesquely up into his mouth. Nina grimaced as Eddie dragged him to the ground. A rapid check of the rifle on his back proved it had withstood the fall far better than its owner. 'Take this,' he said, giving Nina the golden revolver as he hefted the AK.

A burst of bullets fired from above struck nearby rooftops like deadly hailstones. Eddie and Nina flattened themselves against a wall, then ran again. A side alley gave them a glimpse of the lower level – and the men on the ropes descending towards it.

'Eddie, keep going!' cried Fortune, trailing his group across the final bridge. More shots came from the palace's roof, Paris and Ziff firing back to force the snipers to retreat. 'We will be right behind you!'

'So will they,' Nina said in alarm. More figures dropped from the roof, descending spider-like on their lines.

As if that were not bad enough, now gunfire came from a new direction. The Insekt Posse had made it through Solomon's challenges. 'Shit, we're gonna get swarmed,' Eddie said. 'We've got to find that way out!'

The alley opened out into a small square. A stone bowl surrounded by oil casks sat in its centre, other streets angling out of it. 'Which way?' asked Nina.

'Think there was another dead guy down here,' Eddie said, heading for one passage.

Nina started after him, but stopped as she heard Howie shout her name. She turned to see the young man breathlessly enter the square, still clutching the laptop. 'Wait, wait!' he gasped.

'We can't!' she replied. More rifle shots echoed down the cavern, a round ricocheting off a nearby building. 'Come on!'

She followed Eddie, Howie in her wake. The light from the

first hole in the roof made it easier to negotiate the confined alleyways – but it also made them easier to see from above. Bullets smacked against stone—

A high-pitched cry from behind – Lydia. 'Jesus, she's hit!' shouted Fisher.

'It just clipped her arm!' Ziff quickly responded. 'She's okay.'

The New Zealander replied with a screech of both pain and anger. 'That's easy for you to say!'

'Move, quickly!' Fortune snapped. 'Eddie, we are almost at the bottom.'

'So are the militia!' warned Paris.

Eddie scrambled on to a nearby roof. He spun to take in the whole cavern – and did not like what he saw. The first wave of Insekt Posse coming from the palace roof had just reached the ground, with more on the way, and the group descending from the tunnels were now on the second bridge. The expedition was outnumbered at least four-to-one – and outgunned by a much greater ratio. 'Get to the tunnels!' he yelled as he jumped back down. 'Get out of here – just *run!*'

24

Brice heard Eddie's shout from inside the Chamber of the Shamir. 'Yes, you run, Chase,' he said with a smirk. 'We'll see how far you get.'

He had removed the lead box's lid to examine the Shamir. If it was reacting to the infusion of daylight into the chasm, he couldn't tell – the growing vibration of the much larger mineral deposit in the mine was overpowering anything he could feel from its child – but his primary concern was that it was intact and undamaged.

It was. And it was his.

Other shouts outside. 'In here!' he called in French.

Three members of the Insekt Posse ran in. 'Le Fauchet!' shouted one. 'Where are—'

The trio froze as they saw their leader slumped dead. Horror turned to fury, guns coming up to exact vengeance – but Brice was prepared. 'They killed him,' he gasped, feigning shock. 'They murdered Philippe! The bald one executed him, right in front of me – and he would have killed me too if you hadn't blown the roof!'

The militia men stared at him, unsure what to do. All three were obviously on drugs, eyes red – and minds dulled. Mukobo himself never used, Brice knew, but ensuring a ready supply for his men kept them both loyal and unthinking. 'They're getting away!' he went on, taking advantage of their confusion. 'You've got to make them pay for killing Le Fauchet! Cut them up, butcher them like pigs!'

One seemed less addled than the others, hostility in his eyes as he glared at the MI6 agent. Brice felt a moment of worry that the African either didn't believe or didn't care that he wasn't responsible for Mukobo's death . . . but then the other two ran from the chamber, shouting to their comrades. The last man gave him a nasty look, then followed.

Brice turned back to the Shamir. Once Chase and the others were dead, the only people other than himself who knew the ancient relic's power would be a gang of drug-crazed savages – a small smile both at the use of the politically incorrect term and his certainty that it was entirely justified – whose wild stories about a magic stone that could destroy buildings would never be believed.

That suited him perfectly. A plan had developed in his mind after he witnessed what the Shamir could do, and ironically, by killing Mukobo Eddie Chase had made it possible.

He replaced the lid and took hold of the box. The combination of dense stone and lead plates made it a strain to lift, but it was still portable. And he only had to carry it as far as the boats. After that, he could use the satellite phone to call his contacts and get both the Shamir and himself out of the country . . .

He hauled the casket towards the exit as gunfire resumed outside.

'Go, let's go!' Eddie yelled as he hurriedly backed through an alleyway. Nina and Howie were ahead of him, Fortune and his group on a parallel path.

But the Insekt Posse were closing in.

One militia man had started whooping, a demented, almost animalistic sound, and his howl had been taken up by the rest. The terrifying cacophony echoed through the cavern as they bayed for blood.

Eddie had no intention of letting them take any. A screaming man sprinted down the alley after him, AK in one hand and a machete waving in the other – only to tumble gracelessly to the ground as a bullet from the Yorkshireman's own rifle blew a fist-sized chunk from his throat. 'You can fuck off!' he shouted.

But more were coming, and he didn't have enough ammo to take them all down. He turned and raced after Nina and Howie. The two Americans had opened up a lead on him – but to his dismay his wife was now squandering it as she stopped in another little square, Howie continuing past her. 'No, keep going!' he yelled.

'I'm not leaving you!' she insisted.

'Do we have to have this conversation *every fucking time* we get chased?' he demanded. Like the first square, this had a large bowl to provide illumination at its centre, pots of oil around it.

'Do you have to *run so goddamn slow?*' she shot back, setting off again.

Eddie followed her to the crooked alley's first turn – then crouched in an empty doorway, readying his weapon. The Insekt Posse charged into the square. He waited until the first man reached the bowl – then fired.

One of the pots shattered, oil spraying out . . . but it didn't ignite.

'Oh, *arse*,' Eddie muttered. The other howling men raced through the square, guns coming up—

A second bullet smashed another pot – and this time the searing metal ignited its contents.

Fire gushed from the broken vessel, splashing over the spilled oil – which erupted into a wall of flame that swallowed the leading militia. They burst through its other side as human torches, the bloodlust of their screams turning to agony. The Insekt Posse behind them hurriedly halted.

Eddie rose, about to run after Nina. The fire had spread across the whole square. Nobody would be following him—

His satisfaction lasted barely a moment. Rather than turn back, the trapped militia climbed on to the roofs of the surrounding buildings. 'Oh, for fuck's *sake*!' he growled, unleashing a couple of shots that sent two men crashing back on to their enraged companions, before racing away.

More gunshots from another alley: Fortune shooting at his own pursuers, and angry bursts of fire as they retaliated. But there was another sound over the thudding Kalashnikovs. The Mother of the Shamir's subsonic hum was becoming a distinct, audible rumble.

And it was getting louder.

'Eddie!' Nina cried. 'I can see the tunnel!'

'Keep going, don't stop for anything!' A look back spurred him to run faster as he saw the mob leaping from roof to roof in pursuit.

He cleared the village. Ahead was the promised tunnel entrance, a black rectangle cut into the rock wall. Nina reached it, Howie ducking past as she stopped inside the low opening. The rest of the expedition members were heading for her, Fortune and Paris covering their rear.

Ziff had fallen behind the documentary crew, the elderly Israeli struggling to keep pace. He looked back. 'Eddie! Behind you!'

Eddie glanced over his shoulder – and saw one of the Insekt Posse right on him. The tall youth let out a gleeful cry, swinging his machete at his prey—

A bullet whipped over the Englishman's head to strike the sprinter in the face. The African fell.

Eddie looked ahead again to see Ziff standing on a rock, lowering his gun. 'Thanks, Doc!' he shouted. 'But get down! Get to the—'

Bloody holes burst open across Ziff's torso.

The Israeli tumbled to the ground. '*David!*' screamed Nina.

Eddie spotted his shooter: Luaba. He stood on the last building at the village's edge, swinging his smoking Kalashnikov towards the Yorkshireman—

Fortune and Paris both fired at him. The hulking Congolese dived flat. 'Paris, go!' Fortune shouted, heading for the fallen Ziff.

'No, I'll get him!' Eddie yelled. 'Cover me!' He reached the rock, finding the Israeli sprawled behind it. Ziff was still alive, clutching at his stomach. 'Doc! Stay with me, I'll get you up.'

He hauled the other man over one shoulder, then clutched both their rifles by their straps and lumbered towards the tunnel mouth. Fortune kept firing, downing two more militia. 'Eddie, I'm almost out!' he warned.

Paris added his own firepower to his partner's. More screams came from behind Eddie as he struggled onwards. But they were still massively outnumbered even with the Insekt Posse taking casualties – and rapidly running out of bullets.

Rivero reached the tunnel and bent down to enter it, closely followed by Lydia and Fisher. Inside, he switched on his camera's spotlight to reveal that the drainage channel sloped downwards for some distance into the rock.

Eddie reached the opening. 'Nina, help me!' His wife took Ziff's weight as he slid him from his shoulder.

Paris and Fortune, still firing, followed him into the tunnel mouth. 'I'm out,' the tall Congolese barked, discarding his empty AK.

'Take one of these,' Eddie said, dropping the rifles. Fortune collected one, checking the magazine and giving him an unhappy look when he saw how few bullets it contained. 'Don't think the other one's any better.'

To everyone's surprise, Fisher picked up the second Kalashnikov. 'What're you doing?' Nina asked.

'I want to fight,' the director announced. 'If these bastards are going to kill us, I want to take some of them down first!'

'You know how to use a gun?' Eddie asked dubiously as the group headed into the darkness.

'Point, pull trigger, don't hit your friends in the back,' he replied, following Paris's example by supporting his rifle's foregrip in the crook of his right arm. 'I did a documentary about doomsday preppers; they let me fire off a few rounds from an AR-15. Okay, a few dozen.'

'More like a few *hundred*,' said Lydia as she switched on a torch. 'Rambo!' Fisher managed a faint smile.

Fortune took up the rearguard position again with Paris. 'They will reach the tunnel any second!' he warned.

'There'd better be a corner down there,' Eddie shouted to those ahead. 'Or we'll be fish in a very narrow barrel!'

Rivero's reply was both relieved and worried. 'Yeah, there is – but it goes left *and* right! Which way do we take?'

'Don't ask *me*,' Nina protested as she realised the others were waiting for an answer from her. 'It's a drain, so whichever way goes down!'

'They both look flat!'

'Are you *kidding* me? Solomon, you asshole! Not you, David,' she hastily added.

The wounded Israeli gave her a feeble laugh. 'No offence taken. And after all we've been through, I'm reconsidering my opinion of the "great king" . . .'

Nina looked ahead. Howie had let Rivero and Lydia past to light the way. They were indeed approaching a fork in the tunnel. 'Howie,' she said, 'you take David. I need to see where we're going.' Howie tucked the laptop under one arm and waited for her and Eddie to catch up—

A single gunshot from behind made everyone jump, the sound physically painful in the confined space. 'They are at the top!' said Fortune, grimacing at the noise of his AK.

Eddie took Howie's rifle as the young man and Nina switched places, then the redhead scurried down the shaft. 'Why didn't they just shoot us already?' asked Lydia as she caught up.

'You're complaining?' said Rivero sarcastically.

'For one thing, they're all doped-up, so they're not thinking straight,' said Nina. 'For another, I think they'd rather hack us to pieces for killing Mukobo.'

Lydia was startled. 'Wait, Mukobo's *dead*?'

'Ah . . . yeah,' Nina said as she took the New Zealander's flashlight. 'Should probably have mentioned that sooner, huh?'

'No shit!' spluttered Rivero. 'No wonder they're pissed!'

'What happened to him?' Lydia asked.

'What difference does—'

Paris's shout cut her off. '*Grenade!*'

One of the Insekt Posse leaned around the tunnel mouth, about to hurl a bomb—

Fortune fired again. The man's wrist blew apart in a burst of blood and bone fragments – and he dropped the grenade. The militia around him yelled in alarm—

A pounding blast came from the top of the shaft, shrapnel pinging off the stone walls. Paris yelped as a metal fragment slashed his cheek. The explosion's echoes faded, replaced by the screams of the wounded.

'Keep going!' said Fortune. 'That won't stop them for long.'

Nina reached the tunnel's foot. Both new branches ran level for about fifty feet before turning again. 'Oh God, which way?' she said. One seemed no better than the other, but if she picked the wrong path, they would be trapped . . .

Something touched her forehead. She flinched, then looked up to see flecks of grit falling from a crack in the ceiling. In the panic of the escape, she had forgotten the Mother of the Shamir's rising rumble – but now its effects were becoming all too apparent.

Rivero and Lydia arrived, the cameraman aiming his light at the crack. 'It's going to cave in!' exclaimed the frightened sound woman. 'Get out of the way, we've got to move!'

'No, wait!' insisted Nina, watching the falling dust intently. 'Jay, hold still, just for a second.'

He kept the camera upon her. 'What're you—'

'Shush! Don't move! I need to see this . . .'

She stared at the motes dropping through the spotlight beam – then pointed right. 'That way!'

'How do you know?' Rivero asked.

'Remember how I found the map room in the First Temple?' she said as she started down the passage. 'Same thing – the dust's being blown the other way, so the fresh air must be coming from down here.'

'Hope you're right,' said Lydia as she followed. Rivero stayed just beyond the intersection to provide light for those behind.

'Yeah, me too. Eddie, right tunnel, right tunnel!'

More ear-splitting gunfire from the two Congolese as they forced back the regrouping militia – then Paris tossed away his AK. 'I'm out!' he yelled. 'Mr Fisher! Give me your gun!'

Fisher waited for them, but rather than hand over his weapon, gestured for Paris to overtake him. 'You go on!'

'Mr Fisher, that is a very bad idea,' Fortune told him firmly. 'Our job is to protect you, not—'

Fisher held up the stump of his right arm. 'Sorry, but the job? Kinda failed! And I'm in charge of this expedition, I'm responsible for everyone else.' More quietly: 'Make sure Lydia gets out of here. Please.'

Paris exchanged looks with Fortune, neither man happy, but then the shorter Congolese nodded. 'Okay. I'll look after her.' He hurried downhill.

Nina led the way through the new tunnel. She reached its corner, finding to her relief that it sloped downwards beyond the turn. The feeling was quickly tempered by concern as she saw more dust-spitting cracks in the ceiling and walls. 'We've got to move faster! The whole place is going to come down!'

'Like we don't have enough going on,' said Eddie as he reached the first junction. Rivero moved ahead, lighting the way with the Sony. 'Doc, how are you doing?'

'Not . . . very good,' Ziff replied weakly. 'Oh, it hurts . . .'

Paris caught up. 'Mr Pinkett, I can take him. You catch up with the others.'

'Where the fuck's Fisher?' Eddie demanded. 'You're supposed to be protecting him!'

The Congolese took Howie's place, the young American hurrying on past Rivero. 'He wouldn't let me.'

'That's no fucking excuse!'

'It's my decision!' Fisher shouted as he and Fortune approached. 'I'm in charge here, not you!'

'There's a time for heroics and a time for saving your own arse,' Eddie objected, 'and this is an arse-saver!'

The two trailing men reached the junction. 'I agree,' said the director, 'so you make sure everyone—'

'*Grenade!*' Fortune cried, grabbing him and diving into the left tunnel. Eddie rushed back and dropped to the stone floor, Ziff gasping in agony as the Englishman covered him. Paris threw himself after them as a hard metal object clacked down the sloping passage—

The detonation obliterated all senses.

Eddie had managed to cover his ears, but still only heard a piercing, ringing sound for several seconds before other noises gradually returned. None were reassuring. Echoes of falling rock faded, smaller bangs and clunks of stone telling him that rubble was still dropping. The blast had brought down part of the ceiling!

He opened his eyes. The first thing he saw in the light from Rivero's dropped camera was Ziff, face screwed up in pain. The cameraman himself groaned as he clutched at his head. Eddie forced himself up to check on the others.

Paris was behind Ziff. '*Oh, ma putain de tête...*' he gasped, before jerking upright in alarm. 'Fortune!'

'I am okay, I'm okay,' coughed Fortune from several yards away.

'What about Fisher?' Eddie asked. He looked for him, but saw only darkness. 'Steven! Can you hear me?'

'Here, I'm...' The director's reply was slurred, as if half-asleep – then he screamed. 'Oh God, oh my God! My leg!'

'Jay!' Eddie barked. 'I need your light over here!'

Rivero crawled to his camera. He brought it about – and its light revealed a large chunk of fallen stone on the junction's far side, partly blocking the other passage.

Fortune appeared in the gap. 'Eddie! His leg is trapped!' He tried to move the rock. Fisher cried out as it shifted, but it was too heavy to lift.

The Yorkshireman moved towards him. 'I'll help you—'

He jumped back as bullets cracked off the wall at the slope's foot. Above, stuttering muzzle flash lit the way for the Insckt Posse. The crazed whoops and howls of earlier had been replaced by something more chilling: an angry chant of '*Le Fauchet! Le Fauchet! Le Fauchet!*'

They were out for revenge.

The obstruction shifted again as Fortune made another attempt to lift it, but with no better result. 'Too – heavy!'

'Run,' gasped Fisher. 'Fortune, go! I'll – I'll hold them off.'

'They'll kill you!' Eddie protested.

'They'll kill us all in a minute! I'm... not going anywhere.' That last was said almost with resignation.

'Jesus Christ, Steven!' said Rivero. 'We can't leave you!'

'I call the shots, Jay.' Somehow, the words held a hint of humour. 'Fortune, sit me up so I can see over the rock.'

The Congolese reluctantly did so, Fisher letting out another keening cry as the movement shifted his crushed leg. 'Have this,' Fortune said, placing his AK beside the American. 'Two guns – two sets of bullets. Make them count, my friend.'

The director propped his own Kalashnikov on top of the stone, aiming it up the tunnel. 'I should say something cool,' he said, seeing Rivero's camera pointed at him, 'but – oh God, I'm scared.'

'So am I,' said Eddie. 'You're a brave man, Steven.'

'Th-thanks,' Fisher replied, drawing in a deep, tremulous breath. 'Okay. Go on, then, go! They're almost here!'

Fortune's expression was one of shame at having to leave him behind. 'I am sorry, Mr Fisher. I am so very sorry.' He bowed his head to him, then looked back at Eddie and Paris. With bullets still screaming down the tunnel, he couldn't cross the junction to reach them. 'I will see you outside. I hope.'

'So do I,' Eddie replied. 'Fight to the end, Fortune.'

'*Bonne chance, mon ami,*' came the reply, then with a last sad glance at Fisher, he disappeared into the darkened passage.

'Take the Doc and get moving,' Eddie ordered Rivero and Paris. They picked up Ziff and set off as the Englishman returned to the junction. 'All right, you fuckwits,' he growled, switching his rifle to full auto, 'have some of *this*!'

He thrust the AK around the corner and pulled the trigger, sweeping it across the tunnel in a final blaze of fire. Screams echoed from above as bullets ripped into the Insekt Posse's leading ranks. A *clack* as the bolt closed on an empty chamber, but Eddie had counted his remaining shots and already dropped the rifle to scurry after his companions—

The walls behind him shattered under a furious onslaught of fire. Even retreating, he was still in danger as ricocheting bullet fragments shrilled after him. He ducked as low as he could and scrambled around the corner.

The shooting stopped as the militia realised he had discarded his weapon. The horrible chant resumed as they ran to catch their now-defenceless prey—

'Fuck you!' Fisher yelled, opening up with his own rifle. 'Yeah, fuck you, you motherfuckers!' More screams as he cut down the leading attackers. The gun ran dry; he threw it away and fumbled for Fortune's weapon. 'Cut off my hand? I'll cut off your fucking *balls*, you bunch of—'

He brought up the AK, getting off a shot that blew away half the face of a man rushing at him – only for another behind him to open fire. Two rounds hit the American's shoulder, slamming him to the floor. Blood spouting from the wounds, he lay helpless as the Insekt Posse swarmed around the corner and threw themselves over the rock. Machetes hacked viciously at him, his final scream almost drowned out by demented howls of triumph.

25

The sound echoed down the passages below. Lydia froze. 'Oh God! *Steven!*'

'We can't stop!' Nina told her. 'Howie, help her.'

'Come on, Lids. Come on,' Howie said, taking the New Zealander's hand. Numbed, she followed him.

The whole tunnel was now *reverberating* as the Imashamir absorbed ever more energy through the breached lead sarcophagus. Nina's light revealed another turn ahead. She rounded it. The passage sloped more steeply – and she felt a distinct breeze on her face. 'Wait, wait a second,' she told Lydia and Howie as she flicked off the torch. They dropped into darkness . . . but below, a dim glow was visible. 'I can see daylight!' she cried, hurrying downwards. 'We're almost out!'

The others picked up the pace behind her. 'Nina! How far?' Eddie shouted from the rear.

'Almost there!' she replied. One last crooked bend in the passage would bring her to its end. She rounded it, finally able to stand upright. Cut stone was replaced by raw rock. Squinting into the near-blinding daylight, she ran through the opening—

And lurched to a panicked stop as her eyes adjusted just in time to reveal what awaited her.

The drainage tunnel emerged from the promontory above the river – close to a hundred feet over the turgid water. 'Oh, crap!'

Lydia almost ran into her. 'Whoa!' gasped Howie as he pulled her back. 'Not good!'

'No kidding,' said Nina. The drop was near-vertical; probably climbable, given time, but that was a commodity they didn't have. Nothing to her left but an inhospitable rock wall – but on the right—

'This way!' she said, sidestepping on to a narrow ledge.

'Are you out of your *mind*?' Lydia squealed. 'It's like – an inch wide!'

'One inch is better than none!' The New Zealander was underestimating, but not by much. Even with her heels against the wall, Nina's toes overhung the edge. She moved along it as quickly as she dared. 'We can do it – come on!'

'But what if it stops around the cliff?'

'Then we got thirty feet farther than we would have!'

A brick-sized chunk of stone clattered down from above and smashed on the outflow's edge. Howie hurriedly passed Lydia and started after Nina. 'No offence, but I'm gonna go for it even if you're not,' he said, gripping the slim laptop tightly with one hand as the other groped along the cliff face.

Rivero and Paris brought Ziff into the daylight. 'Hey, where'd the others go – oh,' the cameraman said in dismay. 'How the hell are we gonna carry David along there?'

'You . . . you're not,' Ziff said weakly. 'Leave me. Please. Save yourselves . . .'

Eddie arrived behind them. 'We're not leaving anyone else,' he said firmly. 'Paris, Lydia, get your arses along that ledge. Jay, you an' me'll take him. And leave that bloody camera!'

'No way,' Rivero insisted. 'It's made it this far, and it's still recording.'

'Well, the last thing it ever records might be you falling off a fucking cliff – and taking me and the Doc with you!'

'Jay, I'll take it,' Lydia said, to their surprise. 'Hey, I'm already carrying all my audio gear and the backups.' She glanced at her backpack. 'Might as well complete the set.'

'Professionals,' Eddie sighed as Rivero handed her the Sony. 'They're all the bloody same . . .'

He waited for her to get clear, then with the cameraman leading, started to carry Ziff along the new path. The subterranean rumble became more evident as his back pressed against the rock. He dropped his chin to keep falling grit out of his eyes – but knew it would not be long before larger debris started to cascade down the cliff.

And there was another threat almost upon them. The Insekt Posse's echoing shouts grew louder. 'Jay, we need to move faster!' he warned.

'I'm going as quick as I can!' Rivero replied through gritted teeth. The bulky man's injured back was scraping along the rock wall.

'I'm telling you . . . leave me . . .' Ziff whispered. He was barely able to hold his head upright, the hand held to his stomach now drenched in blood.

'Not going to happen,' growled Eddie. 'Stay with us, Doc.'

Ahead, Nina edged around an outcropping. The huge boulder rising from the river came into sight – and between it and the cliff, until now hidden from view, was a steep, narrow slope. It looked as if it would intersect the path linking the ruined city and the river . . .

A jolt almost pitched her over the edge. She threw herself back against the rock wall, only to feel the entire escarpment trembling. It wasn't an earthquake's aftershock, though – rather, the precursor. The Mother of the Shamir was waking from her long sleep.

And she was angry.

Howie yelped as a dry waterfall of stones and dust fell past him. 'Holy shit!'

'Keep going!' Nina cried as she moved on. 'If we can reach that path down there, we can get to the boats!'

'*If* we can reach it!' said Lydia. 'The whole bloody cliff's going to collapse!'

Eddie glanced back at a shout from the drainage outflow. The first of the Insekt Posse appeared. He saw the Yorkshireman and smiled evilly as he raised his gun—

An explosive bang came from above him as rock sheared from the crumbling cliff.

The African looked up – and was crushed flat by a hunk of stone the size of a car. Gore splattered out from beneath it.

Startled cries came from the tunnel. Eddie saw an arm grope around the fallen boulder, but there was not enough room for anyone to squeeze past. The precariously balanced stone wouldn't hold them for long, though. 'Keep going!' he urged Rivero.

'I'm almost there!' Nina shouted back to the others. The drop to the steep path was still too far to risk, but she would soon reach a point where it was survivable – probably. She pulled into a concavity in the cliff. 'Howie, get past me. Drop down to that slope as soon as you can.'

'What're you doing?' he asked.

'Waiting for Eddie.'

He gave her a dubious look as he squeezed past. 'You think he'd want you to do that?'

'I'm his wife, why would I do what he *wants* me to do?' She managed a grin. 'Go on, get to the boats.'

Lydia reached her next, the other woman giving her only an angry look before going by. Nina was about to make a cutting comment, but remembered just in time that her lover had been murdered minutes earlier; there was no need to make matters worse. Instead, she waited for Paris. 'Where's Eddie?'

'On the way,' the mercenary assured her.

She looked past him to see Rivero edge around the outcropping, supporting Ziff. To her relief, Eddie soon followed. 'What about Fortune?'

Paris gave her a grim look as he moved on. 'I don't know. We got separated.'

'Oh, God . . .' She watched the three men approach. 'Eddie! Where are the militia?'

'The first guy's feeling a bit flat,' he replied. 'A rock fell on him and blocked the tunnel. Won't take the rest of 'em long to shift it,' he added, cutting off her premature hope. 'Why are you waiting? Keep going!'

'I'll take over from Jay and help you carry David.'

'I can do it,' Rivero insisted in a strained voice.

'No, you're hurt! The way your back's torn up, I'm amazed you haven't passed out already.'

'What can I say? I'm just that tough,' said Rivero through a pained smile, though he surrendered the Israeli to Nina.

One look at the pale, barely conscious Ziff filled her with alarm. 'David, can you hear me?'

A reply took a moment to come. 'Yes. And . . . I think you're insane for . . . not leaving me.'

'That's the way I work,' she told him. 'You should be used to it by now!'

They set off again. She looked along the ledge. 'Howie! How long before we can get down?'

'Not far!' Howie answered. 'Past those little trees, I reckon—'

A loud crash came from behind – followed by exultant cries. 'They've moved the rock,' Eddie warned. 'We've got to get down to the ground, now!'

'We're too high up!' said Rivero. 'We'll break our legs – or our necks!'

Howie passed some small trees clinging to the slope below. 'Okay, I'm gonna chance it,' he announced. He lowered the laptop as far as he could before releasing it. It fell into a bush, branches crackling as they caught it. 'Thank God for solid-state hard drives, huh?' he said before clambering over the edge, hanging by his fingertips for a moment before letting go. A thud and a loud 'Oof!' came from below – but then he jumped upright. 'I'm down!'

Lydia passed him, traversing the ledge for another twenty feet before fearfully dropping. Her fall was shorter, but she still cried out on landing. 'The camera okay?' Rivero asked as he prepared for his own descent.

'He ought to marry that bloody camera,' Eddie muttered – only to clutch at the rock wall as a tremor shook the cliff. Stones broke loose from above, Nina crying out as a fist-sized lump hit her shoulder.

Cracks ripped through the ledge, a yard-long section just behind them sliding away to smash on the slope below. The subterranean rumble grew ever louder. 'It's gonna go any minute!' said Nina. 'We've got to jump!'

Eddie looked down. The drop to the slope directly below was over thirty feet with nothing but thin underbrush to cushion their touchdown, a bone-breaking or even fatal fall. 'Too high – we'll have to jump into those trees!'

More debris tumbled down the rock face. The couple hauled Ziff along the ledge as stones pelted them. Rivero and Paris made their drops, the others already scrambling up the slope. Nearly at the trees—

Someone shouted. Eddie looked back. The Insekt Posse were catching up, the leader readying his gun.

Still short of the trees – but they were out of time. Eddie was about to order Nina and Ziff to jump—

The cliff behind them gave way.

It was as if a giant scythe had swept through the promontory's end. A great chunk of the towering wall plunged away – obliterating the militia amidst thousands of tons of disintegrating rock.

But Nina and Eddie were still not safe. The ledge crumbled yard by yard as if chasing them—

The Insekt Posse's demise had given them the few extra seconds they needed to reach the trees. '*Jump!*' roared Eddie.

They leapt with Ziff into the scrubby trees below – as the path cascaded after them.

Branches snapped, broken stubs slashing through their clothing – then thicker boughs caught them. The trees lurched violently as falling rocks hit their trunks, roots almost tearing out of the thin soil. Nina screamed as she was snatched away from Eddie and Ziff, dropping towards the churning rubble below—

The air was punched from her chest as she folded painfully over one of the trunk's forks. Gasping, she hung helplessly as broken scree flew around her . . .

The destruction stopped.

Nina strained to raise her head. The trees were partially buried beneath smashed stone, the channel between the cliff and the massive boulder now clogged with debris. Eddie and Ziff were both entangled in branches. 'Nina,' her husband gasped, also winded. 'You okay?'

'Super fine,' she croaked, managing a weak thumbs-up. 'What about David?'

'Oh, shit.' Eddie kicked loose, then clambered to Ziff. The Israeli was bent unmoving over a bough – the sharp stub of a severed branch buried bloodily in his side. 'Doc! Can you hear me?' He checked for a pulse. 'He's still alive,' he reported. 'He's losing blood, though – a *lot* of blood.'

Nina slithered painfully off the tree. The fallen rubble was not secure, stones shifting under her weight – and beneath it all, she could still feel the rumble from the underground chasm. The cliff's collapse was a mere preview of the Mother of the Shamir's full fury.

Eddie lowered Ziff to the slope. The older man had been

unconscious, but the movement woke him. He let out a gurgling cry, blood bubbling on his lips.

Nina gave her husband a fearful look. 'I know,' he said grimly, not wanting to voice the awful truth.

Ziff did it for them, however. 'I'm . . . not going to . . . make it, am I?' he whispered.

'We're not giving up on you,' said Eddie firmly. With Nina's help, he picked up the Israeli and carried him up the hill. The other expedition members waited above, watching anxiously.

'It's not . . . your decision,' Ziff wheezed. 'And . . . Nina?'

He feebly raised a hand; she clutched it. It was as cold as the stones around them. 'Yes?'

'I can die . . . happy.'

'What?' she asked in disbelief. 'Why?'

'Look . . . what we discovered. The lost . . . city. Solomon's palace. His greatest . . . treasure, hidden all this time. But we . . . we found it, Nina. We found it!' He squeezed her hand. 'I spent my whole life . . . searching for the wonders of King Solomon. And . . . we found them.'

'*You* found them,' she told him gently. 'I couldn't have done it without you.'

'Nor I without . . . you.' A very faint laugh. 'I would never have . . . imagined . . . that we would make . . . such a good team. Thank . . .'

She waited for another word, but none came.

Ziff's head rolled lifelessly against Eddie's chest. 'Oh, God,' she said, tears rolling down her cheeks. 'David . . .'

Eddie reluctantly halted and gently lowered the old man to the ground. Above, Lydia made a sound of despair. The Yorkshireman closed Ziff's eyes, then glared at Rivero, who had reclaimed the Sony and, despite his stricken expression, was filming the scene. 'Turn that fucking camera *off*.'

'Eddie, it's okay. He's just . . . doing his job.' Nina had to force the words past the lump in her throat. 'We still need to get out of here.'

'You can't just leave him!' Lydia wailed as the couple stood.

Eddie gestured at the cliff. 'That'll come down any minute. If we don't get to the boats, we'll be buried with him.'

'He's right,' said Paris. 'Come on.' He led the way uphill.

The others followed with varying degrees of reluctance. Nina's was the greatest of all, standing over Ziff until Eddie drew her away. 'Come on, love,' he whispered.

'Those *bastards*,' she snarled. 'Psycho bastards . . .'

They ascended the steep slope. 'Hopefully they're all dead now, so we won't have to worry—'

Everyone reacted with alarm at a shout from ahead. It was not the frenzied howling of the Insekt Posse, though, but a familiar voice. 'Paris! Eddie! Are you there?'

'Fortune?' Eddie exclaimed, surprised. He quickened his pace up the slope, pushing through the thickening undergrowth. 'Where are you?'

'Up here!' The group broke through the bushes to find themselves part-way up the path to Zhakana. Fortune, brushing dust off his clothes, hurried down it. 'You are okay?'

The delighted Paris was first to greet him. '*Mon ami!* I thought you were dead!' said the scruffy mercenary.

'How the fuck did you get here?' Eddie added, shaking his friend's hand.

Fortune shrugged as if the answer was self-evident. 'I followed the tunnel. It came out on the cliff on the far side of the palace.'

The Yorkshireman sighed. 'You really are the luckiest bugger on earth.'

Lydia shot Nina a venomous glare. 'You mean – we went the wrong way? You took us the *wrong bloody way*? Steven *died* back there! He died because of you!'

'All right, that's fucking *enough*!' Eddie shouted. She flinched back. 'We don't have time for this. We've got to get to the boats.'

Howie nodded. 'Yeah, come on. The river's not far.' He jogged down the path, the laptop under one arm.

'Lydia, I'm sorry,' said Nina as the rest of the group followed him. 'But I made the choice based on the information I had.'

'I would also have gone the way you did,' Fortune added. 'Nina did nothing wrong.'

'Yeah, well, tell that to his family,' the other woman snapped, wiping away an angry tear.

The words stung Nina, but she had no time to reply. More shouts came from behind – though these were anything but friendly. 'Oh, shit,' said Rivero, nervously looking back. 'Some of them got out!'

Eddie drew alongside Nina. 'You've still got Mukobo's gun?'

'Yeah.' She handed him the gold-plated revolver. 'I don't know how many bullets it's got, though.'

'Not enough even if it's fully loaded, by the sound of it.' There were definitely more than six surviving militia.

Howie paused beside a tree, the laptop clutched to his chest. 'I can see the boats!' he shouted excitedly, turning to face his companions. 'We can—'

A gunshot cracked through the jungle – and a hole burst open in the computer's casing.

The young man twitched, eyes wide in shock. A thin line of blood dribbled out through the cracked aluminium . . . and he slumped to his knees before toppling dead into the undergrowth.

26

'Get down!' Eddie shouted, pushing Nina back as he used the trees for cover to scurry to Howie's position. He peered around one to see the young American sprawled on the ground, blood oozing from an exit wound over his heart. Shot in the back – but by whom?

A second shot thudded into the tree just above him. Eddie jerked back, but the sound had revealed the shooter's position—

Brice!

The MI6 officer had beaten them to the river. He was untying one of the militia's clustered craft. Two more shots at Eddie to pin him down, then the mooring line came free. He jumped aboard.

Eddie sent a round back at him. Brice rolled behind the boat's cargo, the bullet striking it with a flat smack of lead on lead.

The Yorkshireman instantly recognised it: the Shamir's container. The ancient weapon was now in the hands of the British spy.

The outboard roared. The boat surged away, Brice staying low as he swung it into the river. Eddie fired again, aiming for the engine, but only blew a piece of fibreglass from its casing. 'Shit!' he barked, racing down the slope after him.

But by the time he reached the bottom, Brice was out of range, the boat kicking up a frothing white wake as he threw it into the bend around the promontory. Eddie opened the revolver's cylinder. Only one unused round remained. 'Buggeration and fuckery!'

'Eddie!' Nina cried as the others hurried down the slope. 'Are you okay?'

'Yeah, I'm fine. But Howie's dead. And Brice shot the fucking laptop!'

'For God's sake!' said Lydia. 'Who cares about the laptop?'

'It had Howie's drone footage on it,' Nina told her. 'We filmed Brice confessing to supplying Mukobo with weapons, that he was behind the civil war!'

'But Mukobo's dead,' said Rivero. 'Without him, the civil war's pretty much over, right?'

'Tell that to those arseholes up there,' Eddie countered, gesturing back towards Zhakana. The Insekt Posse would certainly have heard the exchange of gunfire.

'Fortune!' Nina shouted. 'Get the laptop!' The tall Congolese gave her a questioning look, but collected the computer from beside Howie all the same.

One of the expedition's boats was penned in by the Insekt Posse's moored craft, but the other seemed to have been left alone. 'What good'll that do?' Eddie said as he untied their free vessel. 'The bullet went right through it. It'll be fucked!'

'The laptop might be – but the hard drive could be okay.' Nina came to help him. 'If it's not damaged, we'll be able to get the recording off of it. We'll still have the proof!'

Rivero and Paris went to one of the militia's vessels and quickly unmoored it as Lydia climbed aboard. 'That's if we live to show it to anyone,' said the American.

Fortune headed for Nina and Eddie's boat, but the Yorkshireman waved him away. 'Drive the other one! After what happened in Burundi, I know you can handle a boat.'

'Better than you, my friend,' the Congolese replied with a small smile.

'What does *that* mean?' Nina asked as Fortune hopped into the second craft and started the engine.

Eddie grimaced at the reminder as he freed the rope. 'Nothing. Just a small . . . explosion.'

'*What?*'

They both boarded, Eddie going to the motor. 'Dunno why you're worried. You've been with me in boats loads of times.'

'Yeah, and how many of them blew up?'

'Not even half! Probably . . .' He yanked the starter cord. The engine rasped to life.

The other boat was already moving, but rather than swing away from the bank, Fortune drew alongside. 'Eddie! You may need this.'

Paris held up an empty Kalashnikov; the militia had brought spare weaponry. 'Thanks!' said the Yorkshireman, shoving the revolver back into his jacket as the mercenary threw the rifle to him. 'Any ammo?'

'Here.' Paris tossed a couple of magazines after it.

'Nina, load up,' Eddie told his wife. 'We're gonna need it.' She took the AK from him, slotting a mag into the receiver and tugging the charging handle to load the first round. 'You're getting pretty good at that.'

'Not a skill I ever wanted on my résumé,' she said unhappily.

Both boats swept out into the middle of the river. The Insekt Posse charged down the hill after them. 'Take over from me, give me the rifle.'

She switched places, puzzled. 'You know I don't *really* worry about your driving, right?'

'Good to know!' He took careful aim, then sent several shots back at the remaining boats. Shattered wood and fibreglass spat up – and one of the craft blew apart, an oily fireball rising from the thunderous explosion. 'Bollocks!'

'Why? You hit one.'

'I was hoping to blow up *all* of 'em so they couldn't follow us!'

Another detonation – this of shearing rock – rang across the jungle. A house-sized chunk of the clifftop tumbled into the river. The trees at the promontory's edge came with it, for the first time exposing the Palace Without Entrance to view from below. 'Look!' Nina cried. One of the towers crumbled, its ancient stones crashing through the roof. A second followed, demolishing most of the lead-lined ceiling . . . and the Mother of the Shamir's furious roar grew even louder.

The boat rolled as the wave kicked up by the falling debris hit it side-on. Nina grabbed the gunwale for support, Eddie bracing himself as he turned the craft into the crest to keep it from being swamped. Fortune did the same, the speedboat's prow leaping from the water before smacking back down. Rivero, still filming, yelped as he was pitched from his place.

Both vessels straightened out as the wave passed – but bigger ones would soon follow. Nina saw the entire promontory shudder as they rounded it, shedding loose rocks like a wet dog shaking itself off. At its base, the Insekt Posse's boats raced out in pursuit.

Boulders cascaded down the cliff into the water. Eddie swung towards the far bank, gambling that the risk of hitting something in the shallows was less than that of being capsized by a rogue wave. Fortune did the same, cutting across Brice's wake. The Yorkshireman glared after his countryman. There was not much difference in speed between the boats, but the MI6 man still had an advantage, and was edging away from his pursuers.

Gunshots from behind as the militia opened fire, bullets smacking into the water around them—

The rolling thunder reached a crescendo – and the promontory burst apart.

It was as if solid rock instantaneously turned to sand, the whole cliff – the whole *escarpment* – collapsing. What remained of the Palace Without Entrance vanished into the maelstrom, the surrounding jungle falling with it in a storm of shredded foliage. Zhakana was consumed too, the ancient ruins disintegrating before also being swallowed.

Countless kilotons of falling stone hit the water – and hurled up a huge wavefront, an enormous wall of white froth surging outwards at terrifying speed. Nina looked back, and wished she hadn't. 'Oh my *God!*'

Eddie glanced astern. The wave raced after them, bursting the opposite bank and sweeping away towering trees as if they were dry twigs. The last of the Insekt Posse's boats was snatched up. The driver tried to turn to escape, but there was nowhere to go. The craft flipped over, its two occupants flung screaming into the seething waters.

The Englishman knew they would soon follow them – unless—

'Fortune!' he bellowed over the rising noise from behind. 'Turn into it! *Turn into it!*'

He yanked at the tiller, bringing the boat around in a sharp turn to point back upriver. Some of the Insekt Posse saw his move and did the same. But others were panicking, trying to swing out of the wave's path or simply outrun it—

They failed, their boats smashed by the furious flume.

The other craft met it head-on. One had not turned far enough and was bowled over, but three of the enemy speedboats managed to ride up the charging wall of water, tipping almost vertically before disappearing over its crest.

Eddie looked at Fortune – then both men shoved their outboards to full power and drove directly at the wave. Nina held on as hard as she could as the bow pitched upwards—

The hull jolted as it was pounded by debris. Spray soaked them, a broken log lancing past like a spear . . . then there was a sickening moment of freefall as they crested the tsunami.

The landing threw Eddie from his seat. He tumbled down the boat's length—

Though half-blinded by spray, Nina saw her husband bowl past – and desperately grabbed his leather jacket. He thumped to a stop with his legs over the prow.

The boat spun around, smaller waves throwing it about like driftwood. Nina shook wet hair off her face and pulled Eddie back. 'Thanks,' he panted. 'Where's Fortune?'

She saw the second boat off to port. 'They're all okay – and crap, so are those guys,' she added. The jungle around them had been swamped, the river itself littered with flotsam, but those Insekt Posse who had cleared the wave were still afloat.

Eddie scrambled to the stern. To his relief, the outboard was still running. He pulled the boat back downstream, Fortune following.

Nina looked back. The landscape had completely changed. The entire promontory was *gone*, swirling dust all that remained where high cliffs had stood. The plateau on which Zhakana had been hidden for three thousand years was now a shattered crater, only the chewed remnants of trees poking through the rubble. The entire City of the Damned had been swallowed by the earth.

Something else had been buried too. The Mother of the Shamir had fallen silent. The chasm had collapsed on top of it, hundreds of feet of debris blocking whatever caused the destructive effect far better than a few inches of lead. The power it represented, the temptation and the danger it posed, had now been removed – permanently.

The threat from the parent was over . . . but that of its child still remained. Brice had the Shamir – and the British agent had also brought his boat safely over the tidal wave. 'There's Brice!' she said, pointing ahead.

Eddie powered after him. 'His boat's faster,' he warned. 'He'll get away – unless—'

'Unless what?' asked Nina, sure she would not like the answer.

'Unless we cut some corners.' He altered course. The rushing wavefront had broken the banks on both sides of the river, flooding the swampy lands downstream. Brice was still following the waterway's curves to stay clear of the trees – but Eddie was already angling to cut as closely as he could around the inside of the next bend.

'I *really* don't think that's a good idea,' she said, eyeing floating debris in their path.

'You want him to get away with that thing?'

'No, but I don't want to crash either!'

The boat bounded over Brice's wake, broken wood clattering against the prow. 'I can try not to crash into anything *big*. That do you?'

'Not really, no!' she cried as they surged around the bend. One side of the hull scraped against what had been the riverbank, spraying up mud – then Nina saw vines hanging from a low branch rushing at her. 'Aah! *Duck!*'

They both hurriedly dropped, the dangling creepers whipping at the top of Eddie's head as they roared beneath. He glanced back, cringing. 'See? Doddle.'

'Doddle, my ass!' Nina retorted.

He grinned, then looked past her at the river ahead as he pulled away from the waterlogged bank. His plan was working; they had made up ground on the fleeing spy. If they cut a few more corners, he would soon be in effective rifle range of the other Englishman . . .

Brice came back into view – closer than Eddie had expected. He wasn't taking the shortest possible route through the curves, instead following the deeper, safer middle of the waterway. The Yorkshireman realised why. The spy's full attention wasn't on piloting the boat because he was multitasking, one hand raised to his head—

Holding the satellite phone. 'Shit! The bastard's calling for help!'

★ ★ ★

'I don't care,' Brice barked into the phone. 'Get that chopper to me ASAP. If Sir Robert kicks up a stink, remind him who set up his deals in the first place. Just get it done!'

He disconnected and pocketed the phone – then heard another engine. He looked back.

A boat was following him, two familiar figures – one bald, the other red-haired – aboard. '*Really?*' he said with a faint huff that was as much grudging admiration as exasperation. 'What does it take to *kill* you, Chase?'

The engine at full power, he changed course to cut more tightly through the river's bends. Another look back as he sliced around a muddy bank. Chase's boat disappeared behind trees.

Confident that he would reopen the gap, he checked his watch. The helicopter he had summoned should reach him within half an hour, less if his contacts hammered home the urgency of its mission.

And once he was airborne, he could arrange to take care of any loose ends – including those pursuing him.

27

Eddie glared after Brice's craft. Now that the British agent had seen he was being pursued, he was cutting corners himself to maintain or even open the gap—

'Eddie!' They turned to see Fortune's boat behind them – and the Insekt Posse in pursuit. 'They're catching up!' Paris called.

Only one of the three enemy craft had more than two people in it, yet ironically this also seemed the fastest. 'It's Luaba!' Eddie said, recognising the hulking figure in the sleek black-and-gold speedboat's prow.

'Mukobo's buddy?' asked Nina.

'Yeah. And he'll probably be pretty pissed off about what happened to his mate!'

'Oh, you think?'

He looked ahead as Brice went around another curve, then back . . . 'Take over,' he said.

Nina blinked. 'You want *me* to drive?'

'You want to shoot instead?'

'I'll drive.' She hurriedly switched places.

He tipped the AK to drain any water that had collected in the barrel, then lined it up on their pursuers. The leading boat was well within range – but the man in its front seat had an identical weapon to his own—

Fire flashed from its muzzle. 'Split up!' Eddie shouted. Fortune sent his boat to the right, Nina peeling left as rounds kicked up little geysers in the water between them.

He fired back, scoring a hit on the first boat. The gunman

flinched as splinters flew at his face. Luaba's craft pulled out to overtake, the huge man readying his own gun. 'Paris!' the Yorkshireman called. 'You take the—'

'Eddie!' Nina cried in alarm. 'No way through!'

Toppled trees bobbed ahead, forming a literal logjam. A churned line of froth showed where Brice had slalomed between them, but his wake had moved the obstacles, closing the gap—

'There!' Eddie shouted, pointing. The flood wave had inundated another swathe of low-lying marsh – and he glimpsed the curving line of the river beyond its far side. 'Take a shortcut through there, quick!'

'Are you crazy?' she protested. 'We'll hit a tree!'

'You'd rather get shot?'

Nina didn't like either option, but the only alternative was slowing to pick their way between the logs – which at the rate the Insekt Posse were closing would get them killed. She turned towards the drowned bank.

Fortune took another route, however, heading straight for the obstruction. 'Fortune! What're you doing?' Eddie yelled. 'You're gonna crash!'

The Congolese kept going, Paris scrambling into the boat's rear and shouting for Rivero to follow him. The overweight American clambered to the stern . . . and Fortune released the throttle. The sudden deceleration pitched the bow downwards. Rivero lost his balance and fell – as the mercenary jammed the outboard back to full power. The combination of the surge in speed and Rivero's landing flipped the boat's nose back up, out of the water—

It hit the tree, the keel rasping across the wood like a saw blade as the vessel rode over its top. For a moment it seemed too tail-heavy to clear it . . . until Paris threw himself forward, landing beside the shrieking Lydia and bringing the boat see-sawing over the downed trunk.

Eddie stared in astonishment. 'He is the *luckiest* bloody . . .'

The Insekt Posse raced around the bend behind them. The leading boat's driver saw that Fortune's craft was not yet back at full speed and swerved to follow, assuming that if one boat could clear the log, so could another—

He was wrong.

The speedboat's prow hit the tree – and caved in.

The vessel somersaulted into the air and sent its occupants flying. One hit another floating trunk, a broken bough punching through his torso. His companion splashed down just ahead of Fortune's boat. The Congolese twitched the tiller to drive over him. The thunk from beneath the hull as his head bashed against it was followed by a muffled crunch as his face met the propeller.

Eddie winced. 'That's one way to get a really close shave!'

Nina was about to respond with distaste when she realised the other two boats had turned to avoid the blockage – and were coming after *them*. 'Okay, that's not fair!' she said instead as she drove into the floodland.

The boat vaulted over the submerged bank into the muddy new lagoon. The water was deep enough for it to traverse – but only just, the craft lurching as earthen humps beneath the surface punched at its underbelly. She struggled to guide it between the trees as Eddie took aim at the Insekt Posse.

Shots cracked between the boats. Luaba was in the front of the leading craft. He blasted away with his AK, bullets closing on their target—

Nina gasped and ducked as rounds hit the hull, then looked up again. 'Whoa!' she cried. A stand of trees loomed before the bow. She swerved hard left to avoid it. The sharp turn threw Eddie sidelong, sending his shots wide. 'Sorry!'

She straightened out, only to find the way ahead blocked where a huge tree had fallen. No choice but to take the long way back around the stand—

The militia cut right to intercept her.

Luaba's speedboat emerged on the other side, not far behind Nina's – and the faster vessel quickly drew level and swept in for an attack. Eddie fired at the militia leader, but hit only air as his boat bucked through the shallows—

The two boats collided.

The Englishman was thrown to the floor, landing amongst the expedition's spilled supplies. Nina managed to keep hold of the tiller and angle away. She saw Luaba recovering, about to fire at Eddie—

She shoved the outboard hard over. Her boat's bow slammed against the other vessel's stern – and kicked it into a spin.

Luaba was almost flung overboard, sheer muscle power keeping him inside. The driver frantically cut the throttle, the whirling boat stopping just short of a tree. The big man bellowed French obscenities and pointed after the fleeing couple as the other militia overtook them. The outboard roared again, sending the craft back in pursuit.

Eddie opened fire again – then his magazine ran dry. He looked for the replacement, but it was lost amongst the scattered cargo on the floor. 'Bollocks!' he snarled, throwing items aside to search for it. 'Nina, keep ahead of 'em until I can reload!'

'That's what I'm *trying*—' Her sarcastic rejoinder was cut off as bullets lanced past. She dropped behind the engine, realising she had completely lost her bearings. Where was the river?

A glimpse of Fortune's boat through the trees gave her the answer. She turned towards it, carving a serpentine course through the flooded marsh.

The other boats followed, rapidly closing, still shooting.

Eddie threw aside a canister of camping gas, finally seeing the spare magazine under a seat. He slapped it into place—

A Kalashnikov roared. Nina shrieked and threw herself flat as bullets smacked against the outboard, smashing its casing – and puncturing the fuel line. Gasoline spurted out, the engine stuttering.

Eddie raised his head, but the gunman in the nearest boat's bow saw him and fired, forcing him to drop again. Pinned down—

Something he had discarded moments earlier rolled back before him.

'Nina, stay down!' He clicked the AK's selector to full auto, then grabbed the gas cylinder and lobbed it over the stern – and sent a wild spray of bullets after it.

Most went wide . . . but he only needed one to hit.

And one did.

The little gas tank blew up ahead of the leading speedboat. The fireball swept over the gunman, searing his face and setting his hair alight. He screamed and fell backwards, Kalashnikov blazing blindly into the air. The startled driver ducked to avoid both kinds of fire, turning hard—

His boat hit a half-submerged log and launched from it in a corkscrew roll – straight into the thick trunk of a towering moabi tree. The speedboat exploded, showering blazing wreckage across the flooded jungle.

Eddie sat up. Another enemy down, but Luaba's boat was still gaining. He fired again – but the Kalashnikov's bolt clacked on an empty chamber after just a few rounds. Out of bullets . . . and there were no more magazines.

The outboard's cough worsened, the boat slowing. The speedboat rapidly closed in. Luaba grinned in vicious triumph as he aimed at Eddie and pulled the trigger—

Nothing happened. He too had burned through all his Kalashnikov's ammo.

Eddie groped inside his jacket for the revolver, but Luaba had a replacement weapon closer to hand. He snatched his bloody machete from his belt – and made a flying leap into the other vessel.

He landed with a bang in its rear, the huge man's weight violently tipping the boat. The gun thunked to the floor as Eddie was almost pitched overboard. The speedboat pulled alongside, the driver steering with one hand as he fumbled to raise up his AK with the other.

Nina shrieked and rolled as Luaba slashed the machete at her. Its edge thunked an inch deep into the gunwale just above her head, the boat's sway throwing off his aim.

He yanked it out for another strike—

Eddie dived at him, catching the African in a tackle that would have sent any other man over the stern. But Luaba was so solidly built that he only staggered. Nina scrambled clear as the York-shireman drove a punch into Luaba's stomach. The militia man grunted, but in mere discomfort rather than pain. He retaliated by swiping a pan-sized fist at his opponent's head. The blow knocked Eddie on to one of the seats.

Luaba hefted the machete, about to cleave it down into the other man's skull—

'*Tree!*' yelled Nina.

Her cry was aimed at her husband, but Luaba reacted to it, seeing a towering kapok rising directly ahead. He hurriedly grabbed the tiller and swerved away from the obstacle – hitting the speedboat side-on.

The other craft's driver had just targeted Eddie when he was jarred from his seat. Bullets spat from his flailing gun—

One hit the other boat's outboard – and ignited the leaking fuel.

Flames leapt up from the stern. Luaba jumped away in fright. Eddie also scrambled clear – but not quickly enough. 'Ow, *fuck!*' he cried as fire danced over his shin. He clapped his hands over his jeans, but the blaze refused to be extinguished. 'Shit, fuck, wank!'

Nina looked in horror between her husband and the view

over the prow. The river was not far ahead, but more trees blocked the way. Ten seconds, less, before a fatal crash – but Eddie would already be dead as Luaba recovered—

The boat's steel anchor sat in a coil of rusty chain inside the bow. She snatched it up and hurled it over her husband. It hit Luaba squarely in the chest and dropped to the deck with a dull clang.

He reeled back. Nina darted to help Eddie, throwing water over his leg. The flames lessened, but didn't die.

Luaba snarled at the couple – then saw the new danger in their path. Self-preservation overcame anger and he leaned over the flames to pull the tiller. The boat missed the trees by a foot. He hefted his blade again—

Eddie snatched up the anchor and swung it at Luaba's knee. Rust-scabbed metal cracked against cartilage. The Congolese roared as his leg buckled – but still didn't fall, clutching the outboard for support.

'What does it fucking *take*?' the Yorkshireman demanded. He grabbed the chain, then whirled the anchor above his head like a slingshot—

Luaba thrust the machete at his heart.

The point stabbed into Eddie's pectoral as he threw himself backwards. The anchor missed its target and whipped behind the bigger man's back, looping around him before the chain snagged on itself. The steel weight crashed on to a seat, rusted links clattering down on top of it.

Nina saw a flash of gold under a seat. The revolver. She snatched it up – as a thump from beneath the hull warned her they were crossing shallower water.

She looked ahead. Open river was only seconds away – beyond the half-submerged remains of an old fallen tree.

Luaba raised the machete for a final swing—

'Eddie!' Nina yelled. *'We're gonna crash!'*

Luaba froze as he saw the log rush at them. Eddie took full advantage of his hesitation to lunge for the anchor and hurl it over the stern—

The burning boat hit the tree – and rode up over it, vaulting out into the river.

The anchor's prongs thunked deep into the rotten wood behind it. The chain snapped taut—

Luaba's terrified scream was abruptly cut off as the rusty metal carved through his torso like a chainsaw's blade, his upper and lower halves spinning out of the boat in opposite directions amidst a fountain of blood and entrails.

But Eddie and Nina were still far from safe. The anchor chain was fixed to the bow – yanking the boat to a halt mid-jump and flipping it over.

They both screamed as they were catapulted skywards, arcing towards the muddy water . . .

They splashed down – as the burning boat blew up behind them. Its propeller skipped over the water like a razor-edged stone, barely missing Nina as she sank into the filthy depths.

She fought through her panic and righted herself, then kicked upwards to breach the surface. 'Nina!' Eddie gasped, swimming to her. 'You okay?'

'Yeah,' she spluttered, 'but I think I'll need every antibiotic shot they have once we get out of—'

An outboard motor roared behind them.

The speedboat burst from the flooded marsh, its furious driver bringing his craft about to mow down Luaba's killers.

'Split up!' Eddie barked, throwing himself towards the far bank. Nina went the other way. The onrushing boat swung after the Yorkshireman.

He swam harder, but knew he couldn't escape—

The driver's head blew apart.

Nina had brought the golden Magnum above the water and

fired. The dead man slumped over the tiller. The speedboat veered away from Eddie, spinning in decreasing circles until centrifugal force threw the corpse over the side. With nothing holding the throttle open, the outboard dropped to an idle putter, the craft slowing.

Fortune caught up and guided his boat towards the bobbing couple. 'Eddie! Nina!' he called. 'Wait there, I will get you!'

'Thanks!' Eddie replied – then he regarded the abandoned vessel. 'No, wait!'

'What do you mean, "wait"?' demanded Nina, tossing away the empty gun. 'Haven't you seen *The African Queen*? I want to get out of the water before we're eaten alive by leeches!'

'We still need to catch Brice before he gets away with the Shamir,' he said, swimming for the drifting craft. 'And that boat's the fastest thing on this river!'

28

Eddie's hunch proved correct. Once he and Nina had boarded Luaba's boat and set off in pursuit of the British agent, Fortune's craft was soon left behind.

He stared ahead for his quarry. The flood wave had diminished in power the farther it rolled from Zhakana, the riverbanks this far downstream not having burst. That meant Brice couldn't take any shortcuts across flooded land, so the speedboat would eventually catch up. 'What's the plan, then?' said Nina.

'Catch the bugger and shoot him is about as far as I'd got,' he replied. 'After that . . . I dunno. I don't think letting anyone get hold of the Shamir would be a good idea, though.'

'Not even the IHA? It would fall under their remit, after all – it's the Horn of Joshua, a biblical artefact.'

'You think they could keep it safe? Hell, where *could* they keep it? The UN building's not lead-lined, so if they put it in that vault in the basement, the whole building'd probably come down by Tuesday morning. And besides,' he went on grimly, 'I'm not sure I'd trust 'em to keep hold of it. Think how many different countries'd love to get their hands on a weapon like that.'

The IHA's former director felt distinctly defensive about 'her' agency. 'The IHA's an independent organisation under UN jurisdiction,' she insisted. 'They don't have to release anything under their protection if it would endanger global security. When I was running it, I had requests – demands, even – from governments to grant them unilateral access to various discoveries. I always turned them down. My argument was that if something we found was safe for one nation to have, then all nations should have the same access. Funnily enough, none of them liked that, but the IHA's charter gave me full right to control how the things we were protecting were used – or even if they were *allowed* to be used.'

'Yeah, but you're not running the IHA now, are you? You think Lester Blumberg was picked because of how he stands up against the same bloody governments that fund him?'

'So what are you suggesting? Destroy the Shamir, smash it into bits? All you'd get would be a whole load of little Shamirs, like the one King Solomon used to cut the stones for the First Temple.'

He shook his head. 'I dunno. I mean, giving it to the IHA'd be better than letting one country get hold of it for themselves, but—' He broke off. 'There he is!'

Nina glimpsed a distant flicker of colour through the trees. 'He must be over half a mile ahead of us.'

'Maybe – but that waterfall's a few miles from here,' he remembered. 'It's too high for him to go over. He's trapped!'

They swept through more bends, the speedboat's sides brushing against undergrowth along the banks as Eddie carved around them. The other boat reappeared ahead. 'There!' said the Yorkshireman excitedly. 'He'll be in range in another minute. You take over so I can shoot him . . .' He trailed off.

A new sound reached them over the outboard. At first Nina thought it was the waterfall's rumble, before realising it was too regular, mechanical. She looked up. 'Eddie, there!' she cried, pointing.

A helicopter was sweeping towards the jungle.

Brice spoke to the approaching aircraft's pilot via the satphone as he guided his boat downriver. 'Yes, I've just seen you,' he said. 'I don't know how far I am from the waterfall, but I assume you can see it from up there. There was a clearing two hundred metres upstream. You should be able to land and pick me up.'

'Yeah, we saw the waterfall,' replied the pilot. His accent was South African, and he sounded decidedly irate at being rushed into the jungle to perform an extraction, covert operations not being part of his job description. 'It's about three kilometres ahead of you. But you said you're the only person being picked up, right?'

'That's right,' Brice said impatiently.

'Then it looks like you've got some hitch-hikers.'

The MI6 agent looked back upriver. His eyes widened as he saw another boat following him – and even at this distance he could tell its occupants were not Congolese. 'Unbelievable,' he muttered.

He saw the Yorkshireman switch places with his wife. There was only one possible reason for the change of seats . . . 'I'm about to come under fire,' he told the pilot.

'You're *what*? Hey, no one said anything about guns!'

'I won't have time to stop,' Brice went on firmly, 'so you'll have to lower a line to pick me up. The weight will be—'

'What am I, a stunt pilot? I'm not—'

'Oh, *do* be quiet,' he snapped. 'Your orders are to do *exactly* what I say, yes?' The sullen silence from the other end of the line confirmed it. 'Then lower a line and fly overhead to pull me up. The weight will be roughly that of two adult men, so be ready for it.'

He brought the boat around a bend – and the river beyond straightened, stretching out towards the distant edge of the waterfall.

An edge that was getting closer every second.

He looked back up at the descending helicopter. 'How far away am I now?'

'Uh – two klicks, I'd say?'

'Then you'd better bloody get on with it!'

Eddie readied the replacement AK Paris had given to him as he watched the helicopter drop towards the river. 'He's not going to do what I think he's going to do, is he?'

'I think he is,' said Nina as one of the cabin doors opened – and someone inside pitched out a rope ladder. It unfurled like a banner, falling towards the boat below.

'Bloody spies! They really do all think they're James sodding Bond!' He took aim at the chopper – but held his fire.

'What are you waiting for?'

'The ride's too bumpy to hit anything at this range.' The river was picking up speed as it approached the falls, whitecaps forming. 'Keep after 'em!'

'Where else would I go?' she said sarcastically. The speedboat was at full throttle; all she could do was follow the other craft.

The chopper matched pace with Brice's boat, the ladder flapping beneath it. Eddie fixed his sights on the fleeing agent and took an experimental shot. A tiny white speck puffed from the river behind the vessel. He adjusted his aim for a second attempt – which missed by a wider margin, thrown off by the churning waters.

His target would have to be the helicopter. He wasn't happy about that – it was a civilian aircraft – but he couldn't let Brice escape with the Shamir. A couple of rounds hitting the chopper might be enough to scare off its pilot, though. He raised the rifle—

The snaking ladder hit Brice's hull. The spy grabbed a rung with one hand – and hauled up the lead box with the other.

No time left for second thoughts. Eddie opened fire, shots clanging against the helicopter's fuselage. The pilot immediately increased power to gain height, the ladder yanking tight beneath the aircraft—

Pulling Brice out of the boat.

The slipstream spun him around as he was hauled upwards. Eddie kept shooting. Smoke coughed from one of the helicopter's exhausts – but it continued climbing, angling away from the river to seek cover behind the jungle canopy.

Brice and his cargo went with it. Eddie switched targets, unleashing his remaining bullets at the swinging man in a last-ditch attempt to send him plunging to his death.

It failed. The final round cracked from the barrel, but the MI6 officer remained on the ladder as he swept over the trees. 'Buggeration and *fuckery*!' Eddie shouted, throwing down the empty gun. 'The bastard's got away!'

'You hit the helicopter,' said Nina. 'It might not make it out of the jungle – or the Shamir might get too heavy for him and he'll fall off.'

'Yeah, he might. And I might fart angel dust, but it's about as likely – oh, shit! *Turn!*'

She looked ahead – as the empty boat hit rocks on the lip of the falls and corkscrewed over the edge. A boom of disintegrating wood and fibreglass loud enough to be heard even over the water's roar reached them a moment later. Nina jammed the outboard hard over—

The boat turned – but the swollen river's current had caught them, sweeping it relentlessly towards the precipice. The stretch of bank where the expedition had refloated their vessels after hauling them uphill whipped past. 'We won't make it!' she cried.

Eddie scrambled on to the bow. 'Jump for those rocks!' he said. Some boulders lay half submerged close to the bank. 'If we land behind 'em, we'll be out of the current!'

Nina unwillingly followed him. 'They're too far!'

'We've got no choice! *Now!*' He pulled her with him and leapt from the prow.

Nina's cry was cut off as they hit the water and went under.

She lost her grip on her husband's hand. Blinded, she flailed back to the surface, gulping in air – only to choke as a wave hit her face.

The jungle whirled around her. She glimpsed the bank and swam towards it, more waves assaulting her. The boulders loomed ahead. Eddie had been right; the current's grip was lessening. But she still had to reach them . . .

She struggled onwards, her waterlogged clothing and boots pulling her down. The river was still dragging her towards the falls. In the corner of her eye she saw the abandoned speedboat plunge over the precipice after Brice's vessel.

She would soon follow it if she didn't reach safety—

One foot banged against something. Was it just a large stone, or shallows? Nina couldn't tell – but had to gamble that it was the latter. She thrust both feet downwards, probing for solid ground . . .

And finding it.

She thrust herself forward. The nearest rock was ten feet away. She swept her arms through the water to pull herself closer, six feet, three—

Her palm clapped against stone. She gripped it, pulling herself nearer. Where was Eddie?

'*Nina!*'

He was behind her, being dragged inexorably towards the waterfall as frothing waves rolled over him. A few more seconds and he would be past the boulders, beyond any hope of escape—

He resurfaced, thrusting a hand out of the water—

She was there to catch it.

Their fingers hooked around each other. His weight threatened to tear her loose, but she kept her hold through sheer force of will, refusing to surrender him to nature. He swam closer, Nina hauling him in, until his feet finally touched down on the stony river bed.

He waded to the shore, Nina staggering after him. 'God, that was a bit close,' he gasped, slumping on the bank. She flopped down beside him, exhausted. 'Are you okay?'

'I'm fine,' she replied with a half-hearted smile as she squeezed a waterlogged pocket. 'I'm just glad I kept all my important paperwork in a sealed baggie!'

'Might have to put my passport through a mangle,' he said ruefully – then remembered that someone else would be leaving the Congo well before them. 'Fucking Brice!' he said, glaring after the departed helicopter. 'He's got the Shamir.'

'But what's he going to do with it?'

'Won't be anything good.' Eddie stood, shaking off water. 'You heard him talking about regime change and bringing down government buildings – and that was just off the top of his head.'

The distant thrum of an engine caught their attention. The other boat came into sight upriver. Eddie waved until he got a response. 'They've seen us,' he told Nina with relief.

'Great,' she said, trying to wring water from her clothes. 'I don't think I'll ever have been so glad to leave somewhere.' She saw his far from enthusiastic expression. 'What's wrong?'

'I just get the feeling we won't have an easy time getting out of the country. We know enough to cause Brice some big problems. And not only him – the people who sent him too.'

Nina sighed. 'Wonderful. Just what we need.'

They wrapped their arms around each other, waiting for the other survivors to arrive.

29

'We should reach Nakola in half an hour,' Eddie reported, checking a GPS unit. Rather than risk stopping to make camp, they had travelled through the night, he and Fortune trading shifts at the outboard. A misty dawn rose through the trees ahead.

Lydia, sitting sullenly on her own, snorted. 'Yeah, and then it's another day to the airport. If we don't get stopped by the militia again. And if our buses are even still there!'

'They will be there,' said Fortune. 'The people there know me, they will not let anything happen to them.'

'Yeah, well, the guys at the lost city didn't care about your reputation, did they?'

'Hey, Lids, lay off,' said Rivero tiredly. He had finally put down his camera, using Lydia's laptop to back up the contents of its memory card to a solid-state hard drive. 'It's not his fault.'

'Oh, I know *exactly* whose fault it is,' she replied, glaring at Nina. 'And for what? For a fucking television show! We rushed into this whole bloody thing just to satisfy your ego, Nina! And now people are dead!'

Nina's patience had worn to its limit. 'Shut up, Lydia. Just shut the hell up. You think I wanted any of this to happen? Do you think I would even have come here if I'd known it might?'

Lydia was unrepentant. 'I think you'd go *anywhere* for a chance of finding some archaeological crap and getting your face in the news. And you don't care who gets hurt along the way.'

'If you think that's what drives me,' said the redhead, anger rising, 'then you don't know me at all.'

'I don't *want* to know you. I wish I never had. Even before you dragged us into this, you were a horrible person to work with – you're rude, bossy, you don't give a *shit* about anyone else's feelings, and in all honesty?' Lydia's voice rose as she continued her tirade. 'You're not even that good a presenter! You're stiff, and boring. But *no*, you're famous, so the network has to have you. And look where that got us!'

Eddie gave her a warning look. 'Think now'd be a good time to stop talking.'

'Or what? You'll throw me overboard?'

'Don't fucking tempt me.'

Lydia bridled, but said nothing more under his cold stare. Instead she made a sound of disgust and turned away. 'Well, this is . . . jolly,' muttered Rivero to break the uncomfortable silence.

Nina gazed disconsolately at the floor. Eddie gestured for Fortune to take his place at the tiller, then joined her. 'Don't listen to her,' he said quietly, putting a hand on hers. 'She's just angry, she's talking crap.'

'She's saying what she really thinks,' countered his wife.

'If you were like what she said, I wouldn't have married you. I mean, you can get a bit obsessive about stuff, but that's not the same as—'

'*Stuff* like Zhakana, right?' She wiped tears from her cheeks. 'Lydia's right about that part. I pushed to come here; I used my influence to get the network to fund the expedition. And I was so pleased about my . . . my *cleverness* at finding the map room that I thought finding the City of the Damned would be just as easy – and the whole documentary would show off how smart I was to the world. Well, guess what?' She let out a long, miserable breath. 'Nobody likes a smart-ass. And because of me, David and Howie and the rest are dead. Oh, God.' Nina put her hands over her face. 'It's happened again, hasn't it? People have died because I went chasing after another archaeological find – they've died because I put stones and statues ahead of their lives!'

'They're dead because of that fucking arsehole Brice,' Eddie insisted. 'Him and Mukobo. They're the bad guys, they did all the killing.'

'Not all of it.' She finally looked up at him. 'I . . . I still can't believe what you did to Mukobo, Eddie. You just – you shot him!'

'Yeah, and I shot a load of his goons an' all. We'd all be dead if I hadn't. How many people have I had to take down to protect you before now?'

'That's not what I meant. You *know* it's not what I meant. None of the other people you killed were bound prisoners.'

His voice developed an angry edge. 'None of 'em had threatened to rape and kill my daughter either. *After* killing me – and you as well. The world's better off without that piece of shit in it, and I don't know how you can deny it.'

'I'm not *trying* to deny it. What I'm saying is . . . Jesus, Eddie.' A pause before she spoke again, even more quietly. 'You *murdered* him.'

'Not how I see it,' he replied firmly. 'Far as I'm concerned, he was a threat – not just to my family, but to loads more innocent people. By killing him, I've saved their lives, as well as ours.'

'That wasn't your choice to make, though.'

'Then whose was it?' he snapped. 'The UN's? America's? I know it wasn't Britain's, because my own fucking country was backing him!' He shook his head. 'God. Fucking spooks . . .'

Nina glanced at the equipment. The laptop holding Brice's confession was beside Lydia's, but they had no way to know if the recording was retrievable; the machine was too damaged even to power up. 'Maybe we'll be able to get the proof off the laptop when we get out of here,' she said, glad of the chance to move away from a deeply uncomfortable subject on which they would never find agreement.

'Maybe. But we'll probably have more than just Brice trying to stop us.'

'MI6?'

'Maybe the whole government. British politicians'll do anything to cover their own arses – and their mates' arses an' all. They've protected fucking *paedophiles* who're part of the old boys' network. And there've been plenty of convenient "suicides" and "accidents" taking out people who could've caused 'em trouble. Remember when I was talking to Brice, about the Increment and the Removal Men?'

'Yeah?'

'There's been rumours for years that some special forces team was ordered to assassinate Princess Diana 'cause she was protesting against the arms business and wanted to marry a Muslim. Didn't believe them, sounded like a load of conspiracy bullshit – nobody *I* ever knew in the SAS would have followed that order, not against Diana – but after what Brice said about GB63 crashing that 747 . . .' He shook his head. 'If they wanted to be absolutely sure of shutting us up, that'd be who they'd send.'

'So people with the exact same training as you, but younger, and more of them, *and* with the backing of the British government? Great.' Nina gloomily regarded the river ahead. 'So what happens now?'

He considered the situation. 'Brice's probably fucked off with the Shamir already. He'll have got MI6 to extract him.'

'And take him back to England?'

'Probably. But he's still got contacts here. I doubt he'd rely on the militia, especially now Mukobo's dead, but he hired all those mercs we saw at Butembo airport. He might send someone to intercept us before we can leave the Congo.'

'To get the laptop?'

He nodded. 'That video's like a time bomb. He'll do anything to stop it from going off.'

Paris turned in alarm. 'What about a bomb?' His question drew the attention of the others.

Eddie and Nina exchanged resigned looks, then the Yorkshireman raised his voice. 'Okay. There's something we need to tell you all . . .'

The revelation of Brice's true agenda predictably did not lift anyone's spirits. 'Fantastic,' said Lydia plaintively. 'So now the British government as well as everyone else in this bloody country wants us dead?'

'It's us two they want the most,' said Eddie. 'We're the ones Brice actually told what he was really up to.'

'But he'll assume the rest of you either saw the drone recording, or we told you about it,' Nina added.

'Which . . . you just did,' noted Rivero sardonically.

'I doubt he'd accept a plea of ignorance. He won't take the chance that you know nothing about it. He can't.'

'I imagine he will not be satisfied if we give him the recording,' said Fortune.

Eddie shook his head. 'He'll want us all dead, whether or not he gets it. We can link him to Mukobo.'

Lydia put her head in her hands. 'Oh, God. What are we going to do?'

'We're nearly at Nakola,' announced Paris. Ahead, garbage was strewn along the riverbank.

Eddie joined him at the bow. Buildings came into view through the trees. He surveyed the shoreline, wary of an ambush, but saw nobody. 'If Brice sent anyone, they'll probably be coming from Butembo. They might not have arrived yet.'

'But that means they'll run into us on our way there,' said Rivero.

'I know a back road,' Fortune told him. 'It will take much longer to get to Butembo, but there is another way out of here.'

'Brice'll still be looking for us, though,' said Nina. 'Sooner or later, his people'll find us. What do we do then?'

Eddie had no immediate reply. He instead turned his attention to the village. A couple of locals came to the waterfront to watch their approach.

Fortune called to them in French, a brief exchange following. 'They say no strangers have arrived recently,' he reported.

'Good,' said the Yorkshireman. 'Brice hasn't got anyone here yet – so we might have a chance of leaving by the back road before they turn up. We'll need to get everyone into the buses, quick.'

The prow bumped on to land, Lydia immediately disembarking. Paris collected a line and hopped off to moor the boat, but Eddie took it from him. 'I'll do it,' he said.

'Hey, just because I'm hurt doesn't mean I'm useless,' Paris protested. 'I've only got one hand, but it's a good one!'

Nina climbed out after the two men. While Paris had on the surface handled his mutilation with a mix of stoicism and dark humour, during the night she heard him struggling to contain sobs as he hunched up, cradling his missing hand. 'We know – but you *are* hurt. You need a chance to recover, and if you push yourself too hard, that won't happen. Please, let us help you.'

He reluctantly acquiesced. 'Okay. But I'm not going to stand around doing nothing!' He reached back into the boat and lifted out one of the expedition's packs.

Rivero put the surviving laptop in Lydia's backpack before starting to gather his own gear. Nina retrieved its damaged twin. Howie's blood had been wiped off the casing, but there were still dried traces around the bullet hole. She suppressed a shudder, but the underlying pain was harder to push down. She would have to contact the families of all those who had not returned, not only to express her condolences but also to explain how their loved ones had died, and her part in their deaths . . .

The rising rasp of an engine cut through her grim thoughts. 'Someone's coming!' Eddie warned. The expedition's vehicles were parked not far from the shore; he pointed to them. 'Get in, quick!' Fortune jumped from the boat and hurried after Lydia towards the buses, but Rivero remained aboard, stuffing the last of his gear into a bag. 'Just leave it, for fuck's sake!'

'No way,' the cameraman insisted. 'I almost died to get this footage, I'm not leaving it behind!' He yanked the zip closed and grabbed his camera before climbing out, about to turn back for the remaining packs and equipment until he wilted under Eddie's impatient glare and followed his companions.

Everyone hurried to the minibuses. Eddie looked down the village's main street as the approaching vehicle came into sight. It was a dirt bike, riding high on its heavy-duty suspension and chunky off-road tyres: the perfect choice for anyone who wanted to traverse the DR Congo's rutted, broken roads at speed. The rider had a gun slung over his back – not the ubiquitous Kalashnikov of the militia, but its American equivalent, one of the many variants of the M16 assault rifle.

The man drew nearer, his attention fixed upon the minibuses. There was no way the group could make a getaway without being seen . . . 'Nina, give me the laptop,' ordered Eddie.

'But it's our only bargaining chip,' she protested.

'It's also what he's been sent to get – so I'm hoping it'll hold his attention while the rest of you escape.'

'We are not leaving you behind,' Fortune insisted.

'Hopefully you won't have to. Come on, hurry up.'

Nina reluctantly gave him the computer as the rider pulled up near the parked vehicles. The villagers retreated nervously at the sight of his gun. He dismounted and took off his helmet, revealing a tanned Caucasian face and a greasy blond mullet.

'Saw him at the airport,' Eddie muttered. 'One of the mining company bodyguards.'

'Not one of these Removal Men?' Nina asked.

'No, he's just a mercenary – but Brice'll definitely have sent him—'

'Eddie Chase!' the man called in confirmation. 'Nina Wilde! Show yourselves! I know you're here!' His accent was German or Austrian.

'Who's asking?' Eddie shouted back.

'A man called Brice.' He unslung his rifle, a Bushmaster M4 carbine painted in striped jungle camouflage – but rather than ready it, he held it in one hand while he took something from his dark jacket with the other. 'He wants to talk to you.'

'Yeah, to hear our last words,' said Nina, seeing the merc hold out a satellite phone – the one Brice had taken from the expedition. 'Can we trust him?'

'Nope,' said Eddie. 'But he could have just come around here and shot us all if he'd wanted, so . . .'

He stepped out from behind the bus, the laptop in his hand. 'I'm here.'

'Eddie!' Nina gasped, but the mercenary's rifle remained lowered.

The blond man regarded Eddie with suspicion. 'And Nina Wilde?'

She leaned cautiously out from behind the bus. 'Hello, hi.'

He waved the phone impatiently. 'Come here. He's waiting.'

'Keep everyone safe,' Eddie told Fortune quietly before he and Nina went to the new arrival. 'All right. Give us the phone.'

The merc handed it to him, then stepped back. Eddie brought the phone to his ear, Nina craning her neck to listen in. 'Yeah?'

'Good morning, Chase,' Brice replied. 'I'll get straight to the point. You and your wife survived, so I have to assume that your friends did as well – and that you've told them about our little chat at the bottom of the mine.'

'I didn't tell 'em anything,' said Eddie, deciding the lie was worth trying. 'Safer that way.'

'Sadly, I don't believe you. Or rather, I *can't* believe you. Occupational hazard. Considering the circumstances, however, I am prepared to offer you a deal.'

'Which is?' Nina asked.

'Ah, the redoubtable Dr Wilde, sharing your husband's indestructibility as ever. Simply put, I want you to turn over all your electronic equipment to Mr Hapen. Laptops, hard drives, SD cards, phones, anything and everything upon which you might have made a backup copy of the drone recording.'

'You put a bullet through the laptop,' Eddie reminded him. 'And the kid holding it, you bastard. It's wrecked, we haven't been able to copy anything off it.'

'Again, I can't risk believing you. But if you do as I ask, I give you my word that you and your friends will walk out of there alive.'

'And if we don't, we all die, right?' said Nina.

'Oh, much worse than that,' Brice told her. 'Your *daughter* will die.'

The threat sent a fearful chill through her. 'What?' she gasped.

Eddie's response was one of fury. 'You listen—'

'No, *you* listen, Chase!' barked the MI6 officer. 'Macy is currently in Southampton with her grandparents – your father, Larry Chase, and his wife Julie. Quite the age difference there, but that's by the by. My watchers tell me that Macy's wearing denim dungarees with a purple long-sleeved top underneath, and red shoes. Does that sound familiar?'

Macy's parents looked at each other in appalled shock. They did indeed know the outfit. When Eddie spoke again, the anger in his voice was ice cold. 'If anything happens to Macy, when I find you you'll fucking *beg* to end up like Mukobo. Do you hear me?'

Brice's snort of disdain was faint, but still audible. 'You're making a threat you can't carry out, Chase. But you know full well that I *can* carry out mine. And I will – but only if I have to. I'm a professional, not a psychopath. Turn everything over to Hapen, and you'll get to walk away. And so will your daughter.'

'Why would you let us go?' Nina demanded, not believing him for a moment. 'We could tell the world what you were doing in the Congo.'

'This may come as a surprise, Dr Wilde, but outside your insulated little echo chamber of United Nations do-gooders? *Nobody cares*. Nobody cares what happens in the Congo, or the rest of Africa either.'

'The people who live here care,' Eddie growled.

'What they think doesn't matter. Not to me, not to my government – *our* government, I'll remind you – not to any other government in the civilised world. Without proof, you can tell the world whatever you want, but even if you shout it from your media bully pulpit, Nina, *nobody will care*. Anything you say about Mukobo or the crash of Flight 180 will be met with a shrug of indifference or dismissed as a conspiracy theory. The moment you mention Africa, eyes will glaze over.'

'And *with* proof?' said Nina.

'Well, that would be more complicated, wouldn't it? The British government implicated by one of its own operatives in the downing of an American airliner and actively backing a coup in a supposedly democratic nation? It would be . . . troublesome, to say the very least. This isn't 1953 any more.'

'What happened in 1953?' Eddie asked.

The mention of a coup and the date had already given Nina the answer. Ancient history was her passion, but she was still well versed in the more modern variety. 'Iran,' she said. 'MI6 and the CIA overthrew the democratically elected government of Iran to reinstall the Shah as ruler. All because the Iranians wanted to take back control of their own oilfields from British and American companies. And the Shah was a repressive dictator, so there was eventually a revolution against him – which brought the Ayatollah to power.'

'Oh, no blowback there, then!' said Eddie sarcastically.

'It was somewhat more complicated than that – the Shah has been grossly maligned by the liberal media – but still, in hindsight, not one of SIS's greatest successes,' said Brice. 'But it did teach us to be much more circumspect in our regime change operations.'

'Hence your faked resignation,' Nina noted.

'Quite. Which is why I want the recording where I admit to that. That means the laptop, of course, but I still want all your other storage devices as well. Before you have a chance to reach somewhere with internet access and start disseminating copies across the globe.'

'We've got the laptop here,' Eddie told him, still seething.

'Good. Then hand it over to Hapen.'

He reluctantly held it up – but before he could turn it over to the mercenary, Nina stayed him. 'This laptop,' she said, directing her words as much at the blond man as the phone, 'it's really valuable, yes? As in, anyone who had it could potentially blackmail MI6 and the British government for millions of dollars to get it back?'

'That would have very unfortunate consequences for your little girl,' Brice replied coldly.

'I'm not talking about us. I'm speaking – *purely* hypothetically, of course,' she added, her eyes fixed meaningfully upon the mercenary's, 'about somebody else. If they had the laptop, they could demand as much money as they wanted for it, couldn't they?'

Hapen had clearly understood her inference, his gaze locking greedily on to the damaged machine. Eddie also realised what she meant. 'Yeah, they could,' he added. 'Be worth a fortune! Probably a lot more than you're paying to have it collected, right?'

The spy's response was impatient – but couldn't hide a hint of concern. 'I know what you're trying to do, and it won't work. Let me talk to Hapen.'

'Why?' asked Nina. 'Either you trust him, so you don't need to talk to him, or you don't . . . in which case, there's nothing to stop him from doing whatever he wants with the laptop. *Can* you trust him to hand it over without asking for a million dollars first?'

There was a lengthy silence – then to their surprise, a laugh came from the other end of the line. 'Congratulations, Dr Wilde. You found the weak point in my plan. I knew from the start that relying on a mercenary was risky, of course, but unfortunately I didn't have anyone more loyal available in such a short timeframe.'

'Out of the country already, are you?' asked Eddie.

'A long way out, thankfully. I'll be back in England in a few hours. But,' he went on, 'you'll be here with me soon enough. With the laptop, and anything else that might store the recording.'

'Oh, we will, will we?'

'I'm certain of it. Remember, I have watchers keeping an eye on your daughter. They'll take her if I give the word.'

'They wouldn't hurt a little girl,' Eddie snapped.

'They would hurt whoever they're *told* to hurt. Which includes Macy's grandparents as well. Now, here's the new plan. I'm going to tell Hapen to catalogue all your friends' electronics. You will bring everything, including the laptop, to me at Heathrow airport on the earliest possible flight. If I'm satisfied that the recording hasn't been copied or disseminated, Macy will be safe. Otherwise, well . . .'

'We get the picture,' said Nina.

'Good. Now put Hapen back on.'

Eddie returned the phone to the mercenary. A brief discussion, then Hapen gestured towards the minibuses. They went to them. 'Turn out your packs. He wants to make a list of all the electronics,' Nina told the group disconsolately. 'Brice wants everything that might store the recording.'

'Wait, he wants all our backups too?' Rivero asked. 'But – that's *everything* we shot! If he takes those, we'll have nothing!'

'Steven and the others will have *died* for nothing,' Lydia added angrily.

'He's got people watching our daughter,' said the redhead. 'If we don't turn everything over, he said he'll kill her.'

'Then we have to give him what he wants,' Fortune said. Rivero's reluctance was plain, but he started to unpack his bag. The others followed suit.

Hapen recited his findings to Brice over the phone before searching everyone at gunpoint. Finally, he was satisfied. 'Quite the collection,' said Brice after the satphone had been returned to Eddie. 'You can leave the video camera, but I want its memory card, and all the others. Even though it's broken, the laptop is the top priority, of course.' The mercenary had, at his employer's directing, tried to boot up the machine, but it had remained dead.

'Of course,' the Yorkshireman echoed sarcastically. 'So now what? You want us to stuff all this lot in a bag and meet you at Heathrow?'

'Succinctly put, yes. Don't dawdle, though. By my estimation, you should be able to get from where you are to London in forty-one hours. I'll be generous and give you forty-five. Third World airports don't always function smoothly.'

'Gee, thanks,' said Nina.

'The clock starts now, so don't waste any time. By the way,

just so it's clear: I've arranged for GCHQ to monitor the phones and internet of anyone you might think to contact. If you try to warn Macy's grandparents, or your friends at the United Nations, or anybody else in a position to interfere, bad things will happen. The same applies should there be so much as a whisper of online chatter about SIS's activities in the Congo.'

'Tchah! And I had an epic Twitter rant lined up,' Eddie replied.

'I'm so glad I'll be spared it. Now, you have forty-four hours and fifty-nine minutes to reach Heathrow, so get moving.' The line went silent.

Eddie lowered the phone. 'He just gave us a deadline to get to London with this lot,' he told the others, indicating their electronics. 'A tight one, so we need to get started.' He crouched to pick up the laptop.

'Ah-ah,' said Hapen. Everyone froze as he raised his rifle. 'It is worth a lot of money, yes? Then I will take your suggestion – and take *it*. Give it to me.'

Eddie sighed. 'All right, all right. Here.'

He stood – and tossed the computer at him.

Hapen, surprised, fumbled to catch it with his free hand. Before he could recover, Eddie punched him hard in the face. The mercenary stumbled backwards against the bus – where a second punch from Fortune dropped him to the ground, out cold.

'Thanks,' said Eddie.

'No problem, my friend,' Fortune replied, giving the unconscious man a disdainful look. 'No man with a haircut so bad should be allowed to walk the streets.'

Nina retrieved the laptop. 'Okay, so now what?'

Eddie glanced at the boat before regarding the bullet-damaged machine again. 'We do what Brice said.'

'You're going to cave in?' said Lydia.

Rivero was equally unhappy. 'We won't just be giving up everything we filmed, man. This guy won't let you walk away once you hand it over.'

'I know,' the Yorkshireman told them. He took Hapen's rifle. 'So we need some leverage.'

'I don't think they'll let you take that on the plane,' said Paris.

'Wasn't what I had in mind.'

'So what *do* you have in mind?' Nina asked. She could tell that an idea had come to him.

He grinned. 'We'll give him exactly what he's expecting.'

30

England

Grey clouds hung over London's Heathrow airport as the airliner rolled towards Terminal 3. Nina and Eddie's moods were no brighter. Their journey from the edge of the Congolese jungle to Butembo, then flying on to Entebbe in Uganda before taking a commercial flight to England, had left them with very little time before Brice's deadline. They were exhausted from the better part of two days' travel on top of their escape from Zhakana . . . but now, at their final destination, tiredness was not an option. They had to be ready for whatever awaited them.

'Think Brice'll be there?' Nina asked, watching the gate draw closer.

Eddie shook his head. 'Officially, he's not with MI6 any more. He'll have sent someone to get us.'

'These Removal Men you told me about?'

'Dunno. They're a bit . . . unsubtle. I'm hoping he wants to keep a low profile.' The airliner turned to line up with one of the jet bridges.

Some of the passengers were already rising in anticipation of the stop, but an announcement over the PA caught them by surprise. 'Ladies and gentlemen, this is the captain. I must ask everyone to remain seated, as officers of the British Transport Police are waiting to board when we reach our gate. Can passengers Nina Wilde and Eddie Chase please make themselves known to the cabin crew?'

The couple exchanged worried looks. 'So much for arriving incognito,' Nina muttered. 'Should we keep quiet?'

'No point,' said Eddie. 'They know which seats we're in.' He raised a hand. 'Yeah, here we are. Any chance of a last drink?'

The flight attendants regarded them with curious concern, but nobody moved towards them. The plane stopped, engines powering down. Even after the captain's order, a couple of impatient fliers still started to get up, until they were firmly told to return to their seats. The forward hatch opened, a female attendant speaking to someone outside before stepping back.

Three men entered: a burly uniformed police officer, and two in cheap, anonymous grey suits. 'Don't know if they're Increment, but they're probably spooks,' Eddie whispered to his wife. 'They've got shoulder holsters.'

'What do we do?'

'Try to get off the plane before anyone starts shooting.' He slid out the bag containing the expedition's electronics from under the seat in front and extracted the laptop.

'You think we've got a chance?'

'Dunno. I'll just do what I always do – try summat and see what happens!'

The new arrivals approached. 'Nina Wilde, Eddie Chase?' said the cop.

'That's us,' Nina said brightly. 'Is there a problem, officer?'

'Just come with us, please.'

The first man behind him saw the laptop. 'He's got it,' he told his companion, before demanding: 'Where's everything else?'

'In the bag,' Nina told him.

'Give everything to us first.' Behind him, the second suited man's hand slipped inside his jacket.

'Okay.' Nina moved into the aisle, making room for her

husband to stand and pull the bag on to his seat before following her. 'Here,' Eddie told the cop as he held up the computer. 'By the way, I know you're just doing your job, so sorry.'

The officer regarded him questioningly. 'About wh—'

Eddie slammed the palm of his free hand against the laptop's rear – and drove the slim edge of its metal case hard into the cop's face.

Teeth snapped, the policeman stumbling backwards. Before he could recover, Eddie charged into him, driving him into the first agent. Both men fell, the bigger man collapsing on top of the MI6 officer.

The other agent snatched out his gun—

Eddie leapt up, using an armrest like a starting block to propel himself over the fallen men and tackle him to the floor. The laptop skidded under a row of seats. The Yorkshireman glanced after it, then drove an elbow hard into the SIS man's stomach before delivering a pair of fearsome punches to his face. 'Nina!'

She was already moving. The first MI6 man had managed to draw his gun; she kicked it from his hand and jumped over him and the cop.

Eddie grabbed the other agent's Glock 17 and raced for the exit. The cabin crew retreated in fear. Nina followed, vaulting over the broken-nosed man on the floor—

He snatched at her as she passed – and caught her ankle.

Nina tripped. She struggled to break free, but his hold only tightened. He dragged her towards him—

She saw something beneath a seat and grabbed it.

The agent pulled harder – only to lurch back as if taking another punch when she thrust a life jacket into his face and pulled the tab. The bright yellow vest inflated with a bang of compressed gas, wedging itself in the aisle. Nina kicked free and scrambled after Eddie.

They rushed through the hatch and ran up the connecting bridge. 'Outside!' Eddie shouted.

He crashed through an emergency exit at its top to find himself on a flight of metal stairs to the concrete. Nina was about to descend when he blocked her. 'No, go up!' he said, slamming the door.

She climbed on to the safety railing – glimpsing movement through the door's small window. 'Gun!' she warned, seeing the first MI6 man racing up the metal tunnel—

Eddie threw himself sideways as three bullet holes burst open in the door. He blind-fired two rounds from his purloined gun back through it. They did the job, no more shots coming. He jumped up after Nina, seeing that the agent had dived to the floor.

He joined her on the roof. The great concrete expanse of Heathrow stretched out around them, the tails of dozens of parked airliners rising like shark fins. 'Oh, for fuck's sake,' he said, realising they were at the very end of one of the long jetways. 'Why do our flights always have to stop so bloody far from the terminal?' They ran for the main building.

'Why didn't we go down the stairs?'

''Cause we'd never get out of here on foot.' He made a running jump over a set of boxy air-conditioning ducts running the jetway's length, Nina clambering over more awkwardly. A shout as the SIS man started to climb up behind them and called to his companions. He raised his gun—

Eddie fired first. The bullet hit the roof just in front of the man's face. He hurriedly dropped back down.

The Yorkshireman returned his attention to what lay ahead – and below. As he'd told Nina, escaping the airport on foot would be impossible. Heathrow had hundreds of police and security personnel, and they would be surrounded long before even reaching the perimeter fence. They needed an alternative . . .

He spotted one. 'That's our way out,' he told Nina, pointing at a vehicle.

She was not impressed. 'Are you *kidding*?'

'It's that or nick a jet, and the last time I flew anything it crashed into the United Nations!' He spotted stairs descending from another emergency exit. 'Down there.'

'Wouldn't it be better to get inside the terminal and try to sneak out amongst the passengers?'

'Every cop in Heathrow'll have our pictures. The only way we're getting out of the airport is by *breaking* out. And nothing'll stop us once that's moving.'

'It's the *getting* it moving part I'm worried about!' she objected.

The SIS officer peered over the roof's edge again. The two fugitives were out of sight. He cursed.

The bullet-pocked door below opened. 'Where are they?' asked his partner, voice stifled as he held his cracked nose.

'On the roof, but I've lost them. They must be heading for the terminal.'

The other man held up a phone. 'Staite just gave new orders: withdraw and let the police handle them.'

'What? Aren't they a security risk? If they talk to the police first—'

'Our priority now's to secure the laptop and all the other stuff in that bag, and get them to Vauxhall Cross, pronto.'

The first officer climbed back down. Abandoning the pursuit seemed the wrong decision, but orders were orders. 'Have you got them?'

The other man nodded. 'The woodentop's bringing them.' He looked back towards the plane. The policeman – 'woodentop' being derogatory slang for uniformed officers – was approaching with the fugitives' bag in one hand, the other pressed to his bleeding mouth. 'Everything on the list we were given is there.

External hard drives, SD cards, some phones – and the laptop.'

'Their call. Okay, bring that to our car,' he told the cop. 'We've been told to leave catching them to your esteemed colleagues.'

'Hopefully they won't balls it up,' griped the broken-nosed man as they started the long walk through the airport.

Eddie clanked down the metal stairs to ground level. The vehicle he had pointed out was parked nearby. 'Okay, let's roll!'

'*Really* not sure this is a good idea,' said Nina. Before them was an airport tug, a Schopf heavy-duty tractor capable of hauling even super-jumbo aircraft like the double-deck Airbus A380 with ease. The squat, broad machine's wheels were as tall as a man, almost sixty tons of ballast ensuring they remained firmly planted on the concrete no matter how massive its load. 'They'll be able to catch up with us by walking!'

'They're only slow when they're pulling planes around. They're like tanks – once they get going, they're bloody hard to stop.' He opened the cab door. The controls were reassuringly simple, the tug's transmission fully automatic. 'Okay, get in.'

Nina hurried around to the wide cab's far side. Despite the amount of space, there was only one other seat, a simple fold-down bench. 'Oh, comfy.'

'Only the best for my wife,' Eddie said with a grin as he pushed the starter. The tug's massive diesel engine shuddered from its sleep, exhausts spouting dark plumes of smoke. There was a chunky gear selector on the console; he pushed it into drive. 'All right, straightforward enough – like driving a bus.'

'When did you drive a bus?'

'I learned how to drive pretty much everything in the SAS. The bit on my driving licence where it says what I'm qualified for has almost every letter in the alphabet! All right, hold on.'

He depressed the accelerator. The engine thrummed, the tug straining as if simply standing still had flat-spotted its tyres before reluctantly moving off.

Nina regarded the speedometer dubiously. 'Okay, it only goes up to forty, and we're doing . . . five.'

'Give it time! Where's the way out?'

They emerged from behind the jetway – to see two police Land Rovers approaching fast along a taxiway. 'Not that way,' she said in alarm.

Eddie turned away from them, picking up speed as he headed north. Beyond the vast concrete expanse surrounding Heathrow's main terminal complex he saw distant buildings, outside the airport's perimeter. 'We can crash through the fence over there,' he said. 'But . . .'

'But?' asked his wife.

The unwelcome answer came as an airliner screamed in to land on a runway ahead, smoke erupting from its wheels as it whipped past. 'Oh,' said Nina. 'Right.'

'We can make it,' he said, more optimistic than certain. 'We just have to cross the runway when there isn't a plane coming.'

'Uh-huh. And isn't Heathrow one of the world's busiest airports?'

'Nah, I don't think it's even in the top five any more.'

'Oh, so I guess all we'll have to dodge is tumbleweed!'

The tug cleared the terminal complex, open ground spreading out around them. The speedo had now reached twenty, so they were at least outpacing anyone on foot, but the two police Discovery SUVs were gaining on them fast. Beyond the runway, a wide stretch of old tarmac ran all the way to the perimeter fence. 'We can get out there,' Eddie said, pointing at a car park past the high barrier.

'And then what? Drive this thing into the centre of London?'

'I think the bus'd be a bit less conspicuous.'

'I doubt these guys'll let us buy a ticket!' The police vehicles peeled apart, overtaking on each side of the Schopf.

Eddie glanced into the mirrors to see which was closer, then threw the wheel hard to the left. The tug's four-wheel steering veered it around with surprising sharpness. The driver of the nearest Discovery tried to turn away, but too late—

The tractor sideswiped it. The Land Rover was not a lightweight vehicle, but against sixty tons of metal it may as well have been a paper cup. The SUV was swatted aside, nearly rolling over before lurching to a halt – with one wheel hanging off its axle.

Eddie checked the mirror again, seeing the Discovery's stunned occupants sit up, then turned back towards the runway. 'You okay?'

The collision had barely shaken the tug, but Nina saw something that would make much more of an impact. 'Yeah, but – de plane, boss, de plane!' Another airliner was already on final approach.

He looked across to the second Discovery, which had moved well clear. Unlike the vast majority of British police officers, those on duty at airports were routinely armed – and the passenger had lowered his window, bringing up an MP5 sub-machine gun—

'Nina, *down!*' Eddie yelled. She threw herself to the cab floor as he swung the tug away from the police vehicle. Gunfire cracked across the concrete, rounds spanging against the tractor's flank. The cop was aiming for the tyres, not the driver, but the Yorkshireman was sure that would change the moment he realised his bullets were about as effective against the inches-thick rubber as a drawing pin.

They reached the runway. The speedo passed thirty, but the asphalt was wide, the plane still thundering towards them—

The pilot saw the vehicles crossing his path and yanked back the controls, slamming the throttles to maximum power in an emergency abort. The Boeing 787's nose tipped upwards, but the aircraft had not yet pulled out of its descent, on a direct course for the lumbering Schopf . . .

Its landing gear wavered just a few feet above the runway – then rose again as the plane finally climbed.

It shot over the tug and the Discovery, huge twin engines thundering at full force—

The jet blast hit both vehicles. It was powerful enough to make even the tractor skid sideways – but its effect on the Land Rover had the force of a tornado. The Discovery was blown off the ground, bowling over in mid-air and crashing back down on its side. It skidded into the grass, kicking up a great spray of wet soil before thumping to a stop in a drainage ditch. Both cops crawled dizzily from the battered wreck.

The tug cleared the runway, Eddie aiming it down the stretch of old tarmac towards the fence. Thirty-five miles per hour – hardly a breathtaking speed, but with so much weight behind it the juggernaut was now almost unstoppable.

He braced himself, Nina doing the same—

The tug punched through the fence, shredding chain-link and ripping concrete posts from the ground. The impact smashed the windscreen. Eddie stamped on the brake as they careered towards the ranks of high-end cars parked ahead – but now the same inertia that had helped them escape the airport was working against them, the heavy tractor ploughing onwards even as smoke belched from its screaming tyres—

A Mercedes S-class was the first car to be pulverised, mashed into an equally expensive BMW in a chaotic melding of German engineering. Eddie tried to steer away from the other vehicles, but the tug skidded on, carving a destructive swathe through Jaguars, Range Rovers, Audis, Lexuses and Bentleys before the sheer weight of crumpled metal finally dragged it to a standstill.

Relieved, he pushed himself upright. Nina sat up and shook off broken glass. 'There'll be a lot of pissed-off company directors when they get back from their flights,' she said, surveying the wreckage.

'Serves 'em right for not taking public transport,' Eddie replied. They clambered out. 'There's a road over there.' He indicated a set of exit barriers.

'Where are we?'

'North of Heathrow – place called Harmondsworth. We should be able to get into London pretty easily, so long as we're clear before they surround this place.'

They hurried to the gate. A security guard stared in disbelief from his hut at the automotive carnage that had just occurred on his watch. 'Oi!' he cried at the couple. 'Someone's got to pay for all this! I want your names!'

'John Brice, Secret Intelligence Service,' Eddie shouted as they ran past. 'Send the bill to MI6 headquarters at Vauxhall Cross!'

31

The real John Brice was indeed at the SIS building on the southern bank of the Thames. His shabby, dissolute cover persona from the Democratic Republic of Congo was gone, the MI6 officer now shaved, washed and clad in a clean, sharp suit. His presence there was known to very few people, however, and the number who knew *why* he was there was even smaller.

The bunker-like basement levels contained numerous operations centres; they were designed to allow controllers in London to monitor and coordinate activities across the globe, but on this occasion the focus of attention was much closer to home. 'Looks like the police lost them, sir,' reported one of Brice's small team, a young but ambitious woman called Staite. She was overseeing the hunt for the fugitives, while at the same time making sure MI6's involvement remained as discreet as possible. The Secret Intelligence Service's remit was to conduct operations outside British soil; anything on it was the province of its sister/rival agency MI5, the Security Service, and to say that each fist of British intelligence resented interloping on its own turf by the other was a major understatement. 'They've started to search the area around the car park, but haven't found anything yet.'

Staite's partner, an equally youthful Cambridge graduate named Waterford, shook his head. 'How could they lose them? They were driving something that could be outpaced by a Segway!'

'Don't underestimate them – especially not Chase,' Brice told them. One of the op centre's many video screens displayed the passport photos of their targets, the images already acting as reference for MI6's facial recognition software as it scoured London's extensive network of surveillance cameras. 'He's former SAS, and has an annoying talent for survival.'

'Is it wise to let the woodentops handle this, sir?' asked Staite. 'Once we locate them, maybe we should put GB63 on to them instead.'

'I don't want to draw attention, especially not from Five, unless absolutely necessary. All anyone outside this building needs to know is that Chase and Wilde are wanted for reasons relating to external security. What those reasons are, we'll decide once we catch them.' His phone rang. 'Yes?'

'Morley here, sir.' One of the two officers he had sent to collect the fugitives and their possessions. They had failed the first part of their task, but at least the second had been achieved. 'We're leaving Heathrow now. We've got everything you told us to expect.' He ran through a list of assorted electronic items and storage media, but it was the last that most concerned Brice: 'And a laptop – with a bullet hole right through it.'

'Does it boot up?'

'No, sir. I tried, but it won't even turn on.'

'As soon as you get back to Vauxhall Cross, take everything to the techies – Evans is in charge of this operation. When will you arrive?'

'About three-quarters of an hour, traffic permitting.'

'Good. Carry on.' He disconnected and looked back at the screens. One displayed a satellite map with Heathrow at the centre, extending as far as central London on the right edge. Somewhere on it, Eddie Chase and Nina Wilde were on the run . . .

And he had no direct leverage to apply. His watchers were still monitoring their daughter and her grandparents in Southampton, but with no way for him to contact his targets –

their phones were amongst the items Morley and his partner had collected – he couldn't use the threat of violence against her to force them to surrender.

What were they doing? It was possible they would head to Southampton to rescue their family, but the watchers were not merely an observation unit; he had already issued orders for them to take down Wilde and Chase should they show up. And GCHQ was still monitoring all communications with every person they might possibly contact for help, in addition to the agency's standard filtering of the country's news outlets. So far, nothing.

Whatever their plan, he was certain he would figure it out. Wilde might be a PhD, but she was just an archaeologist, not a seasoned covert agent. And as for Chase . . .

Staite gave him a quizzical look. It took a moment before he realised why; he had unconsciously drawn his lips into a dismissive half-smile at the mere thought that some yobbish Yorkshire squaddie might outwit him. Chase relied on brute force and luck, that was all – and both were finite, while he had the considerable resources of one of the world's most powerful intelligence agencies at his disposal. 'We'll get them,' he said, as much to himself as the young woman. 'We'll get them.'

'Do you see her?' Nina asked as she and Eddie made their way through Hyde Park. Their journey into the capital had been lengthy and convoluted as they tried to minimise their exposure to the ubiquitous CCTV cameras. Appropriately for the setting of George Orwell's *1984*, London was the most heavily surveilled city on the planet. The degree to which its tens of thousands of cyclopean glass eyes could be accessed by government agencies had been exaggerated by Hollywood and BBC spy thrillers, the intelligence services not – yet – having real-time access to the security feeds of every pub and corner shop at the click of a mouse, but there were still plenty of official cameras overlooking the streets.

Eddie spotted a familiar figure on a bench near a sculpture of a heron. 'Yeah, there she is.'

They cautiously surveyed their surroundings for signs of anyone paying them undue attention before finally joining the waiting woman. 'There you are!' said Tamara Defendé, in both relief and concern. 'I'm so glad to see you both. When you got off the plane, I had no idea what had happened to you! We heard shots, but nobody would tell us anything.'

'Yeah, it was a bit of a wild ride,' Eddie replied, embracing her. 'But we made it, and I don't think we've been followed. What about you? Did you have any trouble?'

'An African woman travelling alone, having trouble at British customs?' said the Botswanan bush pilot with a sarcastic eye roll. 'They questioned me for thirty minutes about why I was here and how soon I planned to leave – that was the part they cared about the most – before finally letting me go. I'm glad I had a return ticket to prove I *was* going to leave. If I'd arrived on a one-way ticket, I would probably still be at the airport, waiting to be deported on the first flight back.'

'Welcome to England,' he said with distaste. 'But you're here. What about the laptop?'

She opened a large, colourful bag. Inside was a slim computer – with a bullet hole through its casing. Unlike the one on its way to MI6, the damaged circuitry was tinged with red. The laptop Eddie and Nina had brought was Lydia's, the original machine's wound replicated with a shot from the mercenary's Bushmaster – once as many as possible of its files, and those from the backup hard drives, had been transferred to a fistful of SD cards and flash drives bought from a mobile phone shop in Butembo. Nina was unwilling to force the surviving documentary crew to leave empty-handed after everything they had endured. 'Here. The bullet hole didn't help when I was being questioned. I told them I was bringing it to London to get it repaired.'

'Which is kind of true,' Nina said. 'If we can get the video off its hard drive, we've got a chance of exposing the truth about what happened in the Congo.'

'That's if we can get it to the right person,' said Eddie, taking another wary look around. 'And if we can actually trust 'em!'

'I bought some prepaid phones, like you asked,' said TD. She handed him a plastic bag, which contained three identical mobile phones. 'Why do you need so many? Two I can understand, one for each of you, but three?'

'Soon as we finish using one, it goes straight in the bin,' Eddie told her. 'The person we're going to call's almost certainly being monitored – and once they get our number, they can track the phone.'

She nodded. 'Is there anything else I can do to help?'

'I *want* to say "get Macy to somewhere safe",' said Nina, 'but I don't know if we can risk it. We know they're watching her, and if someone they don't know turns up, it would make them suspicious – and they might even target you.'

TD sighed. 'These people, they are bastards. Going after your child? They are as bad as Mukobo.'

'That's fucking spies for you,' said Eddie. 'But you know what's ironic? The only person who can help us right now actually *is* a spy. I just hope he's only the *partial* bell-end I think he is, not a complete one like Brice.' He took out one of the phones. 'You should get moving, TD. Soon as I make this call, there'll be a load of police and God knows who else on their way here, and you don't want to be seen anywhere near us.'

She reluctantly stood. 'I wish there was more I could do.'

'You've done everything you possibly could,' Nina assured her, hugging her. 'Thank you so much.'

'I really owe you,' Eddie added. 'Thanks.'

'Good luck. I hope I see you again.' TD kissed his cheek, then walked away.

He watched her go, then slipped the laptop into the bag with the other phones and started in the opposite direction. 'All right,' he said to Nina. 'You got that number?'

She had transcribed the contact details from their own phones during the flight. 'Yeah, here.'

He began to thumb in the number. 'God, it's been ages since I used a phone with actual buttons.' He had told TD to pick up the cheapest prepaid phones she could find; there was no point buying expensive smartphones just to throw away after one call. 'Okay, it's ringing. Let's hope he answers . . .'

Waterford sat up in response to an alert on his computer's screen. 'Sir, I just got a flash from GCHQ. One of the people on Chase's watch list has just been phoned from an unknown mobile number . . .' He tapped at his keyboard, then listened to the intercepted call through a headset. 'I think it's him, sir! Chase, I mean.'

'Put it on speaker,' Brice ordered. 'Wind it back, I want to hear the whole thing from the beginning.'

The call was being recorded digitally; it only took a moment for Waterford to shuttle to its start. A click of connection, then: 'Alderley.'

'He's calling Peter Alderley?' said Brice, surprised. From what he remembered, his SIS colleague and Chase were acquaintances at best, but hardly friends.

'Ay up, Peter,' the Yorkshireman said over the loudspeakers. 'It's Eddie Chase.'

'Chase?' replied Alderley, surprised. 'Didn't expect to get a call from you. What's up?' A pause, then with a certain dread: 'Oh, God. You've caused another bloody international incident and you need my help, don't you?'

'No, no, nothing like that,' was the not entirely convincing reply. 'Me and Nina are just in town, that's all. We can't talk for too long right now—'

'Obviously telling him that the call's being monitored,' muttered Staite.

'—so it'd be great if we could meet up. What time do you finish work?'

'Five o'clock,' Alderley told him, still sounding highly suspicious. 'Although I generally run late.'

'You're in charge of the department, aren't you? Tell someone else to finish up for you, then hop in that crappy old car of yours and meet us in that square between King's Cross and St Pancras at half six.'

'Battle Bridge Place? I know it, but I did rather have plans for tonight. You know, going home, seeing my wife, having dinner, things like that?'

'Hi, Peter,' said a new voice. 'It's Nina. I know it's short notice, but we *really would* love to see you. Both of us.'

'That's right,' Chase added. 'Nothing I want more right now than to talk to my old mate Peter.'

'O-kaaay . . .' said Alderley dubiously. 'Well, if it's that important to you . . . I suppose I can find the time.'

'All right, great,' said Chase. 'We'll be waiting for you.'

'Anything I should bring?' Alderley asked. 'You know, in case you need it?'

'Just your car so I can have a good laugh. See you there, Peter.' The call ended.

'Did we get their location?' asked Brice.

Waterford checked his screen. 'Sorry, sir. Somewhere around Hyde Park, but there wasn't enough time to get a precise triangulation.'

'Contact the Met anyway,' Brice ordered. 'Tell them to start a search; they might get lucky. And poll all the CCTV resources to see if we can get a hit.'

Staite nodded and dialled a phone number. Waterford, meanwhile, reacted with a start at another piece of data on his monitor. 'Wait, the number he called – it's here at SIS!'

'Peter Alderley is the head of the Africa desk,' Brice told him. 'And he and Chase have worked together before.' The wording of the call was troubling him. Chase and Wilde had clearly given Alderley a coded request for help, but only in the most general way, not providing him with any specific information. Somehow, though, he felt there was more to it, that he was missing something . . .

'Should we pick him up?'

'Who, Alderley?' said Brice mockingly. 'Don't be ridiculous. I just told you, he's a section head. A fishing trip like that would end your career if he really does know nothing about what's going on.' He thought for a moment. 'But put watchers on him, follow him when he leaves the building. They might try to make contact while he's in transit. And get a unit to stake out Battle Bridge Place.'

'Yes, sir,' said Waterford.

Brice regarded the map again, using a tablet to zoom in on Hyde Park. Given such a broad search area it was unlikely that the regular police would catch the fugitives. If he gave an order to designate Wilde and Chase as dangerous, high-priority targets, however, armed response and Special Branch units would cordon off the area and scour every cranny until they were found – but doing so would draw a huge amount of attention, which he didn't want to risk unless he had no choice.

But in a couple of hours, he knew where they would be – or where they *said* they would be. 'Send someone to watch Alderley's house as well,' he told Staite, 'just in case this meeting's a diversion.' It was possible the call to Alderley had been a decoy, as he was sure they knew it would be monitored; but if it was, then to what end?

'Play the call again,' he told Waterford, who dutifully called up the audio file. There was *something* in the short conversation he had overlooked. He just had to figure out what.

The answer had not come to him by the time Alderley approached the rendezvous, though.

'Subject is going into the St Pancras multistorey,' reported one of the watchers tailing the section head. After leaving work, Alderley had travelled by Tube and train to his home, then driven back into central London to make his rendezvous. There had been no sign of Chase or Wilde on either leg of the journey, or near his house. 'Do we follow him in?'

Brice hesitated – having the watchers take their car in behind Alderley ran the risk of his noticing them – but gave an order in the affirmative. 'They might try to meet him inside. Don't let him out of your sight.'

'Roger. Going in now.'

He waited impatiently for an update. More watchers were already in place at the public square between the two railway terminals, but so far none had anything to report. 'He's parked on the second floor,' Alderley's shadow finally said. 'Going past to find a space for ourselves . . . he doesn't seem to have noticed us.'

'Split up,' Brice told them. 'One of you follow him, the other park the car and then catch up. I don't want you to lose eyes on him for a moment.'

'Understood, sir.'

Brice looked up at the operations room's screens. Many showed real-time CCTV feeds from cameras around Battle Bridge Place, little wireframe boxes flashing over the heads of the milling pedestrians as MI6's facial recognition software searched for a match. None yet, though . . .

His phone rang. 'Yes?'

It was a call he had been waiting for. 'I have an update on that laptop,' replied Evans, one of SIS's senior technical specialists.

'Did you recover any files from it?' Brice asked.

'We haven't recovered *anything* from it yet, old man,' said the Welshman with silken pomposity. 'The bullet clipped its hard drive, as well as causing a fair amount of damage to the main logic board. I can give you categoric reassurance that it would have been impossible to boot up after it was shot, though.'

'What about getting data off it? Could anything have been copied even if it couldn't power up?'

'There are ways, yes. But I doubt they could have been employed in the field without specialist hardware.'

'I need to be absolutely *sure*, Evans,' Brice said firmly. 'There's a video file on that computer that's of the highest importance to national security. I need confirmation that it hasn't been watched or copied.'

'I *did* read your request form, old man. Don't worry, we'll get to the bottom of it – just give us a little time. We'll dismantle it and see how much we can tease out of the SSD. Might have to write a custom controller to piece together any scrambled data, but that's why they pay us the modest salaries, right?' He chuckled.

'Just get on with it and report back to me the moment you have an answer,' he said before ending the call.

'Techies, sir?' asked Waterford. 'Always a pain in the arse, aren't they?' Staite smiled.

'Keep your minds on the job,' Brice told them irritably. Based on Evans' report, it seemed unlikely that the incriminating video had been copied – certainly none of the other devices retrieved from Chase and Wilde had contained it – but he needed to be absolutely sure. Once he had confirmation, the threat the couple posed both to himself and SIS as a whole would be drastically reduced. Until that time, though, it had to be considered very great indeed.

'Subject's going down the stairs,' reported the watcher following Alderley.

'Ground units, have someone ready at the bottom,' ordered Brice.

'Already in position,' replied another officer, a woman. Seconds passed, then: 'I see him. He's alone.'

'Nobody passed him on the stairs,' said the man.

'Okay, wait for your partner. Ground units, he's coming your way.' Brice looked back at the screens. One of the CCTV cameras covered the car park exit closest to Battle Bridge Place. A brief wait, then Alderley emerged. 'There he is – track him,' he told Waterford.

Different cameras followed Alderley into the square. He slowed as he neared its centre, looking around. Several watchers announced that they had him in sight. 'No sign of the main targets,' said one.

'Be patient. Let them come to him.' He kept watching the screens. Alderley wandered back and forth, looking hopefully at the stations' exits, but it didn't take long before his body language revealed impatience. He sat on a bench, checking his watch. Even on the CCTV image, his frown was clear.

Twenty minutes ticked by, and still no trace of the people he was supposed to meet. Alderley became increasingly irritated. 'Maybe the woodentops caught them,' suggested Waterford.

Staite shook her head. 'They would have notified us. Sir, this whole thing might be a decoy.'

'I'd already thought of that,' said Brice. The nagging feeling that he had missed something still would not go away. 'But a decoy from what?'

Another ten minutes passed. 'He's moving,' said one of the ground team. Brice looked up from a styrofoam cup of tea. Alderley had finally thrown in the towel, visibly huffing before stalking off towards the car park.

'Looks like he's had enough,' Brice told everyone. 'Stay with him. Mobile units, get back to your vehicles. Wherever he goes, I want him followed.'

'He's making a call,' said Staite, seeing Alderley take out a phone.

'Get it,' ordered Brice. An intercept had already been set up on the section head's mobile by GCHQ; the call came through in real time.

But it was nothing of value. 'Hi, sweetie, it's me,' Alderley said to his wife, who asked how he was. 'A bit pissed off, actually. The people I was supposed to meet never turned up. I'm coming home.' The rest of the call was similarly innocuous.

'Keep some people in the square, just in case they show up,' Brice told Staite, but he was sure now that Chase and Wilde weren't coming.

He glared at the screens. Where were they – and what were they doing?

Alderley returned to his car. The 1971 Ford Capri 3000 GT was his pride and joy, the classic vehicle lovingly hand-restored over two decades as time and finances permitted. It was rare that he actually took the metallic orange coupe out on the road, not wanting to risk damage or – more likely – a breakdown, but the fact that Eddie Chase had been very insistent he bring it rather than his everyday vehicle had caught his curiosity.

So had the rest of the phone call. While he was quite fond of Nina, she was hardly a close friend, and Chase himself was aggravating at best. They would not have contacted him simply to catch up over a coffee. There was something they wanted – *needed* – to tell him. But knowing that all calls to SIS headquarters were monitored, they had been forced to be circumspect.

Except . . . they hadn't turned up. That was both annoying

and surprising – as a former military man, Chase was a stickler for punctuality. Had something happened to them?

That thought had already triggered the innate paranoia of all intelligence officers. He couldn't be sure, but while waiting in the square it did seem that the same faces kept circulating on its periphery . . .

He cautiously surveyed the car park before entering the Capri. A man was just starting his own vehicle nearby. Alderley eyed him. Was it the same car that had followed him in? The silver Vauxhall was exactly the kind of unassuming vehicle that a team of watchers would use.

He waited for the man to depart before starting his own car, the three-litre engine's rumble echoing through the low-ceilinged concrete space. Another look around. Nobody there. Wondering if he was being a bit *too* paranoid, he set off.

Nevertheless, he paid more attention to the view in his mirror on the way home. No one seemed to be following him – though whether that was because nobody actually was, or they were good enough not to be noticed, he couldn't tell . . .

Alderley shook his head as he stopped at traffic lights, smiling to himself. 'There's nobody behind you,' he said—

'Ay up,' said a muffled voice from behind him. 'If you drive over any more bumps, I might have to kill you.'

32

Alderley froze. 'Chase?'

'No, your car's talking to you like KITT from *Knight Rider*. Of course it bloody is!'

'You – you broke into my Capri?'

'The locks are from the Seventies, I could've got in with a pipe cleaner. Why do you think I asked you to bring it? That and being able to find it in the car park. Don't let on that we're here, though. You're being followed.'

'We?'

'Hi, Peter,' Nina added.

'Are you in my boot?' the SIS officer asked. 'And also: why?'

'Long story,' said Eddie. 'But we need your help, and we couldn't talk about it on the phone. The people following you are from MI6.'

'What? Why on earth would my own agency be following me?' The lights changed; he set off again.

Eddie almost had to shout to be heard over the engine and road noise. 'Remember John Brice?'

'Of course I do. He quit two years ago. Why?'

'He didn't quit, he went into deep cover. He was up to some nasty shit in DR Congo for MI6. We caught him at it – and now he wants us dead to cover it up.'

'I'm the head of SIS's Africa desk. If we had an operation in the Congo, I'd know about it.'

'This was the kind of operation that would need total deniability,' said Nina. 'From what Brice told us, only the people at the very top were in the loop.'

'Brice *told* you? That sounds uncharacteristically sloppy.'

'He didn't think we'd stay alive long enough to tell anyone else,' Eddie explained. 'Unlucky for him, we did – and we got it on video.'

Alderley raised his eyebrows. 'I'd . . . very much like to see that video.'

'So would we,' said Nina. 'The problem is, it's on a laptop – and Brice put a bullet through it. So we don't know if we can recover it.'

'We need to get somewhere we can talk properly,' Eddie said. 'By which I mean, not through the back of your fucking car boot. Do you keep this thing in a garage? We need to get out without anyone seeing us.'

'I do,' Alderley told him, only to realise what he meant. 'Hold on. You're telling me that John Brice is still secretly working for MI6 and has assigned watchers to follow me in the hope I'll lead them to you . . . and you want to come to my *house*?'

'Bang on. I can see why they promoted you now.'

'Cheeky sod,' he replied. 'This is a very bad idea, you know. I'm thinking specifically for me, but it won't go well for you either if they realise where you are.'

'We're not asking to rent your spare bedroom,' said Nina. 'We just need you to help us recover the video from the laptop.'

Alderley snorted. 'Or I could just drop you off at the nearest Apple Store.'

'There's more to it than just the video, though,' she went on. 'We were in DR Congo on an archaeological expedition, and we found something in a lost city – something incredibly dangerous. And Brice has it.'

That caught his attention, sarcasm replaced by cautious

concern born of his previous dealings with the couple. 'What kind of thing?'

'It'd be much better if we could tell you face to face. Also, it's kinda cramped in here . . . and it's really starting to smell of gas.'

'It's leaking again? I thought I'd fixed that . . .' Alderley sighed. 'Okay,' he said at last. 'You can get into the house from the garage, so you won't be seen. I'll talk to you once we get there. Having two people climb out of my boot will be quite a surprise to my wife, mind.' Foreboding entered his voice. 'I'll have to warn you, though. If it turns out that Brice really is carrying out an authorised SIS operation, then not only can I not help you, but I'll be obligated to report my contact with you.'

Eddie's own tone became distinctly menacing. 'You'll turn us in?'

'Not on the spot – I trust you that much. But you *would* need to leave pretty sharpish, because I'd have to make the call within . . . five minutes, let's say. First things first, though. I'll hear you out, and see if we can get anything off this laptop.'

'That's great,' said Nina, relieved. 'Thank you, Peter.'

'I'd say "no problem", but I don't know what I'm letting myself in for, do I?' Alderley laughed. 'By the way, Chase?'

'Yeah?' asked Eddie.

'If my car really did start talking to me, and it had your voice . . . I'd have to get rid of it.'

The Yorkshireman's rude retort was drowned out by the rumbling exhaust note.

'Subject has reached his house,' said one of Alderley's watchers. 'He's backing his car into the garage . . . closing the door.'

Brice frowned. There had been no sign of Chase and Wilde on Alderley's journey home. That they hadn't tried to contact him suggested the couple had been somewhere else entirely – so why summon him at all?

'House team,' he said, 'there was definitely no activity at the subject's home, correct? Nobody came or went?'

'No, sir,' came the reply from a unit parked down the street. 'His wife's home, but she hasn't left, and nobody else came to the house.'

'No phone calls to the house or the wife?' he asked Staite, who shook her head. 'All right, then. Mobile units, return to base. House team, stay on site. They might try to reach him during the night. Do you have visibility on the surrounding houses in case they try to come through their gardens?'

'We can see both neighbouring properties,' the watcher told him. 'Access from the rear is blocked by a railway cutting with a high vertical wall.'

'Climbable?'

'Unlikely.'

Another frown. Chase and Wilde's actions made no apparent sense – and an unpredictable opponent was dangerous. 'Double-check that there's no access from the railway,' he ordered as his phone rang. 'Yes?'

'Brice.'

He knew the voice, and immediately became deferential. 'Yes, sir?'

'Anything to report?'

'Nothing yet, sir.'

'Hmm.' For such a small sound, it was laden with meaning: disapproval, and disappointment. Brice felt a flash of humiliation. 'Tell your team to continue, then. The meeting you requested will be in one hour, my office.'

He checked his watch. 'I'll be ready, sir.'

'Some good news would be a helpful ice-breaker, Brice.' The older man ended the call.

Brice lowered his phone, trying to conceal his tension from his subordinates. He had envisioned a world-changing use for the Shamir almost immediately after seeing it in action, developing the plan on his flight from the Congo. When he had proposed it to the man with whom he had just spoken, there had been considerable scepticism – understandable, without a demonstration of the strange stone's destructive powers. But Brice had convinced him enough to take the plan higher . . . and now it would get a hearing.

The future of the entire country hinged upon the decision made an hour from now. He had to push his case as strongly as possible. Ensuring there was no way anyone could prove a connection between the Shamir and SIS would help enormously.

To do that, he had to find – and eliminate – Nina Wilde and Eddie Chase. 'I just spoke to C,' he told his operatives both in the room and in the field with resurgent anger. 'He wants results. These targets are a threat to the security of the United Kingdom. *Find them!*'

Peter Alderley leaned back in a chair, shaking his head wearily. 'Okay, okay,' he said, interrupting Nina and Eddie's explanation of recent events. 'Let me try to get my head around this. You found the lost palace of King Solomon in the jungle, and inside was the actual Horn of Jericho from the Bible – a stone that when it's brought into the light causes some kind of sonic vibration that can literally level cities. Correct?'

'More or less,' said Nina. Alderley's wife Poppy had indeed been surprised that he had brought home guests, but was more annoyed that he had asked her to leave the room so they could hold a private discussion. A compromise had been reached, in that *he* had left the room to talk with his visitors in his small home office-cum-den while she watched television in the lounge. 'I don't think it's so much light as some kind of radiation that activates it, though. Cosmic rays, or neutrinos.'

'Neutrinos,' Alderley echoed dubiously. 'At the same time,

John Brice, who had faked his resignation from SIS to work undercover, was secretly supplying secessionist rebels in eastern DRC with arms and funding so British companies like Monardril could get first dibs on mining concessions in the newly independent state. Yes?'

Eddie nodded. 'You were listening, then.'

'I was, yes. It's the *believing* I'm struggling with.'

'It's all true,' Nina insisted. She held up the broken laptop. 'The proof is on this – if we can retrieve it.'

'That's quite a big if. Bullets and computers generally don't mix. But what you said about Brice freeing Philippe Mukobo from US custody while in-flight over the Atlantic, in the process destroying an American airliner? *That's* the most unbelievable part, never mind magic stones.' Alderley leaned forward, speaking more insistently. 'If he really was acting in the capacity of an SIS officer, it wouldn't just cause a diplomatic incident. It would quite literally be an act of war – against our closest ally!'

'That's what he told us,' said Eddie. 'If we can get the video off that laptop, then you can hear him say it for yourself.'

'It's why he resigned, at least officially,' Nina went on. 'To give the British government total deniability. Hell, maybe nobody in the government even *knew* about it,' she said as a new possibility came to her. 'It might just have been Brice and somebody higher in MI6 acting on their own.'

Alderley shook his head. 'Contrary to popular belief, SIS doesn't start major operations off its own bat. Our job is to implement policy, not create it.' He sensed a certain scepticism. 'What? It's true! I'm in charge of British intelligence activities over an entire *continent*, and I certainly couldn't unilaterally say "the President of Togo's been a bit rude about us lately, I think we should overthrow him. Get to it, chaps!" Something like that would have to be approved at a higher level – a political level.'

'Somebody *did* approve it,' Eddie told him. 'Brice said he had total immunity under the James Bond clause. Someone had to sign off on that.'

'The person who authorises Section 7 immunity for SIS officers is the Foreign Secretary,' Alderley replied – then he froze, eyes widening.

'What is it?' Nina asked.

'The Foreign Secretary . . . Brice resigned, or supposedly resigned, two years ago.' There was a rising undercurrent of alarm to his words. 'Which means his operation in DR Congo was approved at least that long ago, right?'

'Yes?' she said uncertainly. 'And that's sounding seriously bad because . . . ?'

'*Because* the man who was Foreign Secretary two years ago has got a new job since then.'

'Going to guess it's not selling fish and chips at a Harry Ramsden's,' said Eddie.

'Oh, I wish,' Alderley continued. 'The Foreign Secretary two years ago was Quentin Hove.' He saw that they both recognised the name, but pressed on regardless. 'Who is now the bloody *Prime Minister*!'

Brice regarded the Prime Minister of the United Kingdom of Great Britain and Northern Ireland with an expression of neutral deference. Behind it, though, he held the politician in a certain amount of contempt. Quentin Hove had usurped his predecessor in a leadership challenge eighteen months earlier; even though she had put the process of Brexit into motion, it had not been fast or hard enough to satisfy the Europhobic wing of her own party. The smooth-skinned, chinless Hove had been the surprise last man standing after his rivals knifed each other in the back, by all accounts a mediocre intellect despite an expensive education and whose chief achievement as he rose through the ministerial ranks was being less fractionally loathed by the public than his colleagues, using them as lightning rods.

But he was now in charge; other than the monarch, whose role was now almost entirely ceremonial, the highest power in the land. The man Brice had to convince of the importance – and *necessity* – of his plan.

He had begun with the stick rather than the carrot.

'You're telling me that . . . that the mission failed?' Hove had slightly bulging, watery eyes, and his dismay as he realised the implications made him appear on the verge of tears. 'And not only that, but our involvement might come out?'

'We're doing everything we can to minimise that possibility, sir,' Brice continued. 'We've already secured what physical evidence there is, and are working right now to make sure that any hearsay is silenced.'

'Should I ask how?'

'SIS is, as always, doing everything in its power to maintain full deniability, Prime Minister.' Sir Kirkland Armitage, the head of the Secret Intelligence Service – 'C' – was seated behind his desk, having watched impassively as Brice explained the situation to their political superior. 'We'll tell you anything you ask to know, of course, but I sincerely believe it's in your own best interest to leave operational details to us.'

'Of course. Of course,' echoed Hove, taking a couple of paces across the office before turning back to Brice. 'But – you crashed a plane! An American airliner, with over three hundred people aboard!' Despite his efforts to maintain a commanding air, panic was not far beneath the surface. 'That wasn't what we intended!'

'I was authorised to take any and all actions necessary to secure British interests in the Congo,' said Brice. 'Philippe Mukobo was a vital part of that plan, and it was the only way to free him from American custody.'

'But if the Americans even suspect British involvement, it'll be an absolute disaster. Anglo-American relations will be ruined

– no, they'll be *destroyed*! At the exact moment we've pulled away from Europe, we'll have turned our closest friend against us. We'll be left completely isolated, a pariah.' Helpless anger entered the politician's voice. 'And the plan for the Congo, the whole bloody *point* of the exercise, has been wrecked now Mukobo's dead. All those people on the plane, including British nationals – they died for nothing!'

'Not for nothing, sir. There's been . . . a new development.' This was the key moment, Brice's chance to hook him. He waited for Hove's response.

It came with a hint of hope behind the watery eyes. 'What kind of development?'

'Something extraordinary. You've heard of Nina Wilde?'

'The archaeologist? Of course. She found King Arthur's tomb.'

'And a lot more besides. Some of her discoveries have proven ancient myths to be real. What she found in the jungle is one of them. An ancient artefact . . . a *biblical* artefact.' He knew that Hove was a practising Christian; as he'd hoped, the revelation impressed him. 'I've seen its power with my own eyes. I don't know if it really does come from God, but I do know what it can do. What it can do for this country.'

'And what would that be?'

Brice delivered his reply with every ounce of confidence he could muster. 'It will *save* it, sir. It will ensure that you win the election next month. Not only that, it will keep you in office for the foreseeable future, while wiping out the Opposition as a political force for years – and doing the same to the elements in your own party who are working against you. You will not only remain Prime Minister after the election, you'll emerge even stronger than ever.'

The promise of holding on to power in an election where the opinion polls suggested political decimation had indeed hooked Hove. 'How . . . how would it do so?' he asked, licking his lips.

'Prime Minister, that's another operational detail we believe should be limited to those directly involved,' said C. 'However, Brice has told me his plan, and while it's not without risk, I believe it has a very high probability of success.'

'What risk?' said Hove.

'If our involvement became known to anyone outside this room, the consequences would be . . . unfortunate. However,' he went on, before the alarmed politician could object, 'the chances of that happening are small – as Brice said, we are actively working to prevent it. It's what I would classify as a high-risk, high-reward operation. If it comes off, then it will not only keep you in power, but also entirely justify your proposals to strengthen the intelligence services to protect this country – rather than cutting us off at the knees in the name of civil liberties, as the Opposition intends.'

'But if it doesn't . . .'

'If you want us to do nothing, sir, that's your prerogative as Prime Minister,' said Brice. 'I'm merely offering a possible course of action.'

Hove looked between the two men, then went to the large bulletproof window overlooking the Thames and gazed out at the city beyond. 'I have to say that I don't like the sound of this,' he announced after a long, contemplative silence. 'First you tell me that the plan for the Congo has ended in total failure, in a way that could not only damage the country as a whole but implicate me personally. Then, you offer me a solution, but only in the most vague terms, and which seems to rely on the supernatural.'

'Not supernatural, sir,' Brice said firmly. 'I've seen it for myself. It's science, just something we don't fully understand yet. But we will. The artefact has been secured, and even if you choose not to proceed with my plan, it will still be Britain's to study . . . and use. It has enormous potential as a weapon.'

'A weapon?' Hove turned back to him. 'Then your plan – it's some sort of attack?'

Armitage gave Brice an irritated look. The younger man blanched; he had said too much. 'More a projection of force,' C told the politician reassuringly. 'It's not a gun, a missile or a bomb. But just as in the Bible, when it's used, it will be decisive.' He stood and crossed the room to stand beside Hove. 'I can assure you, Prime Minister, that the difference to your election hopes will also be decisive.'

'That sounds almost like a threat,' said Hove, drawing back slightly from the bigger man.

'Not at all. We both want the same thing: to guarantee this country's security and strength in a changing and unstable world. I believe that Brice's proposal will provide it. But it will require great strength and resolution on our own part to see it through. Make no mistake, though,' C continued, 'the entire country will be united behind you. The entire *world*, even. As Prime Minister, everyone will look to you to provide Britain with strong leadership. You will be the man to bring the nation into a new age. The decision is yours.'

Hove licked his lips again. 'I . . . I need some time to consider this.'

'We have a very limited window of opportunity,' said Brice. 'If we're going to proceed, it has to be tomorrow.'

'Tomorrow?'

'We need a decision as soon as possible, sir,' said C. 'Brice has preparations to make.'

'What would I need to do?' asked the politician.

'Just give the word, sir,' Brice said. 'And one other thing . . . I'd strongly suggest that you miss tomorrow's Prime Minister's Questions in Parliament.'

'It's the last PMQs before the election,' Hove objected. 'I can't miss them – it'll give the Opposition a field day! They'll say I'm afraid to stand behind my own government's record. And . . .' He trailed off, a first hint of understanding dawning as he realised the significance of Brice's advice.

Armitage shook his head. 'There will be an extremely urgent national security matter that you need to discuss with me. As Prime Minister, you can nominate any cabinet minister to act as your representative for PMQs. I'd suggest someone who has been . . . challenging.'

Hove looked between the two SIS men again, his expression that of a prisoner – but also one who had seen a way out only reachable by trampling on others. 'A national security matter, yes,' he eventually intoned. 'I have to put the future of the country before petty party politics, of course . . .'

C nodded. 'Of course, Prime Minister.'

Brice stood straighter, like a soldier awaiting orders. 'So shall I proceed, sir?'

There was no verbal answer, but the politician gave a very small nod. Brice responded in kind, seeing that Hove was utterly unwilling – or afraid – to say anything out loud.

'I think that will be all, Brice,' said C.

'Yes, sir,' the younger man replied. 'Thank you for your time, Prime Minister.'

'I never met you,' Hove told him firmly. 'And if asked, I'll deny to my grave that this discussion ever took place.'

C smiled faintly. 'Such is the nature of the job, sir. Brice, you have your assignment. Do whatever is necessary to ensure the security of the realm.'

'Yes, *sir*.' Brice too had a small smile on his face as he left the room, but his was considerably more ruthless.

33

Nina awoke with a start. She and Eddie were in the Alderleys' spare bedroom, a street lamp outside casting a square of light on one wall. The curtains were open; closing them when their hosts were supposedly the only people in the house might have raised suspicion.

That the house hadn't been raided suggested their presence was still a secret, however. She shifted to find Eddie already awake beside her. 'What's the time?' she asked.

'Half five.'

'Really? God.' She sighed. 'That's bad enough in itself, but I hardly slept. I was too worried about Macy. What if Brice already sent his people to take her?'

'Yeah, me too,' he said gloomily. 'Just got to hope he's decided that if he can't contact us, he can't use her to threaten us into surrendering.'

'That's a very big hope.'

'All we've got.' He suddenly sat upright at a noise elsewhere in the house, then relaxed – though still remained alert. 'Ay up. Sounds like Alderley's moving.'

A few minutes later, a quiet tap came at the door. 'Nina? Chase?' Alderley whispered.

'Yeah, we're awake,' Eddie replied.

'Ah, good.'

'No, not particularly,' said Nina grumpily.

A small chuckle. 'This is normally when I start the day anyway, so nobody'll be suspicious. I had a quick peek outside, by the way. There's a car I don't recognise down the street, and from the way it's sitting on its suspension, I'd say there are two quite large men in it.'

'We'll keep our heads down, then,' Eddie said as he rolled off the bed. Both he and Nina had slept fully clothed, knowing they might need to make a rapid departure.

'Come down to my office,' said Alderley, leading them through the house. They entered the room to find the blinds drawn and his computer on, a screensaver cycling through pictures of his Capri. 'I logged into SIS to check the morning's reports and advisories. Last night, around the time you were telling me what had been going on in the Congo, a security alert was issued – for you.' He sat and typed in a password, the car disappearing to be replaced by passport photos of the couple. 'This went to SIS, the Security Service, Special Branch, and the Met and surrounding police forces.'

'Oh, great,' Nina said in dismay. 'We're at the top of the most-wanted list.'

'Hopefully you won't feel too offended that you're actually relatively low priority. The instruction is for you to be detained and brought to SIS regarding, and I quote, "a matter of national security". It saying "detained" and not "arrested" means they don't want anyone questioning you on the record before you get to Vauxhall Cross.'

'Dump us straight into MI6's torture dungeons, eh?' said Eddie.

'We don't have torture dungeons,' Alderley huffed. 'But reading between the lines, this actually gives your story more credence. To me, anyway.'

'Not to anyone else at MI6?' Nina asked.

He shook his head. 'I know you both. Everyone else, though? They'd take what they were told at face value, treat you as a security threat and bring you in – or take you down.'

The couple exchanged glances. 'So much for British hospitality,' said the redhead.

'Oh, it gets worse. There's a small addendum. It says "AFA", which means "all force authorised". That's a polite way of saying that if you happen to get shot dead, there won't be too many questions asked.'

'Huh. Great!'

Eddie brought his right hand towards the flap of his jacket, making sure Alderley saw the movement. 'But you're not going to turn us in, right?'

'Put the gun away, Chase,' the MI6 man sighed. 'If I was going to, I would have done it already. I spent half the night mulling over what you told me. And the answer I came up with is one I really don't like. For John Brice to have gone on a deep-cover mission to overthrow a non-hostile foreign regime, he must have had orders from the very top. That means C. The head of MI6,' he added for Nina's benefit.

'I thought that was M?' she said. Eddie grinned.

Another sigh. 'Only in fiction. But this puts me in quite an uncomfortable position. On the one hand, people whose judgement I trust have brought me intelligence about an operation in Africa that's been kept secret from the head of the Africa desk, and which stands to seriously destabilise a large region—'

'You trust my judgement?' said Eddie, his grin widening into a smug beam. 'Never thought I'd hear that!'

'Maybe I should have said "a person" rather than "people",' Alderley replied, glancing at Nina.

'Tchah!'

'But an operation like that could have major international repercussions. On the other hand, my superior, the person to whom I would normally report such intelligence . . . is the only person who could have authorised such a mission in the first place. And *his* superior is also complicit! I'm sure you can see the problem.'

'Yeah,' said Nina. 'The head of MI6 and the Prime Minister are both bad guys – so who are you supposed to tell?'

'Well, let's not go so far as to say they're bad guys. We need proof first.' He nodded at the broken laptop she was holding. 'But there's a larger issue.' He became positively grim. 'If what you've told me is true, then the head of the British government is directly involved in an illegal attempt to overthrow a sovereign state, the jailbreak of a mass murderer, and the deaths of everyone aboard a civilian airliner. That is . . .' He took a deep breath. 'Quite big.'

'That famous English understatement,' she said.

'We need it to stop us from panicking when we realise the true extent of a crisis,' Alderley replied wryly. 'But something I can't *overstate* is how far the apparatus of the British state will go to protect itself, and its own. And Quentin Hove and Sir Kirkland – C – *control* that apparatus.'

'So what do we do?' said Eddie.

'First thing, we've *got* to get the video of Brice from the laptop,' said Nina. 'Peter, do you know anyone who could do that – someone you could trust?'

He nodded. 'There are people in my department who could handle it, yes. And one of the advantages of being a section head is that generally your staff don't question your orders.'

'So if we get the video, then what?' the Yorkshireman asked. 'Take it to MI5?'

Alderley nodded – though not with much enthusiasm. 'The thing is, for something this big the Director-General of MI5 would report directly to the Prime Minister, just like C. The evidence would have to be absolutely incontrovertible and damning.'

'There's somewhere else we could take the video,' said Nina. 'The US embassy.'

Alderley – and to her surprise, her husband – regarded her

unhappily. 'I . . . I'd really prefer not to do that,' said the MI6 man.

'Why? Brice destroyed an American airliner! We're not just involved, we have a right to know about it.'

Alderley's discomfort was so intense that he was practically fidgeting. 'You'd be telling the US government that a British officer murdered hundreds of American civilians as part of an operation approved at the highest level. The fallout would be utterly catastrophic.'

'Yeah, but it's what happened! Eddie, you can't possibly think this should be covered up.'

'I don't, but . . .' Like Alderley, his internal conflict was so strong that it was becoming tangible. 'When I joined the army, I took an oath – to serve and protect my country. If this came out, I wouldn't be protecting Britain. I'd be fucking *wrecking* it. It'd make America hate us, take us from number one ally to all the way down at the bottom of the shit-list with Iran and North Korea, and I doubt the rest of the world'd treat us any better.'

'Oh, so *now* it's "my country, right or wrong", is it?' Nina said scathingly. 'Even when "wrong" means covering up the murders of hundreds of innocent people?'

'I'm not saying it's good! It's shit, it's horrible. And I'm not saying that Brice and anyone else involved shouldn't be dealt with for what they've done. But . . .' He shook his head. 'I can't chuck my own country down the toilet because of them. I might not live here any more, but it's still my duty to protect it.'

'And what about my duty to *my* country?' she countered. 'Someone committed a crime, a terrorist act, against it. Am I supposed to keep quiet because it's diplomatically inconvenient for the people responsible?'

'That's not what I'm saying,' Eddie insisted.

'Then what *are* you saying?'

'I don't know!' he cried, frustrated. 'There are two countries involved, and I just don't want to make everything worse.'

'Okay,' Nina said, more quietly, 'what would you want Macy to do?'

He was surprised. 'Macy? What's she got to do with this?'

'She's got dual nationality, American and British. So she's involved with *both* countries. What choice would you want her to make – not as a former British serviceman, but as a parent?'

'I . . .' Eddie frowned. 'I'd want her to do what's right,' he finally admitted. 'Whatever that is.' There was a lengthy silence.

It was eventually broken by Alderley. 'If you really are thinking about going to the US embassy,' he said, not remotely enthused at the prospect, 'there are two things to consider. The first is that Brice will almost certainly have placed watchers there. It's an obvious place of safety – well, for you, Nina. You're an American citizen, so once you're inside, you're on US soil and we can't touch you without going through channels. Afraid you're out in the cold, though, Chase.'

'Maybe you should have applied for US citizenship,' Nina told her husband.

'What, and have to start saying "Mommy" instead of "Mummy"?' he retorted. 'What's the other thing?'

'The other thing,' Alderley went on, 'is that you don't have any proof you can *take* to the embassy! Unless you recover the video from that laptop, the only evidence against Brice is hearsay. Since he officially resigned from MI6 two years ago, the government would simply deny any knowledge of his subsequent activities.'

'You said you could find someone to help us get it, though,' Nina reminded him. His sheepish lack of an immediate response spoke volumes. 'Oh, seriously? Now you're going to back out of that?'

'You've put me in an extraordinarily difficult position, Nina!' he said. 'I'm a senior officer of the Secret Intelligence Service;

like Chase, I swore an oath to protect my country – and helping you hand over diplomatic dynamite to the Americans would achieve the exact opposite. *However*,' he went on, raising both hands to silence her before she could protest, 'I also have an obligation to uphold the rule of law and ensure that everyone in my organisation behaves with the highest probity. That includes my superiors as well as the people under my command. The intelligence services have a lot of leeway under the law, but it only goes so far. Section 7 immunity for intelligence operatives only applies to acts committed outside the United Kingdom. Not on home soil. And it definitely doesn't apply to politicians. So if Brice was given an illegal order, the people who issued it are accountable.'

'How would you prove it, though?' said Eddie. 'They'll be covering their arses so hard you'll be able to see their fingerprints pressing through on the other side.'

'I doubt it'd be easy. But the first step, for me at least, would be actually hearing Brice admit to all of this, so . . . I guess I *do* need to help you recover that recording.'

'Peter, that's great,' Nina said, with relief. 'Thank you.'

'That's if there's anything to recover,' he said, eyeing the bullet hole in the laptop. 'But I can also make some discreet enquiries at SIS and see if Brice has popped up on anyone's radar. He certainly wouldn't be able to arrange an extraction from DR Congo and then come back home to put teams of watchers on people – including me! – without leaving a few blips.'

'See if you can find out about the people he's got watching Macy and my dad,' Eddie reminded him.

'I won't be able to poke my nose too far into someone else's active operation without raising questions, but I'll do what I can.'

'What about the Shamir?' asked Nina. 'It's a dangerous artefact, so what would he have done with it?' But as soon as she had posed the question, another came to her . . .

Alderley started to explain that SIS had secure research facilities dotted around the country, but she was no longer listening. 'Wait, wait,' she cut in. 'Forget what he's done with the Shamir. What's he *going* to do with it?'

'What do you mean?' asked the older man.

'He didn't get it out of the Congo just so MI6 could put it in a warehouse like the ending of *Raiders of the Lost Ark*. He had something in mind for it – he wants to *use* it.'

'On what?'

'I don't know, but she's right,' Eddie said. 'When he was talking to us in the palace, part of it was so he could buy time for the militia to get inside, but he also wanted to know more about the Shamir – how it worked, what it can do. And he was really excited about using it as a decapitation weapon.'

Alderley was alarmed. 'You think he's planning to attack a government?'

'I think he certainly had it in mind,' Nina told him. 'And that would be another reason for him to want us silenced, perm-anently. We know the Shamir exists, and what it can do. But nobody else does. So—'

'It would be a weapon nobody could defend against,' he concluded. 'All you'd need to do would be get it into the country undetected. But which country?'

'I'd ask which country Brice has got it in for, but from the way he was ranting on, it sounded like all of 'em,' said Eddie. 'He didn't even sound that keen on Britain. Not from the way things look likely to go after the election, anyway.'

The SIS officer grimaced. 'Yeah, the intelligence services aren't looking forward to what'll happen if the other lot win – which seems likely. Civil liberties are all well and good, but taking away powers that we already have and which every other country uses too, just to win votes from the Edward Snowden crowd, isn't exactly a bright move.'

Eddie shook his head mockingly. 'Glad you think that civil liberties are at least sort of worth having, maybe. Puts you above Brice, at least. But that's pretty much what he said, that MI6 is fucked after the election . . .' His voice trailed off as a thought came to him.

Nina could tell from his expression that it was not a good one. 'What is it?'

'Hove and his lot are probably going to be kicked out at the election,' he said. 'But what if there *isn't* an election?'

'There has to be one,' Alderley insisted. 'The date's been set, and Parliament's about to be dissolved. They can't back out of it now.'

'But they could in extreme circumstances, couldn't they?' said Nina, realising what Eddie meant. 'Like if there was a major terrorist attack?'

'It would have to be more than "major". More like absolutely catastrophic – on the level of 9/11, or beyond. The last time a general election was cancelled was in 1940, in the middle of the Blitz.'

'The Shamir would let him pull off an attack like that, though. Nobody could defend against it, because nobody knows it exists!'

'He could bring down any bloody building in London,' Eddie added. 'All he needs is line of sight, then take the lid off the box. Anything stone or metal goes boom.'

'I can't believe Brice would commit a terrorist act just to secure funding for MI6,' insisted Alderley.

'It wouldn't only be about that, though,' said Nina. 'That's just a bonus. He gives the government carte blanche to bring in whatever laws they like in the name of "security", and nobody would dare challenge them for fear of being accused of going soft on terrorism. You'd have a perpetual state of emergency, and those civil liberties you seem so lackadaisical about?

They wouldn't be a problem any more, because they'd be gone.'

The MI6 officer huffed. 'I am *not* lackadaisical about civil liberties! I actually donate to—'

Eddie interrupted him. 'Wait, that's something Brice actually said to me, in the hotel bar in Butembo. About a state of emergency – he said it was a good way for a government to suspend democracy, something like that.'

'And in the palace,' Nina remembered, 'he described the Shamir as "the perfect tool for regime change". Get all a country's leaders in one place, then drop the roof in on their heads . . .'

Alderley suddenly looked appalled. 'He couldn't possibly . . .'

'Couldn't possibly what?' she asked.

'Parliament is dissolved in the run-up to a general election,' the older man explained, awful realisation behind his words. 'Today's the final session of Prime Minister's Questions before that happens. PMQs are normally packed, and today's will be standing room only. '

'That's the part they show on C-SPAN which makes your politicians look like a bunch of braying schoolchildren, right?'

'It's not a high point of dignity and decorum, no. But just about every MP, from all parties, will be there. If someone really was planning to do a Guy Fawkes and bring the Houses of Parliament down on top of them, that would be the time to do it. It's maximum security, obviously, but . . .'

'But Brice doesn't have to be in the building,' Eddie finished for him. 'He could be sailing past on a fucking duck boat and still do it.'

'And if he's got support from high up, he can get whatever security clearance he needs,' said Nina. 'My God, if he actually *does* have that kind of support, they could still keep the Shamir a secret! They could make up any story they liked about the attack – blame it on Islamic terrorists or whoever. The government gets to stay in power because there won't be an election, and the intelligence agencies get a huge spending boost to fight the new threat, whoever they decide it to be.'

'But there wouldn't be a government to *stay* in power,' Alderley countered. 'You couldn't selectively blow up the House of Commons to take out your opponents while leaving your own side unscathed. It'd be far too dangerous. And I've dealt with politicians – there isn't a single one of them who'd risk sitting in that chamber knowing that the roof was about to come down on them, no matter what their side stood to gain.'

Eddie regarded Alderley's computer. 'Easy way to find out, though. Check if Hove's skiving out of PMQs today.'

'The Prime Minister wouldn't miss Prime Minister's Questions – the clue's in the name,' said Alderley snippily, but he still started pecking at the keyboard. 'By the way, would you mind not looking over my shoulder, please? I'm logging into SIS, so everything here is classified.'

'Ooh, don't mind us,' said Eddie sarcastically as he and Nina begrudgingly turned away.

'I'll remind you that you signed the Official Secrets Act.' Alderley called up an information feed and scrolled through it. 'But anyway, while the PM actually doesn't always attend, it's extremely unlikely they'd miss the final PMQs of a Parliament. There are too many sound bite opportunities to . . .'

'To?' Nina prompted after a few seconds of silence.

'I'm going to risk being arrested and turn around,' Eddie said to her in a fake whisper.

They both faced Alderley again. 'You, ah . . . you were right, Chase,' he said in disbelief. 'There's a first time for everything, but – you were right. Quentin Hove *isn't* attending PMQs today; he's being represented by the Home Secretary instead. Hove's going to . . .' He clicked a link for more details. 'Okay, this is *very* odd. He has what's described as a "critical security briefing" with C at 11.30, so won't be available for PMQs at noon. But if something was *that* critical, he'd have other cabinet ministers with him from the COBRA emergency committee – and the Home Secretary would absolutely be one of them.'

'Also, if it's that critical, why isn't he having the meeting right now?' Nina asked. 'Why wait an extra five hours?'

Alderley dismissed the feed, then faced his guests. 'I'm still finding it very difficult to imagine that Brice is planning to destroy the Houses of Parliament with some lost biblical super-weapon, but . . . the two superiors who would have approved this deep-cover job in the Congo are the same two men who've scheduled a closed-doors meeting in Downing Street at the exact time you'd expect one of them to be grandstanding for the TV cameras in the Commons.'

'So, not a normal situation?'

'Definitely not, no.'

She held up the laptop. 'If Brice really is going to attack Parliament, then we've *got* to recover the video and expose him before it happens.'

'How will that stop him?' Alderley demanded.

'Because on the recording, he talks about using the Shamir to carry out a decapitation strike. So it won't be a secret weapon any more, and it both establishes that he has the means to do it and makes it much harder to pin the blame on someone else. Especially when nobody finds any trace of explosives in the rubble.'

'If the official story is that explosives were found, then believe me, explosives *will* be found,' the SIS officer told her.

'Which is why we have to take the recording to the American embassy. If the US government has proof, they'll have enough leverage to go straight to Hove with it. He and the head of MI6 are the only people who can call Brice back in before it's too late.'

'They'll also have proof of MI6 involvement in the crash of that airliner!' Alderley protested. 'I told you, that would be a diplomatic disaster.'

'Which gives them every incentive to pull Brice in before he can do anything else. Remember, the video shows him *claiming* still to be working for MI6 – but if Hove and C get their stories straight, they can say he's really an embittered *ex*-agent who went rogue, and that everything he told us was a lie. They can't allow him to destroy Parliament if the Americans know about the plan in advance, because it would prove he had MI6 support to get back to England so fast with the Shamir – which in turn proves the British government's complicity in the crash of Flight 180.'

'So they'd sell out Brice to the Americans to save their own arses?' said Eddie. 'Sounds like what politicians would do, all right.'

Alderley's expression became thoughtful. 'If it came to that, I think it's far more likely that Brice would suffer an "unfortunate accident". He'd be a huge liability – they couldn't take the risk that he might implicate his superiors.' He gave Nina a look of faintly amused approval. 'You know, for an archaeologist you actually have quite a devious mind. Have you ever considered a change of career?'

She shook her head firmly. 'No thanks.'

'What are we going to do, then?' Eddie asked Alderley. 'You going to help us?'

He blew out his cheeks, conflicted. 'I'm really, *really* not happy about turning the evidence straight over to the Americans. But . . .' He stood. 'If there's an imminent threat of attack, there isn't time to take this through channels. Hove and C's first instinct, if they are involved, will be to obfuscate and delay so they can protect themselves – by which time it might be too late.'

Nina glanced at a wall clock. It was now after six. 'We've got less than six hours before Prime Minister's Questions start. That's not much time.'

'I know. Which means our *first* priority is to recover the evidence.' He regarded the broken laptop, then frowned.

'Something wrong?' said Eddie.

'Brice – well, someone, certainly – put watchers on me. If I'm under observation physically, then I guarantee I am electronically as well. If the file's retrievable at all, I know someone in my section who'll be able to do it. But if I ring him up, Brice will know about it very quickly.'

'We've got some spare phones you could use to call him.'

'I need more than that, I need cover . . .' He thought for a moment – then smiled. 'Got it. I'll make some calls. Quite a few calls.' He logged back on to the computer.

'What are you going to do?' asked Nina.

'I'm the head of the section – which means I can hold surprise drills at any time. I think today would be a good choice.' He selected a name from a contacts list and dialled their number on his mobile phone. 'Wendy, good morning. It's Peter Alderley. Yes, I'm fine, thanks – but I need everything you have on, ah . . . the secessionist threat in eastern DR Congo ready for a situation briefing at ten thirty this morning. Yes, I know, but it's urgent. Half past ten. Thanks.' He hung up.

'Hiding the needle in the haystack, I see,' said the redhead as he found the next number.

'Information overload's always a good way to beat the system,' he replied. 'Chase, if I can have one of those spare phones, that'd be very useful.'

He made around twenty similar calls, the last to someone called Roy. 'Roy Boxley,' he explained after hanging up. 'He's the chap I mentioned. Young, smart, eager to please, quite the tech-head – I just hope he'll be excited rather than suspicious about being given a secret assignment by his boss.' He entered the number into the prepaid phone. 'Right, since – hopefully! – Roy isn't being actively monitored by anyone, and this phone isn't on any watch lists, the call won't be flagged for attention . . .'

He waited for it to be answered. 'Roy, it's Peter Alderley

again. Okay, listen. Don't worry about the DR Congo briefing, I've got something more important for you to do. I'm going to send some people around to your flat with a laptop. It's damaged, but there's a file on it they need to recover urgently. Just wait there until they arrive, then do what they ask.' A pause as the other man asked a question. 'I told you, don't worry about the briefing. The laptop is your top priority. I don't know exactly what time they'll arrive, but be ready.'

He returned the phone to Eddie, who removed the battery and SIM card, then dropped its body on the floor and stamped on it. Alderley gave him an annoyed look. 'You know, just taking out the battery would have been enough.'

'Yeah, but that was more fun,' Eddie replied with a grin.

'How are we going to get to this Roy's place?' asked Nina. 'If you're being followed, you can't drive us there.'

'I've thought about that,' Alderley replied. 'I've got a tow rope in the garage—'

'You'd need it a lot with a Capri, I suppose,' cut in the Yorkshireman.

'Har har. Har. But there's a railway cutting behind the house. If you tie the rope around a tree, you should be able to climb down. Go left for about four hundred yards, and there's a way up to a bridge.'

'Sounds like you've already checked it out,' said Nina.

Alderley chuckled. 'Hey, I'm a spy. I always know all the possible escape routes!' He stood, becoming more serious. 'When I set off for work, that should keep the watchers occupied enough for you to go out the back way without being seen. I'll give you Roy's address. If you go across the bridge, you should be able to get a taxi. Actually, I'll lend you my and Poppy's Oyster cards as well, in case you need to use a bus or the Tube.'

'Can't we just use cash?' Eddie asked.

'Cash?' Alderley said, smiling. 'That's so last decade.'

'Like my hair. Thanks, then. I'll give you the number of our other phone in case you need to call us. By the way, don't suppose you've got any spare nine-mil rounds, do you?'

'Let me check my kitchen drawers to see if they're in there with the batteries and assorted screws,' the MI6 officer said sarcastically. 'No, I don't. And I'd prefer you not to start any gun battles on the streets of London!'

'So would we,' Nina said firmly. She waited for everything to be exchanged. 'Okay. Thank you, Peter. Let's go.'

34

'Nice place,' said Eddie of the West Kensington apartment building to which a taxi had delivered them. 'Wonder how this Roy can afford it on a spook's pay?'

'Maybe he really is as good as Peter says,' Nina replied, surveying the street. It was now after seven in the morning and people were up and about, but none seemed interested in them. 'Let's see, number twenty-four . . .'

She pushed the intercom button. A short wait, then a man's voice came from the speaker. 'Yah?'

'Roy Boxley?' she said. 'You were told to expect us.'

'Oh, yah, yah. Come on up.' They were buzzed in.

There was a lift, but they took the stairs, not wanting to be sealed in an enclosed space. Their destination was on the fourth floor. Eddie knocked on the door, which was quickly answered.

Roy Boxley did not match their mental image of an MI6 techie. He was in his mid-twenties, tall and broad with the hefty build of a rugby player. Tight ginger curls topped a big, ruddy-cheeked face with an expression of affable curiosity. 'Mr Alderley sent you, yah?' he said in a languid, upper-crust voice.

'That's right,' said Nina.

'Great, great. Come in.' He stepped back to let them enter. The apartment was compact but clearly expensive, bright and minimalist with lots of polished marble surfaces. The huge flat-screen television dominating one wall confirmed it as the home of a young and well-off bachelor. Considering what Eddie had said about SIS pay, Nina imagined Roy had received no small financial help from his family. 'Can I get you anything? Tea, coffee?'

'No, that's fine, thanks.' He gave her an odd look. 'Something wrong?'

Roy tapped his large chin thoughtfully, then pointed at her. 'Nina Wilde! You're Nina Wilde, aren't you? I knew I recognised you.'

'That's me,' she said warily. If the security alert about her and Eddie had gone to all MI6's employees . . .

'Love your show!' he said enthusiastically, holding out his hand. 'Fascinating stuff, Atlantis and all that. Are you doing another series?'

'We've just filmed another one,' she said as his huge fleshy palm enveloped hers.

'Great, great! And I've got the Blu-rays of your films too.' He pointed proudly at a black shelf unit filled with discs of mostly action movies, including the full James Bond oeuvre. 'How close are they to what actually happened?'

'Not even remotely.'

'Oh, shame.' Roy greeted Eddie, then peered at the computer Nina was holding. 'That's the laptop you want me to recover something from, yah?'

She put it down. The young man's eyebrows rose when he saw the bullet hole. 'Yes. There's a video file that . . . well, let's just say it's a matter of national security. It should be the newest thing on there chronologically.'

'And Mr Alderley thinks I'm the man to retrieve it for you? Well, I'm flattered – although I really am,' he added with false modesty. 'But why bring it to my flat? I could have done it at SIS, and probably much faster.'

'The video's of someone *from* SIS confessing to a major crime,' said Eddie. 'Alderley wants to expose them before they can hush it up.'

Roy's eyes went wide – but with intrigue rather than alarm. 'Ah, sounds sauce-ay! Well, if Mr A. wants me to help bust them, I'm in.' He reached for the laptop. 'May I?'

Nina nodded. 'Please do.'

He took it, peering at her through the hole before going to a door. 'Okay, let's see what we have,' he said, gesturing for them to follow.

While the rest of the apartment was clean and fastidiously neat, this room appeared to be occupied by Roy's Mr Hyde. A second bedroom had been turned into a makeshift electronics lab, tall shelves covered in dismantled computer components and no fewer than three working machines on an equally untidy desk. 'Sorry about the mess,' he said as he sat and switched on a powerful lamp. 'My hobby. Learned at an early age that I was very good at dismantling things – like all kids, ha ha – but fortunately turned out to be even better at putting them back together. Useful for my job – I'm sort of the Africa desk's unofficial Q.'

'Can you fix this?' asked Nina.

'Find out in a mo.' He opened the laptop and pushed its power button. When nothing happened, he rummaged through a drawer for a set of small screwdrivers. 'Have to open it up. Make yourselves comfortable, this could take a little while.'

The only potential seating in the room other than Roy's chair being precariously stacked boxes, the couple retreated into the living room. 'What do we do if he can't get it working?' Eddie asked quietly.

'I'm not sure,' said his wife. 'Try to reach Macy, I guess. Oh, God.' She gazed disconsolately at the carpet. 'All this, and we haven't even been able to let her know we're okay. And we don't even know if *she's* okay. What if Brice already sent his people after her?'

He held her. 'Have to hope he's got other things on his mind right now.'

'Blowing up the Houses of Parliament isn't really a spur-of-the-moment thing, no.' She rested her head on his shoulder. 'How do you think he's going to do it? From a boat, like you said?'

He shook his head. 'Changed my mind about that. You've got to aim the Shamir, and standing on a boat in the middle of the Thames pointing something weird at Parliament's going to draw attention. There's a ton of security around there. They're watching out for RPGs, car bombs, mortars . . .'

'So where could he attack from?'

'I dunno. If he really is getting help from the top, he could theoretically get security clearance to walk right into Parliament. But it's more likely he's got enough to get close without making anyone suspicious.'

'In disguise, maybe? As a cop or something?'

'Maybe. But he's still got to carry the Shamir with him – *and* that lead box, or he'll be blowing up buildings left and right.'

'He'd need a car to move it in, then. Or a truck.'

Eddie nodded, but before he could voice any more thoughts Roy reappeared. 'Okay, I've got, as the saying goes, good news and bad news.'

'Let's get the bad out of the way first, huh?' said Nina.

'Ah, a pessimist. Well, the bad news is that your laptop is completely shot, no pun intended. The bullet damaged a load of critical components – including the SSD, the hard drive.'

'I'm finding it hard to see how there could *be* any good news after that.'

'Oh, ye of little faith. The *good* news is that I was able to take out the SSD and connect it to one of my computers. There's still data on it – the problem is that the directory's been corrupted. At the moment, it's just gibberish. But what I can do is clone it on to my own machine, then try to rebuild the directory and recover the files. It'll take a while, but I'm sure it can be done.'

Eddie checked his watch. It was after seven thirty: less than four and a half hours before Parliament would be packed with MPs for Prime Minister's Questions. 'How long? An hour, two, three?'

'Hard to say, chap. Depends how corrupted the files are, and how much data's missing. Based on the size of the drive, at least two hours, though.'

Eddie and Nina exchanged concerned looks. 'Can you do it on a laptop?' Nina asked.

'Yah, but it'll be slower. Why?'

'You might need to work on the move,' Eddie told him.

'What? Why?'

'The thing is,' Nina began, trying not to sound too alarming, 'the person on the video has got watchers out looking for us. Peter's put himself on the line to help us, but sooner or later, this person's going to realise that he has. Once he does, he'll check Peter's phone calls and find you're not at work. So the first place he sends watchers to check—'

'Will be *here*?' Roy said in dismay. 'Wait, am I doing something illegal by helping you? Oh, bloody hell! That's a great start to my career; I've only been at SIS for six months!'

'You're *exposing* something illegal,' she countered. 'And maybe stopping something even worse. That's why we've *got* to recover this file – and why we can't let anyone from SIS catch us first.'

Roy made a sound of anguish. 'They're the people I work for! Ugh. Okay. Let me think. I need to talk to Mr Alderley.'

'They're monitoring his calls,' Eddie warned. 'If you let on anything's happening, they'll be straight round here.'

That did not help Roy's mood. 'Peter was sure you could help us uncover the truth,' said Nina. 'Please, Roy – you're the only person who can do it.' She glanced towards the DVDs. 'Working for MI6 probably isn't like a James Bond movie, but you can still be a hero and save the country. And you don't even need a gun, just a computer.'

'Save the country?' Roy echoed. 'What the hell is going on?'

'Something big,' Eddie told him. 'And we're running out of time to stop it.'

'I really should talk to Mr Alderley again . . .' he said, but his eyes had followed Nina's towards the shelf of movies. 'Is there *anything* you can tell me? At all?'

'The man on the video admits to a terrorist act,' she said, deciding to give him something more concrete in the hope of swaying his decision. 'And we think he's about to commit another, here in London – and we only have until noon to stop him. But without the video, we don't have any evidence. It's our word against his, and right now, he's a lot more likely to be listened to by the authorities.'

'And you say he works for SIS? He's gone rogue?'

Eddie nodded. 'He's responsible for killing a lot of people. And he might be responsible for a shitload more.'

Roy thought hard before finally making a choice. 'All right,' he said, 'all right. I may come to regret this, but . . . I'll help you. If anything goes wrong, though, I'll say you forced me at gunpoint.' He chuckled.

Eddie opened up his leather jacket to reveal the automatic. 'That's plausible.'

'Oh my God. Is that real?' The Yorkshireman's stony expression assured him it was. 'I see. Well, I suppose that means you *could* have forced me at gunpoint if you'd wanted to, but you didn't, so . . . Okay. Let me set things up on my laptop.' He went back into the computer room, pausing in the doorway. 'You know, in an odd way this is actually rather exciting! Terrifying, but exciting.'

Eddie and Nina followed him in, both to see what he was doing and to make sure he didn't try to warn MI6. 'Maybe for you, but I've had way too much excitement lately,' she said.

Her husband patted her on the back. 'Love? I've got some bad news about the rest of the day.'

Brice looked over the vehicle waiting for him in a lock-up a mile from SIS headquarters. It was a white Ford Transit van with a pickup rear body, its paintwork dirty and scuffed from years of solid use. In no respect was there anything noteworthy about it . . . which made it perfect for his purposes.

He checked the pickup bed. SIS's quartermasters had also provided him with suitable props: various tools, warning signs and road cones were stacked in the rear. He hopped up to clear a space for the Shamir's lead box. The ancient weapon was currently in the boot of an equally anonymous car, but he needed to transfer it to something that could stop anywhere without drawing attention from traffic wardens or police officers.

The Transit would fit the bill. Its doors bore the coat of arms of the City of Westminster, the central London borough that was home to many of the city's most famous buildings – including the Houses of Parliament. Anyone looking closely would notice that the vinyl decals were brand new, without the patina of diesel particulates speckling the rest of the van; there were limits to what SIS's people could do on short notice. He doubted it would receive such an inspection, though. A council van working on its own streets was so unremarkable as to be effectively invisible.

He was about to collect the Shamir when his phone rang. 'Yes?'

'I have some good news for you, old man.' Ellis, the senior technician. 'About your laptop.'

'What did you find?' Brice asked cautiously. Ellis's people had been ordered not to watch the incriminating video should they recover it, but it was inevitable that someone would have viewed at least parts of it, if only to check that the picture and sound were intact. 'Did you recover the recording?'

'We recovered *lots* of recordings,' Ellis replied cheerily. 'The thing is, though, they're all audio files, not video.'

The spy felt a rising sense of unease. 'Had anything been copied off the hard drive and then deleted?'

'Doesn't look like it. Even if they'd used a secure delete command, we'd still be able to tell that something had *been* deleted.'

Brice's discomfort grew. Something was very wrong. 'There's nothing at all from the drone?'

'There isn't even anything related to a drone, old man. Apart from the standard system software, all the applications are audio-related. Sound recording, editing, filtering, that kind of thing. Professional-grade software, by the way. I'd say our having this means a sound man's lost their livelihood.'

'A sound *woman*,' he corrected, all the puzzle pieces suddenly slotting together.

'Considering the bullet hole, maybe they lost more than that! But I don't think that you—'

Brice cut off the call. Fighting back anger, he entered a new number.

It was the private secure line of C himself. A reply soon came. 'Armitage.'

'Sir, it's Brice. We have a situation. The laptop we took from Chase and Wilde at Heathrow – it's not the one they used to make the drone recording. They switched it for an identical computer.'

The response was terse. 'Then where's the real one?'

'They must still have it. Maybe they got someone else on the plane to bring it through for them. Sir, Ellis just recovered the data from the laptop in our possession. If Chase and Wilde have done the same with the real one—'

'That would lead to very unwelcome consequences,' C interrupted, making it perfectly clear upon whom said consequences would fall. 'You need to find them, and the laptop.'

'I'm getting ready to start the mission, sir. I need help. If I can have your permission to activate GB63—'

'You have it.' The authorisation came with no hesitation, or emotion.

'Thank you, sir. And there's something else. Chase contacted Peter Alderley yesterday to arrange a meeting, but never showed up. But I think Alderley *must* be involved somehow. He knows something – he might even be helping them.'

'I'll call him in for a chat,' said Armitage. 'Now: is your mission in jeopardy? Will you have to abort?'

'This is the only opportunity we'll have before the election,' said Brice, realising his boss was putting all the responsibility on him. 'If we find Chase and his wife and get the laptop, there's no threat to us.'

'And what if they've already recovered the file and are disseminating it?'

'GCHQ need to monitor for any signs that they might have done so. I can coordinate that through ops. But until I know that there's a definite risk, I'll continue as planned.'

'Very well. Remember, Brice – you can't afford anything to go wrong. Understood?'

'Very clearly, sir.' Brice lowered the phone, realising he was sweating. He rubbed his neck, then made another call, again to SIS. 'Staite? Brice here. C has just approved the use of the Removal Men. Their targets are Eddie Chase and Nina Wilde.' A small smile. 'Turn them loose.'

Peter Alderley looked out from his office at the activity in SIS's Africa section. His unexpected drill was being taken very seriously, his staff working flat out to meet the ten thirty deadline.

He made a mental note to use the same approach again in future; it would keep them on their toes . . .

His desk phone rang. He answered. 'Alderley.'

'Peter. This is C. I need to talk to you. Come up to my office.'

Impromptu meetings with the head of SIS were far from common. 'Sir, I'm just about to hold a staff briefing,' he said, unsettled.

'*Now*, Peter.' He hung up.

'Oh, boy,' Alderley muttered. He had no doubts that the summons was somehow connected to his unexpected houseguests. Had they been caught?

A moment of hesitation – what he was about to do could end his career – then he called the number Eddie had given him. It went through to voicemail. 'Hi, it's me,' he said, trying to sound casual for those monitoring. 'I've just been called into a meeting with the boss, so no idea how long I'll be. You should go on ahead. Bye.' He hoped the recipient wouldn't take too long to check his messages.

A quick apology to his staff for delaying the briefing, then he headed out and took a lift up to C's office near the top of the building. Armitage's secretary told him to go straight in. That in itself was ominous; on the few previous occasions when he had been summoned for a meeting, he'd had to endure the ritual of the powerful, waiting outside like a schoolboy until his superior concluded more important business.

C stood at the window, looking out across the Thames. 'Ah, Peter. There you are.' He did not turn around.

'Yes, sir,' said Alderley, joining him. 'You wanted to see me?'

'Yes, I did.' He continued to gaze at the river. 'I want an explanation.'

'About what, sir?'

'Your contact with Eddie Chase and Nina Wilde last night. They called you.'

'Yes sir, they did,' said Alderley, knowing there was no point dissembling. C would have seen the telephone logs and quite probably listened to the call, GCHQ recording every phone conversation in the country as a matter of routine. 'They said they wanted to meet me, but didn't turn up.'

'And are you in the habit of going out of your way to meet everyone who requests an audience?'

'They're . . . friends,' he said, almost forcing out the word at the thought of describing Eddie as such. 'I hadn't seen them for a while.'

'And were you aware that they are fugitives wanted on a matter of national security? That they instigated a gun battle at Heathrow and caused an enormous amount of property damage in their escape?'

'They, ah, neglected to mention that, sir.'

C finally faced him. The intelligence chief's expression was anything but reassuring. 'I understand that you called members of your department in the early hours of this morning and ordered them to prepare a briefing concerning the Democratic Republic of Congo. Why?'

'A drill, sir. I wanted to test their readiness for an unexpected event.'

'Hardly your usual procedure.'

'The world's changing, sir. We have to change with it.'

C's cold eyes bored into him. Alderley stood his ground, but could feel himself wilting – until to his relief the other man turned away as one of his desk phones rang. He crossed the room to pick it up. 'Yes? I see. Send it to me. No, immediately. Alderley is in my office right now – I want him to hear it too.'

He sat behind his desk, beckoning his subordinate over as if he were an unruly child. Trying to cover his trepidation, Alderley stood before him. 'Hear what, sir?'

'I had our analysts check the phone calls you made this

morning. They also back-traced any other calls received by your people.' He turned to his computer and clicked the mouse to bring up a file. 'One came from a previously unused mobile number. I'd like you to hear it.'

Alderley's heart sank as he heard his own recorded voice. 'Roy, it's Peter Alderley again. Okay, listen. Don't worry about the DR Congo briefing, I've got something more important for you to do. I'm going to send some people around to your flat with a laptop.' His second call to Roy Boxley played through to its conclusion.

C had not taken his eyes from him. 'Explain,' he said. 'Were the people you referred to Wilde and Chase? What was on the laptop?'

'I . . .' Trapped, Alderley hesitated before replying. 'Sir, I was given information by a source I trust,' he said, deciding that if he was going down, he would do so fighting. 'This information regarded illegal operations in DR Congo and a possible conspiracy within SIS itself. In the interests of national security, I decided to begin further investigation on my personal authority as the head of the Africa desk.'

'I see. And do you have the *names* of these alleged conspirators?'

'Yes – but I don't think it would be appropriate at this time to release that information to anyone but the head of an independent investigative enquiry.'

The two men stared at each other. C remained impassive for a long moment – then reached to his intercom. 'Send security to my office immediately,' he barked. 'Peter Alderley is to be placed in custody. There is a man on his staff called Roy Boxley; have him brought up to me at once.'

'Yes, sir,' came his secretary's alarmed reply.

'So you're just going to throw me in a cell?' said Alderley angrily. 'I know about Brice – that his resignation was faked so he could help break up the Congo deniably. And I *also* know he brought something back with him that can be used for a false-flag attack.'

'I'd advise you to keep such conspiracy theories to yourself, Peter,' said C icily. The door opened and a pair of large men in dark uniforms entered, batons and Tasers on their belts.

'If Brice does what I think he's about to, the damage to the country will be on your head. *Sir*,' Alderley added in an acidic tone as the men flanked him.

The intelligence head's response was a dismissive wave of one hand. 'Take him away,' he said, before responding to a buzz from his intercom. 'Yes?'

'Sir, Roy Boxley didn't turn up for work this morning,' his secretary told him. 'Should I try to reach him at home?'

'No,' C replied as Alderley was led away. 'I'll take care of it.'

Fifteen minutes later, a black Range Rover skidded to a halt on the double-yellow lines outside Roy Boxley's home. The four men who jumped out were unconcerned about parking restrictions. As part of their duties, they were exempt from them . . . as well as many other laws of the land.

They did not use the buzzer. The burliest of the group carried a solid metal battering ram, which he swung against the door hard enough to smash the jamb. The others rushed inside, guns drawn.

They pounded up to the other floor. The three armed men took up positions on each side of flat twenty-four's door as the fourth readied the battering ram – and burst it open. His companions rushed in, weapons ready to shoot anyone they found—

Nobody was there. It took only seconds for the other rooms to be checked. 'Clear!' each intruder shouted in turn.

'Control, there's no one here,' the leader reported into his headset. 'I repeat, targets are not here.'

Brice was still in the lock-up, patched into the operation's communications through his phone. 'What about the laptop?' he demanded.

'There are two desktop machines in one of the rooms,' came the reply. 'No sign of any laptops. But there's a space where one might have been.'

The MI6 officer held in an obscenity. 'Withdraw and await further orders,' he snapped. 'Staite, Waterford: get on the CCTV network. If there's a camera near Boxley's flat, go back through the video and see when they left, then track them. You have authority to call on any and all extra resources you need.' He glanced at the van; while he wanted to oversee the manhunt, he also knew he would soon have to leave to reach his target in time. 'As soon as you find them, call me. But *find them*!'

35

Roy gave Eddie an irritated look over his laptop's screen. 'You know, glaring at me won't make it work any faster.'

He and his visitors had decamped from the flat some time earlier after receiving Alderley's message, Roy bringing them to a trendy coffee shop not far from his home. 'I'm a regular here,' he had told them earlier as they settled into a softly lit corner at the rear. 'They'll leave us alone. Oh, and they do the best hazelnut macchiato in London. You should try it.'

Nina had taken his advice, but was less than impressed. She'd held in her critiques so he could work, but it was now after eleven o'clock. They were running out of time. 'How much longer will it take?'

The damaged laptop's hard drive was connected to Roy's machine by a cable, the young man's computer set to remain active even with the lid closed so the scrambled data could be copied and reassembled while on the move. 'It's over eighty per cent done,' he told her. 'So I'd say . . . half an hour before we can check the files.'

'Can't you only recover the video we're after?' Eddie demanded impatiently. 'We don't need anything else.'

'Doesn't work that way, chap. The computer needs to know which data belongs to which file first. Until the directory's repaired, it doesn't know its bits from its bollocks.'

'But it can be repaired, yes?' said Nina.

Roy nodded. 'Looks like there'll be some missing blocks, but considering that someone put a bullet through it, recovering anything at all is a minor miracle. Luckily, you had me on the case.'

'The faster, the better,' said Eddie. He glanced towards the entrance as someone entered the shop, but it was a young woman with a baby. Unless the Increment had really changed their recruitment practices, she was not a threat. All the same, he rechecked that the emergency exit was clear, having chosen their seats for rapid access to it.

'Can you view any of the directory yet?' asked Nina. 'If we can see the dates on the files, we'll know which one we want – it should be the most recent.'

'I can certainly try,' said Roy. He opened a terminal window and entered commands. A list of files scrolled up. 'We've got a bit of it.' He turned the machine to face her. 'Should get more as the directory's filled in, but you might see what you're after.'

Nina read through it. Roy had listed the files by date, newest first, but the topmost were from the day before Brice's confession. 'Damn. It's not there!'

'Wouldn't worry. The bigger the file, the more pieces there are to assemble, so videos will probably be the last to be recovered.' He reached to turn the laptop back—

Nina grabbed his hand. 'Oh, shit,' she gasped.

Eddie quickly stood, hand moving towards his hidden gun. 'What is it?'

She jabbed a finger at the menu bar – and one particular icon. 'You're on frickin' *wi-fi*!'

'Well, yah,' said Roy. 'I told you, I'm a regular – it finds it automatically.'

'Yeah – which means MI6 can find *you*! You work for an intelligence agency, so they'll have a list of all your computers to make sure you're not emailing the Kremlin!'

He blinked. 'Oh. *Oh!* I didn't even – sorry, it didn't even occur to me about the wi-fi. It's just, you know . . . *there*.'

'Some bloody spy you'd make,' Eddie growled. 'Come on, we've got to move.'

'Are you sure?'

'We can't risk staying here,' Nina told him, rising.

'And turn off your sodding wi-fi!' Eddie chided. Roy hastily did so. 'It's like a bloody tracking device. Where else can we go?'

'If we only have to wait a half-hour for the files to be recovered,' said Nina, 'then we should head for the American embassy. And don't start,' she told Eddie. 'What other choice do we have now?'

Roy picked up his laptop, holding it carefully so as not to dislodge the cable. 'Okay, I'm ready.'

Eddie opened the emergency exit. The three piled through, ignoring the shout from a barista. They emerged in a dingy alley. 'I still think giving the video to the Yanks is a bad idea,' he said, 'but you're right, we're out of options. The embassy's in Mayfair – we can get there on the Tube—'

'No, no!' Roy cut in as they hurried along the alley. 'That's the *old* embassy. The new one opened a couple of years ago. It doesn't have a Tube station yet, though – and you won't want to use the one nearest to it.'

'Why not?' asked Nina.

'It's at Vauxhall – right by SIS headquarters.'

'Yeah, okay, somewhere to avoid,' she quickly agreed. 'So what's the best way there?'

They emerged on a main road and looked around. 'Taxi,' said Eddie, before seeing an alternative. 'Or . . . bus?'

'You want to get away from government goons chasing us by *bus*?'

'Well, first thing is that they won't be expecting us to do it. And second, there's one right there.' He pointed at an approaching red double-decker. 'Won't get us all the way, but at least we'll be across the river.'

Nina was dubious, but the trudging pace of the traffic suggested that a cab would be little faster. They jogged across the road to meet it. 'Okay, so we just jump on like in the movies, right?'

'Not any more,' Roy said. 'They banned that when they fired all the conductors to save money. But there's a stop down here.'

They hustled to it, joining the short queue. Eddie looked back. No sign of any speeding cars packed with large men, but after the wi-fi debacle he was sure they would be on the way.

The bus, a new-model Routemaster modelled on the iconic London vehicle, arrived. They boarded, Eddie and Nina paying with the cards lent to them by Alderley. Roy started for the rear, but Eddie called him back, finding seats as close to the driver as possible. 'Just in case he gets any radio messages about us,' he explained quietly.

'You think he might?' Nina asked as the bus set off, heading south.

'There's CCTV everywhere. They might have seen us get on.' He turned to watch as a black Range Rover, flashing blue strobe lights concealed behind its radiator grille, muscled along the other side of the road to head for the coffee shop. 'We got out just in time.'

'Were they after us?' Roy asked.

Eddie nodded. 'You heard of the Increment?'

'Yah, of course, although they're called "E" Squadron now – wait,' he added in alarm, 'they've sent *them* after us?'

'Who did you expect? Austin Powers?'

'Oh, God.' The young man's demeanour had until now been that of someone embarking upon a slightly transgressive adventure, but now the gravity of the situation struck home. 'That's, ah . . . rather serious.'

'No shit,' muttered Nina. She indicated his laptop. 'How much longer?'

Roy opened the machine. 'The directory's almost ninety per cent done. So fifteen, twenty minutes?'

'Keep it going, then,' she told him, looking back after the Range Rover.

Staite and Waterford had been joined in the control centre by two more young and keen operators. 'According to building records, the coffee house has a fire exit into a back street,' one reported.

'Did you hear that?' Staite asked the ground team through her headset.

'Affirmative,' came the reply.

'Got them on cam,' reported Waterford. A screen showed a live CCTV image from the main street, the Range Rover nearing a junction. It made a hard stop at the corner, two men jumping from its rear and running out of frame as the SUV set off again.

'Can we see the shop?' asked Staite.

He checked a grid of smaller images on another display. 'Not directly. There's a camera outside a bank that might have an angle, though. Hold on . . .' His fingers rattled across a keyboard.

'We're here,' the team leader warned. 'Team Two, ETA?'

'Ten seconds. Just reached the alley,' a man replied.

'Got it,' announced Waterford. The view on the main screen changed. The camera was mounted high above the bank's frontage, covering its entrance and ATM, but the coffee shop was visible in the corner of the frame. The Range Rover stopped on the pavement. Its two occupants leapt out and ran to the shop, drawing their weapons.

'Team Two in position,' said the second man.

Staite did not hesitate. 'Move in.'

The pair on screen burst through the shop's door. 'Special Branch!' the leader bellowed, the police undercover unit acting as the cover for MI6's even more secretive operatives. 'Nobody move!' Cries of panic came from the shop's customers, a baby screaming. 'Two men and a woman! They were here – where are they?'

'They – they went out through the fire exit,' someone fearfully replied.

'Team Two, did you get that?' said Staite.

'Yeah,' came the response. 'Door's barred from inside, nobody's here.'

'Team One, search the interior in case they're lying,' she ordered. 'We'll try to pick them up on CCTV.'

A phone rang, Waterford answering. 'Oh, you're kidding,' he said, aggrieved, after listening to the caller. 'It's GCHQ. Boxley logged off the coffee shop's wi-fi over three minutes ago.'

'Good of them to let us know!' Staite said in exasperation. 'Okay, that gives us a new time window. Poll the CCTV on the surrounding streets and wind back four minutes to see if we can spot them. And tell those nerds at the Doughnut' – the nickname for GCHQ's circular headquarters – 'that this is a *real-time* operation, not something to catch up with on iPlayer!'

A report soon came in from the Removal Men that the targets were indeed no longer in the building. 'We'll update you as soon as we locate them,' Staite told him, joining her companions to scrutinise recent footage from the dozen or so cameras covering the area. Minutes passed, Londoners stuttering along the streets in digitised fast-forward. Then—

'There!' cried one of the new operators. He zoomed in on three figures scurrying across a road. 'That's them, isn't it?'

Staite's gaze flicked to another screen showing pictures of the fugitives, now joined by SIS's own identity photos of Roy Boxley. 'Yeah. And they're carrying a laptop! Where are they?'

'North End Road, not far from the coffee shop.' He zoomed out and rewound the footage. 'They came out of the alley behind it.'

'We don't need to know where they were,' Staite chided. 'We need to know where they *are*.'

The young man hastily fast-forwarded. The trio popped across the main road and skip-framed down it until they passed out of sight. Waterford noted the time code, then brought up a contemporaneous image from a different camera. After a moment, their targets reappeared. Everyone watched as they continued down the street – then stopped. 'Looks like they're getting on a bus.'

That was confirmed when a double-decker pulled up. The three targets boarded. 'We've got them,' Staite said into her headset. 'They're on a number 397 bus, heading south down North End Road.'

'Affirmative. Pursuing,' was the hunters' terse reply.

'There are quite a few civilians on that bus,' warned Waterford. 'And Chase has a gun. This could get out of control very quickly.'

'I'll call Transport for London,' said Staite, picking up a phone, 'and tell them to slow the bus down until our teams catch up. If the driver fakes a malfunction, we can get everyone off – right where we want them.'

The bus continued southwards, leaving West Kensington and entering the more downmarket area of Fulham. Eddie kept watch for pursuers, while Nina checked on Roy's progress. '*Please* tell me it's almost at one hundred per cent,' she said.

Roy shook his head. 'Afraid not. But it's getting there. Ninety-three.'

'Great. Once it's done, it might be best if you copy the file on to—'

She broke off as Eddie tensed in his seat, leaning forward to listen in on a radio discussion between the driver and his depot. 'Buggeration and fuckery.'

'What is it?'

'I didn't catch all of it, but it sounded like they want him to tell the passengers the bus's broken down so they can get everyone off.'

Roy raised his head to listen. 'Seems fine to me.'

'There's nothing wrong with it,' Nina realised. 'They know we're aboard. What do we do? Get out and run?'

Eddie looked outside. He didn't know the area, but MI6 would have every escape route mapped in detail. 'If we're on foot, they'll catch up with us in no time. We need to go faster.'

'I think we've picked the wrong vehicle for that,' said Roy.

'I dunno – didn't you see *Speed*?' He jumped to his feet and drew the gun. 'All right! Everyone listen – I'm hijacking this bus!'

'You're *what*?' Nina yelped, but she was drowned out by sounds of alarm from the passengers when they saw he was armed.

Eddie grabbed a handrail in case the driver braked suddenly, then pointed the gun at him. 'Stop the bus and open the doors!' When there was no immediate response from the stunned man, he fired a single shot at the floor. 'I'm not fucking joking – everybody off!'

The terrified driver stamped on the brake, the bus lurching to a standstill in the middle of the road. He opened the doors. The passengers on the lower floor scrambled in panic towards the central and rear exits, more stumbling down the two steep flights of stairs from the top deck. Small screens above the windscreen showed CCTV images of the interior; Eddie waited until both decks were clear before pulling the driver from his compartment. 'All right, bugger off. Nina, take over.'

'What?' she protested. 'You're the one who knows how to drive a bus, not me!'

'Roy's on the computer, I might need to shoot, so that just leaves you. Sorry, love.' He ushered her into the empty seat. 'It's a hybrid, so it should be a piece of piss to drive – like a big Prius!'

'A *very* big Prius.' She reluctantly took her place at the wheel as Eddie ran to the rear. 'Okay, what do I do?'

'If it's like the bus I learned on in the army,' he called to her, 'there should be buttons for the gears and a lever for the airbrake.'

'Buttons, buttons . . . yeah, we got buttons!' There were several banks on the dash, but the three marked D, N and R were the most obvious in function. The squat grey lever beside her right knee was also helpfully labelled 'handbrake'. She put her foot on the brake pedal and pushed the drive button, then fumbled with the lever until it released and pushed it forward. The bus jolted, but remained stationary.

Horns sounded behind her as angry drivers expressed their displeasure at being held up. 'All right, Jeez, give me a chance,' she said, nervously switching her foot from the brake to the accelerator.

The bus crept forward. 'That's it!' Eddie shouted. 'Go faster!'

'Ah . . . I still think it'd be better if you drove!' The huge wing mirrors were convex, giving her a wider view but at the same time distorting it. She tried to compensate for what she thought was a drift to the right only to find herself instead swinging towards the left kerb. 'Whoa! Okay, this is weird.'

'Never mind weird, we need fast!' He saw cars in their wake pull over as something bore down behind them – a black Range Rover. 'They're coming!'

Through the open front door, Nina heard a siren. 'So are the cops!'

'Well, what did you expect?' said Roy testily. 'You just hijacked a bus at gunpoint! Every armed woodentop in London's probably on the way.'

'You just keep watching numbers go up,' Eddie fired back. 'Nina, put your bloody foot down!'

With deep apprehension, she did so. The bus's unscheduled

halt had opened up a space ahead – but it shrank with alarming speed as the speedometer rose. 'Okay, problem – there's a traffic jam!'

Their side of the road was occupied by waiting cars – but the other side was relatively clear. 'Then go around 'em!'

'We'll hit someone coming the other way!'

'They'll move, trust me!'

Nina was almost out of room to manoeuvre. No choice. She threw the wheel to the right to overtake the traffic – and the bus swerved alarmingly, centrifugal force tilting its tall body steeply to the left. She yelled as it veered towards the pavement on the road's right side, pedestrians scattering as she swung back the other way—

A lamp post swept past just inches from the Routemaster's front corner. Nina gasped in relief as she brought the bus back towards the road's centre – only for her to be almost pitched from her seat as the *rear* corner, extending out far beyond the back wheels, clipped the obstacle. Metal crunched, a window shattering.

'Jesus!' Eddie shouted. 'Mirrors, use the mirrors!'

'I'm just trying to use the *steering*!' she cried. The long front and rear overhangs made the bus's handling very different from a car's; each hard turn felt as if she was sweeping sideways rather than forwards. She finally brought the vehicle parallel to the stationary traffic and powered onwards – only for her heart to sink. 'Oh, crap! There isn't enough room!' Even though oncoming drivers had swerved on to the pavement to get clear, the gap between them and the vehicles on the other side of the road seemed much too narrow to traverse.

'Yeah, there is!' Eddie shouted. 'You've got loads of room on the left! Mirrors! Mirrors, *mirrors*! Use the bloody mirrors!'

'You know where you can put your frickin' mirrors?' Nina growled – but a glance at the left mirror told her that he was correct. She was much farther over than she had thought, the combination of her seating position and the Routemaster's size throwing off her spatial perception. A more precise turn of the wheel brought her closer in, just in time to whisk through the gap.

She saw that the road forked ahead. 'We're coming to an intersection! Which way?'

'We're on Fulham Broadway, so . . . right, go right!' Roy told her. 'It'll take us towards the river – we can cross on Battersea Bridge. If we can reach it in one piece,' he added.

'I'll try not to hit anything else!' Nina sounded the horn in a warning blast as she tore through a set of red lights into the junction. Cars scattered like frightened mice as she accelerated on to the new road. 'Roy, what about the laptop?'

'Ninety-five per cent,' he replied.

'Seriously? Can't you speed it up? My parents had a computer with a "turbo" button on it back in the damn Nineties!'

Roy sounded offended. 'It's working as fast as it can!'

Eddie had other concerns. The siren's source had just appeared, a police car sweeping out from the left-hand fork – but rather than follow them, it stopped in the middle of the junction, blocking the confused traffic. The Range Rover entered the other side of the intersection and bullied its way through the chaos.

He thought the police car was waiting for their pursuers to take the lead. But when the Range Rover finally cleared the knot of cars and accelerated after the bus, the cops remained stationary.

There was only one reason why the police would have been instructed to leave the hunt to the Removal Men. Brice and those working with him wanted no official witnesses to their actions when they caught up.

'Nina,' he said, readying the gun, 'you need to get away from these arseholes – or we're going to *die*!'

36

Nina knew the urgency in her husband's voice from far too much prior experience. She pulled out to overtake the vehicles ahead, tearing down the wrong side of the road at forty, forty-five, fifty miles per hour.

The street was broad enough for oncoming cars to swerve clear of the thundering Routemaster, but beyond them she saw buildings blocking her path at a T-junction. 'Crap!' she said. 'Roy, which way?'

Roy looked up from the laptop. 'Left!'

The intersection was controlled by lights, cars starting to come around the corner. 'Hold on!' she cried, releasing the accelerator and curving right – before throwing the bus hard to the left.

The Routemaster tipped alarmingly. The first oncoming car skidded to a stop as the bus tore past – only for a van behind to ram into it and knock it forward. The bus's tail ripped off its front bumper and sent it spinning across the junction.

Nina gripped the shuddering wheel. The speedo was falling, but it still felt as if the double-decker was about to topple over. She braked. To her horror, the bus's list became *worse*, the street rolling before her—

'Don't brake!' Eddie yelled. 'Go *faster*!'

She trusted him to be right. Foot back on the accelerator, hard. The bus lurched, still teetering on the brink of disaster . . . and then the extra power propelled it through the turn.

It swung back upright as she straightened out, straddling the middle of the road between the lines of traffic. 'Glad you remembered your driving lessons!' she called back to Eddie, heart pounding. 'Where are we, and how do we get to the river?'

The bus's drunken reel had almost thrown Roy from his seat. He hurriedly checked that the damaged hard drive hadn't been disconnected before answering. 'The King's Road. Keep going, and there's a turn that takes us to Battersea Bridge.'

'How's the computer doing?'

'Ninety-seven per cent!'

'It's always the last little bit that takes for ever, isn't it?' said Eddie, looking back. Their pursuers had been forced to slow to round the wrecked car, but they wouldn't be delayed for long.

The bus raced on. Bangs and screeches of metal punctuated its journey as it swiped off wing mirrors and scraped against cars that had not given it enough space. 'Ninety-eight per cent!' Roy announced as they hurtled through another set of lights. 'Okay, next right for the bridge.'

Nina heard more sirens. 'Cops are getting closer!'

'So are the goon squad,' Eddie warned. The Range Rover was gaining fast.

Roy pointed ahead. 'Here, go right!'

Nina started to turn – then hurriedly abandoned the move and swerved back on to the King's Road. 'Roadblock!' A police car had stopped across both lanes of the southbound street.

'Why didn't they block *this* road?' Roy asked.

Eddie had the unwelcome answer. 'Because Brice doesn't want the cops to catch us. He wants the Removal Men to get us first – so they can shoot us without anyone asking questions!'

Nina saw a sign ahead. 'Thank God!'

'What is it?' Eddie asked.

'A bus lane!' She found a gap in the traffic she was overtaking, which was comprised almost exclusively of big and expensive SUVs, and darted left into the empty section of road. 'Maybe now we can get somewhere – oh, you've got to be *kidding* me!' What she had hoped would be an escape route came to a sudden end not far ahead. 'It's like two hundred feet long! That's *it*? London, you suck!' There were no spaces in the line of 4x4s to her right, and even with repeated shrills of the horn, none of the drivers were willing to clear one for her. 'Come on, someone get out of my way!'

'Welcome to Chelsea,' said Roy acerbically.

'Don't stop!' Eddie shouted. The Range Rover was gaining.

Nina grimaced, then spun the wheel. The bus scythed into the traffic, sideswiping an Audi Q7 driven by a rail-thin blonde in oversized sunglasses. 'Comin' through! Yeah, I learned to drive in New York, lady. Don't try to block *me*.'

The Range Rover closed in, its front passenger leaning out of his window. 'They're gonna shoot!' Eddie cried. 'Roy, get down!'

Roy hurriedly ducked – as the man opened fire with a handgun. Shots tore across the gap, the Routemaster's back window shattering.

Eddie dived through the open rear doors to land flat on the boarding platform. The Removal Man's gun swung towards him—

The Yorkshireman had already lined up his sights and pulled the trigger. The other man jerked back as blood burst from his shoulder, his gun falling to the road.

Eddie had no time for relief. The bus jolted with an impact, the shrill of metal on metal rising behind him—

He rolled back inside – as they whipped past another bus, the two double-deckers scraping noisily against each other. Pieces of both vehicles' mirrors showered over him. 'Christ! Could you get any closer?'

'I could *try*,' Nina snarked. 'Roy, are you okay?'

Roy looked up from the floor. 'Yah, yah,' he gasped.

'And the laptop?'

'What? Wait – you care more about the laptop than me, don't you!'

'What I care about most of all is not getting killed! Is it still working?'

He retrieved the machine. 'Yah, it is. And it's still on ninety-eight per cent, since I'm sure you want to know!'

'Just keep it running!' Nina glanced at the left-side mirror, only to find nothing there. That would make judging her manoeuvring room even harder – but a quick look in the other mirror revealed a more urgent danger. A man was leaning out of the Range Rover's rear window, holding something larger than a pistol. 'Eddie, gun! *Bigger* gun!'

Eddie pulled himself upright to see the Removal Man readying an MP5K, a compact – but still deadly – sub-machine gun. He took aim again, this time at the Range Rover's driver. Time to end the pursuit—

He fired – but the round glanced off the windscreen. The glass was bulletproof.

The Routemaster's was not. 'Roy, get upstairs!' Eddie yelled, running back up the central aisle. Roy hurriedly scrambled to the forward staircase as the Yorkshireman dived flat—

The SMG blazed, the gunman hosing the bus with gunfire. Bullets ripped through the cabin. Roy shrieked as a round burst through the panel behind him and cracked against the stairs between his legs. He flung himself up the last few steps on to the top deck, clutching the laptop.

Nina heard the bullet strike behind the driver's compartment. She ducked, but knew she was hopelessly exposed in her elevated position. Her pursuers had realised this as well, the Range Rover reappearing in the surviving mirror and pulling out to overtake.

She threw the wheel to the right. The bus tipped again as it crossed on to the wrong side of the road. The Range Rover dropped back. She straightened – but not quickly enough, clipping a car. The windscreen cracked.

'Nina!' Eddie shouted. 'Are you okay?'

'Yeah!' Where were their attackers? No sign of them in the mirror—

Another burst of gunfire blew out the left-side windows. Eddie lunged under a seat as glass cascaded around him. Nina gasped and hunched down again. The Range Rover drew level with the Routemaster's tail. If she swung left again, she could force it to crash—

A thump from behind – and she caught movement on one of the CCTV monitors. To her shock, she saw that the bus had a new passenger. The man in the Range Rover's back seat had thrown himself on to the rear platform.

He still had his sub-machine gun. Eddie snapped up his own weapon—

The man rushed up the curving staircase. The Yorkshireman fired, but hit only metal as his target ran out of sight. 'Roy!' he cried, rising and pounding up the forward stairs. 'He's coming after you! He wants the laptop!'

He reached the stairwell's top, looking over the banister – and hurriedly ducked as the Removal Man saw him and unleashed a burst of bullets. Panels splintered above him. He popped his gun arm around the corner at floor level, sending two rounds down the upper deck. The other man hurled himself on to one of the rear seats, disappearing from sight. Eddie tracked him and fired again, but the bullet didn't have enough power to penetrate all the intervening seat backs.

And now he was out of ammo—

The MP5K rose above the seats and swung in his direction, the Removal Man blind-firing – but only a few rounds lanced up the bus before the clamour of gunfire was replaced by a dry click.

Eddie knew he only had moments before his opponent

445

reloaded. He charged down the aisle. The Removal Man had already ejected the magazine and inserted a new one, springing up to fire—

The Yorkshireman hurled his empty pistol at him. The MP5K snapped up to deflect it, metal clanking off metal – then the savage little gun came around—

Eddie dived over the seats to hit the other man in a flying tackle, knocking his gun arm away. The MP5K went off, a spray of bullets tearing through the bus's side and shattering a shop window on the street beyond.

'Roy, get downstairs!' he yelled. The younger man hurriedly retreated as Eddie prepared to unleash a headbutt—

His adversary beat him to it.

A piercing pain drove through Eddie's upper jaw as a tooth cracked. 'You *fucker!*' he roared, anger powering his fist into the other man's nose. Cartilage crunched, blood spurting. The younger man grunted . . . but didn't go down.

They grappled, lumbering into the aisle. The Removal Man twisted to pitch his target down the rear stairs. Eddie kicked out, catching the safety barrier surrounding the stairwell and propelling both men away from it. His opponent staggered, briefly unbalanced. The Yorkshireman spun, grabbing the other man's gun arm and slamming his wrist against a pole.

The MP5K clattered to the floor. Both men tried to lunge for it while simultaneously forcing the other away. They thumped back and forth against the seats, reeling forward as they struggled for the upper hand . . .

Eddie realised to his dismay that he wouldn't win the contest of raw muscle power. The GB63 member had been through the same special forces training as himself, and more besides after joining the ultra-secret unit – and was both younger and stronger.

Instead he shifted position – and kicked the gun. It skittered up the aisle to the front of the deck, well out of reach.

But the action had saved him from one danger only to expose him to another. His movement gave his opponent extra leverage – and the other man took advantage, forcing him forward and driving his head against another vertical handrail.

If the pain of his broken tooth was piercing, this felt more like being struck by a mallet. Eddie staggered, impossible colours exploding in his vision before clearing – to reveal the Removal Man lunging again. A fist rushed at his face. He jerked up one arm to take the blow, but a second strike thumped into his stomach.

He gasped, stumbling into the front stairwell's safety barrier. Another brutal punch winded him – then a hand clamped around his throat.

The man bent him back over the barrier, fingers tightening like steel cords. Eddie lashed at his head, but scored only glancing impacts. He choked as his enemy's remorseless grip squeezed his airways closed.

The Removal Man pushed harder, about to pitch him head first down the stairs—

The bus tipped violently, flinging both men away from the stairwell.

Nina had seen on the CCTV monitor that her husband was in grave danger and threw the Routemaster sharply to the right, making a tyre-squealing turn down a side street. Roy yelped as he was hurled sideways. He checked the laptop's connections. 'If the cable comes unplugged I might have to start from scratch!' he complained. 'By the way: ninety-nine per cent!'

'Hold it in place with your damn *teeth* if you have to!' she shouted back. Another glance at the screen. Eddie had broken free, but the SIS assassin still had the upper hand – and foot, delivering a savage kick to the Yorkshireman's stomach. Eddie fell back on a seat, his head banging against the window. She gasped.

The Removal Man straightened as if to attack again – then saw something on the floor.

The MP5K was a sinister black shadow at the bottom of the monitor.

Nina looked desperately ahead, but the new street was much narrower than the main road; any turn harsh enough to knock him down would send the bus head-on into a lamp post or parked car. And the Range Rover was still behind them. If they stopped, they would be shot dead . . .

A large red-brick apartment building rose on the left. A driveway ran to it – and *through* it, a tall arched passage leading to another road beyond.

The Removal Man snatched up the gun—

Nina was already turning the steering wheel before her conscious mind could object to the crazy plan. The bus demolished the end of a low wall, the Routemaster bounding over the rubble on to the driveway.

She accelerated, foot to the floor. The bus jolted back towards the vertical. On the monitor, the Removal Man had grabbed a seat for support, but was now recovering. He faced Eddie, raising the sub-machine gun . . .

The archway was just big enough to accommodate the bus – if it went straight through the middle. Nina instead steered to one side. 'Eddie! *Low bridge!*'

Eddie heard her and rolled to the floor—

The Routemaster ploughed into the brickwork.

Masonry smashed and metal tore, the entire frame of the heavy front window ripping loose and slamming across the SIS agent's back. He fell, broken bricks pummelling him.

Eddie shielded his face from flying rubble, then scrambled upright as Nina swung the bus back into the centre of the arched passage. The mangled section of roof crashed to the ground as they burst back into the open.

The Routemaster ploughed through a set of iron gates on to the next street, Nina making another hard right turn. Wind hit Eddie's face through the gaping hole in the bus's front. He looked for the Removal Man's MP5K. It was teetering at the top of the stairs.

The SIS man also saw it. He lunged—

Eddie stamped on his hand. He screeched in pain. The Yorkshireman snatched up the weapon – then twisted to kick him hard in the face with a hideous *snap* of breaking teeth. The younger man slumped nervelessly to the floor.

Gunshots from behind. Windows on the lower deck shattered as Nina swerved frantically from side to side. Eddie ran back down the bus. Below, he saw the Range Rover pulling alongside, the fourth man leaning from a window with another MP5K. The sub-machine gun blazed again, strafing the Routemaster's flank—

Eddie's weapon joined in the staccato chorus. The gunman fell screaming back into the SUV with bloody wounds in his arm and shoulder. The Yorkshireman switched aim, knowing the windows were bulletproof – but gambling that not every part of the vehicle was similarly strengthened . . .

His shots tore into the roof.

The Range Rover was indeed not impenetrable from above. The rounds hit the driver in the legs and hip. The black vehicle abruptly fell back, weaving – then struck a parked car and cartwheeled over it, smashing down on its side.

Eddie hurried down the stairs. 'Nina! Roy! You both okay?'

'I'm fine,' Nina replied breathlessly. The window beside her had been shattered.

'Oh my God!' cried Roy. 'That guy tried to kill us! What happened to him?'

'I took him out,' said Eddie.

'He's dead?'

'No, but I hope MI6's cafeteria has plenty of soup options, 'cause it's all he'll be eating for a while. What about the laptop?'

The young man checked. 'Well, it's still working, somehow, but – oh!' A *ping* came from the machine. 'One hundred per cent. Good timing!'

'It's finished?' asked Nina.

'Yah, yah.'

'Great – but which way do we go?'

Roy looked ahead. 'I'm not sure where we are – no, there!' He pointed. 'Right, then left straight away. I can see the river!'

Nina braked to bring the battered bus through a junction, then immediately turned again to swing it on to a tree-lined road along the Thames's northern bank. She saw a bridge crossing the river about half a mile ahead. 'Can we get to the US embassy from there?'

Roy nodded. 'That's Chelsea Bridge – the embassy's in Nine Elms on the other side.'

'Still got to reach it,' Eddie warned. 'There's probably another half a dozen cars of goons on the way already.'

'Roy, check if the video's there,' Nina said, blasting the horn and swinging the bus around a knot of dawdling traffic.

He quickly checked the newly recovered directory. 'The most recent file is . . . an MP4, about two gigabytes, last changed . . . four days ago.'

'That's got to be it,' said Eddie. 'Play it!'

Roy double-clicked the file. Eddie watched as a video started. Nothing but blackness for several tense seconds, making him worry that the file had been corrupted . . . then lights came into view.

They were inside the ceremonial chamber beneath the Palace Without Entrance, the drone descending towards it. Inside, he saw shadows cast by movement in front of the lanterns – then figures came into view.

Himself, Nina . . . and Brice.

'We've got video,' he told his wife, before looking back at Roy. 'Turn it right up, we need to hear.'

Roy set the laptop's volume to maximum. Echoing voices became audible. 'Cosmic rays, maybe,' said Brice. 'Something that can penetrate so deeply.'

Eddie looked up from the screen. 'We've got it. We've got it – and we've got *him*!'

Nina spotted cars slowing on the bridge ahead – and moving aside to clear a path for something coming up from behind them. 'Roy, have you still got that flash drive?' Having seen several USB sticks on his desk, she had suggested he bring one.

He checked his pocket. 'Yah, it's here.'

'Copy the file on to it.'

'Why?'

'Because a flash drive's a lot harder to break than a laptop! Eddie, bad guys on the bridge.'

Eddie hefted the sub-machine gun and hurried up the front stairs. 'If they stop us, we're dead,' he called back to Nina. 'Keep going no matter what!'

He made sure the Removal Man was still unconscious by kicking him again, then went to the front of the top deck. Another black Range Rover was tearing across Chelsea Bridge. It reached the shore and made a screeching turn through a crossroads to power down the embankment towards them.

He readied the gun, expecting a gunman to lean out – but instead the SUV skidded to a halt across the middle of the road. Other drivers heading in each direction stopped in alarm as a man jumped out and took up position behind it, aiming a gun – an MP5, the full-size, more powerful version of Eddie's own weapon – over its bonnet.

With traffic halted, there was no way around the obstruction. 'Eddie, what do I do?' Nina cried.

'Go through 'em!' he yelled. *'Ramming speed!'*

'Roy, keep down!' Nina shouted as she dropped as low as she could. The speedometer needle rose again—

The man behind the Range Rover opened fire. Nina screamed as the windscreen blew apart – but held her course, foot jammed down on the pedal. Eddie retaliated, bullets twanging off the SUV's windows and bodywork. The man ducked as people nearby fled their cars.

But the MP5K had already exhausted its ammo. Eddie dropped it, bracing himself as the bus surged towards the Range Rover.

The gunman sprang up again – to see a wall of red charging straight at him. He broke and ran—

The Range Rover's driver also realised what was about to happen and threw his vehicle into reverse – but too late.

The bus hit the Range Rover's front quarter at over fifty miles per hour. The SUV was flung around in a mad pirouette, swatting the running man over an abandoned car before smashing into it.

Nina raised her head, squinting into the wind. What had been the platform inside the bus's front passenger door was now folded upwards like crumpled paper, mangled bodywork embedded in it. But the bus was still moving, the long overhang having protected the front wheels. 'Is everyone okay?' she shouted as she turned towards the bridge.

'Somehow, yah,' said Roy, sounding surprised.

'More of 'em!' Eddie yelled from above.

There was indeed another 4x4 charging towards them. 'What, does MI6 have an infinite supply of Range Rovers?' Nina protested.

Too late to turn back. The oncoming SUV braked hard and angled up on to the kerb at the start of the span to block her way, its nose against the sloping metal barrier separating the roadside from the footpath. A window lowered, another MP5 poking out.

The bus roared towards it. 'Hold on!' Nina cried—

The Routemaster smashed into the Range Rover.

The impact slammed the 4x4 up the barrier – and over its top, sending it cartwheeling across the pavement into the bridge's railings. It burst through them and plunged into the murky waters of the Thames forty feet below.

The bus lurched to a stop. Even braced, Nina had still been thrown over the steering wheel. Pained, she remained still for a moment, thinking she could hear a ringing in her ears – before realising it was the sound of distant bells. She sat up. Pedestrians and people in the stationary cars gawped at her. 'Eddie? Roy?'

'I'm still here,' Roy groaned. 'I think . . .'

Footsteps thumped down the stairs. She turned to see her husband carrying the unconscious Removal Man. 'What're you doing with *him*?'

'Getting rid,' Eddie replied, going to the open middle door. 'Don't need him causing you trouble if he wakes up.'

'That sounds like you're not planning to stay around to deal with him,' said Roy.

Eddie tossed the man out on to the pavement as Nina engaged reverse gear and started to extract the bus from the dented barrier. 'You need to get to the embassy. Roy, what's happening with the computer?'

'The file's still copying to the flash drive,' the young man told him as the Routemaster lurched free.

'Still? Fuck's sake, is that laptop steam-powered? Okay, I just heard Big Ben – it's quarter to twelve. If I find Brice before noon, I might be able to stop him. It's about a mile and a half to the Houses of Parliament, so I can make it in time if I run.'

'But you don't know where he is,' said Nina.

'I'll just head for the weird noise.' He jumped down to the street.

'It'll be too late by then!'

'I've got to bloody try! You get that video to the embassy.'

'I'm not leaving you!'

He looked back at her. 'I don't care what Brice says, this is *my* country – and I'm not going to let him fuck it up. Now go!' He vaulted over the barrier and raced away.

'Eddie, wait!' Nina shouted, but he was already gone. 'Shit!' Knowing there was nothing she could do to bring him back, she set her jaw and put the Routemaster into gear.

37

The traffic had cleared the bridge ahead, either oblivious of what had happened behind or wanting to escape the chaos. 'Okay, Roy,' said Nina as she accelerated, 'how do we get to the embassy?'

Roy regarded the approaching south bank of the Thames. 'We've got to get around Battersea Power Station, so . . . okay, head down this road to a roundabout, then go left. That'll take us into Nine Elms – and that leads us straight to the embassy.'

'Great!'

'It also leads straight to Vauxhall Cross, so anyone sent after us from SIS headquarters will be coming down it.'

'Not great!' A flash of alarm as she spotted blue strobe lights in the distance – but again, the police had clearly been ordered not to intervene, the car not moving. Her capture – or elimination – would be left entirely to MI6's assassins.

She raced on, sweeping past expensive, anonymous new apartment blocks on the left, a large park on the right. The roundabout came into view. The road to the left was clear, the police car preventing civilians from becoming ensnared in the chase. She was being channelled, corralled; her pursuers had probably realised where she was trying to go.

Which meant they could wait for her to come to them.

Pushing the grim thought aside, Nina brought the bus through the turn. 'Under the bridge, there,' said Roy.

A broad Victorian railway arch spanned the new road. She

steered beneath it, careful to keep the shredded roof clear of the ironwork. 'How far to the embassy?'

'About a mile.'

'And what about the video? Has it copied yet?'

'Almost done . . . yes! It's just finished.'

'Okay, give it to me.' He quickly unmounted the little flash drive and handed it to her. She shoved it in a pocket. 'Okay, hold on!'

Roy hurriedly retreated and gripped a handrail as she blasted the horn and swung the bus out to overtake more sluggish traffic.

Brice brought his van around the green common of Parliament Square, slowing at its north-eastern corner. Instead of continuing around it, however, he turned on to the pavement. The tourists and passers-by merely flowed around him. The grubby Transit pickup, orange warning lights flashing on its roof, was the perfect stealth vehicle. Nobody would even look once, never mind twice, at a council workman on some mundane business.

He carefully guided the van along the little park's northern side, halting in front of a statue of Winston Churchill. The sight of the great wartime leader gave him a surge of both pride and determination. Churchill had done whatever was necessary to protect his country from the forces seeking to destroy it; now he was going to do the same.

He got out and climbed up into the van's rear. The lead box containing the Shamir was hidden under a dirty tarpaulin. His first task was to line the ancient weapon up on its target.

A glance across the square. The Elizabeth Tower dominated the scene, the clock standing tall over the northern end of the Houses of Parliament. The Victorian-era Gothic edifice was a globally recognised icon of Britain itself, visual shorthand for an entire country . . .

And he was going to bring it down.

He knew full well the damage its destruction would cause to his nation's psyche. Indeed, part of him was appalled by the prospect. But it *had* to be done. The gaping scar in the London skyline would unify the people, bring up the walls necessary to protect against all enemies outside. And once they were in place, the process of rooting out those lurking within could begin.

The purge would begin in Westminster itself. Those in Parliament who were about to weaken and diminish their own country, who would sell it out to foreign powers, could not be allowed to take control. And he had the Prime Minister's authorisation to prevent it.

He pulled the heavy box into position. Once he opened the lid, he would still have to position the strange stone itself to focus its destructive effect upon its target, but then all he needed to do was ensure it remained in place until the job was done . . . and that no one interfered.

He saw someone who might do just that. Parliament Square was the nearest area of open ground to the Houses of Parliament, and as such was under high security, both covert and visible. An example of the latter was now approaching, a uniformed Metropolitan Police officer who had taken an interest in the van.

SIS's forgers had provided him with bogus work orders to justify his presence, but Brice had no intention of wasting time arguing with some dullard of a woodentop. He had taken the precaution of also demanding something that would get rid of interlopers with no questions asked. 'Excuse me, sir,' said the young policeman. 'Would you mind stepping down?'

Brice jumped to the ground, drawing something from an overall pocket: a Met warrant card and badge. 'DI Carver, Special Branch,' he said in a low voice, his smooth elocution replaced by a harsh East End growl. 'I'm on stakeout, and yer gonna bollocks things up if yer don't get moving.'

The officer flinched, but held his ground. 'Uh, sorry, sir,' he said, peering more closely at the ID, 'but you do understand that this is a high-security area? I need to—'

'Course I bloody understand,' snapped Brice. 'Why d'yer think I'm 'ere? We got word that some of our bearded brethren might cause trouble today. Me an' a dozen lads from SO15' – the codename for the Metropolitan Police's Counter Terrorism Command – 'are watching for 'em, but they're not going to poke their bloody noses out while yer standing 'ere like a streak of glowing piss!' He jabbed a finger at the cop's hi-vis vest. 'All right, sonny, now just nod yer 'ead and piss off. You got a problem, report me to yer watch commander. Just do it from somewhere else.'

The policeman was briefly caught between anger and deference. The latter won out; a bad word from somebody in one of the Met's special operations units could be disastrous to a junior officer's career aspirations. 'Okay, sir. Sorry to bother you. I'll be on patrol if you need me.'

'Just make sure nobody else wastes my time,' said Brice, returning to the pickup bed. 'What, yer still 'ere? Jesus Christ, go!'

The cop hurriedly strode away. The spy glared after him, then returned to his task.

Another look at the clock tower. Less than ten minutes before noon.

Ten minutes before Britain changed for ever.

Nina cringed as a jaywalker belatedly ran for the pavement ahead of her. 'What the hell is *with* people in this goddamn city?' she shouted to Roy. 'Big red thing coming straight at them, and they just stare at it!'

'They probably can't believe a London bus is doing more than five miles per hour,' he replied. Then: 'Okay, we're nearly here! Just past these buildings, on the right.'

Beyond a cluster of pricey apartment blocks was what Nina first took as parkland before the building at its heart came into view. The new US embassy in London was a glittering glass cube surrounded by open green space. It was not freely accessible, though; the complex stood atop a small rise, walls spiralling up around it as effectively as a castle's battlements. It even had a moat of sorts, the side facing the Thames separated from the park by an artificial lake. Waterfalls gushed over its sheer inner edge.

There was a pedestrian entrance down a side road on the right, but she would not be able simply to walk in. A pair of the inevitable black Range Rovers waited on each leg of the junction ahead.

But she couldn't stop, not now. She had to get the evidence against Brice and his co-conspirators to the ambassador. But how?

Her only option, insane though it was, struck her. 'Roy!' she yelled. 'Can you swim?'

'Yah, of course, but why—'

Keeping her foot hard on the accelerator, she spun the wheel to aim the ravaged Routemaster between the two Range Rovers. ''Cause we're taking a dip!'

The Removal Men had expected her either to stop or try to round their blockade, crouching behind their vehicles to cover both roads. They hurriedly changed positions and opened fire, but by then the bus had already rushed between them—

It leapt over the kerb, churning up turf as it skidded through the park. People fled, screaming. The remaining windows on the bottom deck exploded under the hail of gunfire.

Splinters stabbed into Nina's cheek as a bullet blew apart the panelling behind her head. She held course as the grassy ground rose up towards the lake. The embassy loomed beyond it—

She screamed as blood sprayed from her left forearm.

The bullet had not smashed any bones, but her hand was now

459

useless, every flex of the fingers agonising. All she could do was grip the steering wheel harder with her right hand as the bus reached the top of the slope—

And vaulted over its summit.

The Routemaster went airborne as it cleared the lakeside, hurtling across the water . . . and arced down into it.

The impact flung Nina against the steering wheel – then a frothing wave crashed through the broken windscreen, sweeping her from her seat.

The world spun, another lightning bolt of agony shooting through her wounded arm as it struck something in the swirl. An echoing boom rolled through the water as the bus slammed down on the lake's bottom. More pain as her head smacked against a seat . . . then something large absorbed the next impact.

Roy. The young man had also been swept up by the inrushing water, but overcame panic to thrust himself in front of her. She heard a gasp as she knocked the breath from him – but he quickly recovered, grabbing a handrail and catching her with his other arm.

He lifted her head above the churning flood. 'The stairs!' he spluttered, pushing her towards the forward flight. 'Get up the stairs!'

'Thanks,' she gasped, spitting out a mouthful of lake as she found footing. 'You okay?'

'Was in the rowing club at uni. Took plenty of unplanned dips!'

Nina staggered up the staircase. The torn hole in the bus's front gave her a clear view of what lay ahead. The Routemaster was about ten feet short of the embassy's wall, a paved plaza visible beyond the waterfall flowing over its edge. Alarm bells sounded inside the compound as its staff reacted to the crash.

But the Removal Men were also responding, running towards the lake. The harsh clatter of automatic weapons echoed across the park, the bus taking more hits. Their orders were clearly to stop her from reaching the embassy at *any* cost – even if that meant gunning her down on the boundary of American territory.

Rounds tore through metal, smacking against seats. Nina ducked fearfully back into the stairwell – but only seconds remained before they reached the lakeside and riddled the entire upper deck with bullets.

She felt her pocket. The flash drive was still there. 'Roy, get back in the water!' she cried, hoping it would offer him some protection – then she sprang up and ran for the front of the bus.

New pain stabbed through her wounded arm, but she forced herself to ignore it, focused on the gap between the Routemaster and the embassy. A mere ten feet, but she had only a short run-up . . .

She leapt, one foot stamping down on the broken window frame to propel her over the gap—

The top of the wall rushed at her.

Too high. She was falling short.

She threw out her arms—

Her left arm again flared with agony even before she hit the barricade. She slammed against it, the wounded limb flopping uselessly to her side – but managed to hook her right arm over the concrete edge.

The waterfall rolled over her, threatening to tear her loose. Nina choked as the deluge hit her face. She clawed for grip, fingers finding a pipe along the inner wall of the pool above her and clutching it as hard as she could.

Shouts reached her over the hissing rush of water. She struggled to raise her head above it. Figures were running across the plaza towards her.

Men in uniform, rifles at the ready. Marines.

They were not the only armed men she had to worry about.

More gunfire erupted from the park, splashes bursting from the falling water around her as bullets struck the wall—

The marines fired back. Clods of earth spat up around the Removal Men as a barrage of automatic fire closed in on them. Outnumbered and outgunned, the British assassins sent a few last rounds at Nina before breaking and running through the trees back to their vehicles.

The firing stopped – but Nina was still in danger. She could feel the pipe buckling under her weight. She tried to scrabble higher, but her feet found no purchase on the smooth, wet wall. And her other arm was useless, pain overcoming her attempts to lift it. She slipped lower, her head dropping back under the relentless waterfall as her handhold tore free—

Someone grabbed her right arm.

She cried out as she was hauled roughly upwards. Two marines had leapt into the watercourse along the wall's upper edge and seized her. They waded back to the plaza and deposited her unceremoniously on the paving. 'She's wounded!' one shouted, seeing blood spreading across her wet left arm.

Nina coughed, trying to clear her airways. 'I'm – I'm Nina Wilde,' she gasped. 'I'm an American citizen – and I've got to see the ambassador! There's a—'

Before she could say anything more, she was sharply brought to her feet. 'Get her to detention,' barked another marine, glaring after the gunmen as their Range Rovers peeled away. 'The embassy's been attacked – we need to lock it down and find out what the hell's going on!'

'I'm trying to *tell* you what's going on!' Nina protested. 'I need to talk to the ambassador, right now! Please!'

But her captors refused to listen, picking her up and frogmarching her towards the embassy building.

Where a cell awaited her – one that she was certain she would still be inside at noon.

38

Brice stood back to regard his handiwork. The lead box, still partially hidden beneath the tarp, was now propped up at one end by tools – directly in line with the Elizabeth Tower.

The great clock told him it was almost noon. He took out a smartphone and brought up an app. It soon confirmed that the part of his plan over which he had no direct control was nevertheless going as expected.

The screen showed a live television feed from the House of Commons chamber. As he had hoped, the green benches along each side of the political duelling ground were full.

The MPs of the governing party were on the left, facing the Opposition. Even on a phone, Brice could see the difference in attitude between the two sides. Those in government, while plainly spoiling for a verbal fight to back up their leader, seemed haunted; the look of politicians who knew they could well be not just out of power, but out of a job entirely, before long. The Opposition MPs were more smug, boisterous – eagerly awaiting one last chance to put the boot into their enemies.

That chance would never come. Brice kept watching as Christian Lombard, the Home Secretary, entered and occupied what would normally be the Prime Minister's place. His appearance prompted mocking boos and catcalls from the Opposition: where was Quentin Hove? Was he too scared to face his critics?

The clock's opening chimes rang across Parliament Square. At the first strike of Big Ben itself it would be noon, and PMQs would begin. Brice crouched beside the box. It was time.

He pulled back the tarpaulin and lifted off the heavy lid. The Shamir rested inside the casket, the odd greenish stone glinting. Almost immediately, he felt it respond to the daylight, the van seeming to buzz as its vibration was transmitted through the metal. He lifted the ancient weapon to aim it at the clock tower.

Another look at the phone. Lombard was now talking. Even with no sound, Brice knew what he was saying; protocol demanded an explanation for the Prime Minister's absence. 'An urgent matter of national security' would stoke the fires of the conspiracy theorists, but within the Commons itself there would be little comeback other than snide mutterings.

And in a few minutes, nobody would be able to deny the urgency of said matter.

He switched off the phone, then dropped down and started to lay out road cones to block off an area of pavement behind the Transit – both so that he appeared to be working, and also to keep passers-by clear of the invisible beam. He couldn't afford anyone to raise an alarm, not now.

The rising noise from the Shamir became noticeable, but over the bells and traffic noise, he was sure nobody else would register it.

Until it was too late.

'Listen to me, *listen*!' Nina cried as the marines carried her into the embassy. 'I've got proof of who brought down Flight 180 – and the same people are planning a terror attack on the Houses of Parliament *right now*!'

Her captors showed no sign of caring. One marine moved ahead to clear the way to a bank of elevators, waving back embassy staff. Nina changed tack, addressing the officials instead. 'I've got the video confession of the man who rescued Philippe Mukobo and killed everyone else on Flight 180!' she shouted. 'If you don't believe me, watch it yourself!' While the claim drew shocked interest, still nobody attempted to intervene. 'My name's Nina Wilde – I saved President Cole's life at the United Nations five years ago, dammit! I stopped New York from being nuked, I've saved the entire goddamn *world* – more than once! Somebody *listen* to me!'

The marines reached the elevators. One pushed a call button. Doors immediately opened, the car beyond waiting to carry the struggling redhead into the building's depths—

'Wait, wait!' someone called behind her. 'Hold on there!'

She desperately turned her head to see a balding middle-aged man carrying a briefcase break from the crowd, holding up his ID badge. 'Anthony Huygens, State Department. That *is* Nina Wilde – I recognise her.' Though Nina generally felt faintly embarrassed about being famous enough to be identified by strangers, this was not one of those times.

'Sir, this woman violated embassy security and broke in here in the middle of a firefight,' the marine replied. 'She's under arrest, and until I receive word from—'

'You're receiving word from *me*, marine!' Huygens snapped. 'We thought Philippe Mukobo was killed on Flight 180. If she's got evidence that he wasn't, we have to verify it. And if there's an imminent terrorist attack on London, then we have to warn the British, right now!'

The marines holding Nina remained still, uncertain whether the official had authority over them. The elevator doors started to close – until she thrust a foot into their path, causing them to retract again. 'The video's on a flash drive in my pocket. Please, just look at it, *please.*'

'Hold those doors,' said Huygens. One of the men in the elevator kept them open. 'I've got a laptop with me,' he continued. 'If she's got nothing, then you can take her away. But I have to check.' There were benches near the lobby's windows. 'Bring her over here.'

The marines turned to the most senior of their number, who looked irate, but nodded. They brought Nina to a bench. 'Okay,' Huygens said. 'Let's see this video.'

'Shit,' Eddie gasped as he heard Big Ben start to strike twelve. He had run through the back streets of Pimlico and Westminster as fast as he could, but even though Chelsea Bridge and the Houses of Parliament were less than a mile and a half apart as the crow flew, the shortest route on the ground was far less direct.

He was also rapidly tiring. At his prime in the SAS, the journey would have been a few minutes shorter and he would have been barely winded by its end. Despite his best efforts to stay in shape, the better part of twenty years had taken their toll.

He emerged from a shortcut through the grounds of Westminster Abbey on to the southern edge of Parliament Square as the bell's last echoes faded. If Brice was going to attack, he was still sure it would be from here. The Shamir needed to be outdoors with clear line of sight on its target, and every rooftop overlooking Parliament would be under constant observation, while any unusual activity on the Thames would draw immediate attention. From what he had seen in the Congo, he didn't think that the Shamir had the range to bring down the building from the river's far side.

That left the square, a busy public place where the MI6 officer could easily hide amongst the crowd. He looked across the road at the park. Even though it was a cloudy day, there were still lots of people, mostly tourists pointing cameras and phones at the clock tower. His gaze darted between them, searching for the spy.

No sign of him – but his view was repeatedly obscured by buses and vans rounding the square. He had to get closer. He waited for a gap, then ran into the road. A speeding black cab's brakes screeched, the driver hooting angrily at him. Eddie ignored him, pausing to let another cab go by before dashing for the safety of the far pavement.

Breathing heavily, he surveyed the square. It was busy enough that it would be almost impossible to check everyone . . .

He felt something, a gentle but rising hum that seemed to be coming from all around him.

It wasn't some reverberation from the bells, or the traffic's endless rumble. He had heard it before. The Shamir, building up power. Brice *was* here. And he was getting ready to strike.

But *where*?

Eddie was about to charge into the crowd — then caught himself. He couldn't just run around at random and hope to spot the rogue agent. He had to figure out Brice's plan, think like him. Where was the best place to put the Shamir, and how would he avoid notice?

A flicker of bright colour drew his attention. A litter collector in a hi-vis vest, pushing his trolley along the pavement. It wasn't Brice — but the man still gave him the answer. The best place to hide was in plain sight, as if he *belonged* there. He would look like some official, carrying out a job . . .

Hi-vis yellow, orange and green were now his target. Eddie hurriedly scanned the park for the giveaway colours. The closest was a policeman on the square's west side, and he saw other cops dotted around its periphery. Was Brice disguised as one?

No. Too much risk of being approached by a real officer who couldn't identify the newcomer, and he would hardly be able to carry the Shamir under his arm while pretending to patrol . . .

More orange, but not clothing. This was a flashing light on a white van across the park. Nobody in the cab — but he glimpsed someone in a yellow vest near the vehicle's rear.

Was it Brice? There was only one way to know for sure. Eddie ran across Parliament Square towards him.

★ ★ ★

'Okay, that's it,' said Nina with relief as the video started on Huygens' laptop. She had been worried that the flash drive's submersion would have damaged it. 'This was filmed by a drone in DR Congo. I'm with my husband, Eddie Chase, talking to an MI6 agent – supposedly an *ex*-agent, but you can hear his own explanation of that – called John Brice.'

The marines leaned closer to watch as the trio came into view, but Huygens was more interested in another figure – an unmoving one. 'That's Philippe Mukobo! He *is* alive!'

'Well, *was* alive,' she corrected. 'Long story. But if you turn up the volume you'll be able to hear what Brice is saying.' He did so. 'Skip forward. Keep going . . . okay, here.'

On the screen, Brice shook his head at Mukobo's corpse. 'And after everything I did to rescue him from the Yanks,' he said, voice echoing and tinny, but still clearly audible.

'How *did* you rescue him?' demanded Eddie. 'He was on a bloody plane!'

'A pilot with some large debts, and a mid-air interception and transfer. GB63 – the Removal Men – pulled Mukobo out through the 747's cockpit escape hatch and winched him up.'

'But . . . then the plane crashed,' Nina heard her past self say. 'What went wrong?'

'Nothing,' was Brice's unemotional reply. 'The plan went exactly as intended.'

Huygens paused playback, startled. 'The NTSB report on the wreckage we recovered from Flight 180 suggested that the cockpit escape hatch had been opened – and found bullet damage to some of the seats in the upper cabin,' he told her. 'But that part was never made public.'

'Brice got him out,' said Nina. 'And if you keep watching, he explains why, and on whose behalf. But there isn't time for that now. The room there, it's underneath a lost city in the jungle.' She sensed disbelief from some of her audience. 'What? You know *why* I'm famous, right? But that box,' she pointed at the lead casket upon the altar, 'contains something called the Shamir – also known as the Horn of Joshua, which brought down the walls of Jericho in the Bible. It's an ancient weapon, an extremely powerful one. And Brice has it. We think he's about to use it to destroy the Houses of Parliament.'

The official boggled. 'Why? You just said he's a British agent! Why would he attack his own government?'

'Regime change. Or rather, *prevention* of change,' she explained. 'The current government's likely to lose the election to a party Brice doesn't agree with. He thinks he's protecting MI6, protecting his entire *country*, by taking out all its politicians – and stopping the election.'

'But if he takes out the politicians, then who's going to run the country? A military takeover?'

'Prime Minister's Questions is just starting. But funnily enough, the PM won't actually *be* there for it.'

He stared at her – then took out his phone and dialled a number. 'It's Tony Huygens. I need to speak to the ambassador – it's an emergency.' As he waited to be put through, he spoke to Nina again. 'And I need you to tell me *everything* you know about this.'

Eddie hurried across Parliament Square. The subsonic hum of the Shamir grew louder as he approached the parked van, people on the green starting to look around in confusion.

The man in the hi-vis vest had moved out of sight. Eddie came around the Transit's front and advanced cautiously down its side. His target came back into view. He was facing away from the Yorkshireman, towards Parliament. His dark hair was shorter and neater than Brice's had been in the Congo . . . but it was almost identical to how Eddie remembered it from their first meeting in Tenerife.

It *was* Brice, he was certain. A glance into the pickup bed confirmed it as he saw the Shamir protruding from its lead box. The attack was taking place, right now.

Closing the box on the strange stone would stop it. But Brice would be armed; he had to deal with him first.

He crept closer, feeling the van trembling as he brushed against it. The ancient weapon was absorbing energy, building up its power – and would release it at any moment. Brice still had his back to him. Eddie emerged from behind the Transit, just ten feet behind the other man. He clenched his fists, ready to strike . . .

Something in the pickup bed rattled as the vibrations intensified. Brice turned to check that the Shamir had not been dislodged—

He saw Eddie – then with lightning speed snatched out a handgun from beneath his hi-vis vest.

Eddie dived behind the statue of Churchill as Brice fired. The bullet smacked against its stone plinth. Screams rose as tourists fled from the gunshot.

The Yorkshireman scrambled around the plinth, but there was no other cover. And Brice was coming for him—

A traffic cone sat beside the plinth's base. Eddie hurled it at the MI6 man as he rounded the statue. It struck his outstretched gun hand, a second shot going wide.

Eddie threw himself at Brice before he could recover. Both men fell. The gun went off again, the bullet searing skywards as they grappled—

The Shamir's deep hum reached a crescendo – and a thunderous *boom* of splintering masonry echoed across Parliament Square as stonework halfway up the clock tower blew apart.

Inside the Commons chamber, the assembled MPs had already heard the low-frequency thrum, the murmurings passing between members on both sides going from curious to concerned as it rose. 'Whatever that noise is,' said Lombard, grateful for the chance to dodge a scathing question on the government's recent record, 'it's preferable to the droning normally heard from the Opposition benches.' The quip, however poor, brought roars of sycophantic laughter from his own side.

'Order, order,' called the Speaker from the elaborate wooden dais at the head of the chamber. The mocking tumult faded, but the underlying noise was still there, stronger than before. The muttered discussions along the benches were now tinged with worry.

One of the Speaker's assistants behind the dais felt his phone vibrate. The number was known only to a few, and those who did had instructions not to call it while Parliament was in session – except in the most exceptional circumstances. He slipped out of sight of the chamber and answered in a whisper. 'Yes?'

'Please hold for the American ambassador,' said a woman. The assistant raised a quizzical eyebrow. Why on earth would the US ambassador be calling?

At that moment, a loud bang came from outside – alarmingly close by.

Eddie looked up in shock as a dust cloud rolled down the Elizabeth Tower, hunks of broken granite dropping from it like giant hailstones. Cracks spread across the clock's western face – then the whole glasswork disc *exploded*, a razor-edged rain showering over the grounds of Parliament.

More stonework shattered under the Shamir's sonic assault, the invisible beam chewing into the tower's south-western corner. The outer cladding broke away to expose the iron beams and girders within – which in turn blew apart, metal as vulnerable as mineral to the ancient weapon's effect.

Even as the architect of the destruction, Brice was just as

shocked by the sight of a national icon crumbling before his eyes. But he overcame it first, slamming an elbow against Eddie's head.

The Yorkshireman still had one hand clamped around Brice's wrist, forcing the gun away from him. He struck back, driving a fist hard into the other man's sternum. The SIS officer grunted in pain. Eddie shifted his grip, managing to dig his fingers in between those of Brice's gun hand.

Brice twisted, trying to get upright. Eddie kicked, catching his ankle and sending him stumbling back to the pavement. But the taller man was now on top of him – and took full advantage, using his elbow again to deliver one, two, three brutal jabs to Eddie's chest and stomach. The Yorkshireman gasped, but refused to relinquish his hold—

The tip of his forefinger found ridged metal: the magazine release.

He pushed it. The magazine popped out, bouncing off Eddie's forearm and clattering to the ground.

One threat reduced – but not removed. There was still a round in the gun's chamber.

Brice shoved his free arm across his opponent's throat, pushing down hard. Eddie gasped, unable to breathe. He swung his fist at the other man's face, but only landed a glancing strike. The SIS officer's grip tightened around the gun, forcing Eddie's straining fingers away.

The Yorkshireman tried to pitch his opponent off him, but didn't have enough leverage. He felt his strength fading, lungs burning as Brice regained his hold on the pistol—

'Drop the gun! *Drop it!*'

An armed policeman at the roadside raised an MP5 at the pair—

Brice snapped his weapon around and fired. The bullet hit the cop in the chest. His body armour took most of the impact, but he still stumbled backwards – and was hit by a car. The policeman was thrown along the road, his gun clattering away.

But Brice's own gun was now empty. He looked down for the magazine—

Its corner slammed against his eye socket.

His weight had shifted when he raised the gun, momentarily easing the pressure on Eddie's throat – and the bald man found a final surge of energy, snatching up the fallen mag and driving it into his adversary's face. Brice fell, blood spurting from a deep cut beneath his eye. The Yorkshireman rolled free, tossing the magazine under the Transit's tail.

Another thunderous crash of falling stone came from the clock tower.

Eddie glanced at Brice – then scrambled to the van's tailgate. The Shamir poked out from the end of the lead box. The lid lay beside it. He clambered into the pickup bed and picked up the heavy slab. If he sealed the Shamir back in its case, cutting it off from its power source, he could still stop Brice's plan—

The Transit jolted as the MI6 agent jumped up after him. Eddie spun, whipping the lid around – and pounding it into his lunging opponent like a club.

Brice reeled back, face twisted in pain. Eddie swung it again to knock him off the van—

This time Brice was prepared. He twisted, catching the lid and trying to use Eddie's own momentum to throw *him* from the pickup.

The Yorkshireman realised the danger just in time to fling himself bodily at the other man—

They both fell, the lid between them. It hit the pavement edge-on – and smashed into three jagged pieces.

Eddie stared at them in horror. There was now no way to shield the Shamir!

The Speaker listened to the urgent message from his assistant, then raised his voice over the growing hubbub of the Commons chamber. Dust and grit began to cascade from the vaulted ceiling as the building shook. 'If I can have everyone's attention, please!' he called, trying to maintain decorum even in an emergency. 'We need to evacuate immediately. If everyone can make their way to the nearest exit, calmly but quickly—'

Pandemonium erupted.

Everyone leapt from their seats in a desperate attempt to flee the chamber. Those on the front rows had the clearest route to the doors with nothing in front of them except carpet, but everyone farther back was penned in by the rows of benches. Men and women were knocked down and trampled as their frightened colleagues piled up behind them.

The first MPs reached the doors and threw them open to flee into the lobbies beyond. But the nineteenth-century chamber had only a handful of exits – and almost six hundred people inside. More were crushed against the walls and door frames by those behind as they tried to squeeze through the openings, choking the escape routes still further—

A terrible noise sounded over the panicked screams, bells ringing all at once in a crazy cacophony.

Another explosion of glass came from the clock tower as a second face shattered. Eddie was shocked by the sight of the structure's upper half visibly rocking, tipping towards the Commons chamber before rolling back with a clamour of bells. More dust and debris erupted below as the Shamir's devastating beam continued to devour the stonework.

The Shamir! He couldn't seal it in its box – but he *could* still point it away from Parliament—

He pushed himself up – only to be slammed flat as Brice hit him across the back with one of the broken chunks of lead.

Groaning, Eddie rolled on to his side to see the rogue agent grab the empty gun and scramble to the van. He clawed beneath it for the magazine.

Eddie forced himself to move. The pain in his back was excruciating, but he clenched his jaw and stood upright.

Brice's hand closed around the mag. He pulled it out, slapping his prize into place and chambering a new round as he turned to find Eddie—

He was already there.

Eddie's fist ploughed into the spy's face. 'Fuck you, double-oh *shithead*!' the Yorkshireman roared. He body-slammed Brice against the pickup's tailgate. 'You're no patriot, you're a fucking psychopath!'

Both men again grappled for the gun. Eddie was still breathless and in pain – but his fury was enough to prevent Brice from overpowering him.

But only just. The SIS officer strained to raise his right arm above his head, using his greater height and reach to inch the weapon from Eddie's grasp. 'I'm doing what has to be done to protect my country,' he rasped. 'I'll let history judge me – but you'll be long forgotten!'

He stretched up as far as he could – and jerked the pistol from his opponent's grip. Eddie clawed for the gun, but it was now out of reach—

He saw something behind Brice – his last chance to save both the day and his own life.

'Know what *you've* forgotten?' he said, abruptly switching his hold to Brice's arm to keep it raised straight upwards. '*The Shamir!*'

He forced Brice's gun hand in front of the ancient weapon.

The pistol blew apart in a shower of razor-edged splinters. Eddie cried out as shrapnel stabbed into his arm and the top of his head – but Brice's wounds were vastly worse. The MI6 agent screamed as his right hand was shredded, splattering both men with blood.

Eddie let go and pulled back – then kicked Brice in the stomach. He crashed against the tailgate. The impact dislodged the Shamir, its horn sliding across the end of the casket. The assault on the clock tower ceased, the invisible beam instead carving into the grey Edwardian headquarters of Her Majesty's Revenue and Customs on the square's north side. Its top floors exploded, the roof collapsing and crushing everything beneath under tons of debris.

Realising lives were still at stake, the Yorkshireman abandoned his attempt to finish off the spy and scrabbled back into the pickup bed. He shoved the Shamir into its box.

But his hope that would end the threat was instantly dashed. Without the lead container's lid, the stone was still being charged by whatever energy it fed upon – and the casket shuddered, the dense metal flaking and cracking as it took the full force of the Shamir's beam.

A glance at Big Ben as the bells continued their mad chorus. The clock tower's top was listing again, a chunk hacked out from below it as if struck by a lumberjack's axe—

The end of the casket succumbed to the Shamir's power and splintered apart. Stone pillars on the far side of the road crumbled, a van passing through the beam ripping open as if slashed by an invisible scythe.

Eddie looked back in desperation at the strange stone. He had to move it – but to where?

The river—

Westminster Bridge was just a few hundred yards away, beyond Parliament. Nina had told him that flood waters once cut off the Mother of the Shamir from its source of power – maybe the Thames would do the same for its offspring . . .

He pulled the Shamir upright, aiming the thrumming stone horn towards the sky, then jumped from the pickup. Brice had gone, but he couldn't spare even a second to look for him, instead piling into the cab. The keys were still in the ignition. He started the engine and jammed the Transit into reverse, looking through the rear window as he set off.

Complete chaos had erupted. People fled in all directions, some drivers trying to weave through the crowd as others abandoned their vehicles and ran. He saw a couple of armed police helping the cop shot by Brice, but the appalling spectacle of the teetering clock tower dominated the attention of all their comrades. Nobody tried to stop him – but nor did they attempt to help him either.

He was on his own.

Eddie sounded the horn, gesturing frantically for people to get out of his way. The Transit somehow reached the road without mowing anyone down, but now he had to go against the traffic to reach the bridge—

A car ploughed into the van's rear. Eddie was thrown across the seats as it spun. He dragged himself upright, looking back at the pickup bed – and saw that the Shamir had been knocked over by the collision. The tax office took another devastating blast as he wrestled the Transit into first gear and swung back towards the river.

London's traditional order had broken down into a free-for-all, cars veering across every lane. 'Jesus Christ!' he gasped, swerving between them. Another glancing strike as he turned hard to avoid a head-on crash – then he was through, the way to Westminster Bridge opening out ahead of him.

The reason for the suddenly clear road was obvious: nobody dared drive past the clock tower. The street near its base was strewn with fallen debris. Traffic coming from the far bank had stopped, the crossing choked at its halfway point as drivers tried to turn back.

An ominous boom from above. The Shamir was no longer pointing at Brice's target, but it had done its work. The tower tilted again, tortured girders screaming – and the clock's north-ern face disintegrated, glass and iron cascading towards the street . . .

Followed by the hands of the clock itself as the mechanism ripped apart.

Eddie had already stamped on the accelerator. The van roared towards the bridge. His view was suddenly obscured by a snowstorm of white glass, a demented drum roll sounding on the roof as broken metal bombarded it. But he didn't dare stop—

The clock's hands stabbed into the road right behind him like colossal spears. The earth-shaking impact of almost five tons of metal kicked the van's rear wheels into the air. He fought to keep control as the tail crashed back down, skidding before straight-ening out. The overturned Shamir cut a line of destruction along the façade of the MPs' offices in Portcullis House as he drove past.

Then he was clear, passing the junction with the Embankment and reaching the bridge itself. He had hoped to reach the middle to dump the Shamir in the deepest water, but there were too many cars blocking the way. Instead he built up as much speed as he could, veering into the oncoming lanes – then turning sharply to the left and aiming straight at the railings along the crossing's side—

The Transit smashed through them, shattered metal spinning over the Thames as it arced towards the brown water below.

Its driver had already bailed out. Man and van hit the surface together, Eddie swallowed by the vehicle's churning splash. The Transit bobbed nose-down for a moment, then rolled on to its back. The Shamir was pitched from the pickup bed and sank into the turgid depths. Its bone-shaking hum quickly faded to nothingness, the water cutting it off from its source of power, just as Eddie had hoped.

Of Eddie himself, there was no sign.

* * *

The great clock's surviving face finally followed its counterparts into oblivion. The empty spaces gaped like anguished mouths, the bells behind them howling out a last discordant cry . . .

And the tower began to fall.

The stonework on the south face sheared away – then the weakened girders beneath buckled and snapped. The entire upper section housing the clock dropped several feet, a halo of pulverised stone blasting outwards before the sheer mass of tangled metal brought it to an abrupt halt.

For a moment, all that moved was billowing dust . . .

That moment passed.

Slowly at first, then with rising speed and inevitability, the clock tower toppled like a slain redwood on to the Houses of Parliament.

It smashed down on to the north wing, utterly flattening it – but the destruction had only just begun.

The remains of the clock itself, inside a huge and heavy cage of Victorian ironwork, broke from their supporting structure on impact with the ground and were flung onwards. Hundreds of tons of shattered metal scythed through the walls of the Commons chamber and the division lobbies on each side. The western lobby, in line with the tower, suffered the worst of the destruction. Politicians from the government's side were torn apart by shrapnel and tumbling debris, Big Ben itself rolling like a juggernaut over the screaming survivors and mashing them into unrecognisable pulp before the great bell shattered against the pillars at the lobby's southern end. Those trapped inside the main chamber suffered an equally horrific fate as the ceiling collapsed, crushing them beneath wood and slate and glass.

Then stillness descended, the cracks of falling stone gradually replaced by the wails of the injured.

It was a scene of unimaginable carnage, the seat of British

democracy reduced to blood-splattered ruins. Hundreds were dead.

But thanks to Nina's warning . . . hundreds more had survived.

39

Nina watched through the windows with Huygens and other shocked embassy staff as a dark cloud drifted across the Thames. The Houses of Parliament were out of direct sight around a bend in the river, but the thunderous boom of an uncontrolled building collapse had already told her enough. It was a noise she had heard before; she had been in her native Manhattan on September 11, 2001, a similar distance from Ground Zero, and its recurrence chilled her very soul.

'Oh, my God . . .' she whispered. 'He did it. He actually did it . . .'

Quentin Hove stared at a television in 10 Downing Street. One of the news channels had a helicopter airborne over the capital, and had cut live to it when it became clear that something was happening at the Houses of Parliament. His face was ashen, eyes wide in shock, but he couldn't avert his gaze. 'What have you done?' he said, voice barely audible.

The only other person in the room was C. 'What have *we* done, Prime Minister,' Armitage reminded him. 'Brice's plan was approved by both of us.'

Hove rounded on the intelligence chief. 'But – I didn't – I didn't know he was going to do *this*!' He stabbed a finger at the television. The helicopter was orbiting Parliament, revealing the destruction in almost three-dimensional clarity. The fallen clock tower had almost totally demolished the north wing of the Palace of Westminster, the House of Commons beyond a collapsed shell.

An urgent knock at the door. 'Prime Minister!' called a frantic aide, rushing in without waiting for a reply. 'It's Parliament, there – there's been an attack!'

Hove hurriedly attempted to compose himself, with little success. 'I know. I know! I'll be out in a moment. Wait outside. Get *out*!' he added, voice cracking, when the man did not immediately retreat.

C felt his phone buzz and quickly checked its screen. He had already ignored two calls from SIS headquarters, which he knew would be his staff trying to inform him about the disaster, but the number told him this was one he needed to take. 'Yes?'

'Sir, the operation is completed,' Brice replied.

'I know, the PM and I are watching on television. What's your status?' The other man sounded as if he was running, but there was also definite stress behind his breathlessness. 'Are you hurt?'

'Yes, sir, but that's not important. I needed to speak to you. Chase showed up.'

C tried to conceal his concern from the politician beside him. 'GB63 didn't catch him? What about the American woman?'

'I don't know, sir. I haven't been in contact with ops. You may need to follow that up.'

'I most definitely will. Where are you now?'

'In St James's Park. I'm going to get clear of the area, then go to the safe house. Sir, I . . . I'll need medical treatment.' The request sounded like an admission of defeat.

'Is that him?' Hove demanded before C could reply. 'Is that Brice? Let me speak to him!'

Armitage shook his head. 'Sir, that would be inadvisable—'

'*Do what I tell you!*' The command was almost a scream. C reluctantly put the phone on speaker. 'Brice, you – you *maniac!*' Hove shouted at it. 'You blew up Big Ben!'

No reply came from the phone, but C spoke for his subordinate, voice calm and cold. 'His inference was quite clear, Prime Minister. When you chose to send the Home Secretary to PMQs in your stead, I took that as confirmation that you were fully on board with the operation.'

'The *operation*!' The Prime Minister's voice rose almost to a screech. 'We – you, you've destroyed *Parliament*! You must have killed everyone inside!'

C stepped closer, both for a better look at the television and to apply subtle physical intimidation to the smaller man. The helicopter was now over Parliament Square, cameras zooming in on the growing crowd spilling out of the building. 'Not everyone, it would seem. There are survivors.' They both kept watching. 'Quite a few survivors.' He sounded almost surprised.

'Sir, if there isn't anything else,' Brice prompted, 'I need to get to the safe house.'

'Go,' C told him. 'I'll send a medic to meet you.'

'Thank you, sir.' He disconnected.

C turned back to Hove. 'I need to return to Vauxhall Cross, Prime Minister. There are some matters that require my attention.'

The Prime Minister's watery eyes widened again. 'What? What do you mean? Have we – have *you* been exposed? If MI6's involvement comes out—'

Armitage cut him off. 'Nothing like that. A cover story's already been prepared, that Islamic terrorists smuggled explosives into the sewer tunnels under the tower's foundations. It gives us both a believable scapegoat, and justification to cancel the election and implement a national state of emergency.' He put a hand on Hove's shoulder; the other man flinched. 'You've done the right thing, Prime Minister. This will allow us to secure our borders and crack down on internal dissent. *You* will be the one to lead us through this most difficult time. You must seize the opportunity – as long as you don't weaken, everything will turn out to the nation's advantage.'

'I . . . yes, yes,' said Hove, nodding. 'I'll prepare a statement immediately.'

'Good. We *will* rebuild, sir. Britain will come out of this stronger than ever before. And so will you.'

The churning ripples from the Transit's plunge into the Thames faded. Despite their fear, some of the people on Westminster Bridge had still rushed to look for any signs of the driver who had crashed into the waters below.

There were none. A man took off his jacket, about to dive after him in a rescue attempt—

'There he is! There!' someone cried.

Eddie broke through the waves, gasping. The sinking van's wake had dragged him down, the Yorkshireman needing all his strength to break free. But now he was being carried along by the strong current, passing beneath the bridge. He struck exhaustedly towards shore – not the one from which he had come, but the south bank. It was farther away, but was clear of the chaos that had erupted around Parliament – and, he hoped, would be free of SIS assassins.

While Nina and Huygens hurriedly discussed events, a member of the official's staff had continued watching the video. 'Mr Huygens, sir!' he called. 'Dr Wilde was right. This guy,' he gestured at a freeze-frame of Brice, 'talks about this Shamir thing being a sonic weapon that can destroy buildings from a distance, and his first thought is to use it for a decapitation attack.'

'Which he's just done,' said Nina. Someone had switched on a television, which was showing grim helicopter footage of the devastation.

'But is there conclusive proof?' Huygens asked. 'This biblical weapon – it sounds too fantastic to be real.'

'How real does it have to be?' she demanded, jabbing a hand at the screen as a replay of the clock tower's collapse began. 'And it's still out there! Brice still has it. Eddie, my husband, went after him, but . . .' She trailed off as an awful thought formed. Eddie had failed to stop the attack – or may not even have had the chance to try. 'You've got to get someone over there to find him!'

'We won't be able to get close,' Huygens told her. The replay continued, the helicopter's cameraman zooming in on fleeing people before pulling back to show the whole terrifying scene. 'The Brits'll close the entire area off, if they haven't already – it's just around the corner from Downing Street and less than a mile from Buckingham Palace.'

'You've got to *try*, though! He might be—' Something on the television caught her eye. A white pickup truck was moving against the other vehicles, heading *towards* the crumbling tower. The cameraman had also spotted the unusual activity and zoomed in again, keeping the building in frame as the truck approached it.

There was a grey rectangular object in the vehicle's bed – its dimensions and colour triggering a jolt of recognition. She darted closer to the screen, but the shape broke down into fuzzy pixels. Was it the Shamir's lead case? She couldn't tell – but there was something inside it, a greenish smear that might have been the strange stone itself . . .

'Holy *crap!*' someone gasped. Nina withdrew – and watched in shock as the clock's hands plunged to the ground, impacting so close behind the truck that it visibly jolted. 'That's the luckiest guy on earth, right there!'

'Where's he going?' asked Huygens, transfixed. 'The bridge is blocked, he can't get over it—'

He broke off as they saw that the driver wasn't trying to cross the bridge. The pickup deliberately swung at the railings – and crashed through, nose-diving towards the water below.

Nina saw the driver bail out as it fell. Another shock of recognition, this time with fear at the sight of a bald man in a leather jacket disappearing into the Thames. 'Oh my God! That was him, that was Eddie!' She stared at the screen, hoping to see him surface, but now the camera had fixed upon the clock tower as it began its inexorable collapse. The room went silent, everyone watching in stunned horror.

The scene played out to its devastating conclusion as a dust cloud swept up from the ruins. The channel cut back to a grim-faced studio presenter. Nina turned to Huygens. 'That was Eddie in that truck, I'm sure of it – and I'm also sure the Shamir was in its back. That means the Shamir's in the river . . . and he might still be alive. You've *got* to get somebody down there to find him. Please.'

The State Department official tore his gaze from the screen. 'I'll . . . I'll see what I can do.'

It took Eddie the better part of ten minutes to find a way up to ground level, penned in by the sheer wall running along the South Bank's waterfront. By the time he did, the streets were filled with the whoops and screams of sirens as emergency services from all over London poured into Westminster. Helicopters buzzed ceaselessly overhead, the civilian aircraft that had been first on the scene ordered away to clear space for air ambulances and police choppers.

He squelched up a flight of steps at a jetty near Lambeth Bridge. The riverfront was thronged by onlookers. He pushed through them to stare back at Parliament, half a mile upriver.

The sight that greeted him was *wrong*, grinding the gears of his mind as it struggled to process the absence of Big Ben from the skyline. The clock tower was familiar to every Briton even if they had never visited the capital, a symbol of the nation that had seemed eternal and unshakeable.

But now it was gone.

Anger surged through Eddie. Partly at himself, for failing to stop the attack – but mostly at Brice and his backers for carrying it out. Despite the agent's sneering claims to be acting for the good of the country, he was no patriot, rather the biggest traitor in Britain's history. Guy Fawkes had only *planned* to destroy the Houses of Parliament; Brice had succeeded.

His fury had no target, though. Brice had escaped, wounded but very much alive. He could now be anywhere. And he had no idea whether or not Nina had reached the American embassy with the evidence against the rogue MI6 man . . .

Images of his wife and daughter flashed through his mind. He *had* to find out what had happened to Nina, and get word to someone who could save Macy from Brice's watchers. He was now only about a mile from the US embassy – but the most direct route to it would take him literally past the front door of SIS headquarters.

He moved back through the crowd and started along the waterfront. Some areas of London, especially along the river, had changed nearly beyond recognition in the fifteen years since he had lived in the capital. He needed to figure out how to get to the embassy without being caught . . .

'Mr Chase? Eddie Chase!'

He whipped around, ready to run – or fight. A large black SUV had pulled up at the roadside, but it was an American model, even bigger than the Range Rovers that had been pursuing him. Its registration plate was a non-standard format, three numbers followed by a 'D' revealing that it was a diplomatic vehicle. The man calling his name had an American accent.

'Who's asking?' Eddie replied warily.

The young man held up an identity badge. 'My name's

Thomas Roston, from the US embassy. Your wife asked us to find you – although we didn't expect to see you right there on the sidewalk!'

'Yeah? What's my wife's name?'

'Nina Wilde. Why, you got amnesia?'

'Funny bastard,' the Yorkshireman rumbled, but the mere fact that Roston was willing to talk rather than gun him down on sight made him more inclined to believe his story. 'Did you get what she was bringing to you?'

The other man nodded. 'The ambassador's watching the video right now. We've been asked to take you to him. I hear you've had some problems with the British security services?'

'You could say that.'

'We'll get you past them. Get in.' He tipped his head towards the rear door.

Eddie was still suspicious, but if Roston's superiors had Nina, he would have to deal with them one way or another. 'Okay,' he said, opening the door. 'Apologies in advance, though.'

'For what?'

He sat down, his sodden clothes squishing under him. 'For ruining your upholstery.'

Roston was indeed telling the truth. It took some time for the SUV to reach the embassy, the police having set up roadblocks and checkpoints at several junctions, but eventually they pulled into an underground parking lot.

They took a lift up into the main building. 'We'll get you some dry clothes,' Roston's driver told Eddie.

'Wouldn't bother,' he replied sardonically as the doors opened. 'Took so long to get here, they've pretty much dried out on their own.'

'You do need a change, though,' said a familiar voice. 'Because they stink.'

'Nina!' cried Eddie in delight and relief as he saw his wife hurry out from a stern-faced reception committee. 'You okay, love?'

Nina held up her left arm, which was now supported by a sling. 'Nope. Got shot. But that's okay, they took care of it – and gave me an injection of something that kinda makes me want to get shot more often.' She smiled to assure him that was a joke, then they embraced.

'Nothing too powerful,' one of the embassy staff said. 'We need you both to be clear-headed.' He extended his hand to Eddie. 'Alvin Crane, Deputy Chief of Mission here in London. The ambassador is currently talking to the President. I can tell you right now, the video your wife brought to us is . . . explosive. If what this John Brice says on it is true—'

'It's true,' Eddie told him firmly.

'Then it's going to seriously impact the US–UK relationship, if it turns out the downing of Flight 180 really was carried out by a British agent with approval from the top.'

Even veiled in diplomatic terms, the Yorkshireman still picked up on the implied threat against his country. 'We don't know if Quentin Hove *specifically* signed off on crashing the plane to rescue Mukobo,' he said, wanting to pin the blame on specific individuals rather than the nation as a whole. 'But it seems like he authorised Brice to do whatever he wanted to start a civil war in DR Congo. Problem was, Brice is a fucking psycho.'

'That's something we can let the investigators and lawyers figure out,' said Crane. 'The first thing is for you to talk to the ambassador and the President, so you can answer their questions and give your side of the story. After that . . . it's up to the President to decide on a response.'

'That sounds ominous,' Nina said quietly.

The diplomat gestured down a corridor. 'Anyway, if you'll come with me, we'll get started. Although first . . .' His nose wrinkled. 'Maybe you *might* like a change of clothes, Mr Chase?'

Eddie shook his head. 'The President can't smell me over a conference call, so let's not waste time. Brice's business is way dirtier than anything I've been swimming in.'

40

One of the first high-level government responses to a terrorist attack on the United Kingdom would normally be for the Prime Minister and high-ranking ministers, security and police officials to convene a COBRA meeting. The menacing acronym had disappointingly mundane origins, standing for Cabinet Office Briefing Room – the 'A' had at one time referred to the specific room used, sticking solely because it sounded impressive.

Today, though, the number of people upon whom Quentin Hove could call had been hugely depleted. While there had been survivors from his cabinet, major figures like the Home Secretary and the Minister of Defence were either injured or in a state of shock, in no condition to make – or question – major policy decisions.

To Hove, this was ideal.

'Gentlemen, welcome,' said the Prime Minister from the head of the table as the other attendees filed in. 'I won't say "good afternoon", because it's anything but. Our country – our *government*, our democracy – suffered a grievous attack less than two hours ago. This meeting is to determine who is responsible, and what action to take against them.'

'We're absolutely certain that it was an attack, then?' asked Sir Michael Orgreave, the Cabinet Secretary and the country's highest-ranking civil servant.

Timothy Blandford, the Director-General of the Security Service – MI5 – nodded gravely. 'There was some kind of explosion in the clock tower. Somehow, somebody was able to get explosives through Parliament's security and detonate them at a time that would cause maximum loss of life.'

'Have – have we got an estimate of the casualties?' asked Hove.

The Director-General checked a tablet computer. 'The most recent figure is . . . out of the five hundred and seventy-three MPs known to be in the Commons chamber, three hundred and forty-seven are alive and accounted for.'

The number brought gasps from around the long table. 'So over *two hundred* dead?' said Tom Kingston, head of the Met's counter-terrorism operations.

'At least. A lot of the survivors are injured, some critically – and we haven't yet been able to compile a full tally of the Parliamentary staff who would have been in the north wing or around the Commons. HMRC was also hit. We estimate over a hundred dead there.'

It took Hove a moment to find his voice. 'So. Who's responsible?'

C, sitting by himself at the opposite end of the table, spoke. 'As you know, Prime Minister, we were discussing intelligence received by SIS concerning a new terrorist threat when this atrocity took place. I've since had further information. It would appear that African Caliphate, a splinter group of ISIS operating primarily out of Libya but with activities in other African states, is indeed responsible.'

The Director-General regarded his foreign intelligence counterpart in surprise. 'Who? I've never heard of them.'

'You'll have all pertinent information by the end of the day,' C replied. 'But to summarise: they're a relatively new offshoot, and it seemed unlikely they yet had the ability to carry out attacks outside their sphere of influence. It would appear that was . . . incorrect.'

'*Incorrect!*' spluttered Kingston. 'They've brought down Big

Ben! That's a bit more than just "incorrect".'

Hove raised his hand. 'Please. Please. C, do continue.'

'Thank you, Prime Minister,' said Armitage. 'The information we received suggested they had obtained a new type of Russian plastic explosive, undetectable by normal chemical sensors, on the black market.'

'The possibility of Russian involvement is extremely worrying,' said Hove. Even though he knew C's story was just that, a fiction, he was still feeling a certain strange enthusiasm at discovering its twists. 'Is there any chance that Moscow might be using African Caliphate as a proxy?'

'Anything is possible with our Russian friends,' Armitage replied. 'The links to other African countries might also spread the net wider. African Caliphate has been connected to secession-ist militias in the eastern Democratic Republic of Congo, for instance, and both Russia and China have been expanding their influence there.'

'You're investigating these links, of course?'

C nodded. 'Of course, Prime Minister.'

'Good. Then the next question is: how to reassure the public that the government is still intact and in charge, and—'

Everyone turned at a frantic knock at the door. COBRA meetings would only be interrupted if there was urgent news about the matter under discussion – or if something else of equal importance had happened. 'Yes?' Hove called.

A Cabinet Office aide hurried through the door. 'Sorry to interrupt, sir,' he said, 'but it's the American President.'

'Probably wants to offer condolences and support,' said the Prime Minister. 'Tell him I'll take his call as soon as this meeting's concluded.'

'No, no, sir.' The official picked up a remote control. 'He's not on the phone – he's making a televised address from the White House.'

'What?' Hove was shocked; for a fellow world leader not to speak privately to the head of a nation hit by a terrorist attack before making a public statement was a serious deviation from protocol. 'What's he saying?'

'I, ah . . . I think you need to hear it for yourself,' said the official, activating the video wall.

Nina and Eddie stood in the office of Simon Nadel, the US ambassador, watching the President's speech on television. Less than half an hour earlier they had spoken to him via teleconference, telling him about events in the jungle; now, he was acting upon their information. 'Just hope he doesn't retaliate by nuking Britain,' Eddie whispered to his wife.

'I don't think he would,' she replied just as quietly, aware that Nadel had been appointed personally by the American leader. 'At least, I *hope* not . . .'

President Michael Schilling continued to speak: ' . . . the shocking and terrible events that took place in London a short time ago. As President of the United States, I offer our nation's full and unconditional support to the people of the United Kingdom in their day of crisis, and I know that every American will do the same in support of our friend and closest ally.'

'We're still friends, then,' said Eddie. 'That's good.'

'He hasn't finished talking yet,' warned Nina. While she had met several of the previous holders of the office, the current president was known to her only by reputation – which was mercurial, to say the least.

Confirmation that things might change came when Schilling's attitude visibly altered, barely contained anger entering his voice. 'However . . . I have received intelligence that identifies the perpetrators of this horrific and cowardly attack. I am here to tell the world right now that, despite whatever rumours may already be circulating, we are certain that it was *not* carried out by Islamic extremists. Instead, we believe that the individuals responsible for the attack on the British Parliament are the same ones who caused the crash of Skyblue Airlines Flight 180 a year ago, with the loss of over three hundred lives.'

Nina gripped Eddie's hand. 'Oh, my God. He's actually saying it straight out. He's not even going to the British government first – he's making an allegation to the world.' Even Nadel was shocked by the bluntness of his boss's declaration.

'We know the identity of the individual who carried out both attacks,' the President continued, staring into the camera as if addressing his suspect directly. 'As for those who *authorised* this person to commit mass murder in pursuit of a cynical political agenda, we also know who they are.' He paused, his gaze intensifying. 'We know *where* they are. Our intelligence agencies are sharing information with their British counterparts as I speak. I trust that the British government will join us in our mission to bring these criminals to justice. Because make no mistake: we are coming for them.'

Brice arrived at his destination, an anonymous terraced house on a west London street. The journey had taken longer than expected. Even outside central London, the city was still in a state of chaos, the capital's main arteries clogged by people fleeing the imagined threat of another attack. He had also had to stop to attend to his lacerated hand. The bleeding was now under control, but he could still feel the metal shards embedded in his flesh.

The safe house door quickly opened after he knocked. 'I'm here to see Bill,' he said, using a simple passphrase. The man who answered nodded and let him in. 'I need treatment for shrapnel wounds,' he went on, displaying his wounded hand.

'I'll take care of it in the back, sir,' said the field officer, directing him down the hall.

A television was on in the front room. Brice glanced in as he passed, seeing another man standing watching it. A news channel showed the American President making a speech. Offering sympathy and assistance to the British people, he guessed; an inevitable gesture, although surprisingly soon after the event.

A table in the spartan kitchen had been covered by a plastic sheet and laid out with surgical items and dressings. 'Sit down, sir,' said the medic. 'Let me see your hand.'

Brice placed his injured hand palm-up on the table, wincing as he opened his fingers. The other man examined it. 'Some of these cuts are practically through to the bone,' he reported. 'Do you want a painkiller?'

'I need to stay lucid,' Brice replied. 'Just get on with it.'

'Okay, sir.' The medic picked up a pair of slender tweezers and began removing the metal fragments.

Brice breathed deeply, trying to focus on something other than the pain. The sound of the television gave him a distraction. Schilling had finished his speech, the news channel's presenters now discussing its content . . .

'He said US intelligence already knows who carried out the attack on Parliament,' said a woman, 'and that it's the same people who brought down Flight 180 last year. The question is: if they knew, why weren't our security services warned?'

A man started to respond, but Brice was no longer listening, trying to contain his shock. The only possible way Mukobo's rescue could have been connected to what he had just done was if Nina Wilde had reached the US embassy with the incriminating video. The Removal Men had failed!

The pain in his hand was all but forgotten as his mind whirled into overdrive. His cover had been blown – which meant he was now the number one target worldwide for US intelligence.

He couldn't allow himself to be captured. The myth of a hardened agent being able to endure torture indefinitely was just that, pure fiction; the reason spies and soldiers were taught about so-called 'enhanced interrogation' techniques was not to resist them, but so they could use them effectively on others. He would break, eventually.

And when he did, he would expose his superiors.

He did not know C on a personal level – very few at SIS did – but professionally was well aware of his reputation as a ruthless pragmatist. Quentin Hove's own reputation, on the other hand, was one of low cunning, opportunism and possessing all the backbone of a jellyfish. What both men had in common, though, was their survival instinct. They would throw their closest friends under the proverbial bus to save themselves . . . and Brice was well aware that he was not even their friend, but an employee. An asset.

A disposable one.

His SIS training had drummed into him the very real possibility that he might have to sacrifice his own life for his country. It was something he was willing to do – but not for this. He had *saved* his country, ensured that the right people would remain in power for a generation or more and set the nation back on the road to greatness. He wanted to see all of that come to pass. And he *would*, he decided with a surge of anger. He wasn't about to let the Americans spirit him away to a black site – or be found dead in a staged suicide, a speciality of GB63.

He knew he was safe for now. If the two men at the safe house had been ordered to eliminate him, he would have been dead within seconds of the front door closing. But that could change at any moment; all it took was a phone call.

A stab of pain from his hand as the medic removed a half-inch sliver of gunmetal. He grimaced, then controlled his breathing once more, listening to the television in the next room – and for the sound of the other man's phone.

★ ★ ★

'I need to speak to President Schilling,' said Hove, struggling to keep his voice from cracking in fear. 'We'll resume this meeting later.' The COBRA attendees filed from the briefing room. 'C, if you'll wait for a moment,' he added as Armitage stood. 'I want to discuss the . . . foreign intelligence implications before I talk to him.'

'Of course, Prime Minister.' C returned to his seat.

The two men waited for the room to clear – then Hove leapt up in near-panic. 'My God. My God! If the Yanks know that Brice brought down that plane, then – then the evidence will point straight to us!'

'There *is* no evidence, Prime Minister,' said C, though he was now hiding his own concern. 'Even if they have this recording of Brice, all they have is the baseless bragging of a former officer who went rogue – and clearly went insane – in a quest for personal glory and riches. There is no *provable* link between Flight 180 and Brice.'

Hove was not mollified. 'And what if the Americans catch Brice? What if he talks?'

'He won't. Sir, I need to return to SIS headquarters to take care of this. But be assured, it *will* be taken care of.'

'Go on, then. Go!' the politician snapped. 'Deal with it!'

'Of course, Prime Minister,' replied C, unctuousness barely covering contempt. He stood, taking out his phone as he headed for the exit. 'This is C. Put me through to the men at the west London safe house.'

'Almost done,' said the medic, carefully drawing a suture through Brice's palm. The stitches in the agent's right hand made it appear to be wrapped in bloodied centipedes. 'I still need to bandage it, but I think I've got all the shrap.'

Brice nodded, but his attention was elsewhere. He had just heard the man in the front room respond to a phone call. He listened more closely. The other field officer lowered his voice, his words masked by the television. There was only one reason he wouldn't want to be overheard . . .

The medic snipped the suture with scissors, then put them on the table and turned to open a pack of sterile dressings. 'Okay, I'll get this—'

Brice snatched up the scissors with his left hand and thrust them into the man's neck, driving their points deep into his carotid artery before yanking them back out. Blood spurted from the wound, the medic staggering back in shock. He clapped one palm over it, the other hand fumbling inside his jacket—

His attacker had noticed the holstered gun during the procedure. Brice snatched it out and shoulder-barged the medic across the kitchen.

A noise from behind. Brice whirled, bringing up the gun—

The second man crashed through the door, his own weapon raised – and took two bullets to the chest. Brice jumped aside as he fell, then whipped around to put a third round into the medic's forehead. A vivid red explosion burst over the white wall behind him.

Brice quickly searched the corpses, taking their spare ammo and a set of car keys. Their phones would be trackable, but he collected one anyway; he had a call to make. His immediate priority was to get out of London before the net closed around him, then leave the country – and a plan to do so was already forming.

He had memorised a particular number, calling it as he headed for the front door. 'Watch unit,' he said. 'This is Brice. Confirm that the target is still in place.'

'She is, sir,' came the reply. 'But after what's happened in London, should we stay on her? There must be more important things for us to do than watch a five-year-old girl.'

'You'll do more than stay on her,' Brice growled as he

emerged on to the street. He blipped the key fob, seeing the lights flash on a Ford Focus nearby. 'I want you to pick her up immediately and bring her to me.' He got into the car. 'Macy Wilde Chase has just become a matter of national security.'

41

Sir Kirkland Armitage put down the phone and went to his office window, staring silently across the Thames. The call had delivered highly unwelcome news. The men at the safe house whom he had ordered to deal with John Brice had been found dead, their weapons missing. Of the deep-cover agent, there was no trace.

He had also learned that both Nina Wilde and her husband were now at the US embassy – and despite demands to turn them over to British authorities, ostensibly to face charges for the swathes of destruction they had carved while evading capture, the Americans had refused. The ambassador himself had made that clear, and C suspected his orders came directly from the White House.

Even without direct evidence to link himself and Hove to Brice's attack, Wilde and Chase would be spilling their guts to the Americans. Suspicions would be raised, connections made . . . fingers pointed. And he had no doubts that Hove would turn upon him in a heartbeat to protect himself. As for what would happen if the Americans caught Brice . . .

C made a decision. He returned to his desk and called a subordinate. 'Is Peter Alderley still in holding? Good. Bring him up to my office, immediately.'

He hung up, then opened a drawer. At the back was something he had never expected to need, but which he had placed there on his first day in the office out of force of paranoid habit gained from working in the field.

A gun.

He took out the Glock and checked it. The magazine was full, the slide moving smoothly when he racked it to chamber a round. Satisfied, he placed it back in the open drawer, within easy reach – but out of sight from anyone before him. Then he sat back and awaited his visitor's arrival.

Alderley entered a few minutes later. 'Wait outside,' C ordered the guards who had escorted the section head. 'I want to speak to him in private.' They left the room.

'What's going on?' Alderley demanded. 'I know something big's happened – I couldn't miss it even stuck in a cell.'

'Sit down, Peter,' C said calmly. Alderley frowned, but took a place in front of the desk. His superior switched on a television, which lit up with a shocking still frame of the clock tower caught mid-collapse. 'There's been a terrorist attack on the Houses of Parliament. The current death toll is at least four hundred, including over two hundred MPs.'

Alderley struggled to overcome his horror. 'So . . . so Nina and Chase were right about Brice—'

'That's why I've called you up here,' C interrupted. 'To find out what you think you know about this alleged plot by a former SIS officer, and how it connects to the crash of Flight 180 last year. Wilde and Chase are both being protected by the US embassy – as is Boxley from your team. Because of what they've said, the Yanks are making some extremely threatening noises towards our country. Not through diplomatic channels either. This comes direct from President Schilling. So: tell me.'

'I'm sure I don't know anything that you don't already, sir,' the moustachioed man said with no small sarcasm.

C jabbed a finger at him. 'Don't get clever with me, Alderley. National security is at stake here!'

'I already told you, before you had me arrested. I was brought intel by a reliable source that SIS was involved in an illegal operation in DR Congo, and that John Brice was in charge with full knowledge and approval from both here and Whitehall, despite supposedly having resigned two years ago.'

'And what about the ancient weapon found by Wilde and Chase in the jungle?'

Alderley eyed him suspiciously. 'The Shamir? So you *did* know about that already. Who told you?'

'Just answer the question.'

'It was Brice, wasn't it? You knew what he was doing all along! For God's sake, sir! I'm the head of the Africa desk, but something this big was going on behind my back? How high does it go? Chase said that Brice claimed to have Section 7 immunity – which must mean that the Prime Minister signed it when he was Foreign Secretary. And I know he didn't attend PMQs today. Did he *authorise* Brice to carry out this attack? Did *you*?' Alderley's voice rose as he became more accusatory.

C's right hand slipped towards the open drawer. 'Are you implying that Prime Minister and I were complicit in today's terrorist attack?'

'I – I think there needs to be an immediate and independent investigation, sir.' Alderley tensed, realising that his superior's bearing had changed, but pressed on. 'Nina Wilde and Eddie Chase evaded SIS watchers – including a team placed on *me*, I might add – to bring me information about Brice, about the Shamir, everything that's been going on in the Congo . . . and the next day, Parliament is attacked. I'm going to assume that whatever official story might have been drummed up, the damage was caused by something more than Semtex or a rocket launcher. Some kind of sonic weapon, maybe?'

C stared at him, his expression as unreadable as a reptile's – then to Alderley's shock raised the gun. 'Your problem, Peter, is that you've practically gone native, wondering how we can help all these pisspot little African nations, when what you're supposed to be doing is using them to help *us*! We're on our own now, and we have to secure our position in the world. Brice's mission in DR Congo was to do just that.'

'By securing *mineral rights*?' said Alderley incredulously, eyes fixed on the gun. 'What about the thousands of people who'd die in a civil war that we instigated?'

'They are *not our concern*,' C stated coldly. 'What *is* our concern as officers of SIS is the defence of the realm, and the protection of this agency. But any revelation of Brice's role in the Mukobo operation threatens both those things.'

'Then I'd say they're already more than threatened! If the Americans have Nina and Chase, and the video of Brice's confession, then they've got more than enough to join the dots and point back to you and the PM. And if it's proved that the Shamir was used to do that,' he pointed at the frozen image of destruction on the screen, 'then . . . then that makes you the greatest traitors in this country's history.'

C said nothing for a long moment, the gun locked unwaveringly upon Alderley. 'If the full truth were to come out, it would be catastrophic for Britain. Don't you agree?'

'I . . . would have to say yes,' he replied uneasily.

'But if anyone who knew the full truth were to be *silenced*, unable to reveal it, then the realm would remain protected. That is, of course, our job as officers of SIS. To serve and defend our country . . . by doing whatever is necessary.'

Alderley's eyes widened in alarm as C stood, the gun still fixed on its target. 'Sir, I don't know the full truth!' he protested.

The head of MI6 regarded him without emotion . . . then let out a small, resigned sigh. 'Which makes you very fortunate, Peter.'

He put the gun's muzzle in his own mouth – and pulled the trigger.

★ ★ ★

Quentin Hove strode angrily into Briefing Room A to find it already occupied. More people than before were present, the previous attendees joined by Claire Parker, one of the junior ministers at the Home Office; though she was relatively young and held only a secondary role in her department, the Home Secretary's incapacitation meant she was technically the highest-ranking minister capable of participating. Also present amongst other new arrivals was Sir Rupert Jennings, the Private Secretary to the Sovereign. Hove was surprised to see him, as national security briefings were not part of his usual remit, but considering the circumstances he assumed the Queen herself had ordered him to find out how her government intended to respond to the attack on the nation.

His anger was because he had not instigated the COBRA meeting. Instead, he had been called – almost summoned – to the Cabinet Offices. 'Right,' he said as the others in the room stood upon his entrance, 'what's going on, and why couldn't I be told over the phone? We can't afford to waste any time in this crisis.'

He took his place, everyone else sitting down. MI5's Director-General was first to speak. 'Prime Minister, there have been a number of alarming developments. The first concerns C.'

Hove belatedly realised that the head of SIS was conspicuously absent. 'Why isn't he here?'

'Sir Kirkland is regrettably unable to attend due to his death,' said Blandford, gravely deadpan.

The Prime Minister stared at him in disbelief. 'What?'

'He committed suicide in his office an hour ago.'

'*What?*' The word was almost a yelp. 'Why?'

'The extremely disturbing intelligence we've received from the Americans may have had something to do with it,' the Director-General went on. 'Evidence has come to light concerning an SIS officer called John Brice, the crash of the Skyblue

Airlines 747 in the Atlantic last year, and secessionist militias in the Democratic Republic of Congo.'

Hove felt a cold fear. 'What has any of that got to do with today's attack? We've got bigger concerns than some jungle backwater.'

'It would appear that it has a great deal to do with it, Prime Minister.' Somehow, the title sounded more like an insult. 'This Brice, though supposedly having resigned two years ago, claimed on camera that he was actually still an SIS officer working in deep cover to aid the secessionist movement. As part of his mission, he freed a wanted war criminal from American custody – while he was aboard an American airliner on the way to the US to stand trial. The airliner crashed into the ocean with the loss of all aboard. If he was indeed a British operative acting under orders, then I'm sure you would agree that such an act would be tantamount to an act of war against our closest ally.'

'People – people claim to be MI6 agents all the time,' Hove managed to say. 'If he resigned, then he resigned. Any actions he took after that would be those of a mercenary – or a lunatic.'

'There, ah, there is something more to it, Prime Minister,' said Parker, sounding extremely nervous as she opened a folder. 'John Brice was given indefinite Section 7 immunity for anything he did relating to a mission in the Congo.' Her hands trembled as she held up a sheet of paper. 'It, um, it was signed by you, sir. Two years ago. When you were, ah, Foreign Secretary.'

'I know what I was doing two years ago!' Hove snapped, recognising his signature and trying to hide his terror behind anger. 'I signed Section 7 orders for dozens of MI6 officers. That doesn't mean I authorised one of our own men to destroy an American plane!'

'It does mean there is a direct link between yourself and John Brice, Prime Minister,' said Blandford. 'Have you had any further contact with him since?'

'I didn't even have contact with him when I signed the order!' Hove glared at him. 'Are you *interrogating* me, Timothy?'

'Merely trying to uncover the facts necessary for the protection of the realm, Prime Minister.' The MI5 head turned to the Director of GCHQ beside him. 'Clive, if you would?'

Clive Collins, head of the communications spy agency, took out a small digital recorder and pushed the play button. Hove flinched in shock as he heard his own voice come from the little speaker – along with those of C and Brice. 'We – you, you've destroyed *Parliament*! You must have killed everyone inside!' the short but damning recording concluded.

All eyes were upon him, the emotions behind them different – dismay, anger, hostility – but none positive. 'Where did you get that?' Hove demanded, knowing his only defence was to attack. 'Politicians are specifically excluded by law from being monitored by GCHQ – especially the Prime Minister! This isn't just inadmissible, it's illegal! It's – it's treason!'

'We didn't intercept this, sir,' said Collins. 'It was given to us by the Americans. The mere fact that they've revealed the NSA can crack our encrypted calls – we're implementing countermeasures already, of course – shows how important they believe this is.'

'It's interesting that you should use the term "treason", Quentin,' Blandford said pointedly. 'Because it sounds very much as if you personally authorised today's attack on Parliament.'

'This is *ludicrous*!' barked Hove. 'I'm trying to deal with an attack on this country, and you're wasting my time with ridiculous allegations! This meeting is over.'

'Actually, Prime Minister,' said Jennings, speaking for the first time, 'it is not.' He too had a folder before him, marked with the Great Seal of the Realm: notice that the documents within had been personally signed by the monarch. Almost regretfully, he opened it and took out the pages within. 'This is an action unprecedented in modern times, but in light of the evidence, Her Majesty is exercising her prerogative to remove a minister of the crown from office pending an investigation. The named minister . . . is you, Prime Minister. I am here to serve you formally with notice of your removal, effective immediately.'

Hove jumped up, slamming his palms on the desk. 'This is *outrageous*! The Queen doesn't have the authority to remove me. I'm not some mere functionary – I'm the Prime Minister! She acts upon *my* instructions!'

Jennings was unruffled. 'Technically speaking, the Prime Minister serves at Her Majesty's pleasure; that is the exact legal term. She has the power to dismiss any member of her government at will. She also has the right in times of grave constitutional crisis – again, the exact term – to overrule the decisions of her ministers. I would consider the deaths of over a third of all Members of Parliament in a terrorist attack to indeed qualify as such.' He slid the papers down the desk to the man at its head. 'Mr Hove, you are no longer the Prime Minister.'

Blandford took over as the stunned Hove regarded the documents. 'It pains me to have to say this, Quentin, but I'm afraid the Security Service need to ask you some questions.' He nodded to an aide, who opened the door. A pair of large, hard-faced men in dark suits entered and moved to flank Hove. 'It would be to everyone's benefit if you would go with them voluntarily, and with dignity.'

Hove was about to protest, but a look up at the looming men dissuaded him. Instead, he made a show of straightening his tie and tugging down his jacket as he stood. 'Very well. But this isn't over. I'll fight this all the way to the Supreme Court if I have to.'

Blandford watched as he was led from the briefing room. 'Make sure he doesn't suffer any . . . "unfortunate accidents",' he told the two guards.

Parker stared after Hove as the doors closed behind him. 'Okay, ah . . . now what do we do?' she said, wide-eyed. 'We don't have a Prime Minister! Who's in charge of the government?'

The head of MI5 gave her a look that was somewhere between amusement and pity. 'Currently? As the senior cabinet member present, that would be you.'

'What?' she gasped. 'But – but I don't know what to do! I'm a junior minister, I've never even run a department!'

'Fortunately, you're in the right place to learn,' he told her. 'The function of a COBRA meeting is to brief members of the government on matters of critical national import so they can decide how to respond.' A small smile. 'So, shall we begin?'

'Are we done?' Eddie said with considerable impatience. 'We've told you everything we know three bloody times over.'

Huygens looked up from his laptop, on which he was reviewing a transcript of Nina and Eddie's statements. 'Almost. You mentioned copying files on to SD cards before you left Butembo. Do you know if the other members of your expedition will have anything pertinent to the investigation?'

Nina tiredly rubbed her eyes. 'There'll be some footage of Brice and Mukobo together when we went through Solomon's challenges, and Jay probably filmed the Shamir in action. That'll let the Brits see that what happened at Parliament was caused by the same thing.' The official nodded, making a note.

'So what's going to happen?' Eddie asked. 'To Britain, I mean. Having the Prime Minister and the head of MI6 be involved in taking down an American plane won't be good for the "special relationship".'

'That's up to the President,' replied Huygens. 'By the way, Hove isn't Prime Minister any more. Seems he was removed from office.' Seeing their shock, he went on: 'The evidence you brought to us played a large part in it. It hasn't been announced

509

to the public yet, but there'll be a statement soon. Looks like the British government wants to do everything possible to make it clear to the President that Hove was the plan's sole instigator.'

'Why just Hove?' said Nina. 'What about C, Brice's boss? He's just as involved.'

'Didn't anyone tell you? He's dead.'

The pair looked at each other in surprise. 'When did that happen?' asked the Yorkshireman.

'A couple of hours ago. Suicide. It seems he shot himself in his office – in front of someone he'd had locked up for helping you.'

'Peter Alderley?' said Nina, worried. 'Is he okay?'

'I think so, but it's MI6; they're not exactly known for their water-cooler gossip.' He finished typing, then closed the laptop. 'Okay. We may want to ask you more questions, but for now, we're done.'

'Great,' said Eddie. 'Then we need a phone to call my dad and make sure our little girl's okay.'

Huygens indicated one of the phones on his desk. 'Be my guest. Dial nine for an outside line.'

'Thanks.' Eddie called his father's home, becoming concerned when he only got an answering machine. 'Dad, it's Eddie – I'm going to try you on your mobile,' he said, before dialling another number.

'They might just be out somewhere,' said Nina.

'They might,' he replied, unconvinced. This time, he got an answer – but the stress in his father's voice immediately set alarm bells ringing. 'Dad! It's Eddie, are you okay? Where's Macy?'

'Edward! Oh, my God,' Larry answered. 'We're at the police station, in Southampton. They – they took her, they took Macy!'

'Who took Macy?' Nina's face filled with fright at his words. She leaned closer to listen to the other side of the conversation. 'The cops?'

'No, I don't know who they were, two men. They – they just kicked down the door and came in with guns! They took Macy away. I – I couldn't stop them, I thought they were going to kill us! Edward, I'm sorry, I'm sorry . . .'

'It's okay, Dad, it's okay,' said Eddie, even as his fist clenched so tightly around the handset that the plastic creaked.

'Are you and Julie both okay?' Nina asked.

'Yes, yes. We're – we're just shaken up. What the hell's going on?'

Huygens had meanwhile taken a call on his cellphone; he urgently held up a hand. 'Sorry to interrupt, but someone's called the embassy's main desk asking for you both. They say it's extremely important.'

'It could be about Macy,' Nina suggested hopefully.

'Hold on, Dad. I've got to take another call.' Eddie put down the handset and took the proffered phone, his wife listening in. 'Hello, yeah?'

'Hello, Chase.' They both froze at the voice. Brice.

'You *bastard*,' Eddie growled. 'If you've hurt Macy, I will fucking kill you.'

'Spare me the threats, I'm not impressed.'

'I'm not trying to impress you. I'm stating a fucking fact.'

Nina whispered a frantic request to Huygens: 'It's Brice! Can you trace the call?' He picked up another desk phone and stabbed in an internal number. Knowing that they needed to keep Brice on the line for as long as possible, she turned back to the cellphone. 'How did you know where we were?'

'Hello, Nina. Well, when someone drives a double-decker into the lake outside the US embassy in the middle of a gun battle, it still makes the news even when something considerably larger has happened. Also, I'd arranged to be notified automatically if you called your father, Chase. I set it up before you even left the Congo, and since nobody told the computers

511

I'm now *persona non grata*, they let me know that you rang – and from where.'

'So you found us,' Nina snarled. 'What do you want?'

'I'm sure you'll consider this very unprofessional, Chase, but I want revenge. Thanks to your handing over information damaging to the country to the Yanks, everything I've worked to achieve is now compromised.'

'Information damaging to the country?' Eddie echoed angrily. 'You mean, you confessing to killing a planeload of innocent people?'

'I'm going to offer you a straightforward swap,' Brice went on, ignoring him. 'Your life, for your daughter's. I'll contact you again later via Peter Alderley to tell you where to meet me. Since I know somebody will be trying to trace this call, I'll save you some time and tell you that you'll need to head in the direction of Southampton. Now don't do anything foolish, Nina, and you'll get your daughter back. See you soon, Chase.'

The call ended. Nina looked at Huygens. 'We didn't get an exact trace,' he said apologetically after listening to someone on his own line. 'There wasn't time. It was a mobile number, and he's most likely on the M3 motorway, somewhere around Farnborough.'

'He's probably chucked his phone out of the window already,' said Eddie, seething. The M3 was the most direct route between London and Southampton. 'Shit!'

Nina heard a frantic voice coming from the forgotten handset. 'Edward! Edward, what's going on?' Larry demanded as she picked it up.

'Larry, it's Nina,' she replied. 'I'm sorry, but we've got to go. The person who's got Macy just gave us an . . . ultimatum.'

'What? What kind of ultimatum?'

'The bad kind,' Eddie told him. 'One way or another, someone dies. Most likely me.'

'My God,' said Larry. 'Edward, oh my God! What about Macy?'

'The deal is: me for her.'

'But you can't just turn yourself over to – to be killed!'

'You'd have done the same for me or Lizzie when we were kids, wouldn't you?' There was no immediate reply. 'Gee, thanks, Dad!'

'That – it's not a situation that would ever have come up!' his father spluttered.

'Yeah, well, it's come up for me. Look, I need to call someone else now. I'll be in touch again later. Or . . . I might not be. In which case, Dad: I'm glad we got over our differences. Well, most of 'em. Make sure you're a good grandad to Macy, okay? Bye.'

Larry started to protest, but Eddie put down the phone. 'What the hell are we going to do, Eddie?' asked Nina. 'That son of a bitch has got Macy – but your dad's right, you can't let him kill you. I won't trade one of you for the other!'

'I dunno what we're going to do,' he said, grim-faced. 'I really don't. Except for one thing – we need to talk to Alderley, right now.'

42

'I don't suppose he said *when* he'd call?' asked Peter Alderley, gazing glumly at the phone on his office desk.

'Sorry,' Nina replied. 'He just said he'd reach us through you.' She and Eddie had contacted MI6 via the US embassy, getting hold of the official after a long wait. Alderley was still somewhat shell-shocked after witnessing his boss blow his brains out, and his subsequent arrest and interrogation – the security guards who rushed back into the room after hearing the gunshot had leapt to the conclusion that he pulled the trigger – had not done anything to calm him. It was only once news of Quentin Hove's removal from office and the NSA recording of the conspirators' phone conversation reached SIS that he was finally released.

'He said he's going to be somewhere around Southampton,' added Eddie. 'After he told his watchers to get Macy from my dad's, he must have gone down there to meet them.'

The older man gave him a doleful look. 'He may well have met them, but we haven't been able to contact them. I have a horrible feeling that they're dead.'

'Why weren't they called off before Brice could tell them to take Macy?' said Nina.

'That's the problem with intelligence agencies,' Alderley said with a sigh. 'Everything's a secret, even from other departments. Because Brice's operation had been authorised by C himself, none of the people assigned to it suspected there was anything wrong – and nobody else in SIS knew what they were doing because the whole thing was compartmentalised. It wasn't until after C killed himself and Brice was named as a suspect in the attack on Parliament that anyone involved started to think, "Wait a minute . . ."'

Eddie shook his head. 'Bloody spooks. And Christ, if he killed them in front of Macy . . . She's five, she shouldn't have to see that shit.'

'I'm *fifty*-five, and I'm not keen on it either,' said the SIS officer. 'I've seen death in the field, but I didn't expect to see it in the office – oh, this could be it.' His phone rang; he answered. 'Alderley. Yes, put him through. Trace it, of course.'

He put the phone on speaker. 'Good evening, Peter,' said Brice.

'John,' Alderley answered warily. 'You should give yourself up. We know you attacked Parliament with the Shamir, and the Americans know you took down Flight 180 to rescue Mukobo. If you really are the patriot you claim to be, you'd turn yourself in rather than damage the whole country.'

'It's certainly an option I'm considering. I *am* a patriot – more so than cowards like C and Quentin Hove. I'm not going to kill myself to avoid embarrassment or try to worm my way out of it by blaming everyone else. But there's something I want to do first. Are Chase and his wife there?'

'We're here, you arsehole,' Eddie growled. 'Where's Macy? Is she all right?'

'She's fine.'

'I want to talk to her,' said Nina.

'She's a little tied up at the moment, if you'll excuse my sub-Bondian pun. But you'll have her back soon if you do as I say. Well, *you* will, Nina.'

Alderley had been checking his computer during the exchange; he reacted to something on the screen with perturbation, then whispered: 'We've found him.'

Eddie nodded. 'What do you want us to do, then?' he said to the phone.

'I want you both to come to my location, which I'm sure SIS has pinpointed by now. Alone, of course. If the police or security services turn up, your daughter dies. And I can assure you that I'll know if they come within half a mile of me. We'll make a straight swap: you for your little girl, Chase. Then, Peter, I'll give serious consideration to turning myself in to you.'

'I expected more from you than petty revenge,' said Alderley.

'It's hardly petty. After all the trouble Chase has caused me, it's actually quite grand. So, get here as soon as you can. I know the traffic out of London is hellish today, but don't worry, I'll be patient. See you soon.' The call ended.

'Well,' said Alderley. 'Now what?'

'We go and get her, obviously,' said Nina. 'And we figure out a way to do it that doesn't involve Brice killing my husband! Where is he?'

'That's the thing. He was using a landline, so we've got his exact location – and it's somewhere I know. You too, Chase.'

'What do you mean?' Eddie asked.

Alderley turned the monitor so the couple could see. It showed a partial map of southern England, Southampton on the left of the screen and the city of Portsmouth on the lower right. A crosshair flashed on the countryside north of the M27 motorway connecting the two ports. 'SIS has a training centre at Fort Monckton near Portsmouth. This,' he indicated the crosshair, 'is one of its associated facilities. It's the Funhouse.'

Eddie was shocked. 'He's taken Macy to the bloody Funhouse?'

'What's the Funhouse?' Nina demanded. 'I'm guessing it doesn't live up to its name.'

'It definitely does not,' Alderley told her. 'It's a testing ground for SIS field officers and potential recruits to "E" Squadron, with mock-ups of different locations. Like a paintball ranch – except with live ammo.'

'Well, now that you know where he is, can't you just send in snipers or something to take him out before he can hurt Macy?'

He shook his head. 'It's indoors – and it's on a secure compound with three-sixty-degree surveillance. Brice wasn't kidding when he said he'd know if anyone came within half a mile. There's no way into the grounds, never mind the building, without being detected. And if he was using the landline, that means . . . he's probably killed the guard staff,' he said with crestfallen realisation, reaching for the phone again.

'What're you doing?' asked Nina.

'I've got to call my superiors,' he replied. 'Brice is the most wanted man in Britain – in the world – right now. We've got to catch him before he has a chance to slip away.'

'But if you send anyone in there, he'll kill Macy!'

'I know this isn't what you want to hear, but that's a risk we might have to take.' He started to tap in a number.

Eddie put his hand down firmly on the phone. 'You're right, I don't want to hear it. And if I hear it again, you know how I've broken your nose twice? It'll be three times, and it won't be the only fucking thing.'

Alderley reflexively touched the crooked lump on the bridge of his nose, a permanent souvenir of prior encounters with the SAS man. 'What else can I do? The country's in chaos, Parliament's been destroyed – and the man responsible,' he pointed at the screen again, 'is *there*.'

'And he'll still be there until we arrive,' Nina said, almost pleading. 'You heard him.'

'He's not exactly the most trustworthy person!'

'You're not fucking gambling with my daughter's life,' said Eddie firmly, his hand still covering the phone. 'Look, you're a high-up at MI6 – you must have some sway. You can tell MI5 and Special Branch and whoever else where Brice is, let them surround the place so he can't get out . . . but get us *in* there first. I'll do whatever I have to do to rescue Macy. And if he kills me,' he added, 'put a bullet in his head the moment he shows himself so I can meet him at the Pearly Gates and kick his arse!'

'You really think you're going upwards?' Alderley asked with the faintest of wry smiles.

'Tchah! I can do your nose *four* times if you want.'

'I'd really rather you didn't.' But the SIS officer's expression had become thoughtful. 'You're right that we can pen Brice in if we move quickly – assuming he hasn't already left the Funhouse, of course. This whole thing could be a diversion to keep us occupied while he escapes somewhere else.'

'My daughter's life is not a "diversion", Peter,' Nina said frostily.

He nodded. 'Not my meaning, but sorry. If you'll take your hand off my phone, though, I can call in forces to surround the grounds. Not to go in,' he quickly added on Eddie's glare. 'Not yet. After what you've done for the country today, I think you really do deserve the chance to rescue your little girl.'

'Okay, so what do we do?' Eddie asked.

'I may be able to get us down there by air, which will save a lot of time,' Alderley replied. 'As you said, I have some sway as a section head – and I doubt departmental budgets will be a priority today.'

'The quicker you can get us there, the better,' said the Yorkshireman, before doing a double-take. 'Hold on. "Us"?'

'John Brice is – was – an SIS officer,' Alderley said, steel entering his voice. 'He not only betrayed his country, he betrayed *us*. There's no way I'm not going with you. I want to see that bastard taken down – one way or another. Besides,' he continued, 'I can use my authority to make sure no police or jobsworth officials mess us around.'

'Okay, if you can help us, then good,' said Nina. She gave Eddie a look; he begrudgingly lifted his hand from the phone. 'Let's get started.'

Ninety minutes later, a helicopter carrying Nina, Eddie and Alderley touched down at Southampton airport. A car waited for them; the SIS officer took the wheel. 'The Funhouse isn't far,' he said as they headed down the M27 into the night. 'About nine miles.'

'I, ah, thought the speed limit in England was seventy,' Nina said in alarm as they rocketed past the handful of other vehicles on the motorway. She had seen from the air that all the roads out of London were jammed, but once beyond the city they became unnaturally quiet, people staying at home out of fear and uncertainty about what might happen next.

'It is – for civilians,' Alderley told her, almost smugly. 'As an intelligence officer carrying out my duty, I'm exempt from speeding tickets.'

'Bet you wish you'd brought your Capri, huh?'

'I doubt that thing'd even *do* seventy,' Eddie said mockingly. Their driver gave him an annoyed look.

It was not long before Alderley exited the motorway, taking the car down ever-narrower roads on to a nondescript country lane. They soon reached an area of land enclosed by a high chain-link fence, with signs warning that the compound beyond was government property and that trespassers would be prosecuted. 'Don't see any cameras,' Eddie said.

'You're not supposed to,' Alderley replied. 'But trust me, they're there. If Brice is still inside, he knows we're coming. Which reminds me . . .' He made a brief phone call. 'As far as we know, he is. Nobody's left the building since we started surveillance.'

'Do you know if Macy's okay?' Nina asked.

'We tried using thermographics to see inside, but it looks like he switched on the Funhouse's climate control. There was too much waste heat venting out to spot anyone.'

'What about ground units?' Eddie asked.

'They're holding back about a mile away. When I give the word, they'll be here in under two minutes.'

'Two minutes is a long time in a hostage situation.'

'Yeah. I know.' He glanced into the mirror. 'Eddie, trust me. I'm going to do everything I possibly can to get your daughter back – preferably while keeping you alive as well.'

'You actually called him Eddie,' Nina noted. If the situation had not been so tense, she would have smiled. 'It must be love at last.'

Both men made hurried sounds of denial, Alderley's a disapproving 'uh-uh' while Eddie's was more of a retch. 'Anyway, this is it,' said the spy. The car neared a gate in the tall fence.

Eddie stared through the chain-link. They were in open countryside, their surroundings cloaked in darkness, but around half a mile away across scrubby fields he saw a large warehouse-like building illuminated by spotlights above its entrance. It was windowless, painted a neutral khaki shade to blend into its environment. 'So that's what it looks like from outside?' he said. 'I only saw a side door when I was being bundled out of a van.'

'It's the inside that's interesting.'

'Hopefully not in the Chinese saying's sense,' said Nina as they approached the gate.

Alderley stopped short of it. 'Ah. That's not good.'

'What isn't?'

'It should be shut.' The barrier was wide open.

A gatepost to one side bore an intercom and a bulbous camera lens. The car's occupants reacted with alarm as a voice barked from it. 'What part of "come alone" was so hard to understand?' demanded Brice.

Alderley hurriedly lowered his window to reply. 'I only came with them so they could get here as quickly as possible, John,' he said. 'I'll drop them off and turn around if you want.'

'Or you could get out and let *us* drive the rest of the way,' Eddie suggested sarcastically.

'No . . . no, bring them to the building,' Brice said. 'But stay in the car. This is between me and Chase, and his wife.'

'And our daughter,' Nina snapped. 'Is she okay?'

'She's fine . . . for now. Macy? Would you like to talk to your mummy and daddy?' The question was asked with an audible sneer.

'Mommy? Daddy?' Macy asked a moment later. 'Where are you?'

She sounded terrified, on the verge of tears. 'Macy!' Eddie shouted through his own window. 'It's okay, love, we're here. We're coming to get you.'

'Did he hurt you?' demanded Nina.

'He . . . no?' came the reply, tremulous enough that it was obvious Brice was intimidating her. Eddie clenched his fists.

'There,' said Brice. 'She's alive. Whether she remains so is now entirely up to you, Chase. Peter, drive up to the car park. Once you're here, Chase and his wife will come inside. I'll tell them what to do from then.'

Alderley drove through the gate, making another phone call as he brought the car down a long driveway. 'Alderley here. Brice still appears to be on-site, with his hostage. We're going in. Wait for my signal before making any move, though. Remember, the hostage is a child.'

They soon reached a small car park by the building, the bushes surrounding it the tallest vegetation in the compound. An awning stood out above a set of security doors – which were open. 'Well, here we are,' said Alderley awkwardly as he stopped outside the entrance. 'Look, whatever happens, we'll get Brice and make him pay for what he's done. So try not to be the last two people he kills, okay?'

'You're goddamn right we will,' said Nina.

'And, Chase?'

The Yorkshireman smiled slightly. 'Back to being formal, are we? Just a one-night stand?'

'Very funny. But here.' The SIS officer took a handgun from his jacket and passed it to him. 'I know that some people in London want Brice taken alive so they can turn him over to the Americans as a sacrificial offering. But if you get the opportunity to save yourself as well as your daughter . . . don't hesitate to take it.'

'Oh, I won't,' Eddie assured him. He quickly checked the gun, then slipped it into a pocket before opening the door. Nina followed him to the entrance. 'Just be ready to get Macy out of here, okay?'

'I will,' said Alderley. 'Good luck.'

'Thank you, Peter,' said Nina as she and Eddie entered. 'For everything.'

Her first sight of the Funhouse's interior revealed a disappointingly mundane reception area, which apart from the preponderance of security cameras could have been that of a hospital or government office. A glass-fronted cubicle adjoined the front doors. The man inside would normally have controlled access to the building – but now he was slumped in his seat with a bullet wound to his face, ghastly crimson rivulets on the wall behind him. The feet of another dead man poked out from a doorway. 'Shit,' muttered Eddie, raising the gun. Brice could be anywhere . . .

The agent's voice echoed from ceiling speakers. 'Ah, Chase. Welcome back to the Funhouse!'

Eddie snapped his gun between all the exits, but there was no sign of movement. 'Where's Macy?' Nina demanded.

'She's fine. She's just chilling.'

Eddie glared at the nearest camera. '*Where?*'

'Inside the test zone, of course. I thought I'd give you a second chance. If you rescue her, you win.'

'I thought you wanted an exchange? Me for her!'

'Oh, I still want you dead, Chase. But if you want your daughter back, you'll have to work for it. I'd recommend that you start straight away – you don't want to leave her in there for too long. Go through the red door ahead of you, then turn right and enter the first room you come to. See you soon.'

'What do we do?' Nina asked as the speaker cut out.

'We've got to go in,' Eddie replied, even knowing they would be walking into a trap. '*I* have to, anyway. You should stay here.'

'I'm not leaving Macy, and I'm not leaving you,' she said firmly. 'Besides, you don't know what's in there. You might need an extra set of eyes.'

He didn't bother arguing; not only would it be futile, but they couldn't waste any time. 'Okay. Then stick close.' He went to the red door, Nina following.

Beyond was a bland white-painted corridor. Another camera silently observed them. Both directions looked equally unassuming, but Eddie went right as instructed to reach a door a short distance away. He gestured for Nina to hold back, then readied the gun and warily opened the door.

The space beyond was a changing room with benches, clothes hooks and banks of metal lockers. He realised he had been there before. 'This is where I got ready for the test,' he said, crossing to the only other exit.

'What's through there?' said Nina.

'Could be anything. I had an Iraqi village; Alderley said his was a submarine.' He yanked the door open and pointed his gun through it. A short grey-walled passage led to another door, this one metal.

'He's still watching us,' she warned, seeing another camera covering the exit tilt to track them. 'He probably isn't with Macy, then. He must be in a control room somewhere.'

'Maybe, but I don't know where it is, and we don't have time to go looking for it.' He reached the door, leaning closer to listen for any noises beyond it – and twitched in surprise as his ear touched the metal.

'What is it?'

'It's *cold*. Really cold.'

'And Macy's in there,' Nina said in alarm.

'"She's just chilling" – that fucker! Shit puns are *my* department! Okay, stay back.' He threw open the door—

A freezing blizzard hit them.

43

Eddie overcame his surprise and squinted into the swirling snow, searching for targets in the semi-darkness. Nobody there – but disorientingly, it seemed as if he were back outside. The Funhouse had been upgraded since his test. The 'Iraqi village' had been an obvious fake, painted wooden flats mounted on scaffolding acting as buildings and sand sprinkled over a concrete floor the extent of the illusion of desert.

This, though, required no imagination to be convincing. 'Damn!' said Nina. 'I didn't know MI6 had a holodeck!'

They had entered a simulated winter, the temperature low enough to make their breath steam. Before them stood a military facility, bleakly functional concrete structures surrounding a tall central control tower. The blowing snow disguised for a moment the true nature of the gloomy twilight 'sky'; the high ceiling was hung with large sheets of a thin gauze, diffusing the glow of an expansive lighting rig concealed above. A glance at the chamber's outer walls, on which were projected images of a mountainous Arctic coastline, revealed that the blizzard was being blasted in through vents. The room was huge, at least two hundred feet along each side.

Eddie had no time to be impressed. 'Come on,' he snapped, running to the nearest building. Nina followed his footprints across the newly lain snow. He peered around the corner. The heart of the fake facility was illuminated by stark floodlights. He saw Cyrillic lettering on one wall. The room had been configured as a Russian military base, MI6's priorities little changed since the Cold War. 'Macy!' he shouted. 'Macy, can you hear me?'

No reply, but the snow blowers' constant drone masked other sounds. 'If she's in here, she'll be freezing!' said Nina, peering in concern through a window. The interior was unlit, but enough light came through from the other side to show that it was furnished. 'Macy!' Still no answer.

'We'll have to search,' said Eddie. He cautiously started down the structure's side wall. More of the imitation facility's set dressing came into view ahead. Stacks of barrels and crates, a couple of Russian jeeps, even a truck—

And an armed man beside it.

Eddie retreated sharply, pushing the startled Nina back, then crouched and peeked out. The man was a Russian soldier, wearing a heavy winter camouflage coat and a dark fur hat. He had an AK-74M rifle in his hands, and was slowly turning to survey the scene . . .

The Yorkshireman relaxed. 'It's just a dummy,' he said.

'But he was moving,' said Nina, still alarmed.

'They had 'em when I was here last. Some are on tracks so it looks like they're patrolling.' He stepped back out, spotting other dummies positioned around the heart of the base. 'Macy! Macy, it's Daddy! If you can hear—'

The soldier pivoted, the rifle locking on to him.

He grabbed Nina and dived – as the AK spat fire.

Shattered plaster exploded from the wall behind them as bullets ripped into it. Eddie rolled, snapping up his gun and firing at the dummy. The first two shots hit its body – but punched straight through the hollow plastic. He immediately switched targets, aiming instead for the rifle. Metal cracked against metal, the AK clattering to the ground with one of the fake figure's hands still clenching the grip.

Eddie fixed his gun upon another dummy under a floodlight,

but it was facing away from them, unmoving. 'You all right?' he asked Nina.

'Yeah, just a minor heart attack,' she replied. 'Jeez!'

A malevolent chuckle sounded over hidden loudspeakers, Brice's voice rolling around the frigid test area. 'Oh, sorry. Did I forget to mention that this is a live-fire scenario?' he said as the couple scuttled to the cover of a pallet of barrels. 'All the guards have motion sensors and will fire at anything that triggers them. Some of them move along pre-set paths – and others I can control directly. Like . . . this one.'

The soldier that had been looking away jerked into motion, swinging around—

Nina and Eddie hurled themselves in opposite directions as another AK-74 blazed to life, the empty barrels jolting under the barrage. The Yorkshireman returned fire, his first two shots again uselessly hitting the dummy – but the third knocked the rifle from the animatronic dummy's hands.

'Poor showing, Chase,' the unseen Brice said mockingly. 'All you ever had going for you was your aim, and now you're losing even that. And you really should be careful where you shoot. Your daughter could be behind any one of these walls.'

'So could you,' said Eddie. He looked for more dummies nearby, seeing none, then hurried to the first he had shot. Its motion sensors were still active, a mechanism clicking inside the stump of its arm as it tried to fire a weapon that was no longer there. He pocketed Alderley's pistol, then picked up the fallen Kalashnikov and made a rapid magazine check. Just under half its thirty rounds remained. He pulled the plastic hand from the grip. 'Fuck off, Thing,' he said, tossing it away.

Nina scurried to the truck and hunched against its front wheel. The cold was beginning to bite through her light clothing. 'Eddie, we've got to find Macy before she freezes!'

'Top of my to-do list!' he replied. '*Macy!*'

He strained to listen over the fans. Nothing – but Nina, her hearing less damaged by years of close exposure to explosions and gunfire, caught a faint cry. 'Eddie, I can hear her!'

'Where?'

'That way.' She pointed towards the centre of the huge room.

The tower stood above everything else, its roof only feet below the overhanging scrims. The top floor was illuminated. 'She's in there,' Eddie realised.

'Great, it's probably surrounded by those dummies!'

He went to the truck's rear and surveyed the scene beyond. Nina was right; an imitation soldier stood guard at the building's door.

The ground floor extended beyond the tower's base, however. 'There might be another way in round the back,' he said. 'Go back the way we came and we'll run around the edge of the room. Careful, though. I wouldn't put it past that twat to have stuck a couple of Russkiebots around a corner to catch us out.'

'You're getting colder, Chase,' boomed Brice as the couple retraced their steps. 'And so's your daughter.'

'We're coming, Macy!' Nina shouted. 'Just hold on, lovely! We're coming!'

They ran through the artificial blizzard around the chamber's perimeter. Eddie checked each gap between the buildings before passing. He spotted a couple of dummies, but all were near the middle of the ersatz base. 'Okay,' he finally said, 'the other side of the tower should be down here. We'll see if there's another door—'

He halted abruptly just short of the corner as he saw a shadow on the snow, cast by one of the floodlights. 'He *did* put another guard here,' he muttered. 'He knew I'd come this way.'

'But does he know that you know that he knew?' Nina asked. 'Because if he did, he might have put another one where he expects you to go instead!'

Eddie shook his head. 'Brice thinks I'm an idiot. All the same . . .' There was a door into the building, but rather than go to it, he instead peered through a nearby window, then used his rifle butt to smash the glass. 'Clear inside,' he reported, sliding through. 'Wait here till I shout.'

Nina crouched outside as he picked his way through the dark room to an exit. He opened the door a crack. No guards in sight – but he was still on full alert. Brice was somewhere nearby, and he was sure he wouldn't be satisfied with killing him by remote control.

But nothing moved except snowflakes. He glanced at the ground. No footprints. No breath steaming in doorways or windows either. He readied himself, then rushed out and whipped around the corner.

There was indeed one of the animatronic soldiers beside the building, gun pointing towards the perimeter. He ran up behind it, expecting it to turn – but it remained still as he tackled it. The gun went off, motion sensors triggered by the fall. A few rounds blew holes in the chamber's outer wall, splinters bursting from the projection of the wilderness, then the firing stopped as the figure's arms broke off at their shoulders.

Eddie rolled off the downed dummy and brought up his own gun in case Brice had prepared an ambush, but the spy still did not make a personal appearance. 'Nina, it's clear.'

His wife jogged to him. 'Funny, I was expecting him to make some dumb-ass quip.'

'I'm not missing them,' he said as he led the way to the central building. 'Huh. Now I realise why people get so pissed off when I make 'em.'

'Don't worry. You're way better at the God-awful puns than he is.'

They reached the door. 'Okay,' said Eddie, deadly serious once more, 'if he's set up a trap, it'll be here. Let me check first.'

He carefully opened the door. The room beyond was a mock-up of a communications centre, lights glowing on various Soviet-styled consoles. They provided enough illumination to reveal a doorway into the tower's base.

No guards. He edged inside and warily crossed to the opening. A flight of stairs beyond led upwards. 'Macy?'

'Daddy!' The fearful cry came from above. 'Daddy, help! Where are you?'

'I'm here, love, I'm here!' he called back, fighting against every instinct to charge up the stairs. 'I'm coming – but I need you to tell me if there's anyone else there.'

'Is the bad man with you?' Nina added as she followed him.

'No, he went! There are only the big doll-men here. Mommy, I'm scared – and I'm cold, I'm really cold!'

'We're almost there, honey!' she said, gripping Eddie's arm in fear and frustration. 'These doll-men, where are they?'

'They're all around me, four of them! He said if I stayed in the middle of them, I'd be okay, but I'm so cold. I want to go home . . .' She started crying.

'We'll be there as soon as we can! Just hold on and don't move, okay?'

'She's surrounded,' Eddie growled. 'They'll be covering the top of the stairs.'

'So how are we going to get to her?'

'If Brice is controlling 'em he'll only shoot at us, but if they're on motion sensors they'll fire at anything moving. If I can stay out of sight on the stairs and hold something up to make 'em use all their ammo . . .' He moved through the doorway—

Something tugged at his ankle.

The faint *ping* of a spring being released as the tripwire tugged out a hand grenade's pin was followed by a clatter of metal – the safety lever popping free to trigger its fuse . . .

He grabbed Nina and ran back. 'Macy, cover your ears!' he bellowed. They wouldn't reach the door in time; all they could do was dive behind the consoles—

They hit the floor as the grenade exploded.

The blast shredded walls and shattered windows. Consoles toppled, chairs sent flying like tumbleweed. Eddie yelled as something stabbed into the back of his leg. Ears ringing, he groped to find a six-inch shard of wood jutting from his calf. 'Shit, *shit*!' he gasped, tugging it out.

Nina sat up. 'Macy!' she cried, looking towards the doorway – and finding it was no longer there. The explosion had not only ripped apart the wooden interior wall, but blown a hole in the building itself – and in the floodlit glare now cutting through the smoke, she saw that the bottom of the stairs had also been destroyed. 'Macy, can you hear me? Macy!'

'*Mommy!*' her daughter wailed from above. 'Mommy, I'm scared, I'm scared!'

'Just stay there, honey, please! We'll be there as soon as we can!' She looked back at Eddie to see him grimacing as he stood. 'Oh my God, are you hurt?'

'Shrapnel in the leg,' he said through his teeth. 'I'm okay – won't be sprinting anywhere, though.' He took a couple of pained steps, then saw the remains of the stairs. 'Buggeration!'

'How're we going to get up to her?' Nina asked.

'Might have to climb up outside.' Eddie retrieved his gun and limped to the hole in the outer wall, checking that no more dummies were lurking nearby before stepping out into the snow. The explosion had revealed that the 'concrete' building was nothing more than a thin skim of painted plaster over plywood panels, like a film set—

A set. That was all the Funhouse was, an elaborate set. Everything was fake: the buildings, the snow, the sky, even the wilderness projected on the outer walls . . .

'Macy, stay still!' he shouted up to the tower's top. 'I'm coming to get you!'

'How?' Nina demanded.

'By thinking outside the box – literally! Come on.' He hobbled as quickly as he could back across the chamber to the dummy he had tackled. 'Grab its gun.'

She picked up the AK-74 and followed him to the perimeter wall. Spots of light marked where the toppling guard's fire had punched through it. Eddie poked a finger into one hole. 'It's just plasterboard.'

'How does that help us get to Macy?'

'This whole thing's like a movie set – and movie sets need lots of lights.' He pointed up at the even blue-grey glow of the fake sky. 'They also need to be able to get to 'em to change the bulbs . . .' He signalled for her to back away. 'Okay, cover your ears.'

Nina hurriedly brought up her hands as Eddie raised his rifle – and emptied the magazine into the wall.

The wooden panelling shredded as bullets tore into it. He swept the gun upwards, carving a ragged line of holes. The AK ran out of ammo; he tossed it away and took the other weapon from Nina, another sustained burst tearing through the drywall before he released the trigger and backed up. 'Okay, coming through!'

Eddie hurled himself at the wall – and smashed through, the bullet-perforated section tearing free to leave an almost cartoon-ish hole. He stumbled to a halt on the other side, raising the rifle.

He had emerged between the test area's outer boundary and the Funhouse's corrugated metal exterior wall. Dismantled sections of what he guessed were set pieces for other scenarios stood in large racks, crates and containers holding props. There was still no sign of Brice . . . and he was getting the feeling that the spy was not as close by as he had thought.

One of the snow machines was mounted on a scaffold nearby, large blocks of ice slowly being fed into it from a refrigerated hopper. But it was what stood beyond – and above – that caught his attention. The lighting grid did indeed resemble that of a movie soundstage, a complex latticework supporting thousands of LED clusters that could be set to any colour and brightness to simulate different conditions. A ladder ran up one of the supports to a narrow catwalk heading out over the enclosed set . . .

Nina came through the hole. 'Okay, how do we get to Macy? We've got to reach her before Brice comes back.'

'I don't think he *is* coming back,' Eddie said, limping to the ladder. 'We almost get blown up, and he doesn't even bother to gloat? He's not watching any more.'

'Then what's he doing?'

'I dunno. But he must have had a reason for bringing us here, and I don't think it was about revenge. If we get killed, that's just a bonus. He wants something else.' He started to climb the ladder, grimacing each time his wounded leg took his weight.

'But what's here that he wants? He killed the staff, so he could have taken anything that was already here—' A gasp as she realised Brice's objective had come with them; had *brought* them. 'Peter! Oh my God, he's after *Peter*! That's why he said he'd contact us through him – because he knew he was the person most likely to help us!'

'Christ, yeah. Alderley's an MI6 agent, and they always have an escape plan – so Brice probably wants to use his!' Eddie dropped the Kalashnikov to her. 'There's a couple of rounds left. I'll get Macy – you warn Alderley!'

He resumed his ascent, pace quickening despite the pain. A green sign on the wall pointed towards an emergency exit, but not knowing how far away it was or where it emerged, Nina hurried in the opposite direction to the main entrance.

★ ★ ★

Outside, Alderley was still in the car, watching the double doors with rising concern and frustration. The bursts of gunfire from within had been followed by an explosion, and a few minutes had now passed since the last exchange of fire.

He knew he had agreed to let Chase and Nina rescue their daughter, but he couldn't allow Brice to escape. A moment of internal debate, then he took out his phone to call in backup—

The front passenger door opened.

Alderley looked around sharply – and saw a Glock pointed at him.

Brice was behind it, hunched down. 'Evening, Peter.' The spy had crept around the building from the emergency exit at its rear, keeping low to use the lie of the land and the bushes surrounding the car park to conceal himself from any distant observers.

'John!' Alderley replied. 'Where are Chase and Nina? What have you done with their little girl?'

'They were alive the last time I checked, but it *has* gone rather quiet, hasn't it?' He had a tablet computer in his other hand, which he placed on the passenger seat. 'Let's have a look, though. I want to make sure they're occupied while we do our business.'

'What business?' Alderley snapped as Brice activated the tablet. 'If you think I'm going to help you—'

'You *are* going to help me, Peter, because I know you'd rather be alive than dead. Poor grieving Poppy would struggle to get by on the parsimonious SIS spousal death benefit, wouldn't she?' A grid of surveillance camera feeds from inside the Funhouse appeared on the screen. 'Now, where are you, Chase?'

He tapped on one image, which expanded to fill the screen. Alderley felt a surge of fear at the sight of Macy, tied to a chair – and surrounded by armed animatronic dummies in Russian uniforms. There was no sound, but he could tell the young girl was in tears and extremely distressed. 'You absolute *shit*,' he snarled. 'You'd use a *child* as a hostage?'

'That's why you never made it to the top tier of fieldwork, Peter,' Brice replied as he dismissed the image and checked other cameras. 'You never had the balls to do whatever was necessary. You're just like Quentin Hove and all the other politicians – happy to give the orders, but too afraid of getting any dirt on your plump little hands.'

The older man noticed a frown forming on Brice's face. 'My hands are *not* "plump",' he said with exaggerated indignation, wanting to distract his captor for as long as possible. If Brice couldn't find Eddie and Nina, then maybe they were outside the test area . . . 'And what do you want from me?'

'What I want,' said Brice, still flicking between the feeds, 'is for you to arrange an NQA flight out of the country from Southampton. I know the airspace is closed and all civilian flights are grounded, but your getting here so quickly tells me you've got the authority to circumvent that.'

'I don't think that my turning up at the airport with the most wanted man in Britain will qualify as "No Questions Asked".'

'Well, that's just it, Peter. I don't need you to think; I need you to *do*.' The frown deepened. 'Where *are* they?'

Eddie sidestepped carefully along the precarious catwalk and looked down through a narrow gap between the scrims. He was almost above the control tower. Once he jumped on to its roof, he should be able to lift one of its corrugated panels and reach Macy.

The last few steps. His wounded calf muscle felt as if someone was slowly driving a corkscrew ever deeper into his flesh, but he took a long breath, willing away the pain as he reached the centre of the tower's roof . . . then dropped.

The gauze beneath the lights tore loose as he fell. He hit the roof with a bang—

And kept falling.

The thin metal folded like cardboard under his weight. Eddie plunged through into the control room with a yelp – and landed heavily on one of the dummies, flattening it.

Macy looked around in astonishment. 'Daddy!'

'Macy, duck!' he yelled as he rolled painfully off the broken figure. There were three other plastic Russians surrounding her – and now they were all turning his way—

'*There* you are!' crowed Brice as one feed suddenly revealed a flurry of movement. He tapped it to zoom in, then another touch of the screen gave him control over the sentries. His target scrambled to his feet as the dummies pivoted towards him, guns at the ready—

Eddie grabbed the fallen dummy's rifle, but couldn't risk firing so close to Macy. Instead he swung the weapon above her head, smacking the AK out of the closest soldier's hands before whirling to take an entire arm off another.

But there was still one left—

He dived forward – wrapping his arms around his daughter and bowling the chair over as the dummy fired.

Macy screamed as they hit the floor, bullets whipping above them. Eddie released her and rolled at the dummy's legs. It lurched, but was attached to a weighted base and sprang back upright, still shooting. The control room's windows shattered.

The rifle jerked mechanically downwards as it tracked the Yorkshireman—

But the soldier's arms had reached the limit of their movement. Eddie jumped up and snatched the AK from the unliving hands – then punched the dummy's head clean off its shoulders. 'Up yours, Charlie Crippen!'

'Daddy!' Macy wailed. He dropped the gun and untied the rope, then hugged her. 'Daddy, you're here, Daddy!'

'Course I'm here, love,' he replied, experiencing a wave of relief so strong that it felt as if his heart would burst from his chest. 'I'll always come back for you, always.' Macy buried her face into his cheek.

But he knew the day was far from over. He still had to find Nina and Alderley – and deal with Brice. 'Come on, Macy,' he said. 'Sorry I forgot to bring you a toy lion; we'll go and find one with Mummy.'

'Mommy,' his daughter automatically corrected. Eddie grinned, then started down the damaged stairs.

'How sweet,' Brice said sarcastically, as the tablet showed father and daughter descending from the control room.

Alderley, engaged in a phone call, glanced at the screen. 'They're okay? Good,' he muttered in an aside.

The ex-spy suppressed his annoyance. Killing Chase, after all, was not the reason he had come to the Funhouse; getting Alderley away from the safety of SIS headquarters had been his true objective. With a gun trained upon him through the open passenger door, the section head had been forced to make arrangements via back-door channels – any officer worth his salt knew ways to bypass the agency's bureaucracy – for a light aircraft flight from Southampton across the English Channel to France. A parachute jump into Normandy, where he had contacts who would either be willing or be given no choice but to help, and Brice would be gone, with the whole of Europe and beyond into which to disappear.

The irony that the one place he could never again go was his home country didn't escape him. Now that he had been exposed, Britain's ruling elite – even though they would benefit the most from his actions – could not be seen to grant him the slightest leniency. But it was a price he was willing to pay for saving the nation.

Besides, even he had to admit that while England had many charms, its weather was not one of them. Heading south had its advantages . . .

'Okay, the plane'll be ready in forty minutes,' said the man Alderley had called. Brice had insisted the conversation take place on speaker so he could be sure a trap was not being set. There was still the possibility that Alderley had used a duress code, but the field agent was gambling that he wasn't nearly paranoid enough to have prepared one for every eventuality. 'The parachute'll be on board.'

'Great, thanks,' Alderley replied. Brice gestured for him to disconnect. 'All right, John, now what?'

'Now, you call off the surveillance teams. Tell them I'd already left before they got here – the whole thing was a diversion.'

'They won't believe it.'

The gun's muzzle tilted towards his head. 'I've got seventeen reasons for you to be very convincing. Now make the call—'

'Drop it or I shoot!'

Brice looked up to see Nina – holding an AK-74. Even with her left arm in a sling, the rifle was aimed unwaveringly at him. 'Nina!' cried Alderley in relief. 'You're okay!'

'Yeah, no thanks to this asshole. Brice, I said drop the gun. *Now.*' Brice let the gun clatter to the ground. 'Now move back.' He slowly retreated, watching her intently. 'Peter, are you okay?'

'Yeah – and Eddie and Macy are fine,' Alderley told her as she rounded the car and kicked the pistol under it. 'He just rescued her.'

'Oh, thank God.' Her gaze momentarily flicked towards the doors, hoping to see her family—

The flat crack of a gunshot and a searing pain in her upper chest came as one.

Nina fell against the car. Agony overpowered any thought of

retaliation as she clutched at the burning wound torn from the side of her left breast to beneath her armpit. Brice had shot her – but *how*?

The answer came as he snatched up her rifle. She glimpsed smoke trailing from his right shirt cuff. Some kind of trick weapon, an ace hidden literally up his sleeve . . .

'It was in the armoury here,' Brice said smugly, tugging back his cuff to reveal a dull grey tube strapped to the inside of his wrist. 'Single shot, triggered by muscle action. James Bond may not be real, but SIS still has its own little gadgets.' He brought the AK towards Nina and Alderley, his face turning cold. 'Now. Peter, make the call. Or she dies.'

'Don't do it, Peter,' Nina gasped. Each breath felt like a glowing poker pressing against her chest. 'He's going to kill us anyway.'

Alderley glared defiantly at his former comrade. 'I know. Go to hell, John.'

'Very well. Goodbye, Nina.' A smile of cold triumph curled Brice's lips as the rifle pointed straight at her face—

'*Brice!*'

The shout came from the building's rear corner, a hundred and fifty feet away. The surprised MI6 man glanced towards it – then looked back at Nina as his finger tightened on the trigger—

The split-second's hesitation saved her life.

Another gunshot – and Brice's throat exploded in a gory burst of blood and torn meat.

He spun and fell, the Kalashnikov's last bullets clanging into the car's flank as his finger spasmed on the trigger. Nina scrambled clear as he hit the ground.

'Nina! Nina!' shouted Alderley, rushing to help her. 'Are you all right?'

'Yes – I mean no, I just got frickin' shot!'

He kicked the rifle away and checked her wound. 'You were

lucky. Those last-resort jobs are pretty low powered and inaccurate.' A brief look at Brice. He was still alive, squirming as he clutched his mangled throat. 'That wasn't, though.'

'Sometimes it *is* all about being a good shot,' said a familiar voice. Nina looked up – and saw Eddie jogging clumsily towards her, Alderley's pistol in his hand. 'Was aiming a couple of inches higher, but from that range, it'll do.'

'Eddie!' she cried. Alderley helped her up. 'Where's Macy?'

'Back there.' He flicked a thumb over one shoulder to where their daughter was peering fearfully around the corner. 'She's okay, thank God.' The Yorkshireman reached Brice. 'Sore throat, Brice? Need some Lockets?' The other man opened his mouth as if to snarl a retort, but all that came out was a slurry of saliva-frothed blood.

Alderley made a hurried phone call. 'We've got Brice. I repeat, we have Brice. Move in and secure the area. He's been shot in the throat; he'll need urgent medical attention.' He turned to the downed man. 'Got to patch you up for your treason trial, after all.'

'Mustn't cheat the hangman,' Eddie added.

Alderley gave him a knowing look. 'Richard Burton?'

He nodded. '*Where Eagles Dare.*'

'Great film. One of my favourites.'

'You know, maybe you're not so bad after all, Alderley.' Both men smiled.

'All right, enough with the male bonding,' said Nina. 'And I don't want Macy to see that.' She nodded distastefully at Brice's ruined neck.

'I'll watch him,' Alderley offered, recovering Brice's gun. 'You go and get your little girl.'

The couple thanked him and made their way to Macy. She regarded them both with tearful concern. 'Mommy! Are you okay? You've got blood on you!'

Nina had done her best to cover the wound, but both her hand and the clothing beneath were smeared with crimson. 'I'm fine, honey. Don't worry about me, it's you who's important. Are you hurt?'

She shook her head. 'No . . . but I want to go home.'

'We will, soon as we can,' Eddie assured her. He picked her up and hugged her, Nina nuzzling against them both as cars sped towards the building.

Epilogue

The Shetland Islands, Scotland

Two months later

Even in summer, the Shetlands were far from warm. Eddie zipped up his leather jacket against the wind as he stepped from the helicopter. Mossy moorland greeted him, the sky and sea beyond a melancholy slate grey. 'Don't think I'll be working on my tan,' he said.

'It's not one of Scotland's top tourist spots, no,' Peter Alderley agreed. The rocky isles were over a hundred miles north of the Scottish mainland, most of the bleak archipelago uninhabited.

Which was why they were there. There were no trees on this particular island, the only thing rising above the rugged terrain a squat blockhouse of storm-scoured concrete. It was an old military facility, a relic of the Second World War when the Shetlands had been home to several Royal Air Force bases.

It had also housed facilities of the Special Operations Executive, the wartime military equivalent of MI6. Ironically, this former SOE bunker now contained a secret of its present-day counterpart. Alderley led the way down to a thick metal door, presenting his ID card to a camera. A brief wait, then a buzzer sounded and the barrier grumbled aside.

The two men entered to be greeted by a pair of uniformed guards. Identities were checked again, scanners passed over their bodies to ensure nothing was being smuggled inside, then one guard signalled to another man in a control booth. A second harsh buzz, and an inner door opened. The visitors were escorted through.

They marched down a stark concrete corridor. Heavy steel doors were set in each wall. Eddie and Alderley were brought to the third on the left side. 'Open number six!' the lead guard called, putting a hand on his holstered sidearm. A sharp bang as heavy bolts retracted, then his companion opened the door.

'I'll wait out here,' said Alderley as Eddie stepped forward.

The Yorkshireman gave him a look of mild surprise. 'You came all the way up here, and you're not going to see him?'

'He's said as much as he's going to say to SIS. Maybe he'll be a bit less on-message with you. Besides, I think what you want to say is between you and him.'

'Thanks.'

'It's the least I could do. Although I'd prefer it if you didn't kill him. He might be *officially* dead, but we may still have some use for him.'

Eddie shook his head. 'You should've made it official. I'd have been happy to help out.' The story given to the media was that John Brice, the renegade ex-spy and latter-day Guy Fawkes who had destroyed the Houses of Parliament, had died from his wounds following a shootout with police. In reality, he had been whisked away by helicopter to a secure government facility for surgery before being interrogated, then eventually imprisoned far from prying eyes.

'I fully sympathise, believe me. But I'm sure that if he were to *somehow* repeatedly fall face-first against a wall, the guards wouldn't rush to help him.'

'Good to know.' Eddie gave him a dark smile, then entered.

The room beyond was square, the walls the same bare concrete as outside. A bed, small desk, plastic chair, steel toilet bowl and matching washbasin were the only furnishings. Cameras in each corner gave the guards total surveillance coverage of the confined space.

Its occupant lay upon the bed, languidly watching him enter. 'They said I had a visitor,' rasped Brice. His throat was a patchwork of Frankensteinian scars, shredded flesh stitched back together. Protruding from it was a slotted metal disc: a mechanical larynx. His voice box had not been completely destroyed by Eddie's bullet, but was damaged enough that he required amplification to speak in anything more than a whisper. 'I didn't expect it to be you.'

'Ay up, Darth,' Eddie replied, folding his arms as the door closed behind him. 'Just thought I'd pop in and make sure you were uncomfortable.'

'Is that all? I'm surprised you're not here to execute me, Chase.'

'Bit hard to execute someone who's already dead. At least, officially.'

'Officially, this place doesn't exist either. And it would eliminate any risk of retribution against the government if the Yanks suspected I was still alive.'

'Well, you got lucky. Alderley told me that the new Prime Minister specifically banned, what did he call 'em? "Extra-judicial killings" by any British agency. So the only reason you're still breathing – well, wheezing – is because the bloke you didn't want to win the election *did* win it.'

Far from gratitude, Brice's only response was contempt. 'Which proves exactly why he's unsuited to run the country. In a time like this, we need strong leadership, not limp-wristed cowards. If he had any balls, he would have had me executed for treason, rather than throwing me in a hole to rot.'

'I'll tell Alderley. Seeing as he's the new boss of MI6, I'm sure he'll pass it on. Maybe the PM'll change his mind, then we'll both be happy.'

A flash of shock before contempt returned, even stronger. '*Peter Alderley* is the new C?'

'Yeah, I think he was surprised too. But he was the only person who stood up to the old one while he was plotting to kill the entire British Parliament, so he got the nod.'

Brice shook his head. 'Then the country's in a worse state than I thought.'

'I dunno, it seems to be bouncing back pretty quickly. They're going to rebuild Big Ben, for a start. And it's not a good time to be a paranoid racist shitmonger, now that everyone knows a rogue MI6 agent blew it up, and why – they look like arseholes by association. Maybe it won't last, but looks to me like the country's going in a new direction.'

'The *wrong* direction. All those lovey-dovey feelings won't last. But by then, it'll be too late to turn back.' The former agent finally sat up. 'You're the *true* traitor here, Chase. You sold out your country's only hope for a strong future, and now you're going to jet off to New York with your family and turn your back on the disaster you've caused.'

Eddie unfolded his arms, making a show of flexing his fists. 'Speaking of my family, that brings me to why I'm here. Wanted to let you know that I've got permission from the new head of MI6 to come and see you whenever I want.'

'No need to put yourself out on my account,' Brice said with a humourless smile.

'Oh, it'll be no trouble. I'll enjoy it.' He cracked his knuckles. 'And I'll be over if, say, I get wind that you've asked any of your mates to come to New York looking for a bit of revenge.'

'And how would I arrange that from in here?'

'You're a top secret agent, I'm sure you've got a plan. But you're not going to carry it out, are you?' The Yorkshireman stepped closer, his expression becoming more threatening. ''Cause if I have to come back here, I'll be the last person you ever see.'

'And I thought Britain had a ban on extra-judicial killings.'

'We just do it under other names. In this case, it'll be "cleaning up a piece of shit".'

'That's something I miss about SIS,' Brice sniffed, unimpressed. 'The repartee is so much more witty—'

Eddie lunged, punching him hard in the face and slamming his head back against the cell wall. Before the shocked prisoner could react, his attacker had grabbed him by the throat, driving his other fist into his stomach. Brice convulsed, choking, as the prosthetic larynx ground into his ruined neck. 'This is one thing I'm not going to fucking joke about,' the Yorkshireman snarled. 'You kidnapped my daughter. Last bloke who touched my little girl got thrown from a seventh-floor window, but you got off easy by just being shot in the throat. Anything happens to my family, though, I *will* fucking kill you. And it *will* fucking hurt.'

He bashed Brice's skull against the wall again, then stepped back. Blood dripping from his nose, the ex-agent gasped for air. 'You're . . . you're not much of a father if you let it happen twice,' he croaked.

'It won't happen a third time, trust me,' Eddie assured him. 'Anyway, I was in London for another debrief, and Alderley let me swing by on the way home so I could let you know the score. Now I've done that, like I said: you'd better pray you never see me again.' He rapped on the door. 'Okay, I'm finished.'

Still reeling from the attack, Brice nevertheless managed to stand. 'Chase!' he barked as the door opened. 'History will prove me right. I was Britain's best hope to return to greatness – Britain's *last* hope!'

'If you're the best we've got,' Eddie said as a parting shot, 'the country really *is* up shit creek.'

'What do we say to Daddy, Macy?' Nina prompted as Eddie entered the apartment to find his family waiting in the hall.

Macy held up a picture she had drawn of a round-headed, pink-faced figure with elongated arms and legs. 'Welcome home, Daddy!' she cried before running to hug him.

'Is this me?' he asked, kissing her before examining the picture. 'It's very good! You got my head just right.'

'Yeah, not a hair on it,' said Nina with a smile as she embraced her husband. 'How did things go in England?'

'Pretty well. Hopefully MI6 is done with me now. Oh, Alderley told me the IHA'll be looking after the Shamir until everyone decides what to do with it.'

'You know you can call him Peter now that you're *Where Eagles Dare* buddies?' He made a mocking face. 'Yeah, I suggested it to Oswald Seretse at the UN, and he passed it on to the White House – and let's face it, the British government wasn't really in any position to refuse President Schilling anything.'

'Not after one of their agents took down an American airliner, no.'

'Oswald asked if I'd be willing to help out with their initial research, since I had first-hand experience of where it was found – and what it can do.'

'Are you going to?' Eddie's question was pointed, but not disapproving.

'I haven't decided yet,' she answered. 'I'm certainly not going to do anything that will take me away from home, though. I even told the producers that if they need me to do any pick-up shooting for the Ark of the Covenant documentary, I'll do it here in New York rather than LA. They're going to dedicate the series to Steven, Howie and the others who died, by the way. After I told them I was donating my fee to their families, I suppose they felt they had to make *some* gesture.'

They went into the living room. 'So, you're staying home for now?'

'Absolutely. Even after two months back in New York, I can safely say I haven't got itchy feet.' She sat, patting the cushion to invite Macy up beside her, then regarded her husband curiously. 'What about you?'

'About what?'

'How itchy are your feet? For England, I mean. You decided where you belong – there or here?'

'Where do I belong?' He smiled and sat with his wife and daughter. 'Right here with the two of you. Wherever here might be.'

Acknowledgements

Many thanks to Morebus for demonstrating what a double-decker bus can do when the driver doesn't have to worry about passenger comfort – and then letting me try for myself!